NACKY PATCHER

AND THE CURSE OF THE

DRY-LAND BOATS

a novel by

JEFFREY KLUGER

with illustrations by

DAVID ELLIOT

To Elisa and Paloma,
mis tigritas mentas;
and to Alejandra,
mi Saturno.

PHILOMEL BOOKS

A division of Penguin Young Readers Group. Published by The Penguin Group.

Penguin Group (USA) Inc., 375 Hudson Street, New York, NY 10014, U.S.A.

Penguin Group (Canada), 90 Eglinton Avenue East, Suite 700, Toronto, Ontario, Canada M4P 2Y3
(a division of Pearson Penguin Canada Inc.).

Penguin Books Ltd, 80 Strand, London WC2R 0RL, England.

Penguin Ireland, 25 St. Stephen's Green, Dublin 2, Ireland (a division of Penguin Books Ltd.).

Penguin Group (Australia), 250 Camberwell Road, Camberwell, Victoria 3124, Australia
(a division of Pearson Australia Group Pty Ltd).

Penguin Books India Pvt Ltd, 11 Community Centre, Panchsheel Park, New Delhi—110 017, India.

Penguin Group (NZ), Cnr Airborne and Rosedale Roads, Albany, Auckland 1311,
New Zealand (a division of Pearson New Zealand Ltd).

Penguin Books (South Africa) (Pty) Ltd, 24 Sturdee Avenue, Rosebank, Johannesburg 2196, South Africa.

Penguin Books Ltd, Registered Offices: 80 Strand, London WC2R 0RL, England.

Printed in the United States of America. Design by Marikka Tamura.

Library of Congress Cataloging-in-Publication Data

Kluger, Jeffrey. Nacky Patcher and the curse of the dry-land boats / Jeffrey Kluger. p. cm.

Summary: When thief and swindler Nacky Patcher and orphaned eleven-year-old Teedie Flinn discover
a huge wrecked boat in a small mountain lake near their town, they try to unite all the inhabitants
to help rebuild the vessel—an endeavor that forever changes all of their lives.

[1. Shipbuilding—Fiction. 2. Cooperativeness—Fiction. 3. Orphans—Fiction. 4. People with disabilities—Fiction.
5. Fantasy.] I. Title.   PZ7.K6875Nac 2007   [Fic]—dc22   2006034534   ISBN 978-0-399-24604-3

10 9 8 7 6 5 4 3 2 1

First Impression

In the wreckage of boats
and the wreckage of seas,
There's a curse to reverse
and a charm to appease.

The basins may fill
and the boats draw new crew,
If the wise spot the course
and the brave sail it true.

—*From the last verse of the*
Songs of the Dry-Land Boats

JIMMER'S HOUSE
WITHIN A HOUSE

BRIGG AND CONSTANCE
KEEPER

THE PADROAD

THE LAKE

THE POUNDS'
HOME

BOWFIN &
KNOCKLE

YULE

MEAT MERCHANT

THE SHOP
AT THE TOP

CHEESE
MAKER

HARDWARE
SHOP

THE SWEET
SHOP

CURIO
SHOP

SHIRT FITTER

SADDLER

INDIGENTS' HOME

ALBERT T. RAIN

EAST
SAWTOOTH MTS

PROLOGUE

Nothing Nacky Patcher and Teedie Flinn discovered in the Yole lake caused them to suspect they were losing their wits. That was good, since what they found in the blackberry water early that night just as the owl light was fading and true dark was arriving would surely have caused most folks to believe they'd come unsprung.

Nacky was well trolleyed on malt, and that could have accounted for what he saw in the little round lake at the center of Yole. Teedie, however, was a boy of eleven, and his eye and mind were unclouded by drink. Yet the sober child and the malt-wobbly man saw just the same thing, as Nacky could tell from the gape-mouthed look on Teedie's pale face.

What Nacky and Teedie found that summer evening they did not find alone. Rather, they were with Nacky's pig—something that made an odd kind of sense, since the last time Nacky encountered this much wood on a wide stretch of water his pig was by his side too. That time, of course, the body of water was a huge, cold ocean, and the wood he saw was the wreckage of the ship that had carried him out there. This time, the water was a mere lake, and a modest lake at that, but the wood still appeared to be a great, broken boat, even bigger than the one on which Nacky had journeyed before.

That was the part that confused Nacky and Teedie so. Judging by the quantity of wood floating on the quiet, blue-black water, this ship would have to have been huge—hundreds of feet long with three towering masts and great clouds of sails, far more suited to the waters between continents than the waters between lake banks. And the banks of this tiny lake were high in the sawtooth mountains of Yole, more than two thousand feet above the level of the coast, which was itself half a day's journey away. It would not have been possible for a person—or even many people—to have carried so much wreckage so great a way and then cast it in the blackberry waters.

The out-of-place nature of the wood gave it a feel less of mystery than menace, and Teedie regarded it with a look of frank fear—an uncommon expression for the brassy boy. The little pink and black pig standing be-tween Teedie and Nacky seemed to feel the same way, snuffling and skit-tering fretfully. Nacky felt no such unease. He had already had his share of curious experiences in the season just past—things that had shoggled his mind and battered his body and left him with a terrible hobbling walk he would carry the rest of his days. In quiet moments, in the privacy of his bed, he was often tempted to believe that those things hadn't happened at all. But he knew that they were real—real as rocks, as his Pippa had liked to say—just as the tons upon tons of planks and masts and frames and stanchions floating and glinting in the lake tonight were real.

Nacky, Teedie and the pig stared out over the water, listening to the low *thunks* the heavy timbers made as they bumped together and watch-ing the twinkly way the planks caught the last of the owl light and the first of the moonlight and flashed it back at them. Slowly, almost as one, Nacky and Teedie eased themselves down on the gravelly bank, feeling the wet pebbles soak through the seats of their trousers.

"Orro," Nacky said to the pig, for that was the animal's name, "I think we been given another ocean ship."

Out on the water, two lengths of timber knocked together once again, providing the confirmation the pig could not.

BOOK ONE

CHAPTER ONE

Four months earlier

A **great many things happened in the** town of Yole in the sixteen weeks before Nacky Patcher and Teedie Flinn found the huge shattered ship in the little round lake. The first and worst of those things happened to Audra and Stolley Pound, when the horses came to pitch them from their home. Home-pitchings were a common enough event in Yole, and most everyone in town had assumed that before long one would be taking place at the Pound house too. Neither Nacky nor Teedie ever found it terribly pleasant to see the horses arrive and do their work, and they didn't particularly want to watch this time either. But both of them had reasons to be there when the Pound family was pitched.

Nacky, as most everyone in Yole knew already, would be going off to prison that morning, getting locked into the penitents' tower on the very same unlucky day on which the Pounds would be locked out of their house. Since this would be his last chance to set eyes on the Pound family for the better part of a year—and perhaps forever, if the home-pitching went badly—he wanted to be present to offer them a nod if they happened to glimpse him in the crowd that would inevitably gather.

Teedie, of course, would be attending the pitching for another reason entirely. For more than a year now, the Pounds' home had been his own home, and he had settled in with Stolley, Audra and their two young sons well—no small thing for a boy who had rarely been allowed to stay in any house long enough to get so much as a clothes hook and a fixed spot at the supper table. Indeed, Teedie had become well nigh a member of the Pound family. All the same, he was not a blood member, and the constable had thus ordered him to leave the house the day before the home-pitching began, the town being liable for any injuries suffered by any nonrelations who happened to be present during the course of an eviction. Teedie, as was his stubborn nature, insisted that he wanted to stay, but Stolley and Audra had been firm, knowing well the boy's reck-less turn of temper—a turn that often brought him to grief when there was danger about.

In just the year Teedie had been living with Audra and Stolley, he'd fallen through their roof trying to mend a hole in the thatching that Stol-ley had clearly told him he'd tend to himself. He'd got half-gored by an oversized he-goat when he'd decided the thing could be trained to pull a cart—knowing full well that was not in the beast's nature. He'd nearly got himself blown into a deep crack in a mountain pass when he'd hiked up there in the teeth of a windstorm, guessing that mountain gales would be a thrill to feel, but forgetting that they'd also be enough to lift a slip of a boy like him straight off his feet. And all of these mishaps had oc-curred after the terrible accident that had crippled his right hand before he ever came to live in Yole—something that ought to have frightened him into taking better care with himself, but that seemed to have just the opposite effect.

"You're gonna get yourself hurt permanent one day," Stolley would warn him after another one of his calamities.

"Been hurt permanent already," Teedie would say, looking at his ruined hand. Then he'd go back to whatever he was doing.

Teedie's heedlessness mystified the Pounds, but the fact was, the kind of hard past he'd had would probably have loosed the wild in any child. A chestnut-haired boy not yet within landfall of eighty pounds,

Teedie was said to be a dead-spit for his mother, though he himself could not have confirmed that, since she died bringing him into the world. His father, who always had a slippery purchase on his reason, lost that footing entirely after he lost his wife. Before Teedie was a year old, the man ran off to live in a tree not far from the family's home in the town of Knockle, convinced that people on the ground were breathing up all the air there was to be had and that the only way to get his fair lungful was to live up above them. The more daft he got, the higher the tree he needed, until one day he found a good hundred-footer, from which he eventually fell and snapped his neck—likely a result of trying to chase off a bird, which he often did when he felt there were too many of them doing too much breathing in branches he had claimed as his own. The mortician who prepared him for burial said he'd never seen so much color in a dead man's cheeks in all his life.

After that, Teedie was delivered by the Knockle constable to the Home for Indigent and Unfortunate Girls in nearby Yole, an orphans' keep that had been established by the fathers of the surrounding communities for abandoned girls from all over the region. The day Teedie arrived it had taken several hours before anyone got around to unswaddling him and learning that the newest member of the girls' home was not suited to the place at all. Teedie was sent straight back to a work school for boys in Knockle and lived there until he was nine years old, when he was expelled for being incorrigible—or at least that's how the headmaster described him. The magistrate then packed him back to Yole, where he was raised in a series of foster homes in exchange for working in the families' shops and kitchens. The Pounds had been the latest—and to Teedie's mind the kindest—of those caretakers.

If there was anyone in Yole who rivaled the Pounds for Teedie's feelings, it was Nacky Patcher, but even Nacky knew it was not an admiration he truly deserved. Nacky was bound for the penitents' tower today on account of all the cheating and swindling he'd done in the past year, mischief for which he richly deserved to be locked away. On more than one occasion, Teedie had boasted that he too was considering a criminal career, and that he was clever enough to be twice the thief Nacky Patcher was—not a hard thing to be, given how often Nacky got caught at his larceny. Teedie had not yet committed even a petty crime, but he enjoyed the stories Nacky used to tell him about the ways he and his grandfather—his Pippa—would fleece the people of Yole and the surrounding communities. More and more, the boy would shadow him about town, requesting advice on how he might get started in the field, and causing Nacky to regret he'd ever filled Teedie's head with his Pippa tales in the first place.

"Reckon I can ask you some questions?" Teedie would inquire, intercepting Nacky on the street or in a shop.

"You know the answer to that," Nacky would respond.

"Reckon I can come with you next time you go fleecing?"

"You know the answer to that too."

Nacky realized that Teedie would be present at the home-pitching today and would no doubt trail along afterward when he was taken to the tower. While Nacky thought it good for Teedie to see the wages of thievery, he also found he was surprisingly uncomfortable with the idea that the boy, of all people, would be watching him as he was led away in wrist cuffs and shackles, no freer to go his own way than a dairy cow being pulled by a neck rope. If Nacky was ever inclined to feel shame—not something he was inclined to do often—he felt it in the presence of Teedie.

It was an unusual coincidence that the home-pitching and Nacky's imprisonment were scheduled for the same busy morning—likely an oversight by the sentencing judge, who ought to have remembered that today was the twenty-first of February. Home-pitchings, as the people in Yole knew too well, took place twice a year, once in the waning days of winter, when the next season's planting was being planned, and once on the twenty-first day of September, when the fruits of that planting were about to be reaped. That was the way it had been since the Baloo family first became the town's principal landowner many generations ago, and that was the way Mally Baloo, the family's current head, still ran things. Baloo seemed to hold the Pounds in particularly low esteem and had been showing uncommon interest in their financial affairs of late, seeming to itch for the change of season so he could get about the pleasure of tossing them from their house. When Baloo took a dislike to a family this way, the pitchings that followed were always grand shows. For days, even well-intentioned people had been coming into Audra and Stolley's little curio shop on the main business street—the only business street—in Yole, as if to confirm that the store was indeed doing as poorly as it always had and that the Pounds would indeed be served their out-with-you papers when the appointed day arrived.

Stolley himself always seemed surprised that his store failed to attract a brisker trade than it did. A little man with tiny gray eyes and vision so sharp he was said to be able to read the lettering on a copper coin from eight feet away at early dawn, Stolley believed he had an equally good eye for fine valuables. His faith in himself was confirmed several years before Teedie ever came to live with the family, when Stolley and Audra were visiting the nearby town of Bowfin and he bought her a used overcoat that turned out to have several forgotten banknotes and a small drawstring bag with a palmful of green gem chips sewn up in its lining. Stolley promptly converted the notes and chips to cash and used the money to open his curio shop, surer than ever that he knew a treasure when he spotted one.

But if Stolley had an eye for valuables, he did not have an eye for business. Most of the porcelain bits, candlesticks, bobs and brooches he stocked in his shop he bought in the first place from the other people in Yole, who would sell them off when times were hard and they needed to raise some fill-the-larder money. Since times were always hard in Yole, however, and people always needed to fill the larder, it was a rare day when anybody would come to the store to buy back the valuables they'd already seen fit to part with, a fact that had always made it likely that the Pounds' business would fail and equally likely that they would one day have to face the horses of the out-with-you wagon, as they would this morning.

Though it was Mally Baloo who ordered the foreclosure on Audra and Stolley's home, it was Chuff the dwarf who would formally bring the Pounds the news. Nobody ever called Chuff the dwarf anything more courteous than "Chuff the dwarf," his small stature—barely forty-five inches from boot-sole to hat—and his apparently small mind never seeming to earn him a more respectful form of address. It had never been established whether Chuff was indeed a simpleton, and there were those in town who wondered if he might not have more sharpness about him than he let on—merely playing at slow-wittedness, since that was the best way to ensure that folks would let him be. Judging by the way Chuff behaved, however, it did seem that his lamps were genuinely dim. He rarely spoke, generally limiting his conversation to answering questions when he was asked them. When he did talk about anything else, it mostly involved his poem.

For as long as anyone could remember, Chuff had been trying to write a poem, though from all accounts, he had not gotten very far. The first stanza, which Chuff would recite to just about anyone who asked—and to many people who didn't—was actually first-rate:

> If it pleases or not,
> I am just as you see;
> I'm a man though I look more a lad . . .

The problem was, no matter how many times Chuff repeated that first stanza, it never led to a second. Instead, his voice would trail off, his watery green eyes would go oddly flat and his mind would appear to go wandering, as if it were trying to chase down the right rhyming words and having little luck finding them. Whenever anyone asked Chuff how his poem was faring, he would always answer the same way.

"I'm puzzling over it," he'd say, neither pleasantly nor unpleasantly.

Most of the time, people saw little of Chuff, knowing only that he lived in a small cabin on the Baloo estate and that when he wasn't composing his poem he did odd jobs in the fields and stables. It was only on days like today, when Chuff was sent on an entirely different kind of errand, that the people of Yole took any notice of him at all.

Chuff set out from the Baloo estate at seven-fifteen in the morning in order to arrive in time for the eight o'clock pitching, his short stride and his sleepy gait keeping him from making the walk any faster. Nacky left his home on a red, pounded-dirt padroad at the edge of Yole shortly after he figured Chuff had set out, reasoning he'd be able to catch up with the little man on the town's main street and follow him the rest of the way to the Pounds'. As Nacky always did when he attended evictions, he tried to comb and tidy himself a bit before leaving the house, believing that people being put out of their homes deserved that much. Combing and tidying was usually a quick matter for Nacky, since he had long ago accepted that no matter what he did, he was never going to be terribly much to look at.

Tall—a good six feet tall and bigger still on those occasions when he remembered to straighten up his sapling of a spine—he rarely carried more than 165 pounds on his frame. Since he had never much cared for the sun, his skin was generally a fish-belly white. His hair was light red and feathery and always looked ready to blow off like milkweed. Difficult as it would have been for so sparse a crop to cover an ordinary head, Nacky's hair had to work especially hard, since it sat atop an unnaturally high crown of forehead. Lately, what hair he did have had begun to retreat even farther, losing more and more ground to the forehead each birthday.

Nacky could not do much about his head or his hair or his skin, but today, as a nod to the Pounds, he did take care to put on what he had come to consider his favorite shirt, a fine blue cotton with a faint bit of white shot through the weave. He had bought the shirt in Audra and Stolley's shop during the brief period they were trying their hands at collecting and selling secondhand clothes. The Pounds had seemed especially pleased when Nacky bought the shirt, confessing that it was their favorite as well. Nacky suspected they would not catch sight of him today, but in the event they did, he imagined they'd be pleased to see the shirt on his back.

Nacky hurried out of his little house, blew on his hands to warm them in a mild late-winter chill that felt more like early spring than late winter, and took the path to town in a light run. When he came within sight of the main road, he saw a small crowd crossing it from east to west, heading in the general direction of the Pound home. At the center of the crowd was a space in which Nacky guessed Chuff the dwarf, lost to view among the other people, was walking. Nacky followed the group through the small padroads and out to the Pounds'. As they moved, more people joined them, until by the time they reached the stretch of red dirt road on which the shuttered house was located, there were at least forty Yole locals—many of whom had nothing much else to do on a weekday morning anyway—surrounding little Chuff. Across from the house, camped alone on the side of the road, was Teedie.

Audra had heeded the order the constable had issued, sending Teedie packing the day before the house-pitching began. Bundling him a bedroll, a change of clothes, a loaf of bread and a portion of sausage, she'd told him to go into town and stay at the abandoned curio store for as long as he could. Teedie left the house as instructed, but went no farther than the other side of the road, where he was determined to keep watch over the house and, he hoped, hold the crowd at a distance when the home-pitching actually began.

As the townspeople neared, Teedie sat cross-legged at a little cook-fire, roasting a link of sausage on a charred, two-pronged fork that he had wedged into the clenched grip of his crippled right hand. When he saw the crowd, he stood up and hastily popped the sausage into his mouth. He discovered too late that the meat was too hot, and he had to puff air in and out around it before he could speak. After a moment, he was able to call out through his chewing.

"Ain't no one home!" he said, with as much brass as he could. A small ripple of laughter came from the crowd.

"So you say," a man answered, as the crowd closed to within a few yards of the house and stopped.

"I do," Teedie said.

"Chimney says something else," the man replied.

Teedie looked up at the square chimney on the Pounds' roof. He wasn't the only one cooking his breakfast at that moment. The crowd laughed again.

"Stomp that cook-fire out, Teedie Flinn, and come over here," the man in the crowd called. "Unless you fancy gettin' arrested."

"Ain't no one gettin' arrested," Teedie said, puffing up his chest to little effect.

Teedie prepared to say something else, but at that moment, Nacky stepped from behind a knot of people at the edge of the crowd. Teedie noticed him for the first time and gave off with a small nod. Nacky affected a stern expression and motioned Teedie over with a sharp tick of his head. Teedie wavered and Nacky narrowed his eyes. The boy slumped and complied, scuffing through the red dirt in the direction of Nacky but stopping just short.

"Fine business you gettin' hurt today too," Nacky muttered.

Teedie folded his arms angrily and looked down at the ground.

With Teedie out of the way, the crowd parted and Chuff stepped forward and approached the house. When he reached the porch, he climbed the steps and knocked on the door.

"That you, Chuff the dwarf?" Stolley Pound's voice called from behind the closed door.

"Yes," Chuff said. There was a silence.

"How you faring on that poem?" Stolley asked.

"I'm puzzlin' over it," Chuff answered. There was another bit of laughter from the crowd.

"I know why you come," the voice said. Chuff nodded and said nothing. A moment passed.

"Chuff?"

"Yes?"

"You know I got me boys in here," Stolley said.

"I know," Chuff said.

"Got me wife, too."

"I know."

From behind Chuff, there was a shifting in the crowd. "You gonna give it up, Stolley?" someone shouted.

"Don't reckon so," Stolley's voice shouted back.

"Good fer you," someone else answered. There was a satisfied murmur of voices.

Nobody expected Stolley Pound to give it up easily, certainly not to Chuff the dwarf. The only reason Chuff was sent at all was to see that everything was kept legal and everybody got the documents the courts of law said they were entitled to get. After that, the little man with the papers in his hand would have finished his work. Then it would be time for the chain-and-ladder wagon to show up. When that happened, the real business of the pitching would get under way. Today, the crowd did not have to wait long.

As Chuff stood dully on the porch and the townspeople shifted nearby, a red cloud kicked up about a hundred yards down the padroad and a loud rattling accompanied it. Though the upward snaking of the road prevented anyone from seeing the source of the disturbance, no one had any doubt what was causing it. Nacky, Teedie, Chuff and the others turned to face the sound. From behind them, someone inside the house opened the shutters a finger's width and peered up the road too.

When the chain-and-ladder wagon at last crested the hill, the crowd drew slightly back. As was customary, the constable, a meaty, red-faced man, was aboard the wagon, while the two beat-men, younger, sturdier fellows, trailed behind. There were two ladders lashed to the wagon's rails—a short one, used during inland evictions like this one, and a long one that was saved for the two-story kitchen houses closer to the coast. Tied to the bed of the wagon lay several canvas sacks and three heavy metal grappling hooks. The wagon was pulled by no fewer than three horses—and three huge horses at that, with hooves like rounded anvils

12

and glistening flanks like great, living boat hulls. Their nostrils breathed steam in the early morning cold. By any measure, this was way too much animal muscle for so small a hitch.

The wagon labored down the road, slowed before the Pound house and came to a stop with its front wheels and its frisking horses standing without a by-your-leave on Audra and Stolley's little parcel of land. The constable jumped to the ground, steadied the horses—which shied as he passed—and strode toward the house. Nacky recognized the lawman from the last time he'd been locked away, but the constable didn't notice him. The crowd, which had begun catcalling and laughing as the wagon approached, now grew quiet.

"Chuff the dwarf," the constable called, "you can stand down now."

Chuff turned to him and blinked, either not understanding what had been said or looking awfully confused for a man who did. "You can step away from the door," the constable clarified. Chuff, with neither a nod nor a word, did step away, backing off the porch and onto the ground.

"Do you have papers for me?" the constable asked.

Chuff handed over the eviction documents. The constable glanced at them without really seeing them and stuffed them into his jacket pocket. Then he stepped forward and climbed up onto the porch of the house.

"Stolley Pound," he called out. "I'm going to ask you and your family to quit your house and come outside."

"We'd fancy stayin'," came the voice from inside.

"What you'd fancy and what you'll do are not the same things," the constable said, and took a step closer to the closed door.

"We know full well what we'll be doin'," Stolley called. "And what we'll be doin' is this."

With that, the shutters in the window to the left of the door opened and a hand appeared, holding a great, black pot filled with bubbling mixabout. In a blink, the hand flicked smartly, the mixabout took flight, and the hot, gray, oatmeal-like mess caught the constable full in the face, causing him to yelp and stutter-step off the porch, whooping in pain. The pot vanished back inside the window, but not before everyone but the constable—whose stung and sticky eyes were tightly closed—could see that the hand holding it belonged to a woman. If Stolley Pound was speaking up for the family, Audra Pound was standing up for the house. The crowd broke into delighted laughter, Nacky—who always suspected Audra had more vinegar in her than she let on—loudest of all. Teedie merely glanced up, then returned his eyes to their spot on the ground, his arms more tightly crossed.

"Stolley Pound," the constable called out, his voice half-muffled by his hands, which were covering his scalded face, "it'll be the tower for the lot of you if there's any more of that! I'm orderin' you to quit this house now!"

"Not while there's more mixabout to boil," Stolley called.

The townspeople laughed again, and the constable spun back toward the wagon. Fixing the beat-men with a glance, he nodded in the direction of the ladders and flicked a hand toward the house. Immediately, the beat-men unlashed the smaller of the two ladders from the rails of the wagon, grabbed up one of the canvas bags and quick-stepped in the direction the constable had indicated. Chuff, who was still standing impassively near the porch, moved slowly out of their way.

Bracing the ladder against the wall, the beat-men climbed sure-footedly up to the roof, carrying the canvas bag between them. With surprisingly catlike ease, they hurried across the roof toward the end of the building where the chimney stood. The cloud of smoke that chugged from the stone stack into the cold air was now gray and thick. Resting the canvas bag at their feet, the beat-men reached inside and withdrew two great armfuls of damp straw. Then they stuffed the straw down the mouth of the chimney, choking off its throat. A hot, wet smell filled the air, and bits of the straw began to whistle and hiss. The beat-men stuffed another armload down after the first, then retreated to the ladder, hurried back down to the ground and returned to the wagon.

"You want your family to breathe, Stolley," the constable called, "you'll bring them on out."

"Family's breathin' fine," Stolley answered, a small cough in his voice. "You reckon we didn't brace up for this?"

The crowd murmured in satisfaction, but uncertainly, as more coughing—this time in the high-pitched tones of a woman and boys—came from the house. For several long moments, no one spoke, listening instead as a growing clatter of urgent footfalls sounded behind the closed door. Once or twice, the front shutters opened a crack and a bit of a face—it looked to be a child's—would appear, draw a breath, and retreat. Then the Pounds grew completely quiet. The family had either managed to put the fire out before the smoke could overwhelm them, or they had succumbed to the cinders and soot they'd been forced to breathe. The crowd, the constable, Nacky and Teedie all listened closely, and then Stolley's voice called out again.

"Hope you've had yer breakfast, constable," he said, "'cause it looks like you've forced us to let our mixabout go cold."

At this, the people in the road lit up with the loudest laughter yet, and the constable spun back around once more toward the wagon. Now the crowd knew he was through fooling with the Pounds. Wordlessly, the three lawmen drew the remaining canvas bags and the three grappling hooks from the wagon, and carried them around to the side of the house, where the plaster-covered wood-beam wall was broken by a pair of high, shuttered windows about five feet apart. The windows were big enough to allow light and air to flow in, but too small to allow anyone but a child to pass through. Picking up two of the grappling hooks and turning them blunt end forward, the beat-men reached up, reared back and smashed the shutters. The crowd jumped back, and Chuff—who was still only a few feet from the house—flinched and blinked. Nacky backed a step away, noticing that his fine blue shirt had begun to feel sticky even in the morning chill. Teedie remained still.

Clearing away the splintered slats, the beat-men attached the sharp, curved ends of the hooks to the sturdy beams at the base of the window-sills. The constable himself then bent down and jammed the third hook sideways between a pair of horizontal beams just three feet up from the ground, twisting the hook so it bit hard into the wood. Withdrawing three heavy ship chains from the canvas bags, the men then attached them to the hooks. Finally, they unhitched the giant horses from their wagon and connected the chains to the beasts' remaining harnesses.

"Stolley Pound," the constable called out, full of purpose, "the horses have been fixed. Quit your house or they'll be switched."

"Switch away," Stolley's voice answered.

The constable turned to the beat-men. "On my sign," he said.

He then raised his arm and dropped it, and when he did, the two other men sharply slapped the rumps of the animals. All three horses whinnied and together pulled. Instantly, the chains stiffened, the hooks dug deeper into the beams, and a webwork of angry spider-cracks appeared in the plaster that covered the wall. The constable watched the horses struggling and called out to the beat-men.

"Again!" he cried, and again the beat-men struck the animals.

The already frightened horses now grew more so, pulling harder until the wall began to creak and pop. The constable watched for a moment longer, then, looking impatient, withdrew his sidearm from his waistband and fired a single, noisy shot into the air. The horses whinnied one last time, gave one final pull, and with a crash, the entire eastern wall of Stolley and Audra Pound's house was no more.

For a moment, silence descended over the scene as the timbers lay on the ground in a haze of dust and the beat-men settled and soothed the horses. The crowd craned forward, attempting to peer into the great, angry maw that the side of the home had become, but try as they might, they could see only darkness. The constable, his eyes dancing uneasily about, turned to the beat-men and shouted.

"Have out with them, then," he said hoarsely. "Have out with them."

With that, the beat-men left off tending the horses, bounded over the rubble of the wall and vanished into the ruined house. After a little muffled scuffling and a few muffled shouts, they reemerged, bringing the Pound family with them. Stolley came first, led by the larger of the two beat-men. Looking even smaller than he usually did, he had a close-cropped head of black hair and a mustache that was blacker still. His clothes and face were smudged from the hearth smoke, and his tiny gray eyes looked like bright buttons against his blackened skin. One of his shoes was oddly missing. After Stolley came Audra, a slight woman with mud-brown hair tied back in a knot. Her face too was soot-streaked, but her dark eyes were cast down and her crumpled expression gave her a more beaten look than her husband's. Her boys, about five and six years old, walked beside her, shoeless, capless, blackened, their gaze cast down like their mother's, their hands tightly holding hers. The smaller of the beat-men followed them.

The Pounds were walked toward the wagon and loaded aboard. The horses were then reharnessed and led through the silent crowd, which parted to let them pass. When the hitch reached the road, the constable and the beat-men hopped aboard and the horses broke into a trot. As they rattled away, Stolley looked back only once. His gaze never fell on Nacky and his fine blue shirt, nor on Chuff and his empty-seeming eyes. They sought out only Teedie, who stood like a rod away from the crowd, almost lost in the cloud of road dust that swirled everywhere. Stolley spotted him and flashed the tiniest twitch of a relieved smile when he did. Teedie did not see it, and in fact did not look up at all until the wagon had crested back over the hill and the Pound family was gone.

CHAPTER TWO

The first few weeks in the penitents'
tower in Yole were the hardest ones because they were the ones a prisoner spent on the top floor, the floor without the roof. The roof of the
tower had blown off in a storm nearly a century before Nacky was born,
and though the local courts considered replacing it, they ultimately decided not to. The high walls and the dizzying height would prevent even
the most industrious prisoner from contriving a means of escape, while
the open sky would provide an exposure to the elements that would
sharpen the punishment and, it was hoped, dull the criminal soul.

Once a penitent endured some time outdoors, he would be allowed
inside, spending the rest of his confinement slowly descending through
different cells on the tower's seven stories—each a bit roomier and pleasanter than the one above it—until at last he reached the bottom and his
sentence ended. Poor conduct could get a prisoner sent straight back
up a floor or two, which was why, as a regular visitor to the tower like
Nacky learned, it never paid to misbehave until you had progressed to
the fifth floor or below, when there would be much less risk of being
sent all the way back up to the roofless roof.

The initial weeks of Nacky's current stay were even harder than usual, since the early spring temperatures stayed low and the early spring drizzle stayed steady, and though the constable provided him with a canvas canopy and a small, metal cookstove, he remained chilled for the better part of twenty-one days. Only when he earned his way to the warm, dry, sixth floor did the time become more tolerable.

Of all the things Nacky generally liked about the interior floors of the tower, what he liked most was that so many of them afforded him a view of the Yole lake. The Yole lake sat at the very center of the Yole mountains, and it might have been a completely unremarkable lake if it weren't for a few things. First of all, it was almost perfectly round, a near-precise, quarter-mile-wide circle broken only by the occasional rip or wrinkle in its banks. The peculiarly round body was also peculiarly deep for a lake so small, sufficient to allow a plumbline to be dropped a good eighth of a mile down before the lead weight at last struck silt.

More distinctive than the odd, pudding-bowl shape of the lake was the odd color of the water that filled it. In general, the water in the local mountains ran a sort of steely silver, tinted both by the stone it cut through and the high ice it melted down from. The water in the Yole lake, however, rarely strayed from a bright, berry blue. Now and again the precise shade of the berry would shift—sometimes it was a deep blackberry, sometimes a softer blueberry, sometimes a still lighter pinkberry or milkberry or skyberry. Whatever its exact shade, a berry blue it generally remained.

For a man like Nacky, who enjoyed his quiet, the opportunity to look out at the lake now and again while pursuing the rest of his confinement routine—which consisted largely of reading, sleeping, eating and receiving the occasional visitor—was, on balance, a passable way to spend a stretch of months. Of course, confinement was still confinement, and most people might have been expected to try harder not to become so frequent a resident of the tower. Nacky, however, seemed destined for the criminal life from the time he was a boy.

Nacky's papa had been a sunny man and had always had proud plans for his only son. Though Dinny Patcher had never settled on what kind of work he liked to do—some years making his living as a roofer, other years getting by as a planter, others working as a peddler or a fruit picker or a horse trader—he had always been very clear that he was bringing Nacky up to go into the silver trade. Nobody in Yole ever believed the silver trade made much sense for local folks, principally because no one had ever discovered so much as a dusting of the stuff in the mountains surrounding the town. Shortly after Nacky was born, however, Dinny was traveling near the coast when he shared a ball of malt in a public house with a local silversmith. The smith told him something that Dinny came to believe was a great mercantile truth.

"No matter how fancies may change, people will always have an eye for a bright bit of silver," the smith declared, holding an ice-bright coin in his small, smooth hand.

There was something about how firmly the man said that and how lovely the coin looked that stayed with Dinny. "No matter how fancies might change," he soon began to tell Nacky, "people will always have an eye for a bright bit of silver." Over time, Nacky came to believe it too.

But silver was not destined to become Nacky Patcher's trade. The winter the boy turned nine years old, his father contracted a severe January grippe that he didn't seem able to shake. After two months, Nacky's mother, who had always looked to Dinny for guidance in important matters, caught it too. By the time the cold weather broke, they were both gone. Quietly, Nacky shut up the family's tiny two-room house and went to live on the other side of Yole with his father's father, the man he called Pippa. There he was taught an entirely new line of work.

For as long as Nacky could remember, he had truly loved his Pippa, and nearly everyone else in Yole did too. Gangly like Nacky, pale like Nacky, Pippa had a crinkly smile and a wily way that his grandson largely lacked. This, most people acknowledged, served Pippa well, since he made it his life's work to swindle as many of the local folks as he could, and the local folks more or less knew it.

Pippa had a lot of schemes he'd use to jolly people out of their money, and most of them worked fine. Sometimes he'd travel from house to house selling titles to cows that, strictly speaking, had not yet been born and, strictly speaking, never would be. Sometimes he'd ride the circuit of the other towns, selling digging rights in imaginary mines or harvesting rights in imaginary orchards or passing on title to bushels and bushels of corn and wheat that grew only in imaginary fields in Pippa's fertile mind.

What made Pippa's swindles work—and kept Pippa's pockets full—was not so much that he told clever lies, but that he told them so well, enjoying both the idea of the fibs and the company of the people he was fibbing to. Now and then, Nacky would come along as Pippa called on someone he was preparing to cheat, and the boy always looked forward to watching how his grandfather did his work. There was a way Pippa had of locking up the eyes of anyone he was talking to, holding on to them tight with his own and tugging them gently back if they started to drift. Then, with a voice that was just a tick above a whisper, he'd begin telling his story, piling picture on picture and promise on promise, until even Nacky half believed what he was hearing. By the time the man Pippa was talking to actually handed over his money, he was so tipsy with the tale he'd been told—and Pippa was so tipsy with the business of telling it—that nobody much cared if the corn or cow or fruit they were talking about was ever delivered at all.

"I did that fellow a good turn today," Pippa would say, as he and Nacky left and he pocketed the money he'd been given. "There's no telling how long that cow would've lived. But that story's going to stay with him forever."

Growing up, Nacky tried as best he could to be the thief his Pippa was, and he seemed to have been born with the temperament for it. Nacky had what his Pippa called the thief heat—a woozy, almost drunken feeling that would come over him whenever he was in the presence of possible plunder. Walking into an empty shop that the proprietor had left untended for a moment, Nacky would look around the room and nearly swoon, knowing that everything in it was there for the filching, provided he had the courage to take it. It never mattered what the untended goods were; Nacky would go just as giddy in a gem store—where the riches had real appeal for him—as he would in a ladies' hat shop, where they had none at all. It was that thrill at the mere business of stealing that was the true mark of the thief heat.

"You've got the taste for it, boy," Nacky's Pippa would tell him proudly, "got it more'n I do even."

But if Nacky had a thief's appetite, he didn't have a thief's talent. By the time he turned fifteen, he was already riding the circuit of the neighboring towns himself, telling the tale of the cow, the tale of the crops, the tale of the mine—and even changing it from the copper mine Pippa favored to a silver mine he imagined Dinny would have preferred. But while Nacky spoke the same words Pippa did, he didn't speak them the same way. He tried the business of locking up the eyes of the man he was talking to, but the man's eyes always pulled free. He tried to pile up the pictures the way Pippa did, but the pictures never seemed to stack. If he walked away with any money at all, he never walked away with much, and within a few days, the man he'd fleeced would usually appear at his door, threatening to go straight to the law if Nacky didn't then and there return every coin he'd gotten from him.

"Do you like these people, Nacky?" Pippa would ask when the man had collected his money and stormed away.

"I do," Nacky would assure him with the brightest smile and nod he could summon.

Pippa would look at him unconvinced. "Because if you don't like them," he'd say, "you can't make them happy."

The truth of the matter was, Nacky didn't have much feeling either way about the people he was fibbing to, which made it more than passing hard to steal from them—or at least to steal from them well. By the time Pippa died, something he did not do until his grandson was close to twenty, the Patcher family, which by now was Nacky alone, did not have any true calling at all. Nacky thus spent much of his adult life inching and pinching in the thieving game, sometimes doing well enough to keep his purse filled, but just as often getting nabbed at it and winding up in the penitents' tower.

Even if Nacky had come up in a different home, of course, it's still possible he'd have had to turn thief to keep himself flush. And for that he blamed Mally Baloo.

Of all the families that lived in Yole, none was more influential than the Baloos. And of all the Baloos, none had made himself more money or collected himself more power than Mally, the current head of the family. The Baloos as a whole had been landowners in the mountains for as long as anyone could remember, holding liens against most of the local homes and shops and charging punishing rents for the privilege of living and working in them.

Few people in Yole could pay their monthly indebtedness, but the regional laws, which favored landowners, who were thought to be fine managers of their local economies, provided a penalty for such a failure. Families that found themselves in arrears in their rent would be required to pay what they owed in assets instead—delivering to the Baloos at least three-tenths of all the crops they grew, four-tenths of all the game they shot, five-tenths of all the cows or sheep they raised and six-tenths of any money they did manage to earn. The debt collectors would visit on the twenty-first day of February and September, and while not a single claim was to be levied between those times, the townspeople were expected to pay what they owed in full when the appointed dates did arrive.

Not satisfied with these cruel rules, the Baloos tightened their hold on the town even further, using their wealth to see to it that sympathetic courts and constables were never established in Yole. Instead, it was left to the judges in other communities to manage the Yole affairs—judges who were well-paid by the Baloos to enforce their claims and who would obligingly order imprisonment not only for locals who missed their pay-ments, but for their family members and even friends, should the debtor try to light-foot it out of town with his accounts unsettled.

Such harsh conditions might have raised up the rebel in other communities, prompting them to stand up and throw off the tyranny of the Baloo family, but not the people of Yole. Their debts may have been held by the Baloos, but their spirits had seemingly been broken by something that lay even deeper. Nobody knew what that something was, but there were whose who believed the answer was to be found in the Songs of the Dry-Land Boats.

The Songs of the boats were not songs at all, but favorite children's fables that generations of Yole boys and girls had learned from the cradle. At least twenty generations back, so the Songs said, the entire mountain region surrounding Yole was a vast inland lake, so vast it was really more of an inland sea. The water that filled the sea was clear, cold, berry blue, and even slightly sweet, or at least some people with sharp tastes were said to insist. Great sailing ships would travel this expanse, transporting goods and passengers to lush and lively towns all along the banks. Eventually, however, local mercantile men, hungry for more land and convinced that rich soil lay in the silt below the water, set about draining the sea—cutting huge notches in the mountain walls and allowing the water to spill out and stream all the way down to the ocean. The water roared from the sea far faster than the mercantile men had imagined, emptying the vast basin in just over a day. Many boats foundered in what became known as the Great Drying, and the lives of many sailors were lost.

The fortunes of all the towns within the mountains changed after that—but not for the better. The fertile soil the industrialists believed was beneath the sea turned out to be nothing but dead clay, hardly able to support a shoot, much less a carpet of crops. The vast bowl where the lake had been thus became an arid crater. The villages along its now-dry banks could make nothing of such sterile land, and with no sea traffic connecting them to one another, they began to turn inward and wither.

Most of the people stranded in the drying mountains moved away, except for the industrialists themselves and their direct descendants, who, it was said, had been cursed for what they'd done and were condemned to establish a new town in the infirm soil at the center of the parched crater. This became Yole. The quarter-mile lake around which the town was built was all that remained of the lost sea—a little like the tiny pooling of tea in the shallow impression at the center of a saucer. Lest the people forget the ruin they'd made of their mountain, they'd be further cursed with a spectral reminder: Wandering through the peaks and valleys of the local mountains, so the stories held, were charmed but ghostly ships, the shadowy remains of the lost vessels that foundered in the Great Drying, always seeking—but never finding—a place in the sea they lost long ago.

Nobody in Yole who was even a bit beyond childhood much believed in the legend, reckoning that their bleak land, cruel debts and general lack of resourcefulness were merely their lot. Nacky Patcher, however, always thought there was something more to the Songs. Many were the times his Pippa would return from his travels with the report that he'd seen one of the dry-land boats, gliding smooth and quiet along the soil of a mountain pass just as the sunlight gave way and the owl light settled in. Nacky's eyes would widen in fright at these tales, but Pippa would insist that the sign was a good one. The last verse of the Songs, he'd remind his grandson, promised that the dark charm that held the town could always be broken, but the locals would have to show themselves worthy of such clemency, watching for the opportunity to redeem their land and seizing it when it arrived. In the twenty generations since the Great Drying, no one had ever figured out just what that meant, but the occasional appearance of the ghostly boats was a sign, Pippa believed, that the promise would yet be kept.

Nacky Patcher, raised on that hope, had lately begun to despair that his faith would ever be rewarded. During this stay in the tower, he found, the view of the lake that he'd once so enjoyed only reminded him of the town's sad past and his own sorry present. A sense of bleakness descended on him, one that seemed to grow worse with each confining day. How he'd endure nearly a year of imprisonment he was not at all certain.

As it turned out, he wouldn't have to.

The poor weather that had been battering Yole of late had also been raking up the shipping lanes, causing an unusually high number of desertions in the commercial fleets that embarked from the towns lining the ocean about half a day's carriage ride from Yole. When shorthanded ships pulled into port, a call would go out for local inmates to fill out the sailing manifests, in return for which they would be given their freedom. Late one morning, as a sleepy Nacky was cooking up breakfast on the tiny stove he'd brought with him from the roof, he heard the heavy key turn in the lock of his thick plank door. The door swung open and the constable stepped inside.

"The clipper *Hoogly* just docked at Twelve Points," the constable said. "They're lookin' for crew."

The lawman spoke brusquely to Nacky as he always did. A resident of nearby Knockle, he'd been in Yole since the morning he'd overseen the Pound foreclosure and would be required to remain as tower guard until Nacky was released ten months hence. Nacky, who was anxious to be free of his confinement as soon as possible, nonetheless didn't care to trade the prison of the tower for the prison of a boat unless that boat was carrying him someplace he wanted to go. He also didn't mind the fact that as long as he stayed where he was, his jailer would feel as jailed as he did.

"Where's the ship bound?" he asked.

The constable looked surprised at the question. "Deep south," he said. "Down to Red Drift."

Nacky chewed on that for a moment, then shook his head no. "Too far," he said absently.

A week later, the constable returned. "The freighter *Princess Arianne* put to port in the M'crooms," he said. "Bound north for New Sweep."

"Too cold," Nacky responded.

Finally, after another week, the constable returned once more. This time, he was carrying word that the *Walnut Egg*, a ship well known for its speed, had dropped anchor in Greater M'croom. It was looking for three or four sailors, and it was heading for the easternmost forehead of

South America, a destination known for gentle weather, fine food and good-natured people. Nacky had no idea if he'd be suited to such an unfamiliar place, but what seemed increasingly certain was that he was no longer suited to remaining where he was. The Songs had always said to look sharp for opportunity, and this, he reckoned, might be his. Without a word, he smiled, gathered his belongings and headed out to sea.

Barely a fortnight later, he'd wish he hadn't.

CHAPTER THREE

After the Pounds were pitched from
their home, Teedie Flinn knew it would not be easy for him to find a
new place to live. Few people in Yole had enough coin to fill their own
purses and feed their own children, much less look after someone else's
forgotten son. The sensible thing would have been for Teedie to avoid
the problem altogether and simply follow the Pound family wherever
they went, and that in fact is what Audra and Stolley and their two
young boys wanted. But Teedie had misgivings.

In the three years he had been in Yole, he'd lived under a lot of
strange roofs other than the Pounds'—enough to know when his stay was
still welcome and when the family had had a full portion of him. Even
in homes in which he'd felt truly welcome, he learned to recognize the
sidelong glance a mother would flash him—sometimes not even knowing
she was doing it—when money was short and food was scarce and he'd
pull up to the table to eat a bit of bread or drink a cup of milk that
would have otherwise gone to one of her true children. It was a look
that made the food choke in his throat, and in all the time he'd been
with the Pounds, he'd never once seen it on Audra's face. Now that she
and Stolley would be hard put merely to care for themselves and their

boys, he knew the side-eyes couldn't be far away, and he didn't want to be there when they came.

More problematic, even if Teedie were welcome in the Pounds' new home, he wouldn't be welcome in their new town. After Audra, Stolley and the boys were pitched, they went off to live with Audra's family in the town of Bowfin, hard up against the town of Knockle, where Teedie was born. Teedie, as the constables of all the local communities knew, was forbidden to live anywhere but Yole, a prohibition that had been strictly enforced and seemed richly deserved, ever since the uprising at the Knockle work home and the fire that resulted.

No sensible person really thought Teedie was at fault for the fire. The problem was, there were a lot of people around who weren't so sensible, and in the days after the tragedy three years back, it was no surprise that they looked for someone to blame, and no surprise that they chose Teedie. Teedie himself sometimes wondered if the finger-pointers weren't right, and in quiet moments at the borders of sleep, he could still sometimes see the terrified look on the other boys' faces as the blackfire roared up and the building came down, and would wake up with a start and think that maybe the fire had been his handiwork after all.

The Knockle work home where the fire occurred wasn't strictly a work home at all. Rather, it was what the locals called a half-home—something quite a bit worse. Work homes were places set aside for ordinary boys who'd been unlucky enough to lose their parents and for whom tough but fair labor would now take the place of a mother's love and a father's rules. Half-homes were for different kinds of boys—ones who'd been orphaned as well, but who'd already proved themselves wild enough that ordinary work would not be sufficient to keep them out of mischief.

Half-homes were so named both because the boys who were sent there were considered halfway to a criminal life, and because the terms of their confinement were modeled after that of prisoners on convict ships, save for the fact that everything was cut in two. It was a practice designed to maintain the boys' health but break their will, and on the whole it worked very well. Penal regulations assured ship prisoners of seven pounds of food each week, so the boys got three and a half. Prisoners got a gallon of water each day, so the boys got a half-gallon. While it was true that none of the boys was even half as large as most of the prisoners, it was also true that they were growing, which meant that their appetites were at least three-quarters as keen. The short portions were guaranteed to keep them from starving, but guaranteed too to leave them always a little bit hungry and parched.

The boys' days and nights were scissored up into half-shares as well. They were allotted a tolerable seven hours of sleep, but that generous stretch was divided into two three-and-a-half-hour naps, separated by four hours of study. Most of the boys never quite adjusted to being rousted twice daily from the deepest patch of slumber and would remain in a cross and cloudy state through much of the day. When they did sleep, it was on cots precisely eighteen inches wide—half the thirty-six inches provided on the convict ships. The only part of the boys' day that was served up in a full helping was the eight hours of labor they were required to perform from late morning to suppertime, and while the work was usually manageable, it was occasionally something else entirely.

Ordinarily the orphans in the Knockle half-home were assigned the job of manufacturing candles and hurricane lamps. It was hot work, particularly when it came time to melt the wax or blow the glass, but it was easy enough once you learned it. Three autumns back, however, the selectmen of Knockle decided to hold a harvest festival and to cap the celebration with a display of fire rockets. Nobody in the region knew how to set the fuses or pack the powder fire rockets required, but given that the boys in the half-home had proven themselves to be an industrious lot, and given that their usual work involved flame and light, they were deemed the best suited to take on the job.

The type of fire rockets that would be used in the festival were more properly known as fruit rockets, owing to the kind of light they produced. The powders used to make the flames burned hot but dark, producing not bright yellows and greens and golds, but deeper shades that called to mind ripe cherries, dusk apples, and black plums. Fruit rockets were best launched not in full dark—when they would be lost against the nighttime sky—but in the owl light just before the sun had fully set, when the lingering glow of the day would frame the flames most brilliantly. Of the few colors the fruit rockets produced, it was the black plum that most thrilled observers. The powders produced a flame that was both utterly dark and brilliantly bright at the same moment. Those who'd never seen blackfire could never precisely imagine what it looked like. Those who had seen it could never forget it.

The boys did their powder-packing in a planked room on the first floor of the half-home with only a few windows admitting any daylight, and those were high on the wall near the ceiling so as not to serve as a distraction. A wooden staircase led up to the second story of the house, where the boys slept; a stone staircase led down to the cellar, where the candle wax, lamp parts, and rocket powder were stored. During the rocket-making, barrels of the powder would be carried up to the work-room, where the boys would scoop it out and mix it with rice starch to hold it all together and pine pitch to help fire it up. Then they would stuff the sticky fuel into paper tubes, attach a short fuse at one end and cap the other with a cone. A few days of working with such harsh, explosive dust and even the fittest boys began coughing like consumptives. The less fit ones could scarcely catch their breath.

"Hold that hacking," the headmaster would bark as he'd stride up and down between the rows of worktables, his own breath protected by a eucalyptus cloth he held to his face.

"Can't help it, lord," a boy would answer. "Can't get free of the powder."

"Them what are coughing can't fairly be working," the headmaster would snap. "Them what aren't working will get pitched out."

Teedie fared no better or worse than most of the other boys, coughing constantly but tolerably. But that wasn't so for Dal Tally, the boy assigned to the spot next to him at the worktable. A small, pale child a full year older than Teedie, Dal actually looked a good deal younger, never seeming able to put much muscle on his bones or much fat on his muscles. He grew flush in the sun and thus avoided it, remaining pale and drawn-looking no matter the season. Even before the rocket work, he often seemed unable to take in enough wind, wheezing pitiably whenever the boys were assigned to dust or sweep and sneezing unceasingly as soon as the flowers appeared in the spring. At his first glimpse of the barrels of powder that would fill the fruit rockets, Dal seemed to know he would suffer terribly.

"You pulling any breath?" Teedie would whisper to him at the table, hearing the wheezing but not wanting to turn away from his own work lest he be called for loafing.

"Enough," Dal would answer.

"Don't sound like enough. Sounds like you're choked off whole."

Now and again when the headmaster was granting himself a smoke outside, Teedie would offer to manage Dal's work so that the smaller boy could catch his wind. But on the few occasions Dal accepted, the double-time scooping Teedie had to do just kicked up more dust, and the coughing this drew from Dal would catch the headmaster's attention the moment he returned, leading him to punish both boys with an extra two hours of work after the others had gone off to sleep. It was all becoming impossible to bear, and one night during the dinner hour, Teedie decided he could take it no more.

The boys ate their meals at the same tables where they did their work, and while the rocket powders would be dumped back into their barrels before the plates were laid, the noxious dust still covered everything, including the boys' hands. Since many of the half-home meals were served without utensils—foods like Navy biscuits and potatoes in their jackets not really calling for any—the boys were forced to touch what they ate with hands that immediately made the meal unpalatable. Even the parts of the food they didn't touch became covered with powders settling down out of the air.

"Can't rightly eat anything," Teedie muttered to Dal one night over a biscuit turned orange from fuel dust, "not without a fork, anyway."

"Ain't likely to get one of those," Dal answered.

"I can ask," Teedie said.

"Don't do it, Teedie," Dal said. "Ain't worth the trouble that's sure to come."

Teedie thought for a moment, then looked over at the headmaster, who was striding between the tables in the stiff-backed way he had at the end of the day when he was tired and inclined to answer any foolishness from the boys especially harshly. Then, before Teedie's judgment could pull him back, he stood up in his place as the boys were required to do when they needed a drink of water or a privy trip during the workday. He called out a question in the brief, unwasteful way he'd been taught to when making all such requests.

"Fork, lord?" he asked, not looking directly at the headmaster.

The other boys, who had been eating silently, stopped and turned. The headmaster, a tall, willowy man with a narrow head shaped like a sweet potato, did the same. He regarded Teedie balefully.

"Did you find bean mash in your dish tonight?"

"No, lord."

"Bread soup?"

"No, lord."

"Then I reckon your hands will serve you fine."

"My hands've gone orange, lord," Teedie said quietly. "Biscuit too."

The headmaster regarded Teedie for a long moment. "I expect we'll have to find another means for you to eat then. Sit, boy."

Teedie did as he was told.

"Hands behind your back," the headmaster snapped.

Teedie did that too.

"Now finish everything that's in front of you—biscuit, potato, tea. And don't move them hands while you do it."

Teedie stole a glance at the man, then bent slowly forward and, as he'd been ordered, began working his mouth around the biscuit in his dish. The thing broke and crumbled and stuck in orange-tinted clumps to his face. The other boys, who might have been expected to laugh at such clumsiness, did not. Teedie worked the biscuit for a moment more, then turned to the potato, a hard-baked thing that was easily too large for his small jaw. He took a couple of tentative snaps at it, but it kept skittering away from him, finally bouncing off the plate altogether and fetching up against his mug of corn-sugar tea.

"That mug too," the headmaster said. "Use your teeth if you have to."

Teedie obediently clamped his teeth on the rim of the mug and tried to lift it from the table, but his purchase was poor. He tried again and failed again, then tried once more and actually succeeded in raising the mug an inch before it slipped from his teeth and tipped over, spilling hot tea across the table and into his lap. Scalded, Teedie leapt to his feet.

"Sit back down, boy," the headmaster ordered.

"But I'm burned, lord."

"I said sit back down!"

Teedie looked down at the mess on the table and the hot stain on his trousers—already turning uncomfortably cold—and felt the orange biscuit crumbs caked to his face. Suddenly, with an anger he didn't know he had inside him, he wheeled on the man.

"No!" he said. "I ain't gonna sit! I ain't no criminal—halfways or no ways—and I ain't done nothing to get treated like one!"

There was silence for an instant as the headmaster gaped at him, and then the other boys in the room let out with a whoop, startling the headmaster and shocking Teedie, who looked around blinking and smiling.

"You're a criminal if I says you're a criminal," the headmaster shouted over the noise.

"No I ain't," Teedie said, emboldened by the boys.

"I ain't one neither," said Dal, fighting for the breath to speak up himself.

"Nor I!" said another boy, jumping up at the next table.

"Nor I," shouted two others, leaping up to join them.

"You boys'll sit or you'll be pitched!" answered the headmaster. "Every last one off to the tower!"

"Tower ain't much different than where we are now," Teedie said.

"Better in fact with no headmaster," another boy said. At that, another—much louder—chorus of whoops rose up from the orphans.

Now the remaining boys who had been sitting down stood up to join the others. As if with one mind, all of them pushed back from their tables, the benches scraping in the rocket dust that covered the floor. They turned to face the headmaster, and he took a tiny step backward, a step that said he'd scanned the group in front of him, done some quick arithmetic, and didn't like what the numbers told him. As on most nights, the headmaster was alone with the boys, the cook having gone home once he'd prepared the simple evening meal, and nobody else much being needed to tend to children who were usually underfed, overworked and, by this time of day, hungry only for their beds. But tonight, the boys seemed hungry for something else. As a group, they took a step forward.

"You hold your ground, now!" the headmaster said.

"We've took enough orders," said one of the bigger boys.

"Not another step," the headmaster shouted, glancing over his shoulder.

"We'll step if we care to," another big boy said, advancing to the front of the group. He was followed by three other boys almost his size. Teedie—far smaller—took a step closer to them. The headmaster backed up farther, bumped a bench and lost his balance. He caught himself before falling completely. The boys let out with laughter and jeers.

"You'll regret crossing me!" the headmaster warned.

"Only regret we have is minding you as long as we did!" said the biggest boy. "But we're done with that. There's pitchin' to be done tonight, but it ain't us what's gettin' tossed!"

With that, the big boys broke and charged. The smaller boys—Teedie and Dal among them—followed, and the headmaster, his face now showing true fear, backed and scrabbled toward the door. He reached it one step ahead of the boys, fumbled with the latch, and flung it open. The boys converged, pushed him out into the cold night, and slammed the door loudly behind him.

Instantly, the room erupted in noise and joy. The boys hugged and cheered and jumped in place. They locked the door and dragged a heavy shelf against it. They leapt up on chairs, climbed up on tables, flung their hated biscuits across the room and stomped their hard potatoes flat. They did all the things they'd imagined they'd do if they were ever through with the horrid headmaster—and then they did one more thing they oughtn't have done.

One of the boys found the unlit tobacco pipe the headmaster had left behind and began strutting around, chewing and puffing it the way the headmaster himself did. This drew much laughter from the other boys, who grabbed at the pipe and took their own turns with it. Still another boy then pulled a matchstick from a cup near a wall lantern, lit it and fired up the dry tobacco in the bowl. He blew hard through the mouth-piece, sending up a shower of sparks and ash that delighted the other boys. The headmaster himself had never done such a clever thing with his pipe, and the boys laughed harder when they thought of that. But there was a reason the headmaster had taken such care. While he might chew his pipe all day long, he never dared actually light it until he was either outside or up in his room, away from the explosive rocket powders scattered about downstairs. The boys did not know to be so cautious.

As the lit cinders that flew from the pipe landed on the floor, they gave rise to a sparking and sizzling from the sprinkling of dust. The boys standing nearby squealed in delight and jumped back, pointing and laughing. But the powder sparks were able to do more than just sizzle. One especially large one jumped high off the floor, struck a boy in the cheek and caused him to yelp in pain. Another leapt to the tattered cuff of a small boy's trousers, setting them smoldering and causing him to perform a terrified dance on one foot while taking the other in his hands and slapping out the little flames.

Now the boys weren't so amused. From one end of the open work-room to the other, the powder covered the floor in a thin, even dusting. The sparks that had begun as a few hot points were now ranging out in a rapidly widening circle. They stung the toes of the barefoot boys standing closest, causing them to hop up onto tables. They advanced on the boys standing farther away, sending them retreating in a frightened stumble. The carpet of sparks spread under tables and chairs, flowed around barrels and workbenches and raced out to the edges of the room. When they reached the wooden staircase leading up to the sleeping chambers, they stopped. The headmaster always took care to brush the boys off before they went up to bed so that they wouldn't carry any powder up with them. When the sparks reached the stone staircase leading down to the cellar, however, they behaved entirely differently.

With barrels and buckets of rocket powder being carried to and from the workroom all day, the cellar steps were fairly smothered with dust. The moment the sparks touched the top stair, there was a bright flash and a loud *whoosh,* and the steps ignited. The boys froze, wide-eyed, knowing they should flee, but too frightened to move. In a flash, the fire raced down the stairs and disappeared into the stone room below. All was silent for an instant, then suddenly from directly beneath the workroom came a thunderous *whump* as one of the heavy powder barrels ignited and blew. The blast shook the building, heaved the floor and flung several of the boys straight off their feet. Now they had no trouble moving at all.

"Get out!" the boys shouted in unison. "Run! Run!"

Teedie and the others broke for the door, which was not only locked but blocked by the heavy shelf. They took hold of the giant thing and began pulling and pushing it in different directions.

As they struggled, there was another great blast as a second great barrel caught. The tremor this time caused two ceiling beams to fall, one square on top of the shelf blocking the door, making it even less passable. The high windows, which might have provided another escape, were entirely out of reach. At the same time the beams fell, a huge wave of yellow-black smoke coughed up from the belly of the cellar, filling the workroom and choking the boys with its searing stink.

"Sulfur!" one of them screamed. "Get down!"

The awful cloud poured through the entire first floor, turning the boys temporarily blind. Those who did manage to open their eyes could see that the room had gone almost entirely dark, the smoke so putrefying the air that the lanterns simply snuffed themselves.

"The stairs, the stairs, the stairs!" the boys who could speak yelled to one another. "Crawl!"

As one, the sightless, voiceless boys did just that, creeping toward the staircase across the wide floor, which bucked beneath them as smaller barrels in the cellar continued to flame and burst. Teedie kept hold of Dal Tally, pushing him along the floor ahead of him, silently imploring the sick, wheezing boy to keep moving lest neither one of them survive. When they and the other boys reached the staircase, they scrabbled up, stumbled to their sleeping quarters and ran screaming to the windows. They pounded on the shutters with their hands and fists until the thin wood splintered away, then they thrust their heads and shoulders through the holes they'd made, frantically gasping the cold night air.

Outside, the headmaster, who had been stalking off to fetch the constable, heard the explosions and saw the flashes of light and came racing back to the house. Now as he sprinted toward it, he saw the boys—black-faced with soot and crying out in fear—half dangling from the windows. There was no doubt in his mind what fuel was driving this fire, and no doubt that there were still more barrels to blow, otherwise the house wouldn't be standing at all.

"Jump, boys!" he shouted. "Jump now!"

"Can't do it!" several of them answered. "Can't see!"

"You don't need to see!" the headmaster shouted. "The grass is soft; I'll break what falls I can. But you got to do it now!"

Just then, there was another *whump* from the basement and another shaking of the house, and all at once, the blind jump into the cold night held no fear for the boys. One by one, then two by two, they climbed up on the sills and leapt from the windows, the headmaster running from one to the other as they were in flight, trying at least to slow their fall with his arms and chest before they could strike the ground. As they hit, he would push them roughly away, forcing them a safer distance from the house where they collapsed in a sobbing, gasping group.

Teedie Flinn, who had been crowded away from the window by some of the bigger boys, was one of the last to jump. He pushed Dal out ahead of him, and the small boy turned out to be so paper-light the headmaster actually caught him on the fly. Teedie wasn't so lucky. As he was leaping free, he caught his foot on the bottom of the sill, pitched forward and plunged to the earth face-first. It was only with the help of the headmaster and Teedie's own outstretched arms that he hit the grass with a force that didn't kill him. Still, as he struck the ground, he felt an explosive pain in his right hand as if all the fine bones from fingers to wrist had broken and burst. He drew himself up into a ball, howling with the hurt and the fear, and rolled back to where the other boys were.

When the headmaster had taken a count of all the terrified children and satisfied himself that they were safe, he moved them still farther from the dying building. Then, as a group, they turned and watched as the remaining barrels of fruit rocket fuel brought down the half-home. First the deep pulpy flame of the ripe cherry fire poured through the windows; then came the ruby purple of the dusk apples, a light so rich it was almost possible to smell the sugar in the fruit the flames were pretending to be.

Finally, there was the greatest explosion of all, and through every window in the house came the plum-colored blackfire. It was, as people had always said, a flame so bright it was hard to look on it full, and yet so dark it seemed impossible to see anything at all. Teedie knelt on his haunches in the grass, cradling his ruined right hand and rocking gently. It was true, he thought, that once you'd seen blackfire you could never forget it. What no one had ever told him was that you'd dearly wish you could.

The Knockle half-home was rebuilt within a few months, and all the boys were sent back there to live—all save Teedie Flinn. The very morning after the fire, the local constable banished him from Knockle, sending him to nearby Yole, where he was ordered to find keep with local families until he came of age. Afterward, he'd be expected to leave the mountain towns altogether, never to return to any of them again. Teedie did as he was ordered, trudging alone toward Yole that very day.

In the three years that followed, he'd taken up residence with no fewer than five Yole families, sweeping up, tending shop and doing whatever else was required of him. The Pound house had likely been his last chance to find a true home, but now that was lost to him too. There'd be no other families inclined to take in such an accursed boy anymore. It might be time, Teedie guessed, to begin the career of thieving he'd been considering for so long.

CHAPTER FOUR

The wave that should have killed
Nacky Patcher struck in the last hour of the tenth day of his first trip
to sea. There were a lot of other waves that hit the ship that day, and
Nacky and the rest of the crewmen weathered them well. But Nacky's
wave didn't strike until very late at night, and the instant it did, he figured he was done.

Nacky was probably the last man aboard the *Walnut Egg* who ought
to have lived through a wave of such size. His poor seaman's skills already made it a bit of a surprise that he'd survived as long as he had. At
first, Nacky was pleased at how much he enjoyed his time aboardship,
at least when he was standing on the breezy bow, with the wind blowing
his feathery hair back around his head and the temperate sea delivering
the odd bump but no belly-churning waves.

Much of the ease he felt in the boat likely had to do with how familiar it seemed to him. The ghost vessels his Pippa had occasionally
described seeing in the dry mountains around Yole were bigger than the
speedy *Walnut Egg* on which Nacky now sailed, and colored a woodier
gold than the grim brown-black of the *Egg* too, which was old and thus
heavily tarred against leaks. But the constant creaking of the masts

was the same Pippa had described hearing across the mountains as the boats would glide by, and the smell of raw rope and cut wood that Pippa claimed wafted from the spectral vessels seemed to come off of Nacky's ship too. The cozy feeling all this gave Nacky did not last long, however—only until the captain actually called on him to work and he realized what the business of serving on a ship really meant.

There were any number of jobs a green seaman like Nacky was thought suitable for, but as it turned out, he muffed them all. There was sail-rigging to be done—work that utterly mystified Nacky and that he was allowed to try only once before making a terrible tangle of it. There was deck-cleaning, a simple enough business but one for which Nacky also proved unfit, since he rarely managed to keep his footing on the slick planks when the ship was stable, never mind when it pitched and listed. Finally, the captain assigned him to the humble business of cargo-steeving, a job even Nacky suspected he could manage, if only because it kept him belowdecks and out from underfoot.

Nacky's new crewmates found much to amuse them in his poor abilities and delighted at watching him go stumblingly about his work. Nacky did not care for being the object of so many low laughs but tried to abide them just the same, performing the jobs he was given as best he could and simply nodding at the needling. It was in the middle of the second week of the *Walnut Egg*'s trip to the forehead of South America that a savage, mid-spring storm rose up, slapping and tossing the ship and threatening to scuttle it altogether. Nacky went tea-china white when the storm hit, but the rest of the sailors, who had much to do to keep the vessel righted, seemed too occupied with their work to worry about it sinking. It was only after nightfall, when the weather grew even worse, causing a rogue wave to crash over the stern end of the ship and smash all the lanterns on the aft deck, that the captain himself appeared concerned—and at last had something useful for Nacky to do.

"Patcher!" he called out, poking his head out of the dry wheelhouse and spotting a dripping Nacky on the listing deck. "Go below to the hold and fetch more lamps."

Nacky blanched, dreading the very thought of venturing down to the stuffy 'tween deck, where the sickly motion of the ship could cause even the strongest seaman to yollick up everything he'd eaten that day. Before he could protest, however, the captain vanished back into his wheelhouse and slammed the door. Nacky thus did as he was told, slipping and skidding over to the hatchway, struggling down the ladder to the dark 'tween deck, then stumble-running the length of the hundred-and-sixty-foot corridor toward a door near the bow that led even deeper down to the huge, black hold. It was only when he reached the hold door that he realized he'd neglected to ask the captain for the key he'd need to open it up. Nacky let out a groan, knowing that the captain would quickly discover the oversight and send another sailor down after him—a sailor who would be carrying not just a key, but a few choice words for the full-grown cargo lad who had once again mitt-handed what was essentially a boy's job. Glowering at the lock on the hold door, Nacky did hear another set of footsteps—two sets, actually—climbing down the ladder to the 'tween deck and hurrying down the dark passageway toward him.

"You along there, Patcher?" one of the voices called.

Nacky recognized the voice as belonging to the bo'sun known as Orro. Nacky had liked Orro from the first time he'd met him, though he couldn't say exactly why. Orro was a big man, the full of a door, with a dark beard, a head of shaggy hair and a pair of hammy upper arms that seemed to have been built for shipboard work. The index finger of his right hand was shorn off clean at the middle knuckle, yet he nonetheless wore a pewter ring on the stump that remained, as if he were determined to do whatever he could to pretty up the ugly thing he had left. On the opposite hand, the middle finger was completely gone. Orro had once made his living as a highwayman, ambushing commercial wagons before being caught and sent to sea for what was now his fourth trip. Many was the time Nacky pictured what it would have been like to confront that forbidding form on a lonely road late on a moonless night.

"Patcher!" Orro called again.

"Here," Nacky shouted. "Up ahead."

"Not bloody far ahead," the second man said, with a snirt of laughter.

This voice, Nacky knew, belonged to Mink, someone he had come to think of as the most disagreeable sailor aboard the ship. Slight, dark and wiry, Mink was a snappish sort, with narrow features and jumpy eyes. Mink had been a burglar before coming to sea, making his living scaling the walls and entering the windows of the kitchen houses near the coasts. Though he insisted sailing was now his life's calling, he looked far more suited to his burglary work. Mink and Orro bounded up the corridor and came to a stop next to Nacky, all three men steadying themselves by holding on to a support stanchion.

"Might have known you wouldn't make it far by yerself," Mink said. "I told the captain we oughta just leave you here, but he wanted to give Orro somethin' to do."

Orro flashed Mink a bull's look and nodded toward the door of the hold. "Open it up," he said.

Mink reached into his pocket and fished out the hold key. Then he pushed Nacky aside, unlocked the door and swung it open.

"Up with you," Orro said to Nacky, with a jerk of his chin to a lantern hanging above the door. "And down with that."

Nacky reached up and took down the lit lantern, and Mink motioned him into the hold. He did as instructed, leaning into the open doorway with the lantern extended ahead of him. He saw nothing but a velvety blackness and a steep ladder leading down into it. At that moment a burst of thunder sounded outside and the ship heaved and bucked. Nacky felt his stomach turn over once. Orro nodded into the abyss.

"Down you go," he said. "Need a half dozen more o' them lamps."

Without protest, Nacky stepped onto the ladder and eased himself down the rungs, holding on with just one clammy hand while clutching the lantern with the other. When he reached the bottom, he felt a damp chill he hadn't felt in the cramped 'tween deck. Turning to face the hold, he held the lantern in front of him and took a moment to look about. The *Walnut Egg* was sailing full on this trip, its gullet stuffed with hogsheads of vinegar, jugs of sherry and crates of filberts and green cooking apples. There was also said to be a pig on board—though Nacky had not yet seen it. Unprotected plunder like this would normally be more than enough to get the thief heat rising in Nacky, and even in the belly of the bucking ship, he felt his heart pick up, his breath quicken and at least a small dreaminess start to settle over him. Just then, however, a voice cut through his reverie.

"Patcher!" Mink's voice called from above. "What're you about down there?"

"I'm lookin' for the lanterns," Nacky called back, agitated.

Shaking off the thief heat, Nacky began moving carefully about the hold, toeing aside a surprising amount of wrecked cargo that had been torn free by the storm and could easily cost him his balance if he didn't tread carefully. He was doing a fair enough job keeping his footing when suddenly, off to his right, he heard something move. He caught his breath and turned, throwing the light of his lantern on a pile of food debris. Next to it, just at the limit of the lamp's reach, stood the rumored pig, a small, pink and black thing no bigger than a good-sized footstool. Nacky let out his breath, smiled weakly and looked at the animal for a few seconds; the animal looked back. Its eyes were small and black like a pig's eyes ought to be, but they moved across Nacky's face with more life and light than he'd ever seen in such a beast. After a moment, the pig broke the gaze and returned to snuffling a mound of spilled filberts.

"Patcher!" Orro's voice called from above. "Don't be hurklin' around down there. If you can't find them lamps, say as much."

Nacky was about to answer, when the *Walnut Egg* hit a steep swell. Stumbling backward, he planted his right heel squarely on the pulp of a squashed apple. He skidded to his side, fetched up against a stack of crates and started to fall forward. On the deck in front of him were several jagged shards of a broken sherry jug. Nacky could see them, but the motion of the boat did not allow him to avoid them. Lurching forward, he planted his right foot squarely on the deck, directly atop one of the largest fragments.

With the force of the stomp and the shape of the shard, the sole of

45

Nacky's shoe gave way to the clay like an over-boiled beet. Nacky cried out once, but caught the sound in his throat so as not to let on he was in trouble. His eyes watering, he plopped to a sitting position, grabbed his foot, and felt the shard protruding from it. Closing his eyes he jerked it free and felt a flame of pain; a warm, wet flow ran over his hand. He tried to wiggle his toes and felt another blaze; the toes did not move. Removing his shoe, Nacky saw red-black blood dripping to the deck. He tugged his handkerchief from his pocket and tied it around the arch of the foot, pulling it so tight his eyes watered again. Then he turned toward the ladder and called out.

"Orro," he shouted.

"What's yer business, Patcher?"

"Bad business. Think I hurt myself."

Even from a distance, he heard another snirt of laughter come from Mink. "I carry the lanterns, you carry Patcher," he said to Orro. "I know'd it'd come out that way."

Orro and Mink hurried down the ladder into the hold, and Nacky stood and hobbled toward them. The weight on his gammy foot caused another bolt of pain to run up his leg and he nearly toppled over.

"Sit, Patcher," Orro said.

Nacky obeyed, dropping down on a broken crate. Orro fell to a knee and picked up Nacky's foot. He studied it closely. "Nasty," he muttered.

"Might just lose that thing," Mink said.

Orro shot him a look.

"I'm sayin' he might," Mink protested. "Seen feet split up like that before. You cut a cord, there's no help for it. Can you wiggle yer toes, Patcher?"

Nacky said nothing.

Mink clucked. "No help for it, then."

"Mink, ya shag-boss, get useful and help me find them lanterns," Orro said, then turned to Nacky. "You sit there and tend to the lamp we do have."

Nacky could see that the lantern needed tending indeed. In the last few moments, it had grown steadily darker in the hold as the flame fought to stay alive on the fading wick. Nacky began worrying the wick-knob, easing it up and down and causing the shadows around him to grow and shrink. As he did, he noticed a troubling sound coming from the ship. Just beneath where he was sitting, a hull plank began to groan. This was followed by another groan and a creak that sounded like soft gunfire.

At the same time the *Walnut Egg* began to speak, it also began to rock. A heavy bird-shot of rain raked the hull, and though the seams between the hull planks ought to have been well sealed with gobs of tarry caulk and long ropes of oakum, Nacky thought he could hear a wind whistling inside the ship. A hard wave slapped the boat and a bright bolt of lightning flickered outside, causing a cat-scratch of lit lines to flash on the wall. Nearby, a high mound of crates toppled over, thundering down onto the deck. Nacky was seated less than five feet away as they fell.

"Get away from there, Patcher, before you get flattened!" Orro called. As he spoke, another even larger pile fell and smashed.

Rising unsteadily on his left foot, Nacky staggered toward the wall, supporting himself with one hand while the other held the lantern. His tittling gait didn't provide much speed as he negotiated the heaving floor planks. With each step, he looked over his shoulder to see how much distance he'd opened up between himself and the cargo behind him, all the while the boat heaving beneath him. On his final glance, he caught a glimpse of the crates, a glimpse of the contents they'd spilled, a glimpse, he believed, of the little pink pig. Then, the world exploded.

With the loudest report yet, the sky shook with a blast of thunder and the *Walnut Egg* reared violently upward, carried by a wave that seemed to lift the ship whole. Nacky, driven to his knees, let go of the lantern, laid his hands on the deck and clenched and unclenched his fingers, looking for handholds the flush-laid planks could not provide. The wave carried the vessel higher and higher, and Nacky grasped for purchase more and more frantically. Then—in a violent instant—the churning ocean seemed simply to flick the boat straight into the air. With a sickening spin, the *Walnut Egg* began to turn completely upside down.

Nacky, with no grip on the planks, flew free like a flung bug. In the blackened gullet of the boat, he heard, for the moment, no sound at all as the airborne vessel rotated around him. Then there was a violent snapping noise as the inverted *Walnut Egg* plunged back toward the ocean, the ship's three great masts impaling the surface of the water like fork tines into food. An eyeblink later, the deck itself struck the flat of the sea. As it did, the entire flying contents of the hold plunged downward and landed with a huge crash. Nacky struck the hardwood planking with a force that his unexpectedly acute senses told him ought to kill him. He bounced once, then twice, then felt his head strike the corner of a beam. He saw a starburst of light and swooned at the edge of unconsciousness. In the moment before he slipped away, he heard debris smash and shatter everywhere. Somewhere nearby, he also heard the thicker, meatier sound of two men and one pig landing. That, for a time, was the last thing he heard.

CHAPTER FIVE

Nacky wasn't sure how long he re-
mained unconscious in the belly of the *Walnut Egg,* but when he woke
up, it was to the chill of seawater lapping about his feet. Sitting up with
a jolt, he looked down and dimly saw that the hold of the *Egg* was in
a very changed state. The great space appeared to be entirely inverted,
with the ceiling now below him, the floor above him, and cargo strewn
all about. The entire ship, he could also see, was no longer level; the
stern part of the vast hold was sharply inclined downward and was beginning to fill with water. Crates that had landed and broken there were
half-immersed and floating, with the occasional apple or jug drifting
around them.

Nacky squinted around in the gloaming and felt a stepmother's
breath of wind. Looking in the direction of the hull planks, he saw that
a number of them had gapped and spread, letting in both a thin hiss of
air and the dim, predawn light. A few feet away, Nacky heard a stirring.
Looking toward the sound, he saw Mink and Orro lying in a heap on
a patch of dry planks, farther along the upwardly inclined hold. The
pig lay near them. Nacky dragged himself up to where they were and

flopped down next to them. The other two men opened their eyes blearily. The animal did the same.

"You all right, Patcher?" Orro asked.

"Mmm," Nacky grunted. "You?"

"Mmm," Orro echoed.

Mink rubbed his forehead and sat up slowly. "Surprised I didn't split me head clean open," he muttered. Then he looked at Nacky. "Looks like you did, though. What ain't runnin' with water is runnin' with blood."

Nacky put his hand to his head and noticed that it felt wet and sticky; his shirt was stained red as well. His foot ached horribly, and a thin trail of watery red ran along the planks behind him. He pulled the foot toward him and tightened the handkerchief wrapped around it.

"Ship finished?" he asked Orro.

"She look ready to right herself to you?"

"No."

"Guess she's finished, then."

"Think anyone is alive up there?" Nacky asked. He looked at the ceiling below him and corrected himself. "Down there."

"Don't hear no voices," Mink said. "Don't hear no splashin'."

As Mink spoke, Nacky noticed that he couldn't clearly make out what the little man was saying. He jammed his index fingers into his own ears and began working them around.

"Little blocked up, eh?" Mink asked.

Nacky nodded.

"Should be," Mink said. "Too much air in here; too little boat to hold it." He pointed to the rising water. "That's only crowdin' it more."

"What's that mean?" Nacky asked. "Ship bursts?"

"No," Orro said. Rising to his feet with a grunt, he picked up a box slat and flung it toward the inside of the hull. It stuck to the wall planks like a wad of wet clay.

"Air's escapin' through them gaps," Orro said. "Your ears oughta feel better once enough leaks off. Course by then, that water will've rose up to take its place."

Nacky stared at the box slat with widened eyes. The wind he'd felt before wasn't entering the hold. It was leaving it, threatening to take with it the men's very breath as well.

"So what are we about, then?" Nacky asked with a crispness that surprised him. He stood up clumsily and Mink did the same.

"Now?" Orro said. "Now we chop ourselves out."

Orro turned to look at the stern end of the hull, and Nacky followed his eyes. He knew what the big man was thinking. Hanging on the rear wall was a pair of hand axes that the stevedores would use when unloading a crate if a knot in a cargo rope became wet or tangled. The axes were kept just at head level, at a spot that made for a convenient reach. In the inverted stern of the boat, however, head level was underwater.

"Think they're down there?" Nacky asked.

"Oughta be," Orro said.

"Expect I oughta get 'em then," Nacky said, hobbling forward.

Orro put a restraining hand on his shoulder. "Siddown, Patcher, you're pancrocked. You'll just start bleedin' and fallin' all over again and then I'll have to come down and fish you out."

Nacky, relieved, flopped on a crate and looked toward Mink, expecting to see him make his way into the water to fetch the axes. But Mink held his ground, and Orro, much the clumsier of the two, trudged toward the stern himself. When Orro hit the submerged part of the hold, he shuddered as the cold water closed around his ankles. He plunged below the surface, and for a few seconds there was no sign of him. Then he shot back up, eyes wild, chest heaving, breath catching—and hands empty. Orro descended again and surfaced again, descended again and surfaced again, each time panting and empty-handed. Finally, the fourth time he burst from the water, he cried out and thrust his ugly left hand above his head, clutching two black-handled axes. Splashing back out of the water, he thumped across the wet ceiling boards, startling the pig as he passed.

"Sharp as shaving blades," he said. "Now we get to work choppin' up a sailing ship."

The plan Nacky, Mink and Orro devised for the work was a sensible one. Picking a clear area on the wall that they guessed was above the waterline, they first stacked several crates into a makeshift pyramid leading up to the spot. Rather than trying to hack a sufficiently big hole in the brick-hard hardwood that made up the hull, they decided to weaken it first. Cutting in a rough circle, they would inscribe a groove that would enclose a space big enough for a human body to crawl through. When the etched circle was complete, they would pry a beam or post from the hold and pound it against the spot like a battering ram, causing the circle to pop out like a giant bung-plug. Then they would leap to freedom and scramble aboard the biggest pieces of flotsam they could find.

Orro and Mink began the chopping, with Nacky helping out when one of them grew tired, handing up a green cooking apple when asked. It had been many hours since the three men had come down into the hold, and with only seawater around them, they had grown powerfully parched. The apples would thus have to do, and while they were a slow and sour way to tame a thirst, they did help.

Finally, after Nacky had begun to think he could no longer take the sound of hacking, Mink and Orro whacked their axes into a beam and stood proudly back to regard their work. In the center of the patch of tarred planks was a raw, white-yellow circle crudely gouged. Nacky looked up and had to admit it was a pretty piece of business, though he had one reservation. As close as he could judge, the circle was not wide enough to serve its purpose. Once the men punched it out, Mink would probably fit through with little trouble. Nacky himself would be a squeeze. Orro would be out of the question.

"That look a tick small to you?" Nacky asked.

"'A tick small?'" Mink mimicked. "You fancy gettin' up here and choppin' it bigger? That look 'a tick small' to you, Orro?"

"It does," Orro said. "Only a tick, but that's all it takes."

"Well, I ain't startin' over," Mink said heatedly. "I'm gonna get me a post, I'm gonna ram that thing out, and I'm gonna go through and see me some sunlight."

As Mink spoke, there was a low rush outside and a wave lifted the boat. It wasn't much of a swell, but gammy and tired as the men were, they all stiffened. In a moment, the boat stabilized, but not before the bolts came loose from a four-foot support stanchion on the other side of the hold and dropped into the water with a soft *plink-pop.* The stanchion splashed loudly in behind it.

Orro stared at the long post with the first true look of fear he'd shown all day. Even on a ship as battered as the *Egg,* a piece of wood like that oughtn't simply come loose. It was almost as if the bones of the boat were somehow coming unpinned. Mink seemed not to notice anything unusual at all.

"There!" he shouted triumphantly. "That's me post!" Mink hopped into the water, splashed across the hold and retrieved the stanchion. Wrestling it back up the pyramid of boxes, he positioned himself in front of the hull.

"You boys ready to leave this coffin?" he asked.

Orro got to his feet. "Hold hard, there. You can't do this by yourself. You take the front, I'll take the hind, and we pound when I say. But if that hole's too small, you're gonna stay and help us hack until we all get free. You hear me?"

Mink nodded and the two men took hold of the post. Orro counted to three, and he and Mink reared back, striking the stanchion against the hull with a mighty thud. Nothing happened.

"Again," Orro commanded.

They pounded once more, and once more there was nothing.

"Again," Orro repeated.

This time, when the two men came forward, the thud was much louder, and Nacky could hear something else too—the sound of splintering wood and rushing air. The rough circle that had been cut in the hull vanished in an eyeblink and was replaced by a rough patch of gray-white sky. At the same time, Nacky felt a colossal gust of wind tear through the hold. This was the same trapped air that had caused the plank to stick to the wall, but with a bigger hole to rush through, the suction was much greater. And with a cold sense of horror, Nacky realized what that meant.

Looking up from his perch on the boxes, he saw Orro standing a few feet back from the hole, clutching the stanchion while his clothes and hair flapped about him. Mink was standing directly in front of the opening, his eyes wide, his mouth working silently, his fingers and hands white against the dark of the hull. And then, all at once, he wasn't there.

In a horrible heartbeat, Mink lost his grip and shot headfirst through the hole like an iron ball coming out of a cannon. Nacky could see his dark, shrinking shape against the day-bleached sky flying twenty, then thirty, then fifty feet away, then falling into the ocean with a small, wet plop. Immediately, Orro dropped the stanchion, pulled a lid off one of the crates, and slapped it against the hole. The lid stuck fast, the daylight vanished and the wind stopped. Nacky looked at Orro, horrified.

"What are you about?" he shouted.

"He's finished, Patcher."

"You don't know that!"

"He's finished, Patcher."

"You didn't even look!"

"I said he's finished!" Orro shouted, turning on Nacky wild-haired, wide-eyed and breathing hard. "The man can't swim. Never could. He shot out too far to find any flotsam, and that's the finish of him. Meantime, every second we leave that hole open's a second less we got. Look around you." Nacky stayed still. "Look around, I say!"

Nacky looked about and saw to his alarm that Orro was right. In the few seconds the hole had been open, the water level had climbed up to the bottom box of the pile on which the men and the pig were perched. Nacky sat and dropped his head in his hands.

"He couldn't swim, Patcher," Orro now said more softly. "Why do you think it was me what had to fetch the axes?"

Nacky and Orro sat for several long minutes in the silent, sloshing hold. Now it was clear to both of them that they were going to die here.

In the time they had left, however, it seemed only natural—if not very sensible—to continue to look for a way out. The only course was to resume chopping, this time cutting a bigger hole that would accommodate both larger men. With some of the air pressure relieved by the terrible burst that had claimed the sorry Mink, they could only hope that the suction wouldn't be as strong when they punched out their hole this time. Without speaking, Orro extended a hand to Nacky, who hopped awkwardly back to his feet. They picked a spot on the wall just to the left of the patched hole, and began wearily hacking.

The two men chopped throughout the morning and afternoon as the boat continued to settle and the water continued to rise. Finally, just two hours before the sun ought to go down, Nacky and Orro had carved out another, much bigger circle. Orro waded into the hold—the water by now rising as high as his chest—fished out three crates of apples and carried them back to the top of the pyramid. He splashed around in the water for another few minutes, looking for the filberts and sherry, but the sherry jugs had shattered and the filberts had sopped up so much seawater they were inedible. Climbing back up the pyramid, he sat down next to Nacky.

"You done good work here for a soft-as-pudge sailor," Orro said. "Mink—I don't much miss 'im much. I'm sorry he's gone, but he was a blister of a man and everyone knew it. You're different. You pull some jig act and drown, I'll be sorely put out."

Nacky nodded.

Orro paused and then spoke again. "And I'm sorry we couldn't keep a sure ship under you this trip. Maybe you'll get to sail again. And when you do, maybe I'll be about—me or my like."

Nacky stared at the big man in confusion, but he couldn't tell if even Orro was entirely sure of what he meant by that. Before Nacky could say anything in response, Orro held up a hand. "All right," he said. "Let's have at it."

The two men got to their feet and picked up the stanchion, with Nacky in front this time. On the count of three, they reared back and lunged; as before, the planks didn't give. Once more, they reared back and hit the end of the post against the dead-on center of their target, and this time—with a great sound of tearing timbers—most of the circle gave way. There was a sudden wind at Nacky's back, though not as powerful as the one that had ripped through the hold before when the air had been more tightly packed. The hole in the hull was not yet big enough to let them pass, but with two more blows, they knocked the rest of the circle free.

Nacky swayed at the lip of the opening and stared at the expanse of ocean and sky. Orro pushed him aside and tossed the crates of apples out. "You're next!" Orro shouted over the rush of wind. Nacky hesitated and the next thing he felt was Orro's hand in his back giving him a powerful shove.

Nacky soared up and out, and for several seconds felt nothing but the wind. Then he heard a loud splash, felt an enveloping cold and realized he was in the water. An instant later, he heard another splash and Orro was in beside him. The two men struggled toward the crates, took hold of them and looked up. It was only then—for the first time—that Nacky felt true terror.

Looming in front of him, huge, close, tarred brown-black, was the mortally wounded carcass of the *Walnut Egg,* upside down and sinking from its stern end. Nacky kicked his feet to back away from the giant dying thing, when a clattering sound made him stop. Standing in the hole in the hull was the little pink pig. Stutter-stepping back and forth, it eyed the water anxiously and then flung itself out, plummeting toward the ocean and hitting it with a fleshy slap. Frantically, the pig paddled toward Nacky and Orro, struggling to keep its snout above water. When the animal was in reach, Nacky extended his arm and gathered it in.

The two men and the pig held their positions for a moment, staring up at the wreck, when all at once, they heard a sound that resembled a gunshot, but with less of a metallic crack about it. Nacky and Orro looked toward the sound and were astounded to see one of the ship's bung-plugs—the coinlike bits of wood that covered the peg-holes in the hull—fly from the planking and strike the water like a bullet. Nacky whipped his head to look at Orro and saw that he was wearing the same disbelieving face he'd worn when the bolts popped free from the stanchion in the hold. There was another report from the ship, and two more plugs fired into the water. Nacky, Orro and the pig paddled frantically backward. Other plugs followed, then more, *rat-tatting* away from the ship and tattooing the ocean like shot from a hundred hellish rifles. Nacky covered his face with his free hand and involuntarily let fly a scream. Orro kicked at the water, pushing himself farther and farther away.

Before all the plugs were exhausted, Nacky noticed another sound, this one an eerie, windy whipcrack. Uncovering his face, he looked up to see a long, tarry rope of oakum waving and flailing like an angry tentacle from the plank seam into which it had been hammered. Quickly, another rope worked itself free, then others, until the *Walnut Egg* looked like nothing so much as a writhing snake's nest. As fast as the oakum ropes had begun to move, they tore completely away from the ship, spun out into the ocean, hit the water and sank.

Now there were more rifle sounds from the *Egg,* this time from the peglike trunnels that the bung-plugs had been protecting. If the trunnels fired off too, the ship itself could not long survive, and with a groaning sound, whole hull planks indeed began dropping into the water. First two or three went, then eight or ten, then dozens. The ship began shedding its hull like so much slatted snakeskin. In less than a minute, the *Walnut Egg* was stripped to its bones, revealing its huge wooden rib cage, its inverted floors and ceilings, even the deep gullet of its hold, now spilling its cargo through the sides. More pegs and plugs fell from the skeleton, and more of the ship began disassembling itself with a deafening sound of final collapse.

And then, in a flicker, it was over. The air fell absolutely silent, the water fell absolutely still. The vast patch of gray sky that had been filled by the cut of the brown-black boat was now gray again. Nearly all the debris on the water slowly vanished, sinking as if it had been made of iron instead of wood. A few small bits remained, but with those fragmentary exceptions, the *Walnut Egg* had completely disappeared. Nacky tightened his grip on the pig and turned to look at Orro, who stared back at him with no expression at all. The sky darkened a shade, and a dry drizzle began to fall.

Nacky Patcher would remain at sea for nearly two more weeks. After the ship vanished, he and Orro and the pig paddled toward a pair of floating doors a few dozen feet away. The men each claimed a door and climbed aboard. They placed the pig in an empty crate floating nearby. Collecting stray bits of rope and oakum, they tied the doors together and secured the pig's crate and the three apple crates behind.

Neither man could say why they had taken the pig along with them. They suspected they might eat it, but they also suspected that without fresh water, the salt in the blood might kill them. So for a time, they figured they'd live on the apples and let the pig get by as best it could. As it turned out, some of the fruit was covered with mold, which caused the men to grow violently ill when they ate it, so they fed those to the pig, who seemed to like them fine. The rest of the apples they ate themselves, slowly, for more than ten days, before they were all gone. Then they cut the fruit crates loose and survived on nothing.

It took Orro—who was a big man and needed a lot to keep himself going—less than two days to die from exposure and thirst. Nacky cried a little—though tearlessly, since he too was parched. Then he patted his friend's ruined hands, rolled him into the deep and cut his empty door loose. He and the pig then floated slowly off, moving away from the forehead of South America back toward the coast from which they'd come— the hard grip of the curse of Yole pulling them sorrowfully home.

CHAPTER SIX

Nacky Patcher had always told Teedie
Flinn that of all the fool careers a boy could pursue, thieving was the
worst. And of all the places to try practicing the art, Yole was the last.
Teedie hadn't fully realized why that was so until he actually began
scouting about town for places to try a little filching and discovered how
many homes and shops had recently come under the black rag.

Black-ragging was a practice begun only in the last few years. When a
family's house or business was seized, it was common practice to padlock
the building to protect whatever valuables were left inside. But padlocks
could be picked, and evicted families became adept at popping them free,
pinching back their confiscated belongings and then relocking the doors
before a visiting constable could tell anyone had been inside at all.

To prevent this from happening, Mally Baloo ordered that doors and
windows of seized buildings whose walls had not already been knocked
down be secured not with locks but with black strips of cloth tied in an
elaborate knot that only the magistrates and a handful of very old sailors knew. The knot could be easily cut or untied by unpracticed hands,
but it could never be retied properly, leaving a sure sign that someone
had trespassed inside. If a building wearing the black rag was illegally

entered, it was usually not possible to determine the guilty parties, but Baloo had made it clear that for every trespass he discovered, one Yole family whose debts he'd so far been tolerating would be pitched in retribution. Since no one in Yole wanted to be responsible for yet another set of out-with-you papers being served, the black rags were generally respected. Until now.

Once Teedie Flinn decided that thieving was the only way he could make a go in Yole, he concluded that black-rag buildings were the best places to begin. If anyone was light-fingered enough to puzzle out such a complicated knot, untie it cleanly and tie it back up again, he guessed he was—a most particular bit of vanity since Teedie didn't even have a full tally of working fingers to begin with.

Teedie's right hand had been as badly hurt as he'd feared it was in his fall from the half-home in Knockle. When he arrived in Yole three years ago, the very first thing he did was ask the way to the local doctor. That doctor, unluckily, was Dr. Mull.

Dr. Mull fancied himself a fine physician, especially gifted at tending to problems of the skeleton and joints, which ought to have been fortunate for a boy with Teedie's injury. The problem was, what Dr. Mull thought of his skills and what those skills proved to be were two different things. A bone repaired by Dr. Mull usually turned out to be an unlovely thing, often needing to be rebroken and reset repeatedly until the doctor and the patient at last considered it either healed up well or so far beyond saving that there was no point in caring for it further.

Dr. Mull made his usual tangle of things when he treated Teedie's hand, splinting and breaking it no fewer than three times before the fingers finally clenched up into an unmoving claw. The gnarled hand was good enough for holding a utensil or a tool, provided Teedie used his left hand to wedge the object into the fisted fingers of the right. But apart from that, it was largely useless. Teedie nonetheless had enough sand in him not to be overly troubled by his misfortune, and he became so smooth at operating his bad hand with the help of his good one that if you didn't look closely, you sometimes didn't notice there was anything wrong with him at all.

It was that nimbleness that helped Teedie convince himself he had the skills to manage the black rags. All he needed was to buck up his courage enough to try. After several nights spent sleeping in the damp wreckage of the Pounds' home and several days without a proper meal, he was ready.

Early one evening when it was still light enough to see what he was doing but dark enough that most people had gone off to their homes, he crept over to the main business street that ran through the center of Yole. The street was built on a long hill running from Gilly Boate's shop at the top—which he called, straightforwardly enough, The Shop at the Top—to the public house and restaurant in a cul de sac at the bottom, which was called, less straightforwardly, the Albert T. Rain. Both businesses were still going concerns, but along the road between them, things were far bleaker.

Everywhere along both sides of the business street, the black rags fluttered thick as crows' wings. Teedie glanced at the shuttered hatmaker's store, the long-closed sweet shop, the little buildings where the meat merchant, the cheesemaker and the shirt-fitter had worked. Last, his eye fell on Audra and Stolley Pound's curio shop. Teedie had not been inside the store since several days before the house-pitching, but he still remembered where the Pounds kept the most valuable bits and bobs. What's more, he remembered where they kept a large barrel of willow nuts—bitter things that were something of an acquired taste, but that Audra and Stolley kept on hand in the hopes of attracting customers. Teedie had never cared for willow nuts, but with his belly as empty as it was now, they started to seem like a treat.

Teedie looked about himself to make sure the street was empty, then made his way in the shadows toward the side of the store where a small window was partially concealed from view. He crept close, squinted at the black rag tied there, then lifted it with his clenched right hand. The knot was indeed a complicated thing, not so much tied as woven. He studied it for a moment longer, then flexed the fingers of his good, left hand and brought them close. A blood-pumping sense of light-headedness came over him, coupled with dreamy thoughts of what he would find inside the store and how easy it would be to make off with it. He'd heard of this feeling before. It was the thief heat Nacky Patcher had often warned him about. Until that moment, however, he'd never felt it. The sensation was a fine one, and Teedie reflected that if this was what being a thief felt like, it was a calling he wouldn't mind pursuing at all. Before he could move any further, there was a voice behind him.

"I'd not touch that rag if I was you, Teedie Flinn," it said.

Teedie wheeled around, gaping, and tried to speak. Nothing came. In front of him stood Emma Hay, her arms folded, her lips tight, her eyes narrowed reproachfully. Teedie had seen that fire expression on her face before, but never directed at him. Whenever Emma aimed such a look at somebody, it did not promise anything good.

Emma Hay was headmistress of the Yole Home for Indigent and Unfortunate Girls. Emma herself had become a resident there when she was just ten years old, shortly after her parents died. Now, more than twenty years later, she still lived in the big house, though these days she ran the place. It was a hard job, and a lot of people worried that Emma was not up to it, particularly after that nasty business involving Mary Berry seven years back. Most people knew that Emma had had no choice but to call the law when Mary tried to escape the home—or at least it would have seemed to Emma that she had no choice. But Mary being who Mary was and things having gone the way they did for her, someone had to take on the blame, and Emma took it without complaint.

So much work and so much care ought to have coarsened Emma's appearance, but she remained quite an eyesweet, or at least that's what the men of Yole said. Her hair was roughly the color of cherrywood, sometimes cheating toward brown, sometimes slipping back toward red, depending mostly on the season. Her smile was a curious thing, not given very freely, and when it was, revealing a line of teeth that were perfectly white and perfectly strong, but also arranged in a this-way-and-that fashion that could give her a snaggly, even snarly, look. When her mood was right, though, the smile grew surprisingly soft, creating the impression of someone so easy and careless she couldn't even be bothered to keep her teeth organized. Tonight, Emma did not appear to be in one of her easy moods.

"What are you about, boy?" she asked.

"Not about anything," Teedie muttered, avoiding her eyes.

"That's not the way it looks. It looks like you're about to fool with that rag. You fancy being nabbed by a constable?" Emma asked.

Teedie shook his head no.

"You fancy a trip to the tower?"

Teedie shook his head no.

"Then I expect you'd best leave that knot alone."

"Anything in that shop belongs to them Pounds," Teedie said.

"Anything in that shop *belonged* to the Pounds," Emma said. "Now it belongs to Mally Baloo. I don't think a kitten like you has the scrap to take him on."

"Ain't no kitten," Teedie grumbled.

"You're not a full-up cat either." She looked him up and down and clucked her tongue. "You'd best come with me," she said.

Emma took Teedie by the wrist and began walking him away from the curio shop and toward the indigents' home on the other side of the street. Teedie was surprised. He had no recollection of the brief hours he'd spent in the home when he was a baby, but he'd heard hard things about the way the girls there lived and the work they were made to do. Whether or not the stories were true was difficult to say, since Emma never allowed any but the indigent girls themselves to set foot inside. Teedie, however, had always had doubts about the state of affairs in the home.

The building, for one thing, looked too well-kept on the outside to be as fearsome as people said on the inside. What's more, the well-washed look of the girls—who rarely appeared in public without Emma close behind and who never appeared in anything other than their matching yellow canvas dresses with the words "Property of the Yole Indigents' Home" stenciled at the hem—did not have the gray, hollow cast that the half-home boys did. Emma's hand, Teedie guessed, was probably a tolerably fair one, but since she never cared enough about people's opinions to answer the dark things they whispered about her, the stories persisted.

Emma marched Teedie across the street and clumped with him up the steps of the big house. She let go of his wrist to fish her key from her apron pocket and began to unlock the door. Teedie stepped forward expectantly, and she looked at him queerly.

"You have a mind to come inside?" she asked, not entirely pleasantly.

Teedie looked uncertain. "Uh, yes," he answered.

"You'd best change it then. You sit; I'll come back."

Teedie did what he was told, settling down on a hard, polished porch bench and craning his neck to see if he could make out anything through the cracks in the closed shutters. Nothing but a butter-yellow light leaked out around the slats. A few moments later, Emma returned with a bedroll, a pillow and a quilt in one arm. She carried a basket in the other hand.

"Around to the left," she said, pointing Teedie to a stretch of porch on the side of the house. She nudged him toward the spot she had in mind, unrolled the bedroll and laid out the quilt and pillow atop them. Then she handed him the basket. Teedie opened it up, and his eyes went wide.

Inside was a crisp loaf of fresh bread, a clump of bright yellow cheese, a jug of cold milk with beads of moisture on the sides and a pair of fat pears—one green, one red. There was a butter knife for the bread and cheese, a cup for the milk and a napkin for his hands.

"Eat that," Emma said, pointing to the food. "And use these," she added, indicating the knife, cup and napkin. "Then you go straight to sleep."

Teedie smiled and nodded, entirely unsure of how to respond to such bounty. Emma seemed to realize that and, sparing him the struggle of coming up with a way, turned to go. After she took a step, however, she turned back, licked her thumb and rubbed it across Teedie's cheek. A clean streak opened up in the gray grime that covered his face. She clucked again.

"And I suppose we'll have to arrange for you to have a bath tomorrow too," she said.

Without another word, Emma turned and disappeared into the house. Teedie stood where he was, blinking with suddenly wet eyes. At such a moment, Audra Pound would have kissed him on the forehead. Emma didn't do that, but she might as well have.

Teedie lived at the indigents' home for weeks without ever setting foot inside. Emma set up a small washtub for bathing on the porch and a screen for privacy beside it. She brought Teedie his meals each day packed in the same big basket, and he ate them on the patch of grass behind the house. Within a week, his hollow cheeks began to round out and his pasty skin began to brighten. He spent his days doing small chores and running errands for Emma in order to earn his keep. At night, he bedded down early and slept well and deeply until the sun came up. The only condition Emma imposed on him for all the trouble she was taking was that as long as he was in her care, he would not even consider thieving.

"You lay hands on another black rag and I'll carry you to the tower myself," she promised. Teedie believed her.

But the Yole Home for Indigent and Unfortunate Girls could not long accommodate an indigent and unfortunate boy. There were two dozen girls living in the house, the youngest just four years old, the oldest nearing sixteen. A boy in their midst—even one kept confined to the porch and out of the way—stirred them into a fluttery state Emma was at a loss to control. They'd giggle behind the shutter slats and peek at Teedie as he ate his meals. They'd contrive reasons to come out to the porch early in the morning, craning their necks for a look at him as he slept behind the screen. They timed their yard chores for when they were sure he'd be around, forcing Emma to invent an errand for him somewhere else. Teedie did not know what kind of work went on inside the house, but whatever it was, it apparently wasn't getting done—at least judging by the put-out face Emma increasingly wore and her repeated mutterings about having too much to do and too few hands willing to do it properly. Finally, she decided that the arrangement could not go on.

"You'll not be living here any longer," she said one day when she brought Teedie his supper. The boy swallowed hard. "But that doesn't mean you won't be looked after," she added.

Teedie would continue to take all his meals at the home, Emma explained. He'd continue to do jobs for her, and she'd continue to promise to hand him to a constable personally if he so much as flirted with trouble. It would only be the business of sleeping on the porch that could not go on; Emma had another place for him to stay.

"Go out to Nacky Patcher's house," she said. "That joxer's gone to sea, and if I know the likes of him, he won't be back, at least not for a long while."

Teedie collected his bedroll and pillow and set out for Nacky's that very evening. He didn't share Emma's low opinion of Nacky, nor her belief that he wasn't coming back. All the same, the weather in the mountains had been poor of late and the people in town were saying the conditions had been the same all the way down to the coast. If the skies had been just as sour at sea, the ships under sail would be having a hard few weeks indeed.

CHAPTER SEVEN

The people of Little M'croom were not accustomed to large debris washing ashore in their town. The powerful waves that crashed into the coast threw most floating rubbish hard against the black stone seawall that lined the quayside, ensuring that anything that did arrive by water was reduced entirely to splinters. That's why the people were so surprised when the salt-bleached door carrying the dead man with the sea-burnt face bumped up against the rocks. They were even more surprised when they saw that the man had a pig with him.

A small crowd approached the quayside, peered at the man and soon learned that he was not in fact dead—though with his swollen eyes, cracked lips and sloughing skin he might as well have been. He also had a nastily bandaged foot that looked like it had long ago bled out whatever it might once have held in its veins. Nonetheless, after a moment, the man sat up, looked around himself unseeingly and tried to blink his unblinkable eyes. Then he crawled out on the low, inclined seawall, absently shooing his pig in front of him and inexplicably dragging his door behind.

When the man reached the top of the quay, most of the crowd

backed away, but two people did step forward, took him by the arms and led him slowly toward a small stone house that served as the quayside infirmary. A third person took hold of the door and the pig.

The man was taken inside the infirmary, where his wounds were dressed and his skin was cleaned and he was laid down in a wood-frame bed with a narrow mattress and scratchy-clean white sheets. He muttered something about his pig and was assured the animal was all right. He muttered something about his door and was assured it would be returned to him.

For more than a week, the man stayed in the bed, slipping in and out of consciousness and trying to swallow the warm tea, cool water and thick spoonfuls of mixabout and honey that were fed to him. As the food and the drink took hold, he had a few clear moments, mostly when someone would come by to unwrap and bathe his foot. The pain of all the poking would stir him from sleep, and when he saw what they were up to, he'd struggle.

"I aim to keep that foot," he'd protest. "Make it right, but don't take it off."

The people would assure him that making the foot right was precisely what they had in mind, and whenever they left him, they left the foot with him as well.

It was not until a drizzly morning on the fourteenth day after the arrival of the half-dead man—who was now able to say that his name was Nacky Patcher—that he was at last well enough to climb out of bed, stand on his one good foot and be on his way. Someone brought him his pig and his door; someone else handed him a crutch. A final person passed him a generous pocketful of coins, more than enough for a carriage trip to wherever he needed to go. Then they led him out the front door and back onto the cobbly quay.

His purse unexpectedly full, Nacky Patcher did plan to hire a carriage to take him straight back home to Yole. Before he left, however, he had one more bit of business to attend to.

The *Walnut Egg*, he knew, had been owned by a man named Alfred

Puddemsey, a wealthy exporter who was rarely seen around the quay and who had a habit of registering his ships under many different names in many different countries. The slipperiness of both the man and his boats meant that if one of the vessels was lost at sea, it was nearly impossible for survivors to make a claim for the entire voyage's wages, which maritime law said they were entitled to receive. With the storm that sank the *Walnut Egg* also lashing the coast, and with reports coming back from the shipping lanes that the outbound *Egg,* which should have been spotted by inbound boats, was nowhere to be seen, it had become clear to the people in Little M'croom that the vessel had almost certainly sunk. Since Puddemsey no doubt kept the ship handsomely insured, it was also certain that either he or one of his jump-boys would soon emerge from the tall grass and visit the harbormaster's office to claim the payment for the lost consignment. When that happened, Nacky would be waiting.

Nacky took a day-room near the docks and spent most of his time sitting on a bench outside the little clapboard building where the harbormaster worked, with his pig and his door by his side. The first day, Nacky saw no sign of Puddemsey. Nor did he spot him on the second. Finally, on the third day, just as his money was starting to run out, he saw a small man—one who moved with the fleetness of the lost Mink but carried a stouter body on shorter legs—hurriedly entering the little building. Nacky had no doubt who he was.

"Alfred Puddemsey?" he asked, entering the office a step behind the man.

The man wheeled and looked flustered but did nothing to conceal who he was. "I'm Puddemsey," he answered simply.

"Nacky Patcher," Nacky said, not extending his hand. "I come from the *Walnut Egg.*"

Nacky allowed those words to settle for a moment and saw Puddemsey struggling for a response.

"The *Egg* is at sea," he protested at last.

"Not any longer," Nacky answered.

Then, with a smoothness Nacky had practiced in his mind a hundred times, he pulled the man aside and told him the tale of the death of the ship, leaving out nothing about just how the lost *Egg* had gone down. He told the story close, his face just inches from Puddemsey's own. He told it soft, making the owner lean in closer still. He told it knowing Puddemsey could not only see the story in his sea-scorched face, but smell it in his salt-pickled skin and his sun-bleached hair. The owner, he could tell, believed him at first and then didn't believe him, then he believed him a bit more, then he believed him a bit less. Ultimately, he settled out on the not-believing-him side, and when Nacky was done with his story—pulling away from the man as quiet and gentle as he'd closed in on him—Puddemsey told him so.

"You're spinnin' silk," he said with a wave.

Nacky gave off with a small, practiced shrug, gathered himself up and said what he'd come to say.

"It may sound like spinnin'," he answered, "but I'd wager I look like I believe it. That either means I'm givin' you the true bill or I've come unsprung." Nacky stepped back and let Puddemsey look his fill at the man who stood before him, with his half-crazed eyes, his half-dead foot and his odd little pig, whose own eyes all of a sudden seemed small and dark and mean. "Meself," Nacky said, "I think I've come unsprung. But I ain't goin' away."

Judging that it wouldn't do to have such a daft, walking ghost following him about, Puddemsey then and there drew up a draft and paid Nacky nearly eighteen months' wages—or more than three times what he would have earned on his sea voyage—extracting in return only the promise that he go away and never bother him again. Nacky pledged that he would, and he meant it. Before the end of the day, he'd hired a noddy and a driver and set out on the road that led back to Yole. On his way, he reflected that Pippa himself could not have managed things better.

CHAPTER EIGHT

Teedie had a rather pleasant go of things living alone in Nacky's home. The house itself was entirely ordinary, a two-room stone cottage at the edge of town. The parlor was sparsely furnished, with only a reading chair near the window, a bookshelf next to the chair and a supper table with two straight-backed chairs of its own near the hearth. The little bedroom had a chest of drawers, a single window and a narrow bed. There was a privy out back.

Teedie set up housekeeping in the parlor instead of the bedroom, having grown accustomed to curling up on the floor in his bedroll and not caring for Nacky's bed anyway, which reminded him of his little cot in the half-home. He'd go to sleep not long after sundown and wake up just before sunrise, then begin his day with an easy sprint into town. If it was a Monday, Wednesday, Friday or Sunday, there'd be a basket of breakfast waiting for him on the porch of the indigents' home.

If it was a Tuesday, Thursday or Saturday, there'd be no basket, but there would be hot water in the washtub behind the screen along with a rough cake of soap and a fresh set of clothes. Once he'd bathed and changed, he'd rap on the front door and Emma would come out to inspect him, taking special care to examine his hair, which he hated to wash and would sometimes merely wet in the hope of fooling her, which he never did. If she was satisfied with his state, she'd hand him his basket.

As Teedie spent more time around the home, he began to see more of the indigent girls themselves, and they started to grow accustomed to his presence, though he was still never permitted inside the house. The younger girls would occasionally stare at his ruined right hand, clenching up their own right hand the same way and then looking at it to see if they'd got it right. The older girls would hiss at them to stop, then steal a sorrowful glance of their own at Teedie's fisted fingers. Teedie was rarely troubled by the attention, having come to think of the hand as nothing particularly special. Soon the girls came to see it the same way.

But if Teedie's physical misfortune held little enduring interest for the residents of the home, his dark past did. None of the girls knew just what to believe about the shadowy things he was said to have done, but they weren't shy about inquiring.

"Is it true you burned down all of Knockle?" one would ask, approaching him in the little yard behind the house as he plastered over a hole in a wall that was letting in mice.

"True bill," Teedie would answer.

"Is it true you used the blackfire to do it?" another would press.

"True too," he'd say, with a finger to his lips suggesting this part of the tale was really not fit to share.

The questions would go on that way until Emma would come out, see what the girls were up to and scold them for their foolishness.

If Teedie sometimes found the girls bothersome, he dared not show that, particularly in front of the ten-year-old girl known as Mag and the eight-year-old Gurtee. Mag and Gurtee were not sisters, though the black hair, pale skin, and berry-blue eyes they shared made them seem so. One other thing they had in common were their wits. Mag and Gurtee were generally considered the cleverest girls in the home, at least judging by how well they performed the lessons Emma gave them to do. Lately, Emma had taken to instructing Teedie in his writing and reading as well, and he'd sometimes approach one of the two girls to help him with a passage he was supposed to copy out of a book or broadsheet, using his good left hand to do the work.

"Such printing," Mag or Gurtee would scold, doing their best to sound put out but actually seeming nothing of the kind. "It's a wonder you know your letters at all."

With his chores and his lessons and a roof over his head, Teedie spent his days as enjoyably as he'd ever spent them with the Pounds. It was only the nights, which Teedie passed alone in Nacky's parlor, that sometimes left him feeling a little melancholy and shadow-spooked. All that changed one morning before sunup when he was sleeping in his bedroll and suddenly heard a clumping and scrabbling at the front door. He awoke with a start to see Nacky Patcher and a small pink pig looking down at him.

"What are you doing here, boy?" Nacky asked.

"Nacky!" Teedie exclaimed, leaping up. He hadn't realized how much he'd been fretting about whether Nacky would make it back from the sea until that moment, and he would have hugged the twig-thin, sun-dried man standing in front of him if he hadn't looked as if he'd snap like kindling at even a baby's embrace. What's more, the little pink pig glared at Teedie meanly, seeming unwilling to have Nacky touched at all.

Instead, Teedie helped Nacky to the reading chair—noticing that something appeared terribly wrong with one of his feet—and began chattering excitedly. He asked Nacky about his ship and the journey and what had happened to his foot and then, before the man could answer, rat-tatted out his own news about his weeks at the indigents' home and the fine meals he was eating there and how he'd almost undone a black rag at the curio store and might do it still if he could get out from under the eye of Emma long enough to try. Nacky said nothing throughout, waiting until Teedie had spent everything he had to say, and then spoke up.

"What are you doing here, boy?" he repeated.

"Living here," Teedie answered simply.

"Anyone give you pass to do that?" Nacky asked.

"Emma did."

"Anyone give her pass to give you pass?"

Teedie shrugged, the energy at last seeming to drain out of him. "I ain't usin' the bed," he said, "just me roll."

Nacky regarded him closely, then let out a sigh. He had not come home from his long and awful voyage expecting to find anyone living in his home. But the fact was, he'd known since the moment he woke up in Little M'croom that he was no longer fit to live alone—at least for a while. Cooking for himself would be hard; fetching wood and water would be well-nigh impossible. And without a wagon or horse, he had no way at all to get into town. If he was going to buy the food and bandages and other things he'd need, he'd have to have someone here to help him. Teedie seemed a handy choice.

"I expect I could find some use for you," he said.

Teedie smiled.

"But you try any mischief . . . ," Nacky said, letting a tone of warning hang in the air.

"I try that and Emma will have at me before you do."

Nacky nodded, satisfied. That very morning, they set up housekeeping.

The man, the boy, and the little pink pig got on well in their modest home, with Teedie keeping his sleeping spot in the main room, Nacky taking the bed and the pig curling up on the floor nearby. Teedie still ate his meals at Emma's house, smuggling back what he could to Nacky and the pig and using Nacky's money to buy the rest at the single grocery store left in Yole. Nacky told Teedie what the pig's favorite foods were—biscuits, cow's milk and turnips, mostly—and instructed the boy to address the animal as Orro, a name, Nacky explained, he'd chosen to honor a lost bo'sun he'd known at sea. When Teedie pressed further into the matter, Nacky, not caring if the boy thought him daft or not, told him everything that had happened on his voyage, much the way he'd told Alfred Puddemsey. The boy accepted it all without question.

The first matter Nacky and Teedie had to tend to after they settled in concerned Nacky's ruined foot. The people in Little M'croom had been telling the truth when they promised Nacky they'd let him leave town with all of his parts. During the ride home in the noddy, however, the foot began to flame up terribly, causing his leg to throb and his brow to break out in fever. The heat and the ache did not abate, and after two days, Teedie ran to town to fetch Dr. Mull. If the doctor had made such a hash of Teedie's hand, it was unlikely he would do much better fixing so sorry a thing as Nacky's foot. By now, however, the foot was probably past fixing and needed instead simply to be taken off, a job that even Dr. Mull could be trusted to manage.

Dr. Mull indeed removed the useless foot and afterward told Nacky about a man from Bowfin who was especially gifted at making wooden replacement parts and was happy to come by and show off his wares. The man paid a visit and filled Nacky's ear with descriptions of the various types of wonderful wood he could choose for his new foot. There was sweetgum, he told him, a good, sturdy wood that could last him a lifetime, but also a very heavy wood—so heavy it wouldn't even float when it was green and freshly cut. There was purple heart, a fine tropical hardwood that had a nicely exotic feel to it, but that could be hard to replace if the foot was ever damaged. Teak and black locust were equally elegant—and could be equally scarce. Ultimately, he recommended, an unremarkable fellow like Nacky would probably do best with an unremarkable loblolly pine, a light wood that was easy to lift, unlikely to rot and simple to replace, should the need arise.

Nacky followed the man's recommendation and spent the first weeks he was home in Yole simply practicing the step-*clump* gait he'd need to learn if he was going to get around. With Teedie helping him, he'd step-*clump* up the padroad, step-*clump* out to his well, step-*clump* around the plank floors of his parlor. After a time, he learned to walk so well he decided he was at last ready to step-*clump* into town. For that occasion, Nacky planned to treat himself to dinner at the Albert T. Rain.

The only true public house in Yole, the Albert T. Rain had been open since Nacky was young, quite a long time for a Yole business to remain in operation. It was originally known simply as Dree's Place, after its owner, a big pot-walloper of a woman who moved to town some fifteen years ago. Yole was an odd place to choose to live—most folks preferring to leave it if they could—but Dree thrived there, keeping her establishment going on the promise of good meats, fine breads and strong malt, which she never failed to deliver. Dree had long been fascinated by maritime matters, accumulating a small library of ship books and papers and keeping them in her rooms above the restaurant, where she would lose herself in them the way other people lost themselves in literature.

About ten years ago, Dree changed the name of the restaurant to the Albert T. Rain, in honor of an old cargo ship that had foundered near the coast between Greater M'croom and Twelve Points, taking the lives of all thirty of its crew members and scattering the shore with debris. Dree was staying at the sea for a holiday at the time of the wreck and helped herself to some of the beached wood, using it as ceiling timbers in her restaurant to give the place a more maritime air. So pleased was she with the results that she made it a point to stay alert to reports of any other wrecks off the local coast, offering to pay handsomely for some of their remains as well.

Nacky set out for his visit to the Rain at the end of an afternoon he'd spent reading, Orro had spent snuffling about on the road and Teedie had spent playing outside somewhere. Rising from his parlor chair, Nacky hopped a few steps to the spot by the hearth where he kept both his wooden foot and his salt-bleached door—his twin mementos from his time aboard the *Walnut Egg*. He plopped down on the floor, regarded the nub of ankle at the bottom of his right leg a bit dourly, then pulled on the special sock the limb-maker had sold him, one made of thick wool with an even thicker flannel pad stitched into the bottom, intended to dull some of the shock the ankle would feel as he hobbled about on the piece of hard pine. He then positioned the ankle in the socketed top of the foot and took hold of the two tanned leather straps attached to it, belting them around his lower leg. He liked the snug feel of the belts and smiled a bit at the entire clever assembly. Then he rose, step-*clumped* across the parlor, opened the door and whistled for Orro, who came running, expecting to be fed.

"You ate a dish of rinds and rubbish not an hour ago," Nacky said, crouching down to pat the animal's bristly side. "It's me what's entitled to supper now."

Nacky clucked his tongue, and together he and Orro step-*clumped* and *clack-clacked* down the two short steps of the house. As soon as they emerged, Teedie's face appeared above, looking down at them from the roof.

"Where are you off to?" Teedie asked, surprised to see Nacky outside.

Nacky jumped, then looked cross. "Boy," he said, "bring yourself down here before you get hurt."

Teedie did as he was told, hopping from the roof to the ground as absently as if he were hopping from a chair. Nacky winced, but Teedie landed softly as a cat.

"Where are you off to?" he repeated.

"Dree's."

"Expect I can come?" Teedie asked.

"You know Dree don't allow none but those of age."

"Expect you can bring me a taste of drink then?"

Nacky rolled his eyes.

"Can I walk with you at least?"

Nacky sighed. "Come along."

Nacky, Teedie and Orro set out along the padroad that led to town, the pig and the boy keeping their pace slow to accommodate the hobbling man. They had not gone more than a few hundred yards when they noticed the silhouette of another man well ahead of them, traveling along the same road in the same direction. Nacky recognized that the shadowy shape belonged to Jimmer Pike. Jimmer was Nacky's junior by several years and looked to be younger still, with his cloud of blond curls, his doughy shape and his big, chubby smile. Nacky always enjoyed Jimmer's absently cheerful disposition, and Jimmer—by virtue of that disposition—never much minded Nacky's more serious temper or criminal past. The two thus got on well.

"Jimmer!" Nacky called to the silhouette ahead of him.

The Jimmer-shadow turned, waved and quick-stepped back in Nacky's direction; Nacky step-*clumped* awkwardly forward. Teedie, unhappy at having the walk disturbed, trailed after.

"That firewood foot still givin' you a bad time?" Jimmer asked, trotting up to Nacky with an ease the one-footed man envied.

"This is a good time," Nacky said. "Bad time, I'd be ridin' me pig."

"Looks like he'd be sturdy enough to take it," Jimmer said, bending down to give Orro a couple of too-rough swats on the side. "H'lo there, Arrow."

"Orro," Nacky corrected, as Orro himself backed away.

"And I see you've got your pup with you too," Jimmer said to Nacky, with a nod toward Teedie.

"Ain't no pup," Teedie grumbled sullenly.

Jimmer laughed agreeably, and the group continued slowly in the direction of town. After a moment, Jimmer chirped up. "I mention I'm buildin' again?" he asked.

"You been buildin' for a while," Nacky answered.

"No, I was buildin' before. Then I stopped. Now I'm buildin' again."

Nacky, of course, knew that Jimmer was building, since that was more or less all he did anymore. For most of his life, Jimmer had been a flighty sort, rattling and prattling about this or that grand plan, but never settling on any one of them. Some time ago, however, he'd taken a holiday in Twelve Points, stumbled across a carpentry book in the town's library and devoted the rest of the time he was there to reading anything else he could find on the topic. When he came home, he announced that putting up houses was going to be his life's work.

Jimmer took up his new profession straightaway, and the first home he started on was his own. Staking out a one-thousand-square-foot plot of land around his family's tiny five-hundred-square-foot house, he began to build four new walls surrounding the ones already there. For several weeks, anyone walking by the Pike home would stop to watch as the familiar house slowly vanished behind the rising facade of the new one. When the walls were done, Jimmer scrambled up on top of them and enclosed the entire structure with a roof.

Now the Pike family had what was essentially a house within a house—an arrangement that suited no one. So for days afterward, passersby heard ferocious hammering and ripping inside the new home, as bit by bit, beam by beam, Jimmer began throwing his smaller house out the front window of his bigger one. His parents seemed much put out by all this and took to staying with friends in Greater M'croom until their boy finished his work. When anyone would ask Jimmer why he didn't build his home in a more traditional way, clearing his land first before starting on the new one, he looked genuinely perplexed.

"I need someplace to live while I'm buildin', don't I?" he'd ask. The question seemed like such a good one, nobody bothered to press the point further.

Now Jimmer was at it again, expanding his one-thousand-square-foot home to at least fifteen hundred square feet—and causing his parents to make what had been a temporary stay in Greater M'croom a permanent one. "The walls are almost up," Jimmer said to Nacky, walking backward in front of him so he could face the group while he spoke. "Next comes the roof, and then she's done."

"And after that?" Nacky asked.

Jimmer beamed. "After that, I make meself available for work. Plenty of little houses in this town in need of expandin'."

Nacky nodded, picturing the big, sprawling, roofless house on the Pike family land and the smaller, trimmer ones on all the other plots around Yole. He reasoned it was best to say nothing.

The group walked farther, passing a handful of those little pocket houses on either side of the road, until at last they approached the one where Teedie and the Pounds had lived. The wrecked home was just as

Baloo's beat-men had left it four months before—its eastern wall demolished, its chimney scorched, its occupants long gone. Jimmer and Nacky stared at it somberly. Teedie turned away.

"Rotten business," Jimmer said, surveying the wreck.

"Rotten," Nacky agreed, casting a glance at Teedie.

Teedie strode ahead.

Eventually, the group reached the end of the padroad and turned left onto the greater road descending into town. The red soil gave way to cobbles and the buildings drew closer together. The houses and shops on the street were mostly dark, either because the people had not yet lit their lanterns for the evening or because the buildings were black-ragged and empty. The only exception, as always, was the Home for Indigent and Unfortunate Girls, which leaked bright yellow light through its window slats and around its sills. On so quiet a street, the illuminated building gave off an odd sense of industry.

Finally, directly ahead in a cul de sac, was the restaurant. The building was constructed of dark, planked wood, calling to mind the flank of a ship. Above the front door, Dree had had a woodcutter carve out the name *The Albert T. Rain* in fancy script. Nacky, Jimmer, Teedie and Orro approached the building and climbed the porch steps. Nacky turned to Teedie.

"You've got a proper supper waiting for you somewhere else," he said, gesturing to the indigents' home.

"I don't care for no basket food tonight," Teedie said.

"You ain't getting any Dree food at all, so you'd best make your choice."

Teedie turned angrily and began to stalk off toward the indigents' home.

"And see that you're waitin' for me on this porch when you're done!" Nacky called after him. Teedie didn't answer.

Nacky, Jimmer and Orro at last entered the restaurant. As they did, they were hit by a familiar scene. The Albert T. Rain was crowded, and with the people, the cooking and the close air of a summer evening, it was uncomfortably warm. Both of Dree's hearths were going, and the aroma of sausages, heavy breads and what Nacky took to be a stew swirled through the room. With so many fragrances in the air, it would be a wonder anyone could smell anything else. But Dree, Nacky knew, had a sharp nose, and one of the things she'd never miss was the smell of pig.

Casting a glance toward one of the hearths, Nacky saw Dree's broad back facing him as she bent over a pot. Dree generally favored dark red dresses and owned, Nacky guessed, at least five or six. Tonight, as on most nights, she was wearing one of them. With her round shape and the deep color, she always put Nacky in mind of a great apple, but he didn't dare tell her that. Once in a while, she'd dress in purple, calling to mind a plump plum, but he didn't dare say that either.

"I believe I smell a pig," Dree now barked without turning around.

Jimmer looked at Nacky; Nacky shrugged and opened the door behind him. He clucked his tongue at Orro.

"Out with you," he said. Orro looked up at him, *clack-clacked* out to the porch and settled himself in a corner. Nacky looked over at the hearth and saw Dree, her back still to him, nod once as the pig smell left the room.

Nacky and Jimmer made their way into the restaurant, passing a table occupied by Brigg and Constance Keeper, a couple in their middle years who rarely went anywhere unless they were together and almost seemed to have come into the world already married. Brigg and Constance frequently ate at the Rain and, Nacky noticed, rarely conversed when they did. Both liked to read, but they could not easily afford books. Instead, they would collect newspapers from other towns, tuck them away for months or years and bring them with them when they went out.

"A good story is a good story," they'd say when asked about the practice, and leave the matter at that.

Tonight, the Keepers were reading as always, and as Nacky passed the table, he accidentally jostled Brigg's chair. Lost in a yellowed paper published in Bowfin, Brigg did not look up.

Nacky and Jimmer at last worked their way to a spot near the bar and sat themselves at the only empty table they saw in the room. When they did, Dree, who could not have seen them sit, turned.

"Are you takin' what you always took, Nacky?" she called.

Nacky gave her a nod, knowing that she knew to bring him a serving of red lead, which was his usual kind of sausage, a square of yalla buck, which was his usual kind of bread, and a large ball of malt.

"Jimmer?" Dree called.

"What are you takin', Nacky?" Jimmer asked.

"Red, yalla and malt."

"The same," Jimmer called to Dree.

Dree nodded. "You finish that house yet, boy?" she asked.

"Expectin' to," Jimmer said, "expectin' to."

While Jimmer and Nacky waited for their food, Nacky looked around and for the first time realized where he was sitting. Directly above his head was one of the pine beams that had come from the *Albert T. Rain*. One table to the left was a pale ash chair and a small table that also came from the sea, hewn from planks from the lost clipper *Whistler*. Off to the right was a larger table hammered together from the bleached remains of the downeaster *Lamplighter*.

Nacky stared at the big table, where the weathered-looking Gilly Boate and three other men were seated, shuffling a deck of flats and playing a spirited round of spoiled five. The cards and the plates and the mugs of malt covered most of the table planks, but a fair bit of the telltale grain of shipboard pine was exposed. Nacky let his gaze linger a moment longer, and Jimmer caught him at it.

"Expectin' it to jump out at you?" he asked.

"Don't much like it, Jimmer. It's bad luck grave-robbin' wrecks like that."

Jimmer shrugged. "Maybe so, but it'd be Dree's luck, not yours."

Nacky nodded, but he wasn't appeased. The fact was, he was convinced that the restaurant was already haunted. Many had been the time he was having a quiet malt at a quiet table, when his ears would prick up at what sounded for all the world like boat timbers creaking. He could never tell exactly where the noise was coming from, and when he cocked his ear to the spot that seemed likeliest, the sound always slithered away to somewhere else. On the one occasion he gathered himself to ask Dree about it, she simply gave him one of her looks that could hard boil an egg and told him to tend to his malt and let her tend to her business.

Nacky's and Jimmer's food soon arrived, and they took their time enjoying it. While he ate, Jimmer kept casting his eye toward the card game at the *Lamplighter* table, until Gilly finally looked up and told him he could either stare or he could play, and seeing as how one of the chairs would be coming empty soon, Jimmer might as well fill it himself.

"Don't mind if I do that," Jimmer said brightly, then turned to Nacky and spoke quietly. "I been watchin', and those boys can no more play that game than sprout wings. Be a shame not to help meself to a bit o' their money."

Nacky waved Jimmer off, content enough to finish up his dinner alone. He took his last few bites of food, step-*clumped* to the bar and paid his bill. He was about to leave the restaurant when he was almost knocked over by Emma Hay rushing in. As always, even a glancing encounter with Emma left him feeling flustered.

Emma and Nacky had been acquaintances since they were both much younger, but they did not see a lot of each other back then, what with all the time Nacky spent practicing Pippa's swindles and all the time Emma spent behind the walls of the indigents' home. Nonetheless, Nacky always had a keen eye for Emma, though she never looked back at him with the same fondness, having no patience at all for his thieving. While she was grateful enough that Nacky was allowing Teedie to stay in his home—and told Teedie to tell him so—she gave him little thought beyond that.

Emma swept past Nacky without seeming to see him and fought through the other customers to the bar where Dree was at work. Nacky gathered himself up and called after her.

"Emma," he said in a voice that seemed to him too loud. She turned, looking briefly put out at having been disturbed. Nacky thought he saw a tiny glint of menacingly flashed tooth, but Emma managed to work up a smile.

"Nacky Patcher," she said. "How are you faring?"

"Faring fairly," Nacky answered, "considering all."

"Of course," Emma said. She glanced downward. "A pity about your foot. Walnut, is it?"

"Pine, actually," Nacky said. And then added with a bit of pride, "Loblolly."

Emma regarded the foot for a moment. "Looks like a clumsy thing," she said in a tone that struck Nacky as gentler than the one she usually used.

"I'm gettin' used to it."

"Yes, I expect you'd have to."

With that, the smile Emma had been able to push up fell away, and without another word, she turned and made her way to the bar. Nacky watched as Emma and Dree exchanged a few words. Dree then went to one of the hearths and returned with two large, hot trays of sweet brick. It was not what Nacky had expected. Of all the things Dree could bake, sweet brick was easily the tastiest—a combination of white cornmeal, pounded nuts and just a shadow of honey. As the thick mix baked up, it fluffed itself into something that was too crusty to be a true cake but too cakey to be a true bread. Whatever it was, it was wonderful, and Dree charged dear for it. Nacky knew from Teedie's dinner baskets that Emma could prepare a considerable meal, but for her to have the money to buy two full trays of a thing as pricey as sweet brick struck him as more than passingly odd.

Emma paid for the bread, turned back around and hurried past Nacky toward the door. With her hands full, she tried to shoulder it open, but couldn't quite manage it. Nacky sprang forward and opened it for her. Emma raced out without a backward glance.

Nacky stood in the doorway of the Albert T. Rain, watching Emma's retreating shape, then clicked his tongue for Orro, who sleepily rose from his spot in the corner of the porch and sniffed the air, as if to confirm that the gangly, wooden-footed man in front of him was the correct gangly, wooden-footed man. Nacky looked out toward the street and whistled once, and Teedie emerged from the darkness a few dozen yards away, having obviously finished his dinner at Emma's and gone to play in the shadows of the darkened buildings. Nacky gave him a close look as he approached, scanning his face for the darting eyes that would suggest he'd been fooling with the black rags again, but the boy looked innocent of any mischief. He fell in step beside Nacky and Orro, and the three of them began walking slowly home.

Night had still not yet fallen in Yole, though the bottom rim of the sun had already slipped partway below the horizon and the owl light was fast gathering. The street was entirely empty, and after the heat and the din of the Albert T. Rain, Nacky liked it like that. Suddenly, for no reason he could determine, Orro broke into a run, speeding off ahead with surprising light-footedness. Nacky stared at Orro's pink, shrinking shape in astonishment, then stumbled into a run after him.

"Orro!" he called. "Orro! You stop that."

"I'll fetch him," Teedie said, and sprinted ahead.

Orro slowed at the sound of Teedie's feet and looked back, and Nacky assumed he was going to stop. But the pig, evidently satisfied he was indeed being followed, turned front again and raced on.

"Orro! I told you to stop!" Nacky shouted. "You mind me, now!"

If Orro heard this time, he simply ignored the command and sped ahead. Teedie continued to give chase, but as fast as the fleet-footed boy could run, he could gain no ground on the fleeter pig. Nacky picked up his pace behind them both, breaking into an awkward run-hop that caused his breath to catch in his lungs, his food to shift in his stomach and the rim of his loblolly foot to bite into the skin of his ankle. Struggling up the downhill road, they ran past the indigents' home, the grocery store, the Pounds' empty shop. Finally, Orro approached Gilly Boate's shop at the top of the hill and stopped. Teedie, breathing hard, stopped beside him. Nacky, wheezing, finally caught up with them both.

He staggered to a halt and leaned forward, bracing his hands against his knees and trying to prevent himself from yollicking his meal.

"What . . . were . . . you . . . after?" he gasped at Orro.

Orro looked back at Nacky and Teedie, cocked his head and waited for them to catch their breath. As soon as they did, he took off again.

Nacky cried out in frustration, and he and Teedie once more lit out after the little racing shape. Now that they were at the top of the town hill, the running was a little easier as they rounded the turn and the upward grade of the cobblestone street gave way to the downward grade of the pounded dirt padroad. They raced along together, until eventually the pig turned off onto a still narrower path that led to a ridge and then down to the Yole lake. The pitch of the terrain on the path was uncomfortably steep and the rubbly footing unsteady, and Nacky reluctantly followed Orro and Teedie, step-hopping and wheeze-gulping across the ridge and down toward the lake bank. Finally, when Nacky and Teedie truly could run no more, the hill reached its bottom, the path reached its end and they found themselves on flatter footing, skidding in the gravel at the lake's northern bank behind Orro. The man and the boy looked out over the water, breathing heavily. Then they let out a scream.

Directly in front of them, floating squarely in the center of the tiny, quarter-mile lake, was the vast, capsized hull of a clipper ship. It was, or surely seemed to be, the *Walnut Egg*—the *Walnut Egg* as Nacky had last seen it, wounded and tipped, inverted but whole, floating keel up in the final moments before it had come undone. At the same time, however, it wasn't the *Walnut Egg*. The *Egg* had been a small clipper, just a hundred and fifty feet long. This one was at least a third again as large—two hundred feet, maybe even two hundred and fifty. Such a big vessel floating on the ocean was a fearsome enough sight. But the same giant object dropped into a puddle of a lake seemed that much bigger, that much more frightful, all the more so when it was turned bottom up—rolled by some obvious violence that likely still lurked. Nacky and Teedie both covered their eyes. Then, slowly, they looked once more.

The boat was gone. As quickly as it had appeared, the wounded clipper had disappeared. The surface of the lake was once again empty, the apparition that had been hanging so huge had vanished completely, leaving no trace of itself behind. Or almost no trace. Suspended in the air, insubstantial as steam, a faint outline of the great bulk of the ship remained. Nacky and Teedie scanned the keel-line and only then realized what the ghostly shape was. As they did, they both let out a shudder of relief.

On the other side of the lake was a flat-topped hill they had seen uncounted times before. Looked at the right way, the hill precisely resembled the hull of a capsized boat, or at least it did when the hour was late and the fading light could fool the eye. Nacky and Teedie stared at the hill for a long moment, and Nacky then felt a nuzzling at his leg and looked down to see Orro nosing at him.

"You saw it too, I wager," he said, smiling down at the animal.

It was then that they all heard a noise. It was a wet sound, a hollow sound, a sound not unlike the rich and resonant clunk wooden beams produce when they bump into one another. It was the sound of wood that was afloat.

Nacky and Teedie looked slowly back out over the water, and what they saw stopped their breath. Wherever they cast their eyes, no matter how deeply they peered into the growing darkness, the surface of the Yole lake was covered with drifting timbers. There were big timbers and small timbers, polished timbers and dull timbers; there were stout, heavy, square-cut ones and long, graceful, fluted ones. And timbers weren't all there were. There were planks, beams, spars, arches, futtocks, stanchions, rails, hatches and rungs. Somewhere else were three—no ten, no forty—drifting doors.

And most gigantically of all, there was a keel. Heeled over on its side, glinting and drifting in the almost-vanished sun, was a vast, curved scythe of wood, two hundred feet long if it was an inch, tons upon tons if it was an ounce. The keel was longer than the *Walnut Egg*'s had been, and yet unlike the *Egg*'s, which changed grain as the wood that made it up changed, it appeared to have been cut from one vast length of timber, without a seam or a joint anywhere in it. It was a fact that was lost entirely on Teedie; but Nacky, who had already seen one ship come unbuttoned, recognized it instantly.

As Nacky noticed that, he realized that all of the countless other pieces of wood littering the surface were made up the same way. They all appeared to be hewn from but one piece of wood each—carved with all the sockets and grooves and bore holes that would be needed to connect them to every other piece, but none of them was in fact connected at all. It was a ship broken down to its structural limits, all there, all preserved, all reduced to its irreducible essence.

Nacky and Teedie took a few tentative steps into the lake, watching as the water surged slightly in and out and the carpet of flotsam moved with it in a single mass. In the ankle-depth water were dozens of wooden bung-plugs and trunnels, schooling in the shallows like baitfish. Nacky bent down, formed both hands into a scoop and picked up several of them, then watched as the water ran out and the pegs and plugs remained. He handed one to Teedie. The two of them had learned much about wood in the time they'd been selecting Nacky's foot, and they immediately recognized the yellow-brown flare of what they held in their hands.

"Teak," Teedie said simply.

They ran their eyes back over the blanket of flotsam everywhere else on the lake. All of it flashed the same elegant color.

As the last of the sun disappeared and the owl light closed in full, Nacky surveyed the scene in front of him and heard the words of Orro— the lost Orro, Orro the man—echoing in his head. There would be another ship, Orro had told him before he died. And now it appeared there was one.

BOOK TWO

CHAPTER NINE

Chuff the dwarf was listening for fish
in the pond outside his cottage when he first learned about the ship
Nacky Patcher and Teedie Flinn had found in the Yole lake. It was Bara
Berry who brought him the news, and the moment he heard her calling
out to him from a little hill on the grand estate where Mally Baloo and
Chuff and Bara and so many others lived, he felt a sense of relief. Had
she not appeared soon, he might never have seen her again.

Nobody in Yole knew just how it was that Chuff the dwarf could
listen for fish, but nobody doubted he could do it. It was when Chuff
was a boy that people first began realizing he might be able to hear
things he ought not be able to hear. There was the time he was serving
Mally Baloo at table and suddenly snatched a fresh apple from the great
man's hand, nearly earning himself a throttling until he explained that
he could hear a large fruitworm moving about inside. Baloo picked up
a heavy beef knife, cut the apple open, and revealed not one, but two
of the slug-ugly things curled up in the core. There was the time estate
workmen were digging a well on the Baloo land and Chuff told them to
move precisely twenty yards east, where he was certain the dense rock
below ground gave way to a reservoir of percolating water—water that

nobody else knew was there but that had kept him awake the night before with its constant churning and gurgling.

Most important, there was the time a twelve-year-old Chuff first went fishing in the Baloo ponds and announced that if he paid close mind, he could clearly hear the whispery *swish* of the sportfish swimming in the dark green water. So good did Chuff become at listening to the pond that he soon learned just where to drop his hook in order to place it straight in the path of an oncoming fish—sometimes even distinguishing between the soft gurgle of a school of finger fish and the deeper, louder sound of a fish that could be a true meal.

When Chuff wasn't fishing, there wasn't a great deal else for him to do beyond helping out a bit in the fields and going into town when there were out-with-you papers to be served. The little man's essential uselessness always seemed to wear on Baloo like rawbark, and most people assumed his services would have been sold off entirely had any other estate been willing to pay so much as a coin for them. But Chuff had been born on the Baloo land. He never knew his father, but his mother had been a maid in the Baloo kitchen. After she died, Chuff stayed on, and with each passing year it seemed increasingly likely that he'd live his entire life on the estate too.

This morning, Chuff was at the pond near his one-room cottage, dropping his hook and line here and there and listening for the fish he hoped would be his breakfast. Chuff's lips were moving as he fished, mouthing the words of his three-line poem—which, just in the past few weeks, had become a six-line poem. "If it pleases or not," the poem now went,

> I am just as you see;
> I'm a man, though I look more a lad.
>
> My sorrows are plain,
> my afflictions are three;
> each cruel and each hard and each sad . . ."

Truth be told, Chuff was not entirely happy bringing the last line up short with so sodden a word as *sad,* and for some time he had been casting about for another one that could pair up proper with the *lad* in the first verse. That was the puzzle he was worrying over when Bara Berry crested the hill overlooking the pond and ran down to tell him about what Nacky Patcher and Teedie Flinn had found in the Yole lake the night before.

Bara Berry was the younger sister of Mary Berry—the only one of Mary's relatives known to be alive. It had been seven years since Mary had tried to escape the indigents' home, Emma Hay had called the law on her, and so much unpleasantness followed. Bara, who had lived at the home at the time as well, was a girl of barely eighteen now, which meant that she had not been more than a child when she and her sister last saw each other.

Like so many of the home girls, Bara was sent to work at the Baloo estate as soon as she was old enough to put in a true day's labor. A post at the Baloos' was said to be a good one, since her food and clothes and cottage would be provided and she'd earn a modest wage besides. The problem was, her living costs would be charged against her earnings, and since the wages were small and the debts were large, she would never get clear. In the eyes of the law, leaving the job was the same as debt-skipping, and Bara—along with most of the estate workers—was thus bound to keep working for Baloo until he either forgave the debt or sold it off to someone else.

Despite this enforced service, Bara worked hard for Baloo. A slight girl, she was judged to be of little value toiling in the fields and was instead put to work assisting the estate leather worker, rebinding the Baloo family's account books and, in her free hours, making shoes for the other laborers living on the grounds. She was exceedingly clever—cleverer than Baloo knew—and always made it her business to look through the books she was repairing, puzzling out for herself what the numbers in the columns meant, and telling the other workers when Baloo's purse was particularly fat and they were likely to get warmer blankets and richer food, and when it wasn't as fat and they'd have to save their scraps and take particularly good care of their bedding. She was clever too about making the shoes.

Every month or two, Bara would be given the leather, wood, cord and nails she'd need to make a dozen or so pairs and would return them completed in lightning time. The workshop manager would always weigh the shoemaking material before he gave it to her, insisting that she return not just the shoes, but every bit of scrap left over. It was the only way he could be sure she hadn't sold off the extra material or made additional pairs for workers whose old shoes had worn out but who were not entitled to a new pair until the following season.

It didn't take Bara long to discover that the workshop manager was a poor judge of weight and often gave her far more material than she needed. When he did, she'd indeed cobble up a few extra pairs of shoes and pass them on to the Baloo workers most requiring them. Then she'd slip off the estate and wheedle a ride to nearby Bowfin, where she'd visit the local carriage maker and offer to carry off some of his cord and leather rubbish. When she had weighed out the right amount of scraps, she'd return to the estate and present them—along with the approved shoes—to the workshop manager. So far, the fussy man had never caught wise.

Yesterday afternoon, Bara had made her most recent trip to Bowfin but was later than usual returning this morning, which was why Chuff had begun to fret that she might have been caught at her mischief and sent off to the tower and why he breathed so much easier when he saw her cresting the hill, running toward him in a clumsy sprint-stumble, a sack of carriage maker's scraps slung over her shoulder. Bara herself appeared to have more on her mind than the mere matter of her own safe return.

"Chuff! Chuff!" she called, half-running, half-tumbling down the hill.

Chuff looked up, smiled, and from what Bara could see from a distance, appeared to nod and say something like, "Yes?" For all Chuff's fine hearing, he never seemed to understand just how loudly he needed to speak for other people to hear him clearly.

"Chuff!" Bara called again, fighting to keep her wind and her balance as she pad-padded through the grass. "There's passremarkable news."

Bara sprinted the rest of the way to Chuff, came to a stop in front of him and dropped the heavy, horse-smelling bag on the ground. Bending forward, she fought to catch her breath. "Something's been found at the lake," she said, gulping air.

Chuff nodded.

"Something big," Bara said.

Chuff nodded again, his eyes looking sleepy. "Finished another verse of me poem," he said.

Bara blinked, brought up short.

"I know," she answered, taking in a swallow of breath and flapping her hand in a never-mind wave. Then she caught herself. Bara and Chuff had been fast friends for a while now—Bara reckoning Chuff needed looking after and Chuff seeming grateful that anyone would bother. Bara had learned some time ago that there were ways to talk to the little man and ways not to, at least if you wanted him to stay the course through an entire conversation.

"I know," she said again, gentler now. "You read it to me. I like the way you brung up the end of that last line." The truth was, Bara didn't much care for the end of Chuff's poem, reckoning the word *sad* sat a bit heavy on the verse. But she figured it didn't hurt to do him a kindness.

Chuff nodded and then appeared ready to take in the first thing Bara had said. "There's something at the lake?" he asked.

"Sure as rocks there is," Bara answered, then ran-stumbled into her story the way she'd run-stumbled through the grass. "I was walkin' on the padroad on my way back from Bowfin, when I looked down the hill at the lake and seen this wood rubbish coverin' it one side to the next. Looks lick-alike a busted-up ship, only the biggest ship I've ever seen. Seen a man, a boy and a pig sleepin' on the bank too and didn't need much guessin' to know that they was Teedie Flinn, Nacky Patcher and that animal of his. I'd've gone down the hill m'self to see for certain, except I couldn't keep my footing with this bag, and besides, I had to get back here to deliver my scraps and shoes. I did run into Meddo Brinn on the road, and he'd already been by the lake ridge and seen it too. Reckon he's passin' the word and folks'll be showin' up there straightaway. Soon's I drop my bag and show my face, I'm goin' back over."

Bara at last ran out of steam, her expression flushed and excited. Chuff looked at her.

"You saw a ship at the lake?"

Bara nodded. "You can come with me to look if you want," she said, in fact hoping that Chuff would decline the invitation, since his short gait and sleepy pace would only slow her down.

"It's a broken ship?"

Bara nodded.

Chuff looked beyond Bara and seemed to be paying attention to something far away. "I guess I would like to see that," he said. "Terrible lot of folks are almost there already."

"How do you know that?" Bara asked.

Chuff considered the question. "Don't know," he said. "I think I can hear them. Wood's doin' a lot of bangin' too."

Bara regarded him curiously.

"I reckon I can hear that as well," he added.

Bara continued to look at Chuff, but he broke the gaze and stared beyond her again, cocking his head in his listening stance. Bara followed his eyes and mimicked his pose, and all at once, her breath was taken back out of her. She had never matched Chuff's gift for hearing and never would. But now, in the quiet of the morning, she could almost fancy she heard the wood bumping too. It was not, she noticed, an especially welcoming sound. Perhaps she wouldn't mind Chuff joining her at the lake after all.

CHAPTER TEN

Chuff and **Bara** did **not** know **about**
the kitchen girl named Brinca who would be put out of her cottage not
long after they hurried off to see the broken boat. It may have been
Chuff's job to serve out-with-you papers to people being pitched from
their homes everywhere else in Yole, but on the grounds of the estate,
Mally Baloo liked to keep such matters to himself, lest Chuff let the
news slip too early and cause unpleasantness. Cottage clearances were
common on the Baloo estate lately, with more and more workers who
displeased Mally Baloo—and even some who didn't—being sent packing.
In just the last six months, no fewer than eight cottages had been emptied, and while there were dozens of others still filled with workers, the
new vacancies were more than anyone living on the land could recall.

When Baloo sold a worker's debt contract, he always demanded a
plump price, made all the plumper by the fact that it was usually the
strongest and healthiest workers he chose to sell. That plus the savings
he realized on the clothes, food and other upkeep for the people he was
pitching meant that clearing a cabin was a very profitable proposition
for him. The workers themselves simply went wherever the new buyer
took them.

Baloo had been eyeing Brinca for eviction for a while now. She was a strong girl, not more than twenty-two or twenty-three years old, and she was stout but solid, giving her a good deal more strength than the ordinary woman and only a bit less than the ordinary man. She was not a clever girl, however, particularly when it came to the crops she tended. She never seemed able to tell her radishes from her turnips or her celery from her rhubarb or even her yams from her common sweet potatoes. It was the yams and sweet potatoes that provoked Baloo most, and when he'd come across a field that was planted with both instead of one or the other, he'd rage at the simple Brinca, who'd often cry pitiably—something that looked odd coming from so large and sturdy a girl.

Baloo was always in fine spirits after he pitched someone from the estate, and he always followed the eviction the same way. First, he'd order up a lunch of mock goose, which was one of his favorite meals. Made of the stuffed, seasoned and roasted stomach of a goat or sheep, mock goose was poor man's fare, not generally found on the tables of folks so well-tinned. But Baloo had developed a taste for the unlikely dish and seemed to enjoy it most on those occasions when he was feeling especially pleased with himself.

After Baloo had had his lunch, he would order that the cottage of the worker who'd just been evicted be demolished and the soil it sat on be turned for growing. For reasons no one had ever determined, crops on the Baloo land thrived when they were planted in the spot where a home once stood. There were those who said the lack of sun over the years had prevented the strength of the soil from being bleached away. Others disagreed, however, believing that, like so much else on the Baloo estate, the crops had simply grown used to things touched by sorrow, and the home of a worker who'd been pitched from the estate and sent to places unknown was one of the most sorrowful things of all.

This morning, Baloo had woken up in a good temper, but it darkened fast when a runner sent by the constable arrived and cheeped to him about something that was said to have been found at the lake. It wasn't long before a visibly angry Baloo decided he needed something to brighten his mood, and called for beat-men to be fetched for a pitching and cottage-razing that very morning and for a young sheep to be tied off for slaughter for a mock-goose lunch later.

Brinca was in a distant field puzzling out her crops while all this was happening, so she didn't hear the bleat of the sheep when its throat was cut, nor see the beat-men when they arrived. She didn't even hear the din they made as they were breaking her walls and demolishing her cottage. It was only when she returned from the fields just after noon to prepare her small lunch that she saw the four men standing before the ruins of what had for so long been her home. When she saw what they had done, a wail escaped her that could be heard in all the corners of the estate for a full minute or more after she released it. Before the sound even died, she was being packed into a noddy and driven out the gate, her debt paper now belonging to a peat merchant who needed a strong back for shoveling and cutting in a faraway bog. Brinca never again set foot on the land of Mally Baloo or even in the town of Yole itself.

By the time Baloo, whose temper had now improved—at last sat down for his mock-goose lunch, the site of Brinca's cottage was already being cleared. He ordered that the little plot forever be planted with both yams and sweet potatoes, so that his field workers could take a moment when they needed and study the difference.

CHAPTER ELEVEN

For the first hour or so after Nacky
and Teedie found the great blanket of floating wood in the Yole lake,
they had no idea what they ought to do, and so they did nothing at all,
sitting on the bank and saying little, with the drifting teak spread out in
front of them and Orro the pig curled up between them. Before long,
however, the warm air and the late hour began to sit heavier and heavier,
and they lay down and slipped into brick-heavy slumber. There's no telling how long they might have remained that way if they hadn't been
disturbed by the voice of Jimmer Pike, cutting through the fog of sleep
sometime the next morning.

"Ho, there," they could hear a Jimmer-like voice call. Nacky muttered something and turned over in the lake bank's damp, rattly pebbles.
Teedie remained motionless.

"Nacky!" Jimmer called again. "Nacky Patcher!"

Jimmer's voice was closer now, and his wet, running footsteps car-
ried it nearer still. "Wake up, there!" the voice finally said, this time in
Nacky's ear, as a hand roughly shook his shoulder. Opening one eye,
Nacky saw an outline of a head and shoulders silhouetted against the

orange light of the east-rising sun. The shadow-head was crowned by the familiar, pillowy curls. Nacky raised a hand to shade his eyes.

"Jimmer?" he asked.

"And lucky it's me first," Jimmer said.

Nacky propped himself up on one elbow, looked about and blinked in the light. "What is it?" he asked.

"I might ask you that," Jimmer said. "I might well ask you that. Of a mind to explain what you're doin' here? Of a mind to explain what all this is?" Jimmer threw an arm in the direction of the lake.

Teedie at last began to stir as well. He sat up and looked at Jimmer, shielding his eyes just as Nacky had done.

"H'lo, Jimmer," he said pleasantly. Jimmer nodded back crisply.

"Jimmer wants to know what this is all about," Nacky said to Teedie, indicating the lake.

"It's still here?" Teedie asked, turning to face the water.

"Every stick," Nacky answered.

Just as Nacky said, the planks and beams and futtocks and frames of the great broken ship were precisely as they'd been last night, bobbing and bumping on the skyberry water from one end of the lake to the other. This was the first time, however, that Teedie and Nacky had seen them in the full light of day, and they were a passremarkable sight. The angled morning sun streaming over the hills fired up the blond-gold teak the way mere owl light had not. The reflected shimmer coming off the wood seemed almost not to be reflecting at all, but streaming from inside the grain itself.

"Lovely thing, ain't it?" Nacky asked, turning back to Jimmer.

"Lovely? Looks to be the better part of a ruined boat."

"Ain't ruined," Nacky said. "And it ain't just the better part; it's the whole thing."

"How do you know that?" Jimmer asked.

Nacky paused and looked at Teedie. "Don't know," he said, "but it's true." Teedie nodded in agreement.

"Who put it here?" Jimmer asked.

"I reckon that ought to be clear," Nacky said.

Jimmer gave Nacky an uncomprehending look. "It ain't clear," he said, "but you better make it clear right soon. Meddo Brinn already peeked down here and cheeped to a constable and who-knows-who-all else. They was halfway here when I run into 'em on the padroad and figured I better double back to warn you. If you done somethin' you oughtn't, you'd best have a way to explain it."

Nacky looked at Jimmer as if he hadn't heard him and began to struggle to stand. Teedie leapt up and helped him rise, and together the man and the boy stepped toward the water with Orro following. Crouching, Nacky picked up a trunnel, a bung-plug and a plank. He turned them this way and that in the morning light, and then, with a quick and seemingly practiced hand, slipped one of the trunnels through a hole in the plank and wedged a bung-plug in behind it.

"Look at this, Jimmer," he called over his shoulder. "Buttons up easy as you please."

"Don't be hurklin' around there, Nacky," Jimmer said, casting an anxious glance up the lake path. "Didn't you hear what I said?"

Nacky waved a hand without looking back. "If we can collect all the bits and they're all cut just so," he said half to himself and half to Jimmer, "I don't expect it'd be any trouble at all."

"Don't expect what'd be any trouble?" Jimmer asked.

"Piecin' it together," Teedie answered for Nacky. "Ain't that so?"

Nacky nodded. "Don't see why not. Got all the parts; got lots of time. No reason we couldn't make us a ship."

Jimmer's eyes went wide. "What are you sayin', Nacky?"

Nacky stood, turned and faced his friend. He locked up Jimmer's eyes with his own and spoke slowly.

"I'm gonna build the thing, Jimmer," he said. "Me and the boy. I already seen how a boat come apart. I always reckoned I was showed such a thing for a purpose. Now I'm gonna put one back together."

Jimmer stared at Nacky and then broke the gaze. "You're away to the hills."

"What else do you reckon we're supposed to do with it?"

"You ain't supposed to do nothin' with it."

"That ain't what the Songs say," Nacky said.

"What songs?" Jimmer asked.

"Them dry-land boats."

"Them's cradle tales, Nacky!"

Nacky merely smiled at Jimmer and looked out at the forest of floating wood. Two of the larger frames bumped together with a thunk that made the men, the boy and the pig jump.

"Tell them beams they're just cradle tales," Nacky said. "You recall any of the verses of them rhymes?"

"Not one," Jimmer answered.

"I do. Recall 'em all." Nacky gathered his thoughts, then began to recite:

> In the wreckage of boats
> and the wreckage of seas,
> There's a curse to reverse
> and a charm to appease.
>
> The basins may fill
> and the boats draw new crew,
> If the wise spot the course
> and the brave sail it true.

Jimmer looked at Nacky uncomprehendingly. Nacky stared back hard. "This here is a ghost boat turned real," Nacky said. "There's a way to break the charm what's holdin' this town, and we just spotted it."

"This here is wood someone else left behind and is gonna come back for," Jimmer said. "You ain't gonna change anything around these parts by buildin' another man's boat."

"I ain't just got to build it. Got to haul it all the way to the ocean too," Nacky said, as Teedie nodded his agreement. Jimmer looked incredulous. "It stands to reason, don't it?" Nacky asked. "You can't free up the town if you don't free up the boat."

Jimmer turned beseechingly to Teedie, who smiled. "That's the way I puzzle it out too," the boy said.

Nacky faced Jimmer and spoke now with a harder edge in his voice: "I'm gonna build it, Jimmer. I'm gonna build it good. If you're of a mind, you can lay off them little houses of yours and come help me. This town could use saving, and this might be the way."

Jimmer struggled for something to say, but just then, a sound echoed through the bowl from the top of the lake path. The men, the boy and the pig turned and saw a crowd of what appeared to be more than two dozen people gathering on the crest of the ragged hill and standing there utterly still. All of them looked out over the lake for a long, puzzled moment—and all of them then broke the gaze and began running and skidding down the path.

From where they stood, Nacky, Teedie and Jimmer couldn't make out who most of the people were, but they did recognize a few of them. At the head of the crowd—as Jimmer had warned—was the letter carrier Meddo Brinn, along with his ten-year-old son. Meddo was a stocky fellow not yet in his middle years who had not much liked Nacky since they were boys, when Nacky sold Meddo's family one of his imaginary cows. Nacky was caught at the swindle, paid the money back and never tried fleecing the Brinns again. Meddo's family was content to let the matter drop, but Meddo himself never was.

Hurrying down the hill behind Meddo were the Dreeboys, a pair of brothers not yet twenty, who looked enough like each other to be dead-spit twins—down to the position of the sun freckles on their faces—except that one of them was a good six inches taller than the other. The Dree-boys lived in a small sidehouse behind the Albert T. Rain and did odd jobs for Dree, which is how they got their name. Most people believed that the Dreeboys were in fact Dree's boys. She was rumored to have been widowed shortly before coming to live in Yole and was said to have grieved the loss cruelly. After that, she dared not mention that the boys were her sons lest she call to mind the man who'd given them to her, and that she could not bear to do. Since she never discussed any of her personal affairs with anyone, however, nobody knew for sure if there was truth to the story. Behind the Dreeboys was old Gilly Boate, the owner of the Shop at the Top; behind him was the beefy, red-faced constable. All the others followed.

Nacky and Teedie watched as the people hurried toward them. Jimmer looked at Nacky and Teedie with a just-as-I-told-you nod. At his feet, Nacky could hear Orro scrabbling nervously and reached down to give the pig's back a pat. In the sky to the east, just beyond the approaching crowd, a small, black thunderhead drifted into view, nipping off a corner of the sun. Nacky and Jimmer didn't notice it. Teedie did.

"Didn't I say there'd be somethin' down here?" Meddo Brinn asked the constable when the crowd had closed to within hearing and come to a stop. "And didn't I say Nacky Patcher was mixed up in it? Looks like he mixed the boy up too."

Nacky squared off his shoulders and tried to work up a smile. The constable, he recognized, was from Greater M'croom. He was in town today, quite likely, to collect a payment from Mally Baloo for his help in the most recent round of house-pitchings.

"H'lo there, constable," Nacky said. "H'lo there, Meddo Brinn."

"Don't need any helloin' from you, Nacky Patcher," Meddo answered. "Just need to hear some explainin'."

"What kind of explainin'?"

Meddo spread his arms to indicate the lake. "What kind do you reckon?" he asked sharply. Nacky stayed silent. "You don't want to talk to me," Meddo said, "I expect you'll talk to the law."

"You know what this rubbish is, Nacky Patcher?" the constable asked.

"We don't know nothin'," Teedie said, stepping forward. Nacky put a hand on his shoulder and held it there hard.

"You mind yourself, boy," the constable said. "Let Nacky Patcher answer for what this is."

"Looks to be a boat," Nacky said.

"You find it?"

"I did."

"With the boy?"

"Yes, with me," Teedie said.

"What about you, Jimmer Pike?"

"I come down here this mornin' lookin' for Nacky," Jimmer said. "Saw what you see now."

Meddo snorted once and exchanged a look with the Dreeboys and Gilly, who snorted back. Nacky darted his eyes over the crowd, which muttered skeptically. Nothing Nacky was mixed up in was likely to sit right with this group, and he'd more or less reckoned that from the start. Those were the wages, he knew, not just of having spent his life thieving, but of thieving badly. Fleece a fellow well and he'll at least tip his hat to your skill. Fleece a fellow clumsily and you've got neither honor nor ability to your name. Meddo Brinn may have been the only one here today who truly carried any ill will toward Nacky, but he was not the only one who didn't much trust him.

"You reckon I put all this rubbish here myself?" Nacky asked the group at large, gesturing toward the lake.

"I don't know what I reckon," Meddo said. "I only know that if it's rubbish, it's rubbish what can fetch a price. Gilly Boate here might like to sell a stick or two in his shop. The Dreeboys might like to carry a piece or two back to the Rain." Gilly and the Dreeboys nodded.

"That ain't the way the law works," Nacky said, turning to the constable. "Wood like this is salvage, ain't it? If I found it, ain't I the one what decides what happens to it?"

"That's what we're tryin' to lay out," the constable answered. "You bein' straight about how you come upon this wreck?"

Nacky nodded and the constable turned to Jimmer.

"You bein' straight about findin' Nacky Patcher with it?"

Jimmer nodded.

"Don't seem no help for it then," the constable said, spreading his hands. "Nacky Patcher, it's your wreck. Share it with the boy if you choose."

Meddo Brinn cursed and turned away. Nacky lit up and looked at the constable in surprise. The last time the two men had seen each other was three years ago, during one of Nacky's earlier imprisonments, when the constable had had to stay in town for six months to tend to Nacky in the tower. When the lawman released him, he had seemed happy to see the back of him. Now he was taking Nacky's part against the rest of the town.

"So you're just plannin' to stay here all day and prevent anyone from makin' off with Nacky Patcher's wood?" Meddo asked the constable.

"Didn't say that," the constable answered, taking a step away from the water with his hands clasped behind his back. "All I'm settin' down is who has rights to what. You folks don't agree, it's a matter for a judge."

"Then if someone was to help himself to a piece of that plankin' . . . ?" Gilly Boate asked.

"It'd be up to Nacky Patcher and the boy to go to the courts about it. Until then . . ." The constable turned his palms up and looked at Nacky.

Now it was Nacky's turn to curse and Meddo's turn to brighten. "That's as fine a readin' of the law as I've ever heard!" Meddo said.

"That ain't right!" Teedie cried. "This here's our find!" The crowd gave off with a laugh at the boy's sass.

"I told you to stay aside, boy," the constable said. "I imagine you'll be findin' your way to the tower soon enough, but today ain't the day."

Nacky looked at Teedie and nodded him silent. Meddo Brinn grinned again, took his son by the wrist and stepped into the skyberry water. He bent down and fished out a handful of bung-plugs, bringing one up to his eye like a jeweler studying a stone. Then he turned around and tossed the plug to Gilly, who bobbled it once, then twice, then caught it just before it hit the ground. Nacky and Teedie winced. In the sky to the east, another dark tuft of clouds joined the one already there. Teedie looked up at it, but no one else did.

107

"Some fine hardwood, eh, Gilly?" Meddo said. "These bits burn as hot as I think they will, I'm comin' back with my ax and choppin' up enough to keep me warm all winter." He passed a plug to his boy and jiggled the rest in his palm, producing a heavy rattling sound.

Nacky reddened and took an angry step forward. Jimmer seized hold of his arm.

"Don't be pancrocked," he muttered. He extended his other arm in front of Teedie. "You neither."

With Meddo and his boy in the lake, Gilly gathered himself to follow, casting his eye toward a length of polished planking floating a few feet from shore. Wading into the water, he took hold of the wood and dragged it back onto the bank, leaving a ragged trail behind him. He dropped the plank with a clatter and headed back for more. The Dree-boys, watching Gilly, smiled at each other and bounded into the lake as well, splashing in the general direction of what looked to be a spar or a bowsprit floating a hundred feet from shore. The remaining crowd held back for only a moment, and then, as if with one mind, broke for the water together. Calling and pointing, laughing and pushing, they plunged into the shallows and began flailing about for planks, beams, trunnels, even heavy frames and futtocks. The constable surveyed the scene serenely. Nacky and Teedie watched with climbing ire, their eyes slit, their breath quickening.

"Lay that off!" Nacky shouted to no one in particular.

"Leave that be!" Teedie called.

Jimmer put a restraining hand on Nacky's arm.

"It ain't proper!" Nacky said.

"Proper don't have no business here," Jimmer answered.

Before they could say any more, there was another sound at the top of the lake path, and they turned to see more people cresting the hill, gazing at the spectacle of the wreckage and skidding clumsily down the path. This group was louder than the first one, and—with the lake already full of splashing people—bolder too, running across the bank and high-stepping into the shallows without so much as a pause. They grabbed at planks, hoisted themselves up on frames, flopped on their bellies on drifting beams.

As Nacky and Teedie watched, red-faced, they noticed a shadow fall over the lake. Teedie looked up and saw still more black clouds rolling in. Nacky and Jimmer cast their eyes up too and seemed surprised.

"Been gatherin' for a while," Teedie said.

With more and more of the sun hidden behind the clouds, the skyberry water in the lake began turning a deeper pinberry, and the pinberry gave way to a still darker blueberry. A thin wind broke over the western rim of the bowl, streamed down the hill and caused Nacky's, Jimmer's and Teedie's clothes to flap and their skin to stand up in goose bumps.

"They noticin' this?" Jimmer asked, regarding the people splashing in the water.

"They don't seem to be," Nacky answered.

The wind rose higher and the sky grew darker, and as it did, the competition for the best bits of wood floating in the lake started to grow keen. Two men about Meddo Brinn's age swam out to a choice piece of frame and began shoving and arguing over it. A young couple raced an older couple to a cylindrical spar, hoisted themselves up and tried to balance on it as if it were a great, polished log. Nacky and Teedie silently took in the whole splashing scene, and then suddenly, Teedie had had enough. He pushed past Jimmer and broke toward the water.

"Teedie!" Nacky shouted, and tried to hurry after him, hobbling in the wet pebbles of the bank. He took no more than a few steps before he skidded and fell.

Teedie ignored Nacky's call and his fall and ran into the lake, plunging face-first into the cold water. Thrashing and choking, he regained his footing in the shallows and began to throw himself at anyone in his path, batting away beams and snatching back planks. No sooner would he reclaim a piece of wood than he'd lose his balance again and fall back under the darkening water, dropping the teak he'd grabbed in the process. So unhinged did Teedie seem and so fiercely did he fight that nobody thought to lash at him in return. Instead, they simply splashed backward, trying to put as much distance as possible between themselves and the savage, wild-eyed boy flailing toward them.

As Teedie fought, the shadows darkened by yet another shade, casting the lake in dusk light, and this seemed to pull his attention. He stopped his struggling, stared up and froze at what he saw. Enough thunderheads had now rolled in that the sunlight was blotted out altogether—or it should have been blotted out. But the white sun behind the dark clouds was so torch-bright it seemed to shine right through them. The sky was both brilliant and black, both lit like noon and dark like midnight. It was beautiful and horrible all at once. It was, Teedie realized, a sky full of blackfire.

Nacky looked up and saw it too, and his eyes went as wide as Teedie's. Then he looked back over the water. At the limit of his vision, something caught his notice and seemed to stop his heart. Deep in the debris field, floating alone like a vast carved raft, was a glinting teak door—bigger than Nacky's *Walnut Egg* door, but a door all the same. A lone man was standing on it, laughing and hooting at the low, dark sky, a mound of boards and trunnels piled at his feet. Nacky felt his eyes go full, his skin go cold, his throat go choked and swollen. Then he threw his head back and let fly a furious cry that emptied his lungs and shredded his throat and startled the people near him to stillness.

And in that instant, the sky opened up. With a boom and a crack the likes of which Nacky had not heard since the night of the death of the *Walnut Egg,* the blackfire clouds split wide and a hot rain began to pour from them. The first great gush hit both Nacky and Teedie full in the face, knocking them backward and striking them briefly blind. Teedie wrestled back to standing, regained his purchase in the water and began desperately chesting his way back to shore. On the bank, Nacky picked himself up as well and reached his arms out toward the struggling boy.

"This way, this way!" he called.

Through the curtain of rain, Teedie could just see Nacky and, behind him, Jimmer, crouching in the pebbles and holding on to Orro. Teedie fought through the water, hit the bank and staggered toward Nacky, who gathered him close and forced them all down into a clinch, showing only their backs to the rain. Below him, Nacky could hear Orro's, Jimmer's and Teedie's ragged breathing. All around him, he could hear the rush of the rain and, distantly through it, the cries of the townspeople being tossed about on the water. With his right hand, he gave Teedie's wet back a reassuring pat. With his left, he did the same to Orro's.

"Easy now," he said to the boy and the pig. "Easy."

Nacky himself was not much troubled by the ferocious storm. The rain felt pleasingly warm against his neck and shoulders; the wind felt pleasingly bracing. Both had quickly extinguished the fury he had felt only a moment before. Out on the water, he knew, the people would not be so calm—paddling and gasping and fighting for shore, while the claw of the rain pulled them back. On the bowl of hills surrounding the lake, anybody who had already started to make off with plundered wood would come skidding back down, the dry red soil turning to slick red mud beneath their feet. All of the people would be shoggled and startled. None would be seriously hurt. Nacky knew the character of a storm that was likely to take lives, and this wasn't it.

"How much longer till this breaks up?" Jimmer asked in Nacky's ear.

"Not long now," Nacky answered evenly, "not long."

Smiling slightly, he inclined his head upward and opened one eye into the hash of falling rain. Already he could see a crack of light in the blackfire clouds.

CHAPTER TWELVE

It was hard to recall a time when the
Albert T. Rain was as crowded as it was in the hour after the sudden
storm struck the Yole lake. By ten-thirty in the morning, well before
Dree ordinarily opened her doors for her lunchtime customers, there
was not a table or seat or square foot of floor space left to claim in the
little restaurant.

Most of the people at the lake waited out the storm on the banks or
in the water, then lit out as soon as the downpour stopped, struggling
up the mud-slick hill and sloshing back down the padroad to town. Dree,
who had seen the crowd going out to the lake and watched from a distance as the blackfire thunderheads grew and burst, reckoned that when
the people returned, they would want to gather at the Rain to dry off,
warm up and puzzle out what had happened. And when they did that,
they'd likely have a thirst for her malt—never mind the early hour.

Dree stationed herself on her porch, and when she indeed saw the
crowd approaching, crossed her formidable arms, stepped in front of
her door and told them they were welcome inside, but not until they
removed their shoes, lest they track red mud on the plank floor she took

such care to sweep and polish. When Nacky, Teedie, Jimmer and Orro showed up, she made them leave not only their mud-splattered boots outside but Nacky's mud-splattered pig as well. She sized Teedie up with a narrowed eye, strict as ever about keeping children out of her establishment, but reckoning that on this occasion she could make an exception. She motioned him inside.

"But not so much as a dram for you, boy," she said.

When they were past Dree, Nacky took Teedie by the shoulders. "And not so much as a word out of you neither," he whispered. "You don't say nothin' here about curses nor ghost boats nor anything else we talked about. You hear?"

Teedie nodded, and he and Nacky and Jimmer made their way through the restaurant, the eyes of the other people in the room turning toward them as they passed. In the close quarters of the Rain, the attention from all the others made the three of them uncomfortable, particularly Nacky, who felt self-conscious step-*clumping* into the Albert T. Rain in his stocking-clad left foot and his naked, wooden right one. As quickly as he could, he thus made straight for the safety of the closest empty table—the one, he noticed uneasily, that was made from the light brown ashwood of the lost clipper *Whistler.* He and Teedie and Jimmer seated themselves there and looked around. Everyone who had been at the lake this morning was here, with the exception of the constable, who had evidently used the storm as his opportunity to take his leave and return to the better weather and less-complicated affairs of Greater M'croom. Even without the lawman, it did not seem to be a friendly crowd.

Dree let them all settle and mutter for a full twenty minutes, moving from table to table with the wet, barefoot Dreeboys, serving up mugs and learning more about the morning's events. Nacky would have liked to have stood and called the crowd's attention, reckoning that the first man to speak would have the strongest claim on the thinking in the room. But the Albert T. Rain belonged to Dree, and she would be the one to decide when she had sold all the drink she could and was ready to let a matter of business proceed. Finally, she threaded her way back to her familiar position behind the bar—the Dreeboys joining her there—and rapped her calloused knuckles against the hardwood surface. The conversation in the room fell away, and all heads turned to her.

"So what do we do with Nacky Patcher and the Flinn boy's boat?" she called out. "What do we do with this rubbish in the lake?"

"Still ain't settled that it's their boat," Meddo Brinn said.

"Still ain't settled that it's a boat at all," Gilly Boate added, "'less you're assumin' it sailed up from the sea by itself."

A snirt of laughter came from Meddo and a few others.

"It's a boat all right, Gilly," said the bigger of the Dreeboys. "Nothin' else it could be."

Dree looked scissors at the boy and he fell quiet. "We ain't here to settle what it is or where it's been sailin'," she said. "Where it's goin' is what we're takin' up."

"Captain Patcher already made clear where it's goin'," Gilly said. "He aims to gather it up and carry it home." A bigger ripple of laughter ran through the restaurant.

"And what if he does?" Teedie said, half-standing. "He's the one what found it—him and me." Nacky pulled him back down in his chair.

"You'll speak when you're spoke to," Meddo said. "Mouse like you don't even belong in here."

"The boy's speakin' the truth, though, ain't he, Nacky?" Gilly said. "You're claimin' that wood for yerself and plannin' to haul it off."

Nacky looked at Gilly hard and then stood, pushing back his chair with a scrape on the floorboards that made Dree wince. "I never said I aim to do that," he said.

"What you say ain't never had much to do with the truth," Gilly answered. "Ain't that what earned you all that time in the tower?"

The crowd murmured its agreement, looking at Nacky with the slitted eyes honest folks always use when sizing up a thief. Pippa had told Nacky that he'd have to learn to like the people he planned to fleece, and Nacky guessed the same applied to people he wanted to lead. What

114

Nacky hadn't realized until now was that the people would have to come to like him too.

"Thievin' and cheatin's all behind me now," Nacky said.

"So you say," Gilly responded. "But you're still claimin' that boat's salvage, ain't you?"

"Yes," Nacky said.

"So that means it's yours."

"Yes," Nacky repeated.

"And you ain't plannin' to give it away, are you?"

"No."

"Nor just let it molder there?"

"No."

"Then what do you figure to do with it, if not haul it off?"

Nacky let the question hang for a moment. In the flush of dawn at the edge of the lake with the carpet of teak floating in the skyberry water, it had been a simple matter to tell Jimmer and Teedie what he fancied doing with the wood. In the close and stuffy Albert T. Rain, with the malt flowing and the mood darkening and too many eyes looking at him in too suspicious a way, it would be another matter entirely. Nonetheless, if the law was the law, then the boat was his boat, and if he didn't lay claim to it now, that claim would surely be jumped. Nacky gathered himself up and straightened his long sapling of a spine.

"I aim to build it," he announced to the room at large.

For an instant, there was not a sound in the Albert T. Rain, as if each person in the room was trying to puzzle out what Nacky had said. Then, at once, a whoop of laughter broke out. It was a cross and dark laugh, without the light and air most laughter had. It was laughter intended to bite.

"Where you aim to sail yer boat, captain, the other side of the lake?" called out Jenner Rind, the town's roofer.

"Hope you signed a crew already," Meddo said, "unless that pig o' yours can ship a line."

"Don't need my pig to sail that boat," Nacky shouted. "Don't even know that it'll sail at all, but I aim to see."

"Fine business buildin' a ship what ain't got nowhere to go," Gilly Boate called out. "Leastways you won't get lost."

"It'll sail fine once I get it to the ocean," Nacky said.

The laughter grew louder and Nacky grew red-faced. He looked around the room with his ire rising, but held his tongue. Teedie, however, didn't.

"You'll be pleased enough when that boat's built and this town gets freed!" he shouted, leaping up.

Nacky flashed him a hot look, but it was too late to call back what the boy had said.

"Freed?" Meddo asked. "From what?"

"From the charm, the charm in the Songs."

"What songs?" Jenner Rind asked incredulously. "Them dry-land boats?"

Teedie nodded a firm yes, and Jenner, Meddo and the others turned to Nacky. He stayed motionless for an instant and then nodded as well. At that, the room burst into the loudest, blackest laughter of all.

"That beats the best!" Meddo hooted. "Never seen a child past five who believed them tales, and now I see a half-growed boy and a full-growed man. That shipwreck o' yours left you pancrocked, Nacky Patcher. Either that or this is the worst thief's fib you ever told."

"And how do you reckon that wood got put here if it ain't a charm o' some kind?" Nacky shouted over the noise.

"Maybe someone dumped it," Gilly said. "Maybe some wagons tipped when they was carryin' them pieces to the coast."

"A whole boat's worth o' pieces?" Nacky asked. "And what about that storm? Why do you reckon it swelled up just as you was all making off with them parts?"

"Ain't nothing strange about that kind of storm this time of year," Brigg Keeper called out, sitting with his wife at his customary table and gesturing to his customary pile of yellowed newspapers. The Keepers had not been at the lake this morning but had come to the Rain as they usually did at this hour of the day. "Something like this always hits sudden before summer sets in hard. Happened in Bowfin last year; happened in Knockle the year before that. This ain't magic weather; it's mountain weather."

"As long as we're settled there ain't no spooks," Meddo said, slapping his hand against the tabletop and standing, "I'm gonna go help meself to some of that wood. Anyone in this room with any sense ought to do the same."

"That wood's meant for buildin'!" Teedie shouted.

"I told you to hush that pup, Nacky Patcher!" Meddo said. "There's a reason there ain't a family in town what'll take him in. He was the ripseed what started all that trouble in Knockle, and he's come here to try the same mischief. Just sorry we don't got no half-home for you to burn down, boy."

Teedie looked stunned, and Nacky wheeled on Meddo.

"Now, that's a full portion of you!" he shouted.

"I'll say when I've said enough!" Meddo answered. "I want that boy gone, and I want that boat sold!"

"It ain't up to you!" Nacky said.

"I ain't gonna allow this, Nacky Patcher!" Meddo answered.

With that, Meddo lunged from his spot at his table and sprang toward Nacky. Nacky, without thinking, sprang to meet him. Between the two tables, a great swirl of shouting and shoving went up. Dree rapped her knuckles hard against the bar, but this time no one heard. Suddenly, from the door, a clear, high voice cut through the din.

"Nacky Patcher is right," the voice shouted. "That boat needs to be built, and it needs to be built quick."

Nacky snapped his head toward the sound, and nearly everyone else in the restaurant followed. Standing in the doorway, her eyes bright, her face flushed, her hair blown about her head, was Bara Berry. At her left side stood Chuff the dwarf. They were free of mud and almost entirely dry, having been slowed enough by Chuff's sleepy pace to have missed the storm at the lake entirely. For a moment, no one said anything, and Bara stayed rooted where she was, staring about and breathing hard.

"Don't expect you have any business here this morning, Bara Berry," Dree said from behind the bar. "And I know Chuff the dwarf don't. That little man waits outside—same as the pig, same as the shoes."

Bara looked at Chuff apologetically and inclined her head toward the porch. He stared back at her without reacting. Taking him by the shoulders, she turned him about and gave him a gentle push out the door. Then she turned back and addressed the room.

"I got business, all right," she said. "Bad business, and it's comin' soon. Mally Baloo's gone bust. Man still lives like he's tinned as a prince, but there ain't much more than threads in his pockets. If the bank-men ain't come callin' on him yet, it's only a question of when."

"How's a man like Mally Baloo go pauper?" Dree asked.

"Speculatin'," Bara said. "Diamond mines what don't have diamonds; nut groves what don't grow nuts. It don't make any difference. He's been tryin' to raise money sellin' off his workers, but that ain't nearly enough. The man's down to stribs and don't look likely to come up rich again soon."

"Then I reckon we better serve up a round and drink to Mally Baloo's empty pockets," Meddo said.

"Wouldn't do no drinkin' yet," Bara answered. "Mally Baloo's hard times're likely to become our hard times. Come the first day of fall, he's gonna be collectin' on whatever debts he can—even the ones he's been forgivin' so far. Those of you what ain't made your rent had better take hold of your purses and your houses."

"How's the likes of you know the likes of this?" Dree snapped. "That's Mally Baloo's business."

"It's the likes of me what puts the leather on his ledgers," Bara snapped back. "You don't think I take the time to read what I bind?"

"This girl's havin' us on," Gilly said with a wave.

"Ain't havin' nobody on," Bara said, "especially not you, Gilly Boate. Your house is one of the ones what's gonna go first." Bara looked around the restaurant, pointing as she spoke. "And the same goes for you, Brigg

Keeper, and you, Jenner Rind—and you too, Meddo Brinn. I know what you make carryin' letters in a town what don't get no mail."

Now the Albert T. Rain fell completely quiet and Bara Berry turned to face Nacky Patcher and Teedie Flinn. She sought out their eyes and, wordlessly, with a single hard glance, told them the rest of what she had come here to say. With a nod, Nacky took it in.

If Mally Baloo was really so stribbed, he wasn't going to have his beat-men stop with houses. The local laws gave him leave to seize a share of almost anything that could be bartered or sold, and the mountain of teak Nacky and Teedie had found had more value than just about anything in Yole. Selling off its bones to build homes or carriages could buy Baloo months of peace from the bank-men who were after him. If the locals tried to haul the planks out of town and sell them on their own, Baloo would simply seize his share of the money they earned. If they burned the planks for fuel, he would claim the cost of the lost wood. Even if Nacky contrived a way to build the ship, no sooner would the last spar be in place than Baloo would declare the completed vessel his own. The only way to save the boat was to build it up now and haul it to the ocean, outside the reach of local laws—and do it before collection day arrived in the fall. Nacky and Teedie may have been alone in believing that the dark charm of the dry-land boats had piece or part of this, but no one could deny that building the boat and hauling it to the coast was the only way to put it outside the reach of Mally Baloo.

"You've all got cause to look after this boat now," Nacky said quietly, "no matter what you call a cradle tale."

At that instant, there was a shuffling and clacking at the door, and the people in the Albert T. Rain turned to see Chuff the dwarf wandering back in, his shoulders slumped, his expression dreamy. Half a step behind him was Orro the pig, scrabbling loudly on the planks of the floor.

"I said you was to wait outside, Chuff the dwarf," Dree barked. "And that pig can go with you."

Chuff did not react. Dree turned to the Dreeboys standing on either side of her and nodded. The brothers stepped from behind the bar and began making their way menacingly toward Orro and Chuff. Nacky, alarmed, lurched forward, but the press of the crowd prevented him from moving. Chuff stood his ground, appearing to notice nothing. The Dreeboys strode across the restaurant, closing in on the little man and the little pig. As they did, however, a deep creaking began to fill the room, as if the shiplike planks that made up the building had begun reseating themselves. It was the loudest groaning Nacky had ever heard in the Albert T. Rain—one that Dree herself could not have denied. The creak was followed by another one, and then a third. At Nacky's table, the ashwood chairs of the lost clipper *Whistler* gave off a faint tremble. The lathed posts and flat planks of the *Lamplighter* table did as well. At the same time, the very floor of the restaurant seemed to shift and breathe. Around the room, people who were standing took hold of the nearest wall or chair back. People who were seated gripped the edges of their tables. At the front door, Chuff the dwarf still stared ahead, but now wore a look of unaccustomed clarity on his face. Then, in a strong, unhurried voice, he began to speak:

> If it pleases or not,
> I am just as you see;
> I'm a man though I look more a lad.

> My sorrows are plain,
> my afflictions are three;
> each cruel and each hard and each sad.

> First is my stature,
> my well-suffered shame;
> next are my wandering wits.

Last is my parentage,
blood without name;
a weight that most heavily sits.

Such a person as I
can be rightly forgot,
for what after all is my worth?

Yet from so low a man,
can come much that is not
constrained by my meanness of birth.

A forest of trees
may grow where they stand,
with no one to tend or to see.

But the same stand of trees
need the care of a hand,
when they float where they oughtn't to be.

So do what you will
with this rubbish you find,
though a gift may emerge from the silt.

And try to hold fast
in your heart and your mind:
What is broken must one day be built.

Chuff fell silent, dropped his head and then slowly lifted it again, looking about himself and blinking. The flat light had returned to his eyes, the blank look to his gaze. If he was aware at all of what he had just said, he had already begun to forget it. In the utterly silent Albert

T. Rain, however—where the timbers had stopped popping and the floor had stopped creaking—Chuff's words hung heavy in the air.

Nacky Patcher looked around with the same expression of stupefaction Chuff showed. He too was briefly struck dumb, but his mind was alive with thought. For the first time, he knew with certainty that he'd be building his great teak boat. And no matter how little the townspeople trusted him or liked him, he suspected they'd now be willing to help him in his work.

CHAPTER THIRTEEN

The tall man with white hair had an easy time walking along the ridge and down the bowl that led to the lake. By any measure, it ought to have been a harder business, partly because the footing was still wet from the storm that had passed through that very morning, and partly because it was now deep night, with only moonlight to point the way around the ruts and rocks that made the purchase poor even when the soil was full dry and the sun was full noon. The tall man's long stride, however, made it easy for him to high-step around even the worst footing, certainly easier than it was for the stable boy accompanying him, who was skidding and stumbling on the sodden ridge and once nearly pitched over the edge and down into the lake bowl altogether, until the tall man caught him by the arm.

"Mind yourself," the man said in a stone tone that made it clear he didn't much care what happened to the boy but very much cared that they complete the job they'd come here to do.

It had been a long walk on the dark road to the lake tonight. The stable boy had been surprised they'd come the entire distance by foot at all. The tall man rarely walked when he could as easily take a carriage, nor took a carriage when he could as easily take a grander carriage. But tonight the man seemed not to want to call attention to himself and told the boy they'd be walking instead. Before the boy could ask why—which he was about to do—the man fixed him with a hard look.

"Mind yourself," he'd said, that time with a faint wisp of menace in his tone. The boy held his tongue.

It wasn't until they reached the ridge, picked their way down the lake bowl and stood on the moonlit bank that the stable boy began to reckon why they were here. Spread out in front of them, bank to bank, shoreline to shoreline, was precisely the drifting, bumping carpet of teak that the townspeople had been cheeping about since this morning. It was as grand as they said, as mysterious as they said and even—to the stable boy, at least—as frightening as some of them said. The tall man with white hair seemed interested, but he did not seem afraid.

Folding his arms across his chest, he walked one hundred yards clockwise along the periphery of the lake, turned around, retraced his steps, and then walked a hundred more counterclockwise. All the while, he kept his eyes fixed on the wood in the water as if he were hunting for something. Finally, he stopped, squinted into the darkness and turned back to the stable boy. He signaled to him and pointed to an irregularly shaped piece of wood floating just at the limits of vision. It glinted in the moonlight like all the others, but somehow more brightly. The man ticked his head once, motioning the boy into the water. The boy hesitated and the man ticked again, firmer this time.

The stable boy waded into the lake and shivered at the chill. He breasted his way through the water until he could no longer stand, then splashed and kicked to the spot where the thing he'd been pointed to was floating. He looked long and hard at it, frozen for a moment by its surprising loveliness. Then he gathered it in, kicked in to shore and climbed onto the bank. The object in his arms was more than half his own size and yet he carried it easily, almost as if its obvious worth made him heedless of its weight.

"It's wonderful," the boy said, panting from the exertion. "Something this fine is part of all the rest?"

The tall man regarded the wood with narrowed eye. Wonderful it was, passremarkably so. And it was indeed part of all the rest, perhaps the most important part. It was also now his. He had not known precisely what he was looking for when he came here tonight, but this would be more than suitable to his needs. He ticked his head once toward the lake trail, and he and the boy left the bank and walked back into the night.

BOOK THREE

CHAPTER FOURTEEN

The day the people of Yole began building Nacky Patcher's and Teedie Flinn's boat was unusual for a lot of reasons—but mostly because it was the first day anyone could remember that the bird wagon didn't come around. No one could say just when it was the bird wagon began traveling about Yole, but given all the years it had been making its rounds—and given the fact that it managed to turn up even on days when the rains were falling or a freeze had set in or summer had descended and the red road had turned to a baked hardpan that broke up into a powdery cloud by afternoon, choking the bird wagon's driver and horse and probably the birds themselves—the first day the wagon went missing was not likely to be forgotten.

It was old August Ren who dreamed up the idea of the bird wagon, back in the days when he was a young August Ren. August had always fancied birds and often traveled to the libraries in Greater M'croom, Little M'croom and Twelve Points to read the small collections of birder books and papers that were kept there. For a man who had taken such a shine to birding, there were better places to live than Yole, not least because there simply weren't many birds that called the place home. There were some who said that if there was indeed a dark charm holding

Yole, this might be a sign of it, songbirds spooking easily and avoiding a place under so obvious a cloud. But it was only the very young, the very old and the very superstitious who believed this. Most others concluded that birds go where they fancy and they simply didn't fancy Yole. Whatever the reason, the fact remained that apart from the occasional raven or starling or odd, noisy shrike, most of the better birds never did come around.

August was more troubled by this fact than most, and a long time ago he decided to do something about it. Lingering about the quays in the M'crooms and Twelve Points, he would wait for ships that had been running the animal trade to the Americas or Africa to pull into port. When they did, he'd bribe his way down into the hold, looking for any canaries or finches or other songbirds the boats might have brought back. When he found a few birds that appealed to him, he'd pay whatever the stevedores demanded for them and then carry them back home in a big, roomy cage he had built in the back of his wagon, one that allowed the birds to flap and roost and even fly a bit.

Once August had collected about two dozen strong birds, he set about putting them to work. Each morning before the day broke, he'd climb into the wagon cage, tie a long stretch of cord to the right foot of each bird and tie the other end to one of the cage's roosting branches. Then he'd take to the padroads of Yole, driving by the houses and farms and little shops before most of the people who lived in them had even woken up. At each home he passed, he'd stop and swing open the hinged top of the cage. On cue, the birds would fly out in a great, colorful, musical cloud, flapping up to the branches of the nearest tree and lighting there, their long strands of cord running back to the wagon like harp strings. For several minutes, August would stand by as the birds sang and twittered; then he'd tug on the strings, summon them back to the cage and drive on to the next stop. August would spend hours each morning releasing and collecting his swirl of birds, sometimes not finishing until well into the afternoon. Now and then, if the weather was pleasant and he was feeling inclined, he'd go back out again after sundown, bringing with him this time a smaller flock of nightingales and other evening birds he occasionally liked to show off as well.

August grew old caring for his birds, spending decades riding his wagon without doing any other work anyone could identify. Shortly after the great wrecked boat appeared in the Yole lake, however, Nacky Patcher had another job for him to do.

Since the first moment they saw the remains of the boat, Nacky and Teedie had been trying to determine exactly how many bits of wood made up such a vessel. While Teedie could not even venture a guess, Nacky believed he might know. During the days he'd spent adrift on his *Walnut Egg* door, he'd run the picture of the collapsing ship through his head again and again, and had in fact asked Orro how many parts he thought had fallen away from the vessel before they all sank. Orro, who had learned something about boats during his other ocean voyages, guessed about thirty thousand. Since the broken ship in the Yole lake looked a third again as big as the *Egg*, Nacky assumed it had a third again as many parts, and the more he considered that number, the more certain he became of it.

"It's forty thousand," he'd tell Teedie. "Not a beam more, not a spar less."

However much wood was on the Yole lake, collecting so much free-floating debris would be surprisingly easy—at least when it came to the small parts like plugs and trunnels and planks, all of which could be hauled to shore with little more than time, patience and a good fishing net. Catching and beaching the bigger pieces would not be so simple.

The futtocks and keelson that helped form the ribs and spine of the ship weighed several tons each. The keel itself was far larger and far heavier than both. As with all great sailing ships, the keel of a clipper was not a tall and tapered fin that slashed a deep cut in the water. Rather, it was nothing more than a long, wide, slightly bent beam. So flat and fat was the bottom of the keel that a well-balanced clipper could usually stand by itself on a beach or bank, something many of them did as they were being built. Hauling the enormous keel—as well as the other larger pieces of the boat—would take muscle, preferably animal muscle, and that meant horses.

For several days after the meeting in the Albert T. Rain, Nacky and Teedie busied themselves traveling from house to house along the padroads of Yole, begging and cadging any field horse or other strong-backed nag people might be willing to lend out. Not a great many Yole locals owned something as dear as a healthy horse, and those who did would not usually be willing to trust it to someone else, no matter the reason it was needed. Nacky and Teedie thus carefully chose how to approach each particular house to make the request. People Nacky had fleeced in the past would not be likely to trust him again, so Teedie would do the asking there. People who'd already refused to take Teedie into their homes for fear of his blackfire past would be similarly disinclined to do business with him, so Nacky would make those requests. Occasionally, a door would be slammed in their faces no matter which of them approached, and they'd both be cursed as thieves and firestarters. Nacky shrugged when this happened, reckoning that a thief was precisely what he was. Teedie would glare and grow quiet when the house-burning charge was thrown at him.

"Never mind what they say," Nacky would tell him. "Mules and fools, the lot of them."

Eventually, Nacky and Teedie did manage to wheedle five strong horses that looked like they'd be up to the work. But with all the wood that had to be hauled, they guessed they needed at least one more, especially big-muscled beast. And that meant calling on August Ren.

"I'm going to have to ask after borrowing your horse for a few days," Nacky said as he and Teedie approached August one morning when the old man was readying his bird wagon for its early rounds.

August didn't answer at first. "Business with the ship?" he asked at last, looking through Nacky and Teedie and letting his gaze rest on the chittering birds.

"Yes," Nacky answered.

"Bad piece of work, that."

Nacky shrugged. "Ain't nothin' but a boat, really."

August looked at him and then glanced up at the sky, where the sudden storm clouds had gathered just a few days before. Nacky followed his gaze upward but wouldn't meet his eyes when he looked back down.

"You take my horse for a coupla three days, that's a coupla three days my birds can't come around," August said.

"I know."

"Ain't never happened before."

"I know."

August thought for a moment. "When you gonna need it?"

"We plan to start the work on the boat tomorrow," Nacky answered.

"You reckon you can really build this thing?"

"I do."

August turned to Teedie. "You?"

"Yes," Teedie said.

"You reckon you ought to?" August asked. Teedie started to answer but August held up his hand. "That ain't a question for a child." He turned back to Nacky. "You think this is wood what was meant to be touched?"

"Yes," Nacky answered. "I do. There's a verse from the dry-land boats songs what tells it true. You believe in them songs?"

"I know 'em," August responded, in a way that did not answer Nacky's question and perhaps wasn't meant to.

"Care to hear it?" Nacky asked. August waved his hand for Nacky to proceed and Nacky did.

Of the seven great timbers
from dogwood to pine,
there is none that's so stout
or so sturdy or fine,

Or that braces so straight
in the face of a gale,
that it can't be made more
with the kiss of a sail.

Nacky finished and looked at August to gauge his reaction. For a
long moment, August stared back at him expressionlessly. "Hmph," the
old man said at length, then turned and began to walk toward his wagon.
Before he reached it, he stopped and turned back.

"I'm gonna let you use the animal," he said, "'cause it's best for everyone if you finish this fool business quick. Course, I can't say I'm sure
a light-finger like you will ever bring a strong horse like that back."

"I'll bring it back," Nacky answered, stung.

August looked unconvinced. "I'll give you three days' use and no
more," he said. "It don't do to trade my bird music for your boat magic
any longer than that."

August turned again, climbed into his hitch and slowly drove off
on his morning rounds. As Nacky watched him pull away, he reflected
that for the first time he could recall, the birds in the wagon had gone
completely silent.

CHAPTER FIFTEEN

During the few days Nacky and
Teedie spent gathering up horses to work on the boat, Bara busied herself gathering up townspeople. The folks of Yole could be a forgetful
lot, especially when there was work to do, and though most of those
who were in the Albert T. Rain and heard Chuff's poem on the morning of the storm looked ready to march back down to the lake that very
afternoon, it would take the passage of but a single night before they
would begin convincing themselves that the little man's words were mere
rubbish and the boat might be a matter they'd best not meddle with
after all.

For this reason, Nacky instructed Bara to call on as many houses
in Yole as she could, keeping the people's minds focused on the work
ahead. To sweeten the prospect of spending the summer hauling and
hammering beams, he instructed her to promise the townspeople that
anyone who helped in the building of the boat could also share in the
owning of it. Once the thing was out at sea, it ought to be a fine source
of revenue—enough to pay off any debts anyone owed Mally Baloo and
more besides for the builders' own pockets. It would remain to be seen

whether the people retained enough of the fear they had of Chuff's improbable poem to accept the deal.

When the morning to begin collecting the boat parts finally arrived, Teedie and Nacky rose before the sun was even up, ate a hurried breakfast of tea and biscuits, then rousted Orro the pig from his sleeping spot. The three of them clumped and clacked out of the house and headed up the padroad toward town. By the time they reached the rim of the bowl that surrounded the lake, the sun had risen clear of the mountains and the brightening sky illuminated a surprisingly busy scene.

Clustered at the ridge of the hill were what appeared to be fifty-odd people, milling about, talking quietly to one another and peering down warily at the berry-blue, wood-strewn water that lay below. Near them, several carriages had pulled up and stopped, and their owners were hopping down and unhitching their horses. August Ren's bird wagon was among those here, and even from a distance, Nacky could hear the singing of the birds in the spacious wooden cage and see them beating their wings against the bars.

As Nacky and Teedie drew closer, they noticed Bara Berry circulating among the people, taking note of who was there and scratching their names in a small leather ledger. Bara spotted them and waved them over. Teedie hurried ahead and Nacky and his pig followed.

"Startin' to think I was gonna have to tend to all this myself," Bara said as they reached her. "I've got four dozen people lookin' for somethin' to do and the ones what say they own the boat can't be bothered to come themselves. Half of 'em was already grumbling that they always knew you wasn't to be trusted."

Nacky shrugged and gestured apologetically to his foot. "Who-all do we have?" he asked.

"A lot. Them Dreeboys, the Blands, most everyone who was in the Rain that morning. There's plenty here to do what needs doin', assumin' half of them don't break their necks walking down that trail."

Nacky turned and watched a wobbly line of people picking their way down the pebbly path to the lake, some of them leading their horses. He frowned. "What about Jimmer?" he asked.

"Got here half an hour ago and told me he's all finished with that capstan o' yours."

Nacky lit up. He had known from the start that even with the help of horses, hauling the giant keel and heavy futtocks out of the water would not be easy. What was needed was something that would multiply the animal muscle they had on hand, and Nacky thought he had the answer. In the short time he had spent around the coastal towns, he had seen boatwrights repair the damaged hulls of ships not by hoisting the vessels into dry dock, but simply by tipping them onto their sides when they were still in the water and working on them there. They performed such an improbable job by attaching heavy ship chains to the upright boats' masts, running the other ends back to shore, and connecting them to a stout wheel or capstan mounted horizontally on a stumplike hub. The wheel was equipped with four heavy spokes, and to each spoke a powerful dray horse was hitched. At a signal from the lead man, the horses would start to walk, clopping around in a circle and taking up the chain slack on the rim of the wheel. As they did, the boat would tip further and further, until at last it was lying flat on its side, allowing the boatwrights to clamber on top. Nacky admired the capstan as a neat solution to a knotty problem and reckoned if a wheel and chains could move a whole ship, they could certainly drag a keel and frames onto the land.

For the last three days, Jimmer had been down on the bank building Nacky just the capstan he needed, scraping away a portion of the bark of a sturdy black walnut tree, then building and fitting the wheel around the clean patch. He borrowed horse harnesses from the same townspeople who were lending their animals today and borrowed chains and grappling hooks from a smith he knew in Bowfin. Now Nacky looked down at the bank and saw Jimmer bent over the finished wheel attending to some small detail, while the heavy chains and their glinting hooks stretched across the bank to the water.

"He got it done," he said to Bara with a smile.

"As I said."

"How'd he get that smith to lend him that grade of chain?"

"Wheedled it. That boy smiles right, he can shine-talk just about anything out of just about anyone."

Nacky happily clucked his tongue for Orro and stepped gingerly onto the trail, with Teedie and the pig following. They reached the bank and hurried over to Jimmer.

"Passremarkable piece of work," Nacky enthused.

"Should do the trick as long as it spins proper," Jimmer said.

"You reckon it will?" Teedie asked.

Jimmer looked at him, a bit put off by the question. "I reckon it will. Greased up that bare patch with about a cow's worth of tallow and got more here just in case."

Nacky and Teedie looked at the ground next to Jimmer and saw a large bucket filled with yellow-white animal fat. A long-handled wooden scoop was sticking out of it. Teedie wrinkled up his nose, picked up the scoop and spooned up a messy dollop of the stuff, then let it fall back in the bucket with a wet plop.

As Jimmer returned to fussing over the wheel, Nacky faced up the hill and let out a loud whistle. Bara nodded and shooed the remaining townspeople down to the bank. They all assembled at the bottom of the hill, waiting for Nacky's instructions. Nacky looked at the crowd uncertainly and tried to affect the tone of voice he had heard the lost Orro and the other ship's chiefs use at sea.

"I need four of you folks with horses to take your animals over and hitch them to the spokes," he said in a clear tone. "I need a dozen more what can swim strong to paddle out a hundred feet and start pushing the heavy pieces to shore."

The people shifted, but stayed where they stood. Borrowing a gesture he also copied from the boat chiefs, Nacky now simply pointed to the four largest horses—August Ren's among them—and waved them over to the wheel. Then he pointed to the dozen strongest people—the Dreeboys among them—and waved them into the water. Nacky had been surprised to see the two brothers here, given how snarly they'd been about the boat a few days earlier. But the lure of the work had probably been too much for them, and without a word of protest, they—along with the others—plodded off to do as he said.

The horses were hitched quickly, and not long after, the dozen people paddling about in the lake brought the futtocks and keel to shore, pushing their leading edges up onto the stony soil, while the long trailing ends floated behind. The sheer weight of the beams would keep them in place for a time. Nacky once again signaled to the Dreeboys, summoning them out of the lake and pointing them toward the pair of glistening hooks at the ends of the chains stretching across the bank. "Into the wood," Nacky instructed, pointing toward an enormous futtock.

The Dreeboys stepped toward the big piece of timber and stood astride the beached end. They raised the hooks above their heads and, with a grunt, brought them down against the teak. The sickening sound of metal wounding wood echoed through the lake bowl as the hooks buried themselves in the flanks of the futtock.

Nacky now turned back to the wheel, where the four horses were harnessed and their four owners stood by their sides. Jimmer stood at the ready, his tallow bucket in hand. Bara stood a few steps away, one hand on Teedie's shoulder to prevent him from getting too close to the dangerous work.

"Together on my signal!" Nacky called, raising his arm. He held it for an instant, then dropped it with a snap. Immediately, the owners slapped their horses' rumps, and the animals began to dig and push. The chains running across the bank snapped and straightened, and the crowd on either side of them jumped farther back.

"Stand away in case them hooks pull free!" Nacky shouted.

At the wheel, the four owners leaned in close to their animals, murmuring into their ears and stroking the lengths of their necks. On the bank, the blunt front of the futtock crept slowly out of the water, plowing out a mound of soil in its path. The more the horses plodded, the more the piece of wood climbed, creeping farther and farther onto the bank like a sea creature fighting to beach itself. Finally, the entirety of the heavy beam had been hauled out of the water and lay dripping on the ground.

"Stop the wheel!" Nacky shouted. The men at the capstan pulled back their horses and the chains went slack. A cheer went up from the crowd. Nacky bounded several clumsy steps toward the wheel with Orro scrabbling behind him and grabbed Jimmer in a rough hug.

"As fine a piece of buildin' as I've ever seen," he shouted over the noise.

With the wheel proven, the cautious crowd grew a good deal friskier, and Nacky had no trouble dispatching other people into the water to nudge other heavy frames to shore. For most of the morning, the wood was hooked and pulled, hooked and pulled, until all the heaviest parts were ashore, with the exception of the vast keel, which still lay with its nose on the bank and the rest of its length swaying and floating behind it. Nacky himself stood astride that great piece of teak and swung the hooks into its sides. They bit deep and held fast, but Nacky still regarded the keel doubtfully. No amount of horse muscle looked up to the job of moving so huge a thing.

"On my signal!" he nonetheless called again to the men at the capstan. One last time, he raised his right arm and let it fall with a snap, and one last time, the men swatted the horses and the chains drew tight. This time, however, the teak didn't budge.

"More," Nacky called out.

At the wheel, the men struck the horses again and murmured still closer in their ears. The animals dug their hooves into the soil, causing the veins to bulge in their flanks and the cords to stand out in their necks. Jimmer spooned more fat onto the tree and then more. Still, however, the keel didn't move. Nacky watched for a moment, then leapt for one of the chains and took hold of it himself, digging both his real heel and his wooden one into the bank and leaning back as far as he could.

"Them what can help had better help!" he grunted out.

A dozen men broke from the crowd and divided themselves between the two chains, seizing the links and pulling. Still the keel went nowhere. "More!" Nacky called, and the first dozen people were joined by a second. Teedie cast a glance at Bara, who was still holding on to his shoulder. Then he twisted free of her grip and sprang ahead.

"Teedie Flinn!" she called, but the boy made it to the chain in a blink, positioning himself at the very front of the line of people, where he'd be first to be struck if the hook pulled free. He grabbed one of the links with his good left hand and wrapped his right arm as tightly as he could around the cold, heavy metal.

"Pull!" several of the men now yelled to one another.

On the bank at the edge of the water, the great mass of teak at last began to move, inching forward with a low, scraping sound the crowd could actually feel vibrating through their feet. Nacky tightened his grip on the chain and pulled harder, fighting for balance on the damp bank. Teedie clamped his arm and clenched his hand as tightly as he could. All around them, the twin lines of people pulled and strained.

Link by bright link, the chain was taken up on the wheel like thread on a spool, and inch by slow inch, the keel climbed up onto the bank, making its way to the very center of the vast clearing, with its leading edge pointing toward the trail that led out of the bowl. This was precisely the spot where Nacky and Teedie had calculated there was enough room for a sailing ship more than two hundred feet long to sit as it was being built. With a final gasp, Nacky released his grip, fell away from the chain and staggered backward.

"Hold!" he called, with the last of his breath. "Hold!"

But he had called it an instant too late. The hook in the right-hand side of the keel had taken more strain than it could stand and, at that moment, jerked free of the teak with all the violent power of the horse and human strength that was pulling on it. The glinting thing snapped back through the air with a murderous hiss, heading straight for Teedie at the front of the line. The boy's wits, however, were as sharp as the hook, and his reflexes were sharper still. He dove to the ground just in time, and the angry, business end of the hook flew by and barely grazed the side of his head—lightly enough that he could feel the awful chill of metal against scalp, but nothing more. Behind him, the chain and hook clattered into the crowd, sending the others screaming and scattering.

"Teedie!" Bara shouted, dropping her ledger and sprinting toward him across the bank.

Nacky, who had himself been struck in the chest by the chain, staggered backward. He regained his balance and leapt toward Teedie as well, falling on him at the same moment Bara did. Together, they gathered the boy up.

"I'm all right," Teedie said, struggling from their hold. "I ain't hurt."

"Ain't hurt?" Bara asked. "You was almost killed! Look at your head; that thing parted your hair. Parted it clean as a barber would."

Nacky took the boy's chin and head in his hands and turned him slightly sideways. Bara was right. There was a line in the hair down to the skin, from the front of his head to the back. "Hook like that coulda just as easily parted your skull," Nacky said scoldingly.

Teedie grumbled and pulled away, and Nacky stood and turned to the rest of the crowd. "All right, then," he called out. "We had us a scare and we'll know better next time. But we got our wood beached and our lake clear. We done what we come here to do today."

Suddenly, however, from the edge of the clearing, a man's voice cried out—more in a moan than a shout. Nacky, Teedie and the others turned toward the sound.

The cry had come from old August Ren, standing frozen by the capstan wheel. In front of him, his horse had fallen to its knees, its mouth foaming, its sides lathered in sweat, its eyes rolling wildly. The other three horses hitched to their spokes whinnied and backed away, as August's horse twitched and thrashed and fought for breath. Finally, with a fierce twist of its stout neck, it ripped its harnesses free of the wheel, fell to its side and lay still, its chest no longer rising and falling, its eyes still open but no longer rolling. August dropped down beside the animal and covered his face with his leathery hands.

Nacky stared at the scene for a terrible instant and started to turn away, but not before August could part his hands and fix him with a stare. Nacky held the old man's gaze, his own face twisted in regret. Then he pulled away and looked back up to the top of the bowl surrounding the lake. For the second time in the last week, he noticed that the birds in August's wagon had gone completely still.

CHAPTER SIXTEEN

The *Duchess Isabel* had a terrible go before it put to port in the town of Little M'croom. Most of the sailors on the *Isabel* did not especially care to stop in such a modest coastal village—so accustomed were they to the grand cities of the grand lands they usually visited. But the terrible go the ship was having made stopping necessary.

The *Isabel*'s troubles had begun when it was still well out at sea, a good three days from the closest port. A ship like the *Isabel* was not especially well-suited to traveling such great distances. As merchant vessels went, it was a small one, built more for coastal runs than cross-ocean trips. But the captain of the ship made it plain from the day each voyage began that he preferred to sail only the deepest waters and that the people who owned his vessel trusted him to do so. His crew could either come with him or stay behind and let others fill their berths. Such bold talk was usually nothing more than that, but the *Isabel*'s captain said it so simply and expressed it so sure that most sailors were inclined to follow him. For their trouble—and for their trust—they were rewarded with marvelous journeys they'd carry with them the rest of their lives.

Given the skill of the captain and the calm of his crew, few people would have expected the *Duchess Isabel* to have the trouble it had on this trip. But deep into the journey, an early summer squall appeared from nowhere and began to claw at the sea and the ship with a force all wrong for that time of year. For the better part of two days, the crewmen fought to keep the *Isabel* afloat, swimming the winds and playing the sails and driving the boat harder than they had ever had to drive it before. And at the end of those two days, they seemed to have made it through. With the clouds dissolving and the sky clearing, they shook the rain out of their sails and tacked off toward the port in Bretony far to the north, which was their intended destination.

It was then that the captain heard an odd *plink-pop* as he was walking along the 'tween deck in the direction of his cabin. A *plink-pop* was not the kind of thing he had ever heard in the belowdecks of any ship he had sailed before, and when he looked in the direction of the sound, he was surprised to see that a bung-plug had dropped from its spot in the ceiling where it covered a peg that helped hold a stanchion in place. The plug clattered to the deck and bounced along the planks. A moment later, there was another *plink-pop* and the peg itself followed. The captain recovered the two small bits of wood, looked at them both, then tucked them in his pocket and chewed over the problem.

Over the next half day, crewmen brought him other troubling stories. There was a hinge that *plink-popped* out of a door in the second mate's quarters. There was a pot peg that *plink-popped* out of a wall in the galley, sending a heavy tureen crashing to the floor. And there was a plank that *plink-popped* out of the hull above the waterline and fell square into the ocean below. It was the plank that settled the matter for the captain, who ordered his helmsman to come about and set a course for nearby Little M'croom.

The *Duchess Isabel* docked in the town not long after. The seamen hurried onto the quay and found their way to the closest public house, where they ordered up malts and tried to decide whether to stay ashore or go back aboard a ship that just might be haunted. The captain himself was not nearly so troubled. After the crew was gone, he took a long, slow walk through the empty ship, then returned to his cabin, gathered up his belongings and stuffed them in his seabag. Leaving his cap behind, he left the ship and walked to the harbormaster's office out on the quay.

"*Duchess Isabel* is in port," he said.

The harbormaster made a notation in his book.

"She may be needing some repairs, and she may be needing some crew," the captain went on.

The harbormaster looked at him curiously.

"She'll surely be needing a new captain."

Turning about without another word, the captain left the office and proceeded back along the quay. The *Isabel,* he knew, was still a sound ship. The few parts she'd shaken off were the only ones she was going to lose. After so many years spent sailing, however, he'd learned to read the messages of the sea, and the *plink-pops* had been one. It was a message that had not been meant for the crew and had not been meant for the blameless ship. It had been meant for him. He had business on shore now, he guessed, though he had no idea just what it might be.

CHAPTER SEVENTEEN

For nearly four days after the horses
and capstan pulled the keel and futtocks from the lake, the people who
had volunteered to build the ship worked hard to salvage all the other
pieces still adrift in the water. From the moment Nacky guessed that
the vessel was made up of precisely forty thousand parts, he'd grown
increasingly convinced that he was right. He could not say why he was
so wholly certain, but he nonetheless was—and he wanted to be sure that
every one of those wooden bits was collected and saved.

Teedie insisted he could help out in the job, but Nacky said no,
arguing it was not safe for a one-handed boy to go splashing about in a
lake where the water was so deep and cold. Teedie disagreed, claiming
he could swim like quicksilver, and before Nacky could stop him, sprang
into the lake and began proving the boast. The boy's small size indeed allowed him to slip through the water easily, and what he may have lacked
in strength he made up in sheer speed, spinning his arms and kicking
his legs in a blur of limbs and spray. Even his fisted right hand did not
seem to slow him down, striking the water with more of a malletlike
splash than a knifelike slice, but pulling him ahead all the same. Nacky
had to allow that the boy was fit for lake work.

With Teedie leading the way, the workers pushed floating planks and stout stanchions back to shore, gathered up pegs and plugs and dowels by the handful and bagful. As all of the parts were pulled from the lake, Bara would note them in her neat little ledger in her neat little hand. Bara had been spending nearly all of her daylight hours helping out with the ship, working late into the night to finish her shoemaking and bookbinding for Mally Baloo and then slipping off to the lake in the morning. Nacky stayed close by Bara's side as she tallied up the wood, counting the parts himself as the number rose toward forty thousand. After four days went by and what appeared to be the last of the parts was found and logged, he could see that the total in the book was going to come up at least a hundred shy of the necessary figure.

"Ain't enough," he said. "It needs to be more."

"How do you know that?" Bara asked. "The lake looks empty, and the shore looks full. Seems like we got 'em all."

"If it ain't forty thousand, it ain't everything."

"Why don't you just mill up the pieces we're missing?"

Nacky shook his head sternly. "Wouldn't do," he said. "As long as all the parts have been put here, it ain't for us to replace 'em."

Bara continued to protest, but Nacky stubbornly put out word that while construction would begin within the week, the hunt for the missing pieces would go on. There would be a reward of an extra half share in the boat to anyone who found and returned five or more of the lost parts. Bara warned Nacky that giving away too many half shares could soon enough mean giving away more than the entire boat, something simple arithmetic—to say nothing of the law—said he couldn't do.

"You get yourself sent back to the tower now," she warned him, "and I ain't turnin' a hair to get you out."

"You just worry about addin' them numbers," Nacky answered. "I'll worry about the tower."

To Nacky's delight, the idea worked, and other townspeople began finding teak where no one had ever thought to look. Some of the trunnels and bung-plugs had fallen from hands and pockets during the storm and got set like raisins in hardtack in the now-dried mud of the lake bowl. Some had washed under flat rocks scattered around the rim of the lake and could be recovered only by a back-bending business of pulling up one stone at a time and peeking underneath. As each new piece came in—pushing the total closer to forty thousand—Nacky would page through Bara's book, counting the hash marks and smiling an increasingly self-satisfied smile. Bara would snort in response.

Even if the townspeople could indeed turn up the ship's final parts, Nacky, Teedie and Jimmer still had to puzzle out how to put them all together. There was no denying Jimmer had a wizard's way with carpentry. He was able to assemble things and take them apart in his head before even picking up a hammer and beginning the job for real. There was also no denying that Nacky himself had lately acquired a feel for the guts and bones of sailing ships, having watched the *Walnut Egg* unbutton itself the way it did. Teedie had no special boat wits of any kind, but he was a fast study and a willing worker and in any case would not abide being left aside when the construction began. All three of them knew, however, that before they could turn even a shaky hand to the business of the building, they'd have to call on Dree.

No one in Yole had ever actually seen Dree's collection of ship books and papers. All the materials were kept in her rooms above the Rain, and none but Dree herself ever went up there. But she had boasted of it often, and if the collection was as fine as she said it was, it might tell Nacky, Teedie and Jimmer all they needed to know to begin their work.

While Bara and the boatbuilders searched for the missing wood, Nacky thus put a quiet morning aside to visit the Albert T. Rain. He gave a lot of thought to what time he should arrive and finally settled on half past eight—late enough so that Dree would have already got her ovens fired and her morning contrariness out of the way, but not so late that she'd be itching for the arrival of her lunchtime customers. It was also an hour when Jimmer would already be busy at the lake and Teedie would still be at the indigents' home finishing his breakfast. Nacky guessed Dree might not especially welcome an early-morning visit by even one unannounced guest; she'd surely not open her door to three.

As Nacky step-*clumped* toward the Rain that morning with only Orro accompanying him, he saw that the door to the restaurant was closed and the shutters were locked down tight, but the chimney was chugging white smoke, a sign that a fresh fire had just been lit and was steaming the dampness out of the wood. The quiet part of Dree's workday had begun. Nacky climbed the three stairs to the porch, stepping as lightly as he could with his clumsy foot. He pointed Orro to a corner, telling him with an uncharacteristic hiss to stay there, then turned toward the door and prepared to knock. At that moment, he heard a voice behind him.

"Nacky!" it said in a whisper.

Nacky wheeled around. Standing in front of him was Teedie, his arms folded.

"What are you about, boy?" Nacky snapped.

"Reckon I'd ask you the same," Teedie answered. "You got business here?"

"Yes, I do."

"Boat business?"

"Yes."

"Then it's my business too."

"Not if you want the business to get done," Nacky answered. "Don't you have breakfast to attend to?"

"Done with that."

"I still can't have you with me right now."

"You expect me just to wait in the road while you have dealings about my ship?" Teedie huffed.

"Wait in the road, wait with the pig. I don't have time to quarrel with you."

Teedie scowled, but Nacky scowled harder, and the boy finally turned on his heel and stomped off. Nacky watched him retreat up the street, then turned back around and faced the door. He drew a breath and knocked lightly. There was no answer. He tried the knob and found that the door was unlocked. Glancing at Orro, who was watching from the corner, he pushed the door open a crack and peeked inside.

Near the bar, at the white wood table made from the lost clipper *Whistler,* sat Dree, bent over what appeared to be a business ledger. A small pair of spectacles Nacky had never seen her wear before were perched on her nose. She squinted at the page, then looked up toward the ceiling, appearing to count up a line of figures in her head; then she looked back down and made a notation in the book. Behind the bar, the two Dreeboys were cleaning mugs and stacking plates, saying nothing to each other or to Dree. Nacky edged the door open another inch and it creaked loudly. This time, Dree and the boys looked toward him.

"Nacky Patcher," Dree said without a hint of surprise. "Been expectin' you'd come by."

"Reckon I've been expectin' it myself," Nacky said, poking his head and shoulders farther into the room, but not stepping inside.

"It's early yet," Dree said, glancing at the still-low sunlight streaming through the shutter slats.

"Too early?" Nacky asked, withdrawing his head a bit.

Dree sat back, smiled a faint, unexpected smile, and with a wave, gestured Nacky to come in. Nacky nodded his thanks and opened the door farther. Before he could take a step inside, he felt Orro at his feet, wriggling past him and *clack-clacking* without a by-your-leave into the room.

"Orro!" Nacky snapped, with a nervous glance toward Dree. "I told you to stay outside!"

To Nacky's surprise, Dree again gestured casually. "Pig can stay," she said with a shrug. She then looked over her shoulder at the brothers behind the bar. "You boys can go." The boys flushed and stared at her. "Nacky Patcher has something he wants to ask me," Dree said, "and I expect he's more comfortable askin' it alone."

Dree inclined her head toward the door, and the brothers shuffled out from behind the bar, glaring at Nacky and jostling him with their shoulders as they passed. They exited through the front door and closed it with a bang. Nacky clumped over to the *Whistler* table and sat; Orro followed and settled on the floor beside him. Dree closed her ledger, removed her spectacles and rubbed her eyes.

"You need to borrow me books," she said.

Nacky nodded yes.

"Me papers too."

Nacky nodded again. "I'll bring 'em back," he hurriedly added. "My word's good."

"No it ain't," Dree answered, "but that ain't what I got doubts about. You really think all them pages are gonna tell you how to build your boat?"

"They won't?"

"They will. Tell you everything you need to know from keel-layin' to deck-plankin' to mast-raisin'. Won't do you no good, though."

"No?"

Dree shook her head. "Bein' told somethin' ain't the same as under-standin' it," she said. "Suppose you spent a day with me watchin' me make my sweet brick and yalla buck. Think that means you could bake 'em up fine as I do?"

Nacky shook his head.

"A boat's the same way."

"I still aim to try," Nacky said.

Dree nodded. "I know that," she said and then squinted at him curi-ously. "You really expect you can get this boat built and haul it to the ocean by fall?"

"Yes," Nacky answered.

"You really believe that rubbish you were saying—that that'll break some dry-land charm?"

"I do," Nacky answered. "Do you?"

Dree looked at Nacky, then smiled a smile he'd never seen her smile before. She did not seem to expect the question, but she appeared to admire him for asking it.

"Yes," she said. "Now and again I do." Then her smile faded and her features hardened up again. "I'm gonna help you, Nacky Patcher. The books are yours to use on two conditions. First, you keep your promise and bring 'em back to me as clean and whole as you take 'em away. Second, come September, when your boat ain't built and you're left with nothin' but a wreck, I get me pick of the parts."

Nacky thought for a moment and then stood and shook Dree's hand. A few minutes later, he struggled out of the Albert T. Rain carrying a stack of books and papers that nearly tipped him over. The Dreeboys, glowering on the porch, did not help him with the door as he left.

CHAPTER EIGHTEEN

Teedie Flinn did not go far after he strode off the porch of the Albert T. Rain. He marched up the hill of the Yole business street, passing the indigents' home, the grocery store and the empty shops where the hatmaker, the sweet-baker and the meat merchant once worked. It was only when he passed Audra and Stolley Pound's vacant curio store—with its knotted black rags fluttering slightly in the breeze—that he slowed and stopped. He stood in front of the store, staring at it and breathing hard. Then, without a thought, he stalked around the shadowed side of the building, took hold of the rag tied to the window and carelessly unknotted it. He opened the window, hoisted himself up and leapt lightly inside, leaving the rag on the ground behind him.

The thief heat hit Teedie the instant his feet struck the floorboards, coming on faster than it had the first time he'd experienced it. He felt dizzy at the idea of where he was and what he was doing, and dizzier still when he considered that everything here was his for the filching. Then, however, he remembered who it was who rightly owned all of the bits and bobs he might care to steal, and at that the heat went quickly cold.

It was hard to see in the shadowy shop, especially with the morning light outside still lingering in Teedie's eyes. Nonetheless, he could tell that the place was just as he'd last seen it on the day before Audra, Stolley and their boys were pitched. The bits and bobs and porcelain brooches that the Pounds had laid out for sale were still arranged on the shelves and the counter, neither filched by a clever thief nor gathered up to be sold off by Baloo—the value of the things evidently not worth the bother of either the stealing or the selling. This made Teedie unexpectedly sad, far sadder than he'd have been if the place had been stripped clean by greedy folks come to take the treasures Audra and Stolley had accumulated over the years.

Next to an array of stickpins and strung beads on the counter, Teedie saw Stolley's biscuit plate, the one he'd use at four each afternoon when he'd close the store for half an hour to enjoy a pot of tea and a small meal. Stolley had never, as far Teedie could recall, had to ask any customers to leave when the time came to close the door, nor had he had to rush through his tea to reopen the shop for other ones who'd collected on the porch. Nonetheless, he always took care to post a sign in the window promising to reopen at precisely four-thirty and always swung the door wide with an expectant smile at no one at all when that time arrived.

Next to Stolley's biscuit plate, Teedie saw Audra's cap and, on a hook on the wall behind the counter, her overcoat—the one in which Stolley had long ago found the drawstring bag with the green gem chips he'd used to buy the shop. Now the coat was empty of the gems, and the shop was empty of the Pounds.

Teedie walked slowly around the room, grabbing a handful of willow nuts from the barrel in the middle of the floor, tossing them into his mouth and chewing them sourly. Then he turned back to the counter and without really planning to, scooped up a handful of the things laid out there. He didn't really look at what he'd taken—worry stones, hair combs, a watch chain most probably; he stuffed them all into his kerchief, which he then stuffed into his trouser pocket. Drawing a long breath, he took a lingering look around the store, then turned back to the window, hopped up on the sill and leapt lightly back down to the ground.

Lying in the soil next to his feet, just as he had left it, was the limp black rag that had bound the window. Teedie looked down at it fretfully. It had been one thing to untie the carefully knotted cloth, and at the moment he did it, it had seemed like the right thing too. But now, his temper cooled by the dark of the store and the melancholy look of the things inside, he wondered just what he had done. The loose rag would surely be discovered by Baloo or his beat-men, and it wouldn't take much reckoning to guess who would have had both an interest in trespassing in that particular store and the brass to go ahead and do it. Teedie believed that the threats of tower time for rag-tampering were the true bill, and he all at once felt hot and swoony at the idea that that was indeed where he was headed.

Without giving the matter even a moment's more thought, he bent down and shoveled up the black rag in his bad right hand. Then he turned on his heel and lit out down the padroads off the main business street as quick and quiet as a frightened cat—which at that moment, he guessed he might as well have been. He discarded the black rag somewhere in the scrub by the side of the road and did not return to the business street until the next morning, when he came to the indigents' home to fetch his breakfast. Even from a distance, he could see that a new rag had been tied on the latch of the curio store window, knotted as true and perfect as the one he'd filched had been. That was a sight far more frightening than no black rag at all.

CHAPTER NINETEEN

Nacky, Teedie and Jimmer spent the next three days reading through Dree's books and paging through her papers. Teedie decided that he would not mention anything to Nacky about what had happened at the curio store, reckoning that if there was trouble coming from his filching it would come no matter what, and if there wasn't, there was no point stirring Nacky up about it. The work with Dree's books and papers would take so much thinking from all three of them, they couldn't afford to have anything else on their minds.

Nacky's little house was too small to allow the two men, the boy and the restless pig to spread out comfortably, so they worked instead inside Jimmer's new, half-finished home. The roofless walls of the fifteen-hundred-square-foot building stood around the completed thousand-square-foot house like the high fortifications around a castle. Jimmer had already abandoned the smaller house and moved his furniture into the dirt-floored outdoors enclosed by the walls—the better to prod himself to finish his construction work before winter set in. A simple canvas canopy supported by poles protected him in the event of rain. For fourteen and fifteen hours at a stretch, he and Nacky and Teedie sat at a wobbly table underneath the canopy, the ship books and papers open in front of them.

They said little and read much in that time, passing books and pages back and forth, pointing out paragraphs or diagrams or whole chapters they'd have to understand.

Nacky took in the new material slowly, and Teedie slower still, both of them needing to puzzle through each passage two or three times before they got the full sense of what it was saying. Jimmer required no such study, speeding through the pages and often stopping before a section or a paragraph was at an end, fully understanding what he had read so far and knowing in advance what the text that followed would say. With each passing hour, Nacky and Teedie grew less sure that they had any idea how to put the boat together. Jimmer grew more sure, and early on the fourth morning of their work, he and Nacky and Teedie came to the lake ready to build.

When they arrived at the ridge overlooking the bank that morning, it was clear the workers had not been idle. Under Bara's eye, the wood that had been hauled from the water had been painstakingly organized into dozens of separate piles, with trunnels stacked only with trunnels, planks stacked only with planks, fittings and posts stacked only with fittings and posts—all of them logged into Bara's tidy ledger. Standing among the wood piles was also a thirty-foot-tall, three-legged pulley that Jimmer had dreamed up several days earlier and had instructed the Dreeboys and several of the workers to build. The pulley looked like a rickety affair, seeming ready to collapse at the first gust of wind. But Jimmer promised it would be indispensable in assembling the huge vessel, grappling and lifting all but the very heaviest pieces and easing much of the muscle work. Many of the people on the bank this morning were standing near the giant tripod, looking up at it with their hands on their hips, apparently trying to determine for themselves if it was really up to the job it had been built to do.

Nacky turned to Jimmer skeptically. "You certain that thing ain't gonna topple?" he asked.

"I designed it to stand," Jimmer said. "It's gonna stand."

"Capstan was supposed to work just so too," Nacky said. "But it near killed the boy."

"It weren't the wheel that was at fault," Jimmer said indignantly. "Ain't my blame if the hook couldn't bite the wood."

Nacky let the matter drop and looked around him at the scene atop the ridge. As busy as things were down on the bank, they seemed equally so up here. For all the townspeople who had accepted Nacky and Teedie's invitation to work on the boat, many others had declined, either unwilling to put their trust in the likes of Nacky Patcher or reckoning that a share in a vessel that would likely never sail was not fair compensation for a full summer's labor. Instead, they took to gathering on the lip of the lake bowl early in the mornings, lighting cook-fires, roasting breakfast meats and spending the day eating and watching the activity below. Gilly Boate, Meddo Brinn and a handful of other men usually showed up first, playing their games of spoiled five, eating their sausages from sticks and, after the sun passed noon, drinking ale or malt from mugs and wineskins. Farther back from the edge of the ridge, several families would join them, the adults preparing meals over their own cook-fires, the children playing or running among them. Near the families, Brigg and Constance Keeper would station themselves, sitting in a pair of bent cane chairs, a stack of their yellowed newspapers resting on a clean cloth at their feet. And near the Keepers, August Ren would stand.

In the days since August's horse died, he had maintained a vigil by his immobile wagon, going home only to gather up a cot and blankets, a water jug and dinner plate, and a canvas and poles with which he could construct a crude shelter for himself and his birds. He spent his days tending the birds, saying little to anyone and taking his rest on his cot at night. Once, Nacky appproached and asked him why he didn't go home, and the old man explained that if his now-horseless wagon couldn't move, he wouldn't either. When Nacky offered to borrow another horse for him and even pay any fee the owner might charge, August flashed hot, explaining that over the years, the old horse had learned to read the birds' songs, knowing when he was jouncing them too roughly over the padroads and when he was riding smooth. Until he could find a horse of equal wits that could treat his birds with equal care, he would not budge. Nacky did not press the question further.

This morning, the crowd on the ridge was so thick that August did not even bother to release his birds for a flap at the ends of their tethers, fearing the noisy townspeople would spook the tiny animals. As Nacky, Teedie and Jimmer wove through the milling people, the air thick with the smell of grilling sausage, Nacky looked concerned.

"I didn't want it to turn circus like this," he said. "Too much show above, it's hard for anyone to stay fixed on work below."

Jimmer waved off Nacky's concern and stepped over the ridge and onto the path that led down to the bank. Nacky and Teedie took a step after him, but as they did, Nacky noticed something at the edge of his vision—a smudge of color that reminded him of cherrywood. He snapped his head in that direction and about twenty yards along the ridge saw Emma Hay, her crown of red-brown hair lit up bright by the low, gold sun. Emma was standing just at the lip of the bowl, not far from August Ren's horseless wagon, staring quietly down at the lake. Two young indigent girls, wearing yellow canvas dresses with the words "Property of the Yole Indigents' Home" stenciled on the hems, were flanking her. The girls were the ten-year-old Mag and the eight-year-old Gurtee, the ones who'd given Teedie so much help with his lessons. They pressed close against Emma, who kept an arm draped around both, holding them snug by the shoulders.

Clucking his tongue for Orro, Nacky began weaving through the crowd on the ridge toward Emma and the girls. Teedie held back.

"We got business below," he said.

Nacky turned around, grabbed a bit of Teedie's shirt and pulled him along with him. "We got business this way first," he said.

As they drew closer to Emma, however, Nacky began to slow, his face growing hot, his heart picking up and his doubt growing about whether he ought to bother her at all. Teedie noticed Nacky flushing, smiled and nudged him from behind. "We got business," he mimicked. Nacky glowered, but it was too late. Emma had noticed their approach and turned toward them.

"Nacky Patcher and Teedie Flinn," she said. "And Nacky Patcher's pig." She offered a hint of her crooked-toothed smile. "You're all looking fit." Mag and Gurtee glanced up at Emma and giggled.

Nacky beamed a little too brightly. "I didn't reckon you'd come around here," he said, then added hurriedly: "Happy you did, though."

"I didn't reckon I'd come either. But my girls wanted to see a boat getting built, so I brought them." She looked down at the girls. "Big one is Mag, little one is Gurtee. Girls, this here is Nacky Patcher, captain of the boat. And I know you know Teedie Flinn."

The girls looked at Teedie and giggled again. Teedie looked down and grumbled.

"You picked a good mornin' to come see the work," Nacky said cheerily.

Emma cast her eyes down at the dismembered boat on the bank. "It doesn't look like much yet," she said.

"No," Nacky allowed. "But it will be soon. We're plannin' to start piecin' it together this morning, just as soon as I say a few words—what they call a keel-layin' ceremony."

Emma squinted back down the hill at the vast scythe of keel resting in the middle of the clearing. "Looks fairly well laid to me already," she said.

"It ain't official till you say some words. It's the worst kind of luck if you don't." Nacky flushed a little, glanced away and then glanced back. "Care to come hear the remarks? I been thinkin' of 'em for a while."

Emma said nothing, seeming to consider the question; a small lick of wind blew a shock of cherrywood hair across her forehead. Nacky reddened and the indigent girls giggled again.

"Fancy hearin' Nacky Patcher make some remarks?" Emma asked

them. The girls looked down but nodded yes. Gurtee wrapped an arm around Emma's waist. Emma turned to Nacky. "Reckon you better lead us down to your ship."

Nacky broke into a smile, stepped aside and inclined his head toward the lake path. He started to extend an escorting arm toward Emma, then withdrew it uncertainly, then half-extended it again, creating an odd flapping effect. The girls and the pig glanced at him curiously, but Emma did not seem to notice. Teedie rolled his eyes.

As they stepped toward the path and began picking their way down—Nacky and Orro in the lead, Emma and the girls following, Teedie last—Nacky prattled on about his boat, pointing out various piles of wood and explaining what each one appeared to be and what purpose it likely served. Emma asked some polite questions and Nacky answered them happily.

At the bottom of the hill, Nacky led Emma and the girls toward a stack of lathed stanchions, an especially pretty pile of wood that he reckoned they'd find appealing. As he did, he looked around edgily for Bara Berry and was relieved to see that she was nowhere nearby, apparently busy with her ledger and her wood-counting elsewhere on the bank. Bara still blamed Emma for cheeping to the constables about her sister Mary seven years back, and the two of them rarely passed each other without sharp words or at least sharp looks. That kind of snapping was not what Nacky wanted this morning. Flashing Emma and her girls a last smile, Nacky bounded a few steps toward the keel. He climbed on top of it with unaccustomed ease. Teedie followed and stood near him on the ground. Orro sat at Teedie's feet.

"I need to say some words," Nacky announced. The crowd didn't seem to hear, and he cast a self-conscious glance toward Emma. "I need to say some words," he shouted, louder this time. Still there was no reaction. Teedie placed his index fingers in his mouth and let fly a sharp whistle that silenced the noise. Heads turned in the boy's direction, and he pointed them toward Nacky. Nacky frowned slightly at Teedie and cast one more self-conscious look at Emma. Then he turned back to the crowd.

"Be buildin' in just a gust," he said, "but we've got to make sure we're ready first. Bara Berry?" he called out, scanning over the dozens of heads and faces. Bara waved a hand holding her ledger and scrambled up onto a small pile of deck beams.

"Over here," she called.

"How close are we to bein' full up on parts?" Nacky asked.

"Still three dozen short of your forty thousand—assumin' you're right about the forty."

"I'm right."

"Then we ain't full up."

Nacky looked toward Jimmer, who was leaning casually against his tripod. "Thirty-six short is all right with you?" Nacky asked.

"It's enough to start," Jimmer said with a shrug. "Shy of enough to finish."

"That pulley o' yours ready?"

"Jig," Jimmer corrected.

"Jig. Is it ready?"

"Been ready. You ready?"

The crowd laughed.

"I am," Nacky said. "I just wanted to say a word about this keel we laid here." Nacky looked out over the crowd and broke a sheen of nervous sweat. The expressions on the faces that looked back at him were different from any the townspeople had ever shown him before. They still weren't the faces of people who appeared to have a great deal of faith in him, but nor were they ones that distrusted him entirely either. They were the looks of people who simply expected him to make good on a promise. Nacky coughed a cough he didn't strictly need to cough, then went on.

"We ain't never done much that amounted to anything in this town," he began. "Or leastways, I ain't. I spent me years either thievin' or scheming about thievin'—me and me Pippa both. Most of the time, folks just let us take what we wanted. And when the Patchers weren't takin' from you, the Baloos were, and when the Baloos weren't, the law was always there, promisin' to take more. Folks may laugh at cradle tales about dryland boats, and maybe it's only fools what believe in charms and curses. But this ship here is real as rocks, and this keel I'm standin' on is the first piece of it. I don't know what broke a thing like this up, but I ain't never doubted we're meant to put it together." He took a long pause. "Me, I'd like to get about it."

Nacky looked out over the silent crowd, this time more calmly. He searched out the face of Emma Hay, who was looking back at him. She didn't offer up a smile, but she didn't break the gaze either.

CHAPTER TWENTY

Even Chuff the dwarf often found it hard to hear Mally Baloo enter a room. The morning Baloo summoned Chuff to his home to talk about Nacky Patcher's boat was no exception.

It wan't often that Chuff was permitted inside the main house of the Baloo estate. On those rare occasions when he was, it was generally to carry a bushel of food into the pantry or a bin of rubbish out from the cellar, jobs that kept him mostly confined to the low parts of the home, where Baloo himself was unlikely to be. Nonetheless, now and again, Chuff had reason to venture into the house's upper halls and parlors and sometimes encountered Baloo there. When he did, he almost never heard the great man coming.

The fact that Chuff, of all people, could not hear Baloo approach came as a surprise to the other estate workers, who were well aware of Chuff's remarkable gift of hearing and often used it to make great sport of him. Whenever Chuff was in the house, two or three kitchen boys would shadow him through the cellar's long flagstone corridors, lingering just out of sight in the lantern-lit gloom. When they were sure he didn't know they were there, they would whisper his name or drop a handkerchief to the floor and watch to see if he would react. The boys would wager on the results, with the winning purse going to the boy who produced the softest sound from the greatest distance that Chuff the dwarf nonetheless heard. Most of the time, Chuff did hear the all-but-unhearable noises, but if he ever realized who was behind them—or ever grew tired of being tweaked that way—he never showed it.

On the morning Mally Baloo wanted to talk to Chuff about Nacky Patcher's boat, Chuff was at home in his cottage, preparing his breakfast in his small stone hearth. It was one of the stable boys who was sent to summon him to the main house. Chuff saw the stable boys almost every day, since the paddocks and barns were not far from his cottage, but he never seemed to recall any of their names. If anyone pressed him to guess—something they often did when they were of a mind to tease him about something other than his hearing—he'd always guess Birl. Long ago, when Chuff was a boy, there had been a horse groom on the estate named Birl who would occasionally bring him fig paste or almond cups or other small treats and linger to talk with Chuff and his young mother. Though Birl had long since died, the memory of his name—and perhaps his little kindnesses—had stayed with Chuff. This morning, Chuff wasn't expecting a visit from anyone at all, but no sooner had he lit his breakfast fire than he heard the soft, running steps of the stable boy padding through the grass outside his cottage and came to the door to see who was approaching. When the boy saw Chuff appear at the door, he slowed his run to a trot and shouted out to him.

"Got a message for you, Chuff the dwarf," he called.

Chuff nodded, though at such a distance, the boy couldn't see it.

"Said I got a message for you!" the boy repeated, looking put out and picking up his pace again until he came to a stop in front of Chuff.

Chuff nodded again.

"Don't you want to know what it is?"

"Yes," Chuff answered.

"I expect you would. It's from Mally Baloo himself."

The flat look in Chuff's eyes took on a flicker of interest.

"Reckon that woke you up," the boy said.

166

Chuff nodded.

"Ain't gonna' tell you what the message is, though."

"No?"

"No. Not till you tell me me name."

Chuff looked at him blankly.

"You know. Me name," the boy said. "What's me name?"

Chuff reflected for a moment. "I reckon it's Birl," he answered at length.

The boy let out a bark of laughter. "Reckoned you'd reckon that," he answered. Chuff said nothing, and the boy gave a weary nod. "Don't know why Mally Baloo would want to talk to the likes of you, but that's the message I'm carryin'. Baloo told the house manager to tell the stable boss to tell me that he wants to see you in the main house. Main dining parlor, even."

Chuff's flat eyes lit a bit again.

"And you ain't supposed to make him wait neither," the boy said. "Baloo ain't had his breakfast yet and he wants to see you before he does, so you'd best quit yer daisy-gatherin' and move."

Chuff nodded at the boy and then walked past him, trudging in the direction of the estate house.

"Any guess what he'd want you for?" the boy called after him. Chuff shook his head no without turning around. "Can't be nothin' good then," the boy called. "Reckon this might be good-bye to you, Chuff the dwarf."

Chuff nodded again and continued to walk. "Good-bye, Birl," he said, still facing ahead. As always, he spoke too softly to be heard.

It took Chuff nearly fifteen minutes to plod from his little cottage to the great house in the center of the grounds. When he entered the kitchen door—one of the few doors he was allowed to use—he bumped into a tall, broad-beamed pantry girl whose cross expression and tapping foot suggested that she'd been waiting for him for a while. The girl was young but had already taken on the coarse looks and ways of a far older

167

woman. Her strong arms were folded across her chest in a manner that called Dree to mind, but with none of the sun Chuff could sometimes see behind the storms on Dree's face.

"Oughtn't take a quarter hour to travel from your cottage to my kitchen," the girl said snappishly, "'less you went willowin' in the nut fields on your way." The girl looked down at Chuff's shoes, which were flecked with dark clumps of crop sod. "I see that you did. You best stomp that dirt off before you go trackin' through the main house."

Chuff began marching slowly in place to shake the soil from his shoes. The girl let him complete only three or four steps before taking him roughly by the arm and leading him out of the kitchen and down a large hall in the direction of the main dining parlor.

Chuff, like most people, did not care for the main dining parlor of the Baloo home. The room was made entirely of some variety of veiny, gray stone that resembled the color of meat turned bad, and it had a perpetual chill about it, taking on a frozen cold in winter and a damp cold in summer. Over the years, no fewer than four fireplaces had been built into the room's walls to remedy the problem, but none had seemed to make a difference. On a few occasions, Chuff had served Mally Baloo and his dinner guests at table, and had found the meals to be awkward affairs, with the gloom of the room and the chill in the air keeping appetites poor and conversation spotty. Only Baloo himself seemed to enjoy these evenings, working contentedly through his dinner and never appearing to notice the silence around him at all.

As Chuff approached the open door of the dining parlor today, he saw that none of the fireplaces was lit, and he gathered his shirt tighter around himself. In the shadowy expanse of the room, he could see a solitary man seated at the table, staring ahead toward one of the cold hearths. When Chuff and the girl entered, their footsteps clacked loudly on the stone floor, and the man turned. Chuff's ordinary eyes were no match for his extraordinary ears, but even from a distance, he could see that the man appeared to be Meddo Brinn. Wrapped in half-darkness, the Brinn figure leaned forward and squinted.

168

"Chuff the dwarf?" he called out. "That you?" The voice indeed belonged to Meddo, though it sounded a bit hoarser today than it usually did, softer and less certain.

Chuff nodded yes in response, a tiny bob of his head Meddo could not see.

"Reckon it must be you," Meddo said, " 'less there's someone else your size." Meddo laughed his rough little laugh, but again, some of the muscle seemed to be missing from it.

"No cause to question who else is here," the kitchen girl answered brusquely. "You just concern yourself with why you was called."

Meddo, uncharacteristically, said nothing in response and sat back in his chair. Chuff felt the girl poke him in the back, hurrying him the rest of the way to the table. When he got there, she pointed him to a tall chair next to Meddo's. "Man your size can manage a chair like that?" she asked.

Chuff nodded yes.

"Then climb up and wait," she said. Without another word, she turned on her heel and walked away, her retreating footsteps tattooing off the stones until she vanished through the door.

Chuff regarded the heavy, high-backed chair in front of him, pulled it back and struggled up into it. The table was set as if ready for a meal, but near as Chuff could recall, he hadn't seen company come to the Baloo home for the better part of two years. He tilted up the edge of a heavy pewter dinner plate and peered underneath it. The circle of tablecloth that had been hidden by the plate was faintly whiter than the cloth around it.

"I'd set that back down," Meddo said. "Reckon them plates're worth more than you are." Chuff continued to stare at the cloth for a moment more, then slowly lowered the plate.

"Ain't never been inside this house before," Meddo said, looking around.

Chuff offered a small nod.

"Always this cold in here?"

Chuff nodded yes.

"Know what kind of humor Mally Baloo's in today?"

Chuff shook his head no.

"Don't s'pose you know what he fetched us here for either."

"Only know that Birl said Mally Baloo wanted to see me," Chuff answered.

"Who's Birl?" Meddo asked.

"Birl. The boy. He's with the horses."

"Didn't see no horses, didn't see no Birl," Meddo said.

"No," a voice behind them answered. "And you're not likely to either. There hasn't been a Birl on these grounds for years."

Meddo and Chuff jumped and turned as one. Only feet away from them stood the tall figure of Mally Baloo, still as a statue. Meddo Brinn looked at Baloo and went fish-belly white. Chuff stared too but did not otherwise react. Baloo looked back at them both and smiled.

By any measure, Mally Baloo was an agreeable man to look at, or he ought to have been. Tall—at least six feet worth of tall, and likely two or three inches beyond that—he held himself straight and squared himself off wide, filling a doorway without overfilling it. His hair was white and full, not in the great, unruly curls of Jimmer Pike, but in a series of thick, snowdrift waves. His skin was ruddy and weathered but not too deeply cut with lines. When he gave off with a smile, which he did often enough, his face stretched out easily and brightened up readily.

For all Baloo's pleasant, plumebird looks, however, people never seemed to take to him—and Baloo himself knew it. His smile had a jagged edge to it, lighting up too sudden and winking out just as fast, without any of the slow buildup or melt-away most other folks' smiles had. His hair swooped and swept, but never seemed to change or move, the shape of each snowdrift staying more or less the same day after day. His fine skin sometimes flushed from ruddy to flat-out red, the blood seeming to percolate up inside him even as he kept his smile in place.

Some time ago, Baloo had begun trying to gentle up a bit and decided that if he couldn't soften himself, he could at least soften what he wore. Though he had fancied fine jewelry and glinting shirt fittings, he slowly began to do away with them all. He wore no rings and carried no watch, keeping the hard glint off his hands and the bright fob and chain off his vest. He fastened his cuffs not with polished links, but with small, silk loops. He pinned his collars down with stitches, not studs, and even replaced the bone buttons on his shirts and coats with tiny turned berries made of braided thread. With all that, Baloo believed he grew easier—and certainly friendlier—on the eye. Most folks, however, thought just the opposite. The hard, squared man looked just as hard as he always had, but now he seemed somehow more shadowy too, moving in a soft, secretive whisper even when he wasn't trying to. That's what made it so difficult to know exactly when Mally Baloo was entering a room—and hard to be absolutely sure he was gone when he left.

"I'm sorry to have startled you," Baloo said with one of his flash-powder smiles. "I always forget to announce myself when I arrive. Chuff here is used to it." Meddo nodded, unable to speak. "I'm happy you both came here today," Baloo went on. "I wanted to talk to you about Nacky Patcher—or really, Nacky Patcher's boat."

"Ain't a boat yet," Meddo said unsteadily, clearing his throat and finding his voice.

"I know that," Baloo answered. "I wanted to talk to you before it became one." He pulled a chair away from the table with a loud scrape against the stone floor and sat down with a soft swish of cloth. Chuff and Meddo turned their own chairs about so that they could look at Baloo more directly. "Just how big a ship could this be?" Baloo asked.

"They only just begun piecin' it together, so I ain't seen it whole," Meddo answered. "But I seen the keel and the arms comin' up from it, and heard people sayin' it should measure out more than two hundred feet."

"I don't suppose you heard how it came to be in the lake."

"Reckon no one knows that."

"Nacky Patcher didn't put it there?"

"Don't see how he could've. Don't see why he would."

"Is that what the builders think?"

"They do. They seem to take Patcher at his word."

Baloo looked mildly surprised. He turned to Chuff, and the flint-spark smile flashed across his face again. "Do you know where that wood came from, Chuff?" he asked. Chuff looked at him for a long moment and shook his head no. "And yet your poem had a lot to say about it."

Chuff brightened slightly. "You heard about me poem?" he asked.

"From some who heard it, yes," Baloo answered.

"Ain't finished it yet," Chuff said. "Got six lines, though. 'If it pleases or not, I am just as you see, I'm a man though I look—'"

Baloo cut him off. "I know those lines. How did you come by the other ones?"

Chuff looked confused. "Ain't no other ones," he said.

Baloo's eyes narrowed and Meddo spoke up. "I expect he's tellin' the truth. People been askin' him for days to repeat what he said that mornin' in the Rain, and he ain't come up with a word of it yet. It was his voice talkin', but he didn't seem to be behind it."

Baloo looked suspicious for a moment, then sat back in his chair and allowed his expression to turn to one of thoughtfulness. "I imagine the kind of wood they're fooling about with down there would fetch quite a price," he said, "that is, if you were to sell it off instead of building with it."

Meddo nodded yes. "I told them that."

"And what did they say?"

"They're still plannin' to make a ship out of it."

"Did they say what they plan to do with it?"

"Haul it to the coast."

Baloo looked as if he'd expected that. "Nacky Patcher's just the sort who'd believe that hen-fluff about dry-land charms."

Meddo nodded. "He said as much."

"I'm not surprised. If those fables say that boat has to reach the sea before that spell or whatnot can be broken, that's what he'll do."

Baloo spoke contemptuously, but there was also a flicker in his usually unreadable expression. Meddo—a mean man, perhaps, but not a simple one—caught it. To him it looked an awful lot like fear. Nacky Patcher, it appeared, might not have been the only person in Yole who believed in hen-fluff. Baloo shook off whatever it was that had rattled him and his face closed up again.

"Actually," he said, "it doesn't really matter what they plan to do with their boat, since they don't even have enough parts to complete the job."

"They know that," Meddo answered, "but they're gettin' close."

Baloo smiled. "There's one they'll never find," he said. He turned back and looked toward the door of the dining room. A stable boy entered, different from the one who'd summoned Chuff here this morning. He carried something large and apparently heavy in his arms, something covered by a coarse blanket.

"We paid a visit to the lake several days ago to see what all the fuss was about," Baloo said. "Those teak pieces were so lovely, we couldn't resist helping ourselves to one." He summoned the boy forward, then reached out and threw the blanket back. Meddo's eyes went wide and even Chuff's opened a little. Despite the gloom of the room, the thing the boy held was remarkable, far richer and prettier than it had been in the mere moonlight of the lake. It took Meddo a moment to find his voice.

"It's splendid," he said softly.

"It is," Baloo answered. "It's also mine."

Chuff stayed silent but looked at the stable boy. Then, with what almost passed for a tone of reproach, he spoke a single scolding syllable. "Birl!" he said. The stable boy dropped his eyes and looked away, finding nothing to amuse himself in Chuff's mistaken use of the name.

Baloo shooed the boy from the room, then turned back to Meddo. "That bit of wood will stay with me under lock and key, and when I'm not here, the stable lads will see to it. If Nacky Patcher really believes those dry-land Songs, he won't move that boat until every last piece is in place."

Meddo nodded and then, all at once, Baloo brightened, as if in his worry over the boat he'd neglected something much more important and a good deal pleasanter. "But I haven't asked after you, Meddo Brinn. How is your work? Is the letter-carrying keeping you busy?"

Meddo shifted in his seat.

"I haven't received any mail lately," Baloo said. "Have you, Chuff?" Chuff did not respond. "It must be hard for a man to keep his purse filled doing a job when there's no job to be done," Baloo went on. Meddo fidgeted and his hands began to work the arms of his chair. "A fellow without income could easily fall into arrears on his rent, by . . . what? Ten months so far?" Meddo nodded a tiny yes. Baloo clucked with tin sympathy. "Hard to imagine keeping hold of a home when you're ten months behind the drift. Of course," Baloo said, "debts aren't always paid in money. It's possible to settle them with labor."

Meddo's hands stopped working the chair. "What kind of labor?" he asked.

"Boat labor," Baloo answered crisply.

"You want me to work on Nacky Patcher's boat?"

"I do."

"But you don't want them to finish it."

"I never said I want you to help them finish it. I want you to see to it that they don't. If that wood's still here come the first day of autumn, the worth of it is mine. I may not see how it's possible for them to do what they want to do in the time they've got left, and I may not think Nacky Patcher will move it anyway without all its parts. But if you'd asked me a few weeks ago, I'd've said I couldn't see how wood like that could turn up in the first place. Things that should be happening and those that are happening seem to be turning top-bottom, and I aim to set them right."

Baloo now turned to Chuff. "Chuff the dwarf, I want to know how you know what that poem shows you know. And I'd be disappointed to hear that you can't recall. It might be hard to continue keeping a man like yourself in cottage and food if that man won't offer me help when I ask for it."

Chuff, uncharacteristically, nodded as if he understood.

"Meantime," Baloo said, "I'll see if I can't come up with a way of my own to deal with Nacky Patcher—something more lasting than sending him to the tower."

Meddo went pale. "You aim to have him done in?" he whispered.

Baloo looked disdainful. "Nacky Patcher may be a matchstick of a man," he said, "but it's still easier to break his will than his bones. I have a plan for him."

"And the boy?" Meddo asked. "It's as much Teedie Flinn's boat as it is Nacky Patcher's."

Baloo smiled cheerlessly. "Teedie Flinn's been trespassing somewhere he's not supposed to step. Caused me to send a constable out to retie a rag in the middle of the night—a nuisance for everyone concerned. But now that the boy's run afoul of my laws, I can pluck him up anytime I want. I just need to pick a moment when I can take him with a minimum of fuss. Teedie Flinn's not heading to sea on a boat; he's heading for a stay in the tower."

"I don't know that the builders will abide it if you lay hands on a boy," Meddo said warily.

"The builders will abide what I give them to abide!" Baloo snapped, even the icy light of his moon-cold smile now gone from his face. "You mind your own concerns. You've got a family to look after, Meddo Brinn. If you do what I tell you to do, they'll have a roof over their heads for the rest of their lives. If not, who's to say what becomes of them?"

Meddo looked at Baloo for a long moment. He slowly nodded yes once, and then again—the second time with more certainty. Baloo nodded back, then rose and walked out of the room. His shoes made no sound at all on the hard stone floor.

CHAPTER TWENTY-ONE

Teedie was surprised that no one seemed to be worrying as much as he was about the matter of the sails and ropes. He himself had been fretting over them since the first moment he and Nacky found the broken ship in the Yole lake. What concerned Teedie most was that they simply didn't exist.

For all the floating timber that was hauled onto the bank, a lot of the townspeople still doubted that it would ever be enough to build the entire vessel. Even the biggest wooden sailing ship, after all, was made of many things besides wood—metal, for one. There were huge belowdeck keel bolts, heavy topdeck rigging straps, tiny door hinges, elegant hatch latches, and hundreds upon hundreds of fittings, screws, and nuts, all of which were made of iron or brass or decorative copper. In the case of the Yole boat, all of these parts were indeed found in the mountain of wreckage that was hauled from the lake. All of them, however, were made not of metal, but of polished, rock-dense teak.

If the hard parts of the ship were all there, the soft parts were a different matter—the clouds of cloth that made up the sails, the miles of rope that made up the rigging and the tarry cables of cordlike oakum that were hammered into the gaps between the hull planks to seal the vessel against the waves. None of this material could be replaced by any kind of wood—and none of it was found anywhere in the lake.

Teedie had often raised the problem with Nacky, but to his surprise, Nacky seemed untroubled by it. Having already seen one boat collapse into nothing, and the pieces of another rise up in its place, he seemed oddly content to trust that anything else he required would be provided to him whenever he set about looking for it.

"We'll find what we need," he'd tell a skeptical Teedie.

"How?" Teedie would ask.

"I don't know," Nacky would say with a shrug that maddened the boy. "I just know that we will. Leastways, that's what the Songs say."

If the sails and rope weren't giving Nacky cause to worry, the job the workers were doing was. The first day the building began, things had gone promisingly. The moment Nacky finished the keel-laying ceremony, the townspeople went straight to work and kept at it for fifteen unbroken hours. With the help of Jimmer's sharp eye, they found the keel shoe and the keelson, the sister keelson and the garboards, spotting each from the pictures in Dree's books and hammering them into place.

As the work proceeded, Jimmer's jig whirled and spun and rose and fell, hauling the heaviest pieces of timber from their piles and lowering them featherlike onto the keel mass. It was only when the sun was completely gone and the moon rose that Nacky, Teedie, Jimmer and the others finally stopped the jig, put down their tools and backed away to see what they had built. The boat was still nothing like a boat. Nearly all its wooden bones lay in their huge, stacked piles. But several great ribs now rose from the keel, arcing upward and embracing the air like the legs of an enormous beast resting on its back. The ship—as all ships must—was at last beginning to enclose open space.

In the week since, however, things had not gone so well. Racing to beat the pace they had maintained that first day, the workers grew careless, raising rib after rib and attaching them to the keel, only to have half of them groan and fall back down as soon as they stepped away.

"Take care with that teak!" Nacky shouted at them as the first piece came crashing to the bank, realizing only after he spoke that while the rib itself survived the fall, two of the workers almost didn't, barely missing being crushed by the tree-sized beam. "And mind yourselves too," he added hurriedly. The workers cast him a chilly look.

Nacky's answer to the problem of clumsy builders was to recruit still more of them. Eventually, even Meddo Brinn quit his game of spoiled five, packed up his blanket and wineskin, and came down to see if he too might be of assistance. Nacky accepted his help agreeably.

"Are you away to the hills trustin' Meddo Brinn near your boat?" Bara asked him in a hissing whisper. "Man's got as many faces as he's got fingers."

"He's also got two hands," Nacky said, "and both of 'em can swing a mallet."

Finding a job for Teedie Flinn wasn't nearly so easy. The boy's hammer work was poor—his right hand hurt him powerfully if he tried to wedge a mallet handle into it for too long a time, and his left hand and arm had only a boy's strength. Carrying planks and other large parts was equally wrong for such a flyweight child, and he refused to be called to fetch small parts like bung-plugs and trunnels.

"That's mimma's work," he'd say huffily, and in fact it was, this being the job Nacky assigned to the three older women—grandmothers all—who'd volunteered their help.

After much quarreling, Nacky finally agreed that Teedie deserved a position of real authority, and gave him his own work team—a group of ten sorters, carriers and mallet-men—to oversee. Though Nacky feared the workers would bridle at being ordered about by a boy, Teedie showed such a bull's will when he applied himself to something, that they seemed to tolerate the arrangement, if not always happily. When Meddo Brinn came down to the lake, Nacky assigned him to Teedie's group, smiling inwardly as the young boy with the crippled hand crisply pointed the grown man where he was needed. Meddo accepted the work without complaint.

One afternoon, Jimmer was off in Greater M'croom buying mallets for the new workers while Nacky oversaw the building by himself. With his unsteady footing, he rarely ventured up into the ribs of the boat himself. Instead, he'd do much of his work at a table near the edge of the bank, where he and Jimmer and Teedie kept Dree's books and papers, referring to them continually to direct the day's building and solve any construction problems that came up. Today, Nacky was standing at the table looking up a detail on futtock bolting when he heard a row breaking out on the far side of the ship. Ordinarily, Jimmer would have settled any arguments among the workers, which was fine with Nacky, since he never had much patience for other people's dustups. Today, however, the unpleasant job of peacemaking would fall to him.

Nacky glanced toward the spot where he heard the voices, but from his position at the book table, Jimmer's jig and a large pile of frames blocked his view. He sighed, clucked his tongue for Orro, who had been lazing by his feet, and began hurrying toward the noise. Reaching the bow of the boat, Nacky and the pig crossed over to the starboard side and then came to a stop where the crowd of arguing people stood. Most of them were gesturing and staring upward as they quarreled, and Nacky followed their gaze to the skeleton of the ship looming above him. He let out a small gasp.

Rising twenty or more feet up the ship's frames and running at least another twenty from bow toward stern was a large patch of shiny hull planks covering the ribs, giving the spindly vessel its first covering of wooden hide—and its first bit of beastlike bulk. Two ladders were positioned in front of the planked area, and the Dreeboys, each with a mallet in hand and a waist-bag full of trunnels and bung-plugs, stood atop them. Teedie and the other workers stood at the base of the ladder. Near them was Bara Berry, her leather ledger under her arm. Chuff stood beside Bara. Nacky surveyed the entire scene crossly.

"When did this plankin' start?" he asked.

"This mornin'," Teedie said. "Before sunup."

"And it's right good plankin'," the bigger Dreeboy said. "That work's as fine as what any boatwright could do."

Nacky ignored the Dreeboy. "Did you know this was happenin'?" he asked Teedie.

"I only just got here from Emma's. This is the first I seen of it."

"You knew?" Nacky asked Bara.

"Saw it when I got here and it looked fine to me."

"It ain't fine," Nacky said. "It's too soon."

"Too soon for what?" Bara asked.

"Too soon for these parts," Nacky answered.

"That's what I told 'em," Teedie said.

"Don't seem to matter when parts go on," Bara said. "It just matters if they hold."

"It matters dear when they go on!" Nacky answered. "Thing's gotta grow the way it's s'posed to grow, otherwise it won't keep together. And it's too soon for planks." He turned to Teedie. "You explained it that way?"

"I told 'em true. Think they listened?"

Nacky put his hands on his hips and faced up toward the ladders. "You Dreeboys drop them hammers and climb down here. It ain't time for plankin'."

"It ain't time for anything at the pace you're workin' it," the bigger Dreeboy answered. "Reckoned someone had to start makin' this thing at least look like a proper ship."

"Never mind that," Nacky said. "You come down like I tell you."

"You gave us one share of this boat apiece," the smaller Dreeboy said defiantly. "We figure those are the shares we're hammerin'."

The bigger brother nodded his agreement, then chose a fresh bung-plug from his waist-bag, placed it in a plank bore and prepared to hammer. At that moment, Jimmer came running through the crowd, carrying his bag of new mallets.

"What's the stir over here?" he shouted, dropping the bag as he ran. "Who gave the go to start that plankin'?" For the first time, the bigger Dreeboy looked uncertain and let his hammer hand fall to his side.

Teedie and Nacky turned to Jimmer, wearing relieved smiles. "Where'd you brothers fetch them boards?" Jimmer snapped.

"From the plank pile," the bigger brother answered.

"Which plank pile?"

"Don't know. Don't expect it's important."

"Important's exactly what it is!" Jimmer said. "There's port-side planks and starboard planks. The lake warped 'em up so much you can't tell 'em apart easy by lookin'. But the boards still want to go just one way and won't stay if you hammer 'em the other."

"Look at this," the bigger brother said, striking the fat of his fist against the hull. "These boards is hammered fast!"

"They're hammered bad," Jimmer barked, "and they need to be set right!"

"Hammered bad? You fancy comin' up here and fixin' them yourself?"

Before Jimmer could answer, an odd lick of cold wind broke over the lake bowl and a small cloud—dark as blackfire—peeked over the ridge from the west. Nacky and Teedie both looked up. Teedie narrowed his eyes and took a step back. Nacky shivered, less at the sky or the wind than at the brother's words. Nacky had heard those words before—or something frightfully close to them—spoken in precisely the same way, with precisely the same heat. All at once, a sense of dampness and air-lessness closed in on him, and he knew who had said them first. It was Mink, the lost Mink, standing on a stack of crates in the dark belly of the *Walnut Egg*, gesturing to an undersized, yellow-white circle chopped into the planks of the boat.

A tick too small? Nacky could hear Mink saying. *You fancy gettin' up here and choppin' it bigger?*

Nacky could smell the mold of the hold, could feel the weight of its air, and in his mind, the finish of the doomed Mink played itself out a second time. Teedie looked at Nacky.

"What is it?" the boy asked.

Nacky didn't answer but instead sprang toward the ladders, shouting at the Dreeboys. "Move!" he cried. "Get down, get down!"

The brothers turned to him, startled, and the moment they did, there was a gunshotlike report from the hull as one of the freshly hammered bung-plugs fired itself from the end of the plank, rifled into the crowd and ricocheted off a rock. An instant later, there was a second shot, this one from the trunnel beneath the plug, which rifled in a different direction, sending the crowd moving the other way. Screams broke out around the bank, and the Dreeboys, startled, dropped their hammers. At that instant, the port-side plank that had lost its trunnel popped free with a loud *twang* and struck the boys square in the chest, knocking them from their rungs and sending them flying through the air. They traveled out and down in an arcing fall, landing with a bone-jolting thud in the scrabbly soil. Above them, the half-freed teak plank sprang back and forth, giving off the metallic sound of a wood saw as it did.

For a moment, there was silence as the crowd stared slack-jawed at the two unmoving bodies. Then the bigger brother sat up dizzily and rubbed his head; the smaller brother did the same. The crowd gawked at the swinging plank and the shoggled boys and then broke into loud laughter. Nacky watched the brothers as their cheeks flamed red and their jaws worked, and suddenly found himself laughing as well.

"Now," he called to the Dreeboys, "p'haps you want to pull them planks free and carry 'em back to where you found 'em."

The people in the crowd laughed harder, and Nacky cast his eyes over them smilingly. Several steps away, near a wood pile, he thought he spotted Meddo Brinn. But when he looked again, the man was gone.

CHAPTER TWENTY-TWO

The Albert T. Rain was pleasingly quiet when Nacky and Jimmer arrived there late that afternoon. The Dreeboys took their fall at the lake at about nine in the morning, and what with sorting them out, getting the builders back to work and keeping watch over them to make sure they had the early wildness out of them, it wasn't until well after the lunch hour that the two men could at last break away and slide off to the restaurant for a malt and a talk. There were only two tables occupied in the Rain when Nacky and Jimmer entered, both by men with a large stand of empty malt mugs in front of them. Dree was paying them little mind. She was off behind the bar tending one of her hearths, where what smelled like sweet brick was baking.

As Nacky and Jimmer made their way to their own table, Nacky cast his eyes toward a small slate board on the wall behind the bar and smiled. From the moment Dree lent Nacky her books, she said little to him about the boat, seeming to leave him to build the thing—or, more likely, fail to build it—on his own. Nacky, however, suspected that she was more interested in the work than she let on. That suspicion had been confirmed a week ago when he stopped by the Albert T. Rain for dinner and noticed that the slate board had been prominently posted with a running tally of the number of small parts Nacky, Teedie and the builders had yet to find scratched onto it. At the time, the number was thirty-four, but as the days went by and boat workers dropped in with word of this or that plug that turned up under this or that rock, the figure fell further and further.

"Got tired of people askin' me the number," Dree growled at Nacky when she first noticed him noticing the board. "Reckon if I post it before they ask, they'll leave me be." Nacky nodded wordlessly and said nothing more about it.

Today, the number on the slate board was down to twenty-three, and with a clutch of five trunnels having turned up this morning in a tangle of water weeds on the north edge of the lake, that figure would fall even further. "She's behind the drift on the count," Jimmer said to Nacky.

Nacky grunted. "With eighteen still lost, reckon it's us what's behind."

As Nacky and Jimmer reached their table and sat, Dree turned from the fire, drew two malts and brought them to them. "Early for you," she said, setting down the mugs. "Ought to be four hours of light left at that lake."

"Jimmer and me got some things to talk out," Nacky said. "I left Bara Berry and Teedie Flinn to mind the work."

"One-handed boy and a high-handed girl," Dree grumbled. "Don't seem no way to get anything built."

She turned and walked away. Nacky and Jimmer lifted their malts and sipped off the top inch. "We got troubles, Nacky," Jimmer said simply. "I don't like the state of that wood."

"I ain't so worried about the wood," Nacky said. "Least we got that. What we don't have is sails and rope."

"Teedie Flinn musta come to you."

"He's been comin' to me about this all along. I told him I'd attend to it when the time got ripe. I reckon it's ripe."

"Sails and rope ain't your biggest problem," Jimmer said with a wave of his hand, "not if your wood's flat spoiled."

184

Nacky swallowed. "You said it just needed switching around."

"That's what I'm hopin', but I don't know. Freshwater's no good for wood like that, only salt. The big pieces like the futtocks ain't been hurt much. But the planks and beams soaked up so much lake water they may be far and gone."

Nacky looked down at his malt and shifted in his seat. Beneath the table, the rump of his right ankle ached in the socket of his loblolly foot. "So what do we do to set it right?"

"Don't know that we can do anything," Jimmer said. "Unless we try and build a steambox."

Nacky had been afraid Jimmer might say that. There had been a lot in Dree's books about the business of steamboxes—and none of it had pleased him much. When warped wood needed to be rebent, shipbuilders would light fires, boil up water and run the steam that was produced into long metal boxes. Planks and beams wrapped in wet rags would then be set to cook in the boxes, soaking up the steam until they grew springy as saplings. When the hot boards were pulled out, they could be bent to just about any angle, precisely following the curves and sweeps of just about any boat.

Steamboxes sounded like handy things, but the same books that told Nacky how they worked also told how they sometimes didn't work—how wood that was already wet could soak up too much steam, softening and coming apart like honey cake in the hands; how dry wood could soak up too little, bending only so far before snapping like a bird bone; how overfueled ovens could swell and burst from the pressure of the steam. With Nacky hunting down every last trunnel and plug, he didn't care to take the risk of mishandling the wood and losing even a single part. Mishandling the steambox itself and losing any of his workers he didn't even want to consider.

"I don't like the idea of foolin' with that kind of thing," he said at last.

"I didn't expect you would, but I don't know that I can offer up anything else," Jimmer said. "You really aim to pull this boat all the way to the coast?"

"Only way to break the charm," Nacky answered.

Jimmer rolled his eyes. "I don't believe in no curse, Nacky. Even if I did, that ain't what the Songs say. That's just your readin' of them."

"It's the right readin'," Nacky answered.

"All the more reason the planks got to be hammered true, then."

"You hurt that boat with your steamer, I can't even pull it off the bank."

"Them planks keep poppin' free, I can't even build it."

"And suppose you hurt my workers instead of my wood?" Nacky asked. Jimmer said nothing. Nacky looked at him and shook his head a deliberate no. "Can't abide it, Jimmer. I just can't abide it."

Jimmer pushed aside his malt and leaned forward. "Hear me, Nacky Patcher," he said, sharpening his tone. "I ain't never done this kind of buildin' before, but I know what this wood needs. If I was workin' in a shipyard, I'd have boatwrights doin' me hammering, hoists haulin' me parts and all the time I needed to get the work done proper. But I'm workin' at a lake, which means I've got the likes of Meddo Brinn swingin' mallets for me, a jig I built meself liftin' for me and just eight weeks before autumn arrives and Mally Baloo comes along to seize up everything. That ain't much, but it's what I been given, and I'm answerin' with what I can. You got to decide if them answers is good enough."

Now it was Nacky's turn to fall silent. Jimmer, he knew, was right. He'd asked his friend to do this job, and if it was going to get done, he would have to stand aside and let him do it. Nacky looked toward Jimmer and at that moment, there was a creak from the front door. He turned, and even before his eyes could focus properly, he caught the color of cherrywood. Standing at the entrance of the Albert T. Rain was Emma Hay, her eyes bright, her red-brown hair windblown, her skin flushed from the afternoon sun. She was accompanied by a pair of young workhouse girls—no more than five or six years old—who stood on either side of her and held her hands fast. Emma looked at Nacky, and he flashed her an awkward smile; she smiled back with a crisp nod.

Stepping into the restaurant, Emma and the girls walked toward the bar, where Dree was laying out two trays of sweet brick. Nacky watched as Emma dug into her purse for the money to pay Dree. He let his eyes fill with the scene—the peach pink of her hands, the cherrywood tangle of her hair, the amber brown of the steaming bread. Then he took in the two workhouse girls and noticed, as if for the first time, a different color—the coarse yellow of their rough, matching dresses. Nacky smiled a broad smile as many things all at once came clear in his mind.

"Build your boxes," he said absently to Jimmer. "Build your boxes."

Nacky had told Teedie that what they'd need would come to them when they needed it. And now, he guessed, it had.

CHAPTER TWENTY-THREE

It was easy to see something odd was
going to happen the moment the water in the rock basin turned a bright
berry blue. Not many people in Little M'croom ever saw the rock basin,
but the man who used to be the captain of the *Duchess Isabel*—the man
who owned the land on which the odd little pond was found—saw it all
the time. From day to day and hour to hour, the basin seemed to change
colors as if they were moods. Early mornings it tended toward a metallic gray. Late afternoons it favored sea green. At night, the green turned
shimmery black. Blue, however, was a shade it never took on, so when
the color changed this time, the man who used to be the captain of the
Duchess Isabel guessed it had to mean something.

Few folks in Little M'croom knew that the onetime sea captain had
been a captain at all, and so they never called him by that form of address. What they came to call him instead in just the short time he had
lived in the town was Weaver—a name he didn't care for at all, mostly
because he just didn't look the part. He was a big man, the full of a
door, with a pair of hammy upper arms that seemed to have been built
for hard work. The index finger of his left hand was shorn off clean at
the middle knuckle, yet he nonetheless wore a pewter ring on the stump

that remained, as if he were determined to do what he could to pretty up the ugly thing he had left. On the opposite hand, the middle finger was completely gone. He had a generous head of hair and a wide, full beard, both of which were a uniform silver color; not a single hair or whisker was holding back black, not a single one was proceeding on to white.

Much as a name like Weaver seemed a poor choice for the big, silver man, the fact was it suited him perfectly, because weaving was what he did these days. When he first arrived in Little M'croom, he used a portion of the savings he had accumulated in his decades at sea to buy himself a small house on a generous patch of land and quietly settled there. Weaver made no friends in the first weeks he lived in the house, and he appeared to have no family either. It was said by some people on the quay that he did have a son, a similar slab of a man who cut a similarly fearsome figure. But it was also said that the son had come to no good and that Weaver had lost contact with him.

Whatever the truth of the matter, Weaver clearly had no need of company and might have spent all his time entirely alone had he not soon found himself growing restless. After so many years of work, most recently aboard the *Duchess Isabel,* he badly needed something to keep his idle mind and his half-ruined hands busy. Returning to the quay for a visit one day, he secured himself employment in the Little M'croom net and line workshop, signing on for a job knotting hemp and manila cord into gear for the town's growing fleet of fishing boats. Weaver worked as hard as anyone in the shop, showing up early and leaving late, but wasting little time in conversation.

With no one in town winning Weaver's confidence, there was no one for him to talk to the day the water in his rock basin turned a bright berry blue. Weaver had not paid much mind to the perfectly round, twenty-foot pond near the giant loblolly pine tree on his land when he bought his house. He could see from the lip of the basin that the entire depression was lined not only with muck and silt like a proper pond, but with a brittle layer of black, porous rock beneath the mud. Weaver had heard of such hard-shell formations before. They were said to have appeared long ago, when the land was hot and soft and the ground would occasionally call up a great gaseous belch that would rise to the surface and burst like a slow bubble in warm pudding. When the land cooled, it kept the shape of the bubble that had briefly been there.

There were thought to be other such bubble basins in the coastal and inland communities near Little M'croom. One of them, in the town of Yole, was rumored to be a full quarter-mile across and filled with the blue dregs of what, so the fables said, had been a vast inland sea. Finding out for sure if such a story was true, of course, required a visit to Yole, a nuisance trip to a dreary place that few people in so busy a town as Little M'croom could be troubled to make. Weaver himself would certainly never have entertained the idea—had the water in his own basin not turned colors.

The morning Weaver awoke to find that the water had changed he could not strictly be said to have awoken at all, because he never fell fully asleep the night before. What passed for sleep had been continually disturbed by vivid dreams filled with feverish images—something involving pigs; something involving dwarves; something involving a gangly man with a terrible limp and a sapling boy with a fisted hand; something involving trunnels and plugs and stanchions and planks falling into the ocean with resounding *plink-pops.* It was the *plink-pops* that finally jolted Weaver awake, causing his heart to race and his breath to catch.

Rising in the early-morning light, he staggered out of his house into the clear air. In the distance where the bubble basin lay, he thought he saw an odd shimmer. He walked to the pond, and when he drew close and saw the pale blue water lapping and glinting where green or gray ought to have been, he merely nodded and sat himself down on the ground. He had known from the moment he left his house that he would find something like this. In fact, he had known from the moment he arrived in Little M'croom. It might, he thought, have a lot to do with why he had been brought here in the first place.

CHAPTER TWENTY-FOUR

At the same moment the man known
as Weaver was gazing serenely into his bubble basin, the constable from
Knockle was gazing in wonder into a drawstring bag. It was no surprise
that this particular constable was entrusted with this particular bag. He
was the same constable, after all, who'd always done such a fine job of
pitching Yole families like the Pounds from their homes, usually getting
the houses cleared quick and clean with a minimum of unpleasantness.
A man like that could surely look after a bag like this, but even so, he
was surprised when he discovered the contents. There were six sparkly
gems in the bag, two of them a deep blue, two of them a rich green, two
of them as clear as rain ice. All the gems were no bigger than a cherry
pit, but from what the constable knew, gems like this did not have to be
big to be dear—and dear was what he reckoned they were.

In addition to the gems, the constable had been given a piece of
paper—an old, half-brown thing, the color of spilled tea, filled with script
so curly he couldn't make out most of the letters. The paper was folded
in thirds and tucked into an equally old envelope, which he in turn had
tucked protectively into his jacket pocket. The paper, he had been told,

was worth as much as the gems—which didn't surprise him, given the kind of paper it was.

It was Mally Baloo, of course, who'd given the constable both the bag of gems and the document. And it was Baloo who told him what he was to do with them, summoning the lawman to his estate not long before dawn one morning and dispatching him straightaway on the job he had in mind for him. That job would take the lawman straight to Nacky Patcher's house, and there he was to settle at last the matter of the boat.

The route to Nacky's house passed through the business street of Yole, a straight enough path, but one that pleased the constable little since, for a job like this, he didn't figure it would do for him to be seen. He was thus happy when he arrived at the top of the cobbled road and saw that all the houses were still entirely dark—all except Emma Hay's indigents' home, which shone a deep gold through its slats and cracks, as it always seemed to do. The constable nodded in wonder at that and unconsciously took a step deeper into shadows as he passed the home so as to conceal himself further. At that very moment, the door of the house opened and three girls stepped out onto the porch with linens they proceeded to unfold and shake. The constable—feeling more thief than lawman—averted his eyes and hurried shamefully off, and the girls finished and went back inside, entirely unaware of his passing.

When he finally made his way to the little house on the little square of land where Nacky Patcher lived, the constable was surprised to see a lantern lit here too—a single flame showing through the parlor window. Climbing the steps to the small porch, he rapped louder than would have been polite at this hour if he'd not reckoned someone was awake. He heard four or five dull thumps inside, each a bit closer than the one before it. Then the door flung open to reveal a cross-looking Nacky Patcher.

"Sshh!" Nacky hissed angrily, without even seeing who was calling so early.

The constable jumped, not accustomed to being snapped at so, least of all by a man he'd himself locked away more than once. He leaned in closer to let the faint light from the parlor reveal who he was. "Constable calling, Nacky," he said, "on constable business."

"Sshh!" Nacky repeated, ticking his head back inside. "Don't matter who you are. The boy's sleeping." The constable peered around Nacky to see Teedie Flinn still tucked in his bedroll on the parlor floor. "He sleeps till sunup," Nacky said. "I don't, not when my foot pains me."

It was only then that the constable looked down and noticed that Nacky was standing on his stocking-clad left foot alone, balancing himself by holding on to the doorknob, his wooden foot nowhere in sight. The lawman looked away. It was Nacky's hopping that had accounted for the thumping he'd heard.

"What is it you want?" Nacky now asked impatiently. "Ain't broken no laws and don't need no visits."

"No you ain't," the constable agreed. "As I say, I'm here on business."

At that, the constable reached into his pocket and produced the drawstring bag. He opened it up and poured the colored gems into the palm of his hand. The gold light of the flickering lantern barely illuminated the porch, but the little shimmer that reached this far combined with the faint light of the predawn sky lit the gems up just enough to make it clear what they were. Nacky looked at them, and despite himself, his eyes widened and a faint and familiar dizziness came over him.

"Come outside," the constable whispered. "As you say, we don't want to wake the boy."

Nacky hopped out to the porch, closed the door softly behind him and sat with a grunt. The constable sat on the step beside him, gestured for Nacky's hand and poured the gems into his palm.

"They're what they appear to be?" the constable asked, paying Nacky the compliment of deferring to his thief's eye, even though he was certain the gems were genuine.

Nacky looked at the stones with all the knowledge his Pippa had given him. "They are," he said after a moment.

The constable nodded. "They're yours." Nacky looked up, startled. "Got something else for you too," the constable said. He reached into his jacket, produced the envelope and handed Nacky the tea-colored paper inside. Nacky unfolded it.

"A deed of land," Nacky said.

"Near the ocean in Greater M'croom. Not a big patch," the lawman said, "but not a small one either. A lot more'n what you have now."

Nacky looked at the paper and the gems, and the low dizziness gave way to the true thief heat. It was a feeling he hadn't had since returning from the sea, but now here it was again, roaring through him as big as ever.

"I ain't interested," Nacky said, his mouth dry.

"That ain't the look you got on your face. What I see there is a whole lot of interest."

"Don't matter what you see," Nacky said hoarsely. The constable looked at him hard, and Nacky turned away for a long moment. "What would I have to do for 'em?" he said at last.

"I expect you know."

"My boat."

"Just so," the constable answered. "Weren't never your boat, though. You know that. It belongs to the man what owns the town. All you got to do is walk away and let him have it."

"He thinks that boat's worth more than the gems and the land?" Nacky asked.

"Maybe not. But I guess he reckons if he lets the boat go, he lets the whole town go. You ain't the only one what believes in curses and fables, Nacky Patcher."

"They ain't fables," Nacky answered quietly.

The constable shrugged indifferently. "As you've said. All the same, Baloo's offer is this: You figure out a way to get them builders off that bank for one day, maybe two, so he and his men can get in, and them stones and this paper come to you."

"It's the boy's boat too," Nacky said.

"Mally Baloo's got other plans for the boy."

Nacky looked startled and straightened his spine. "I won't allow no harm to come to that child!" he hissed.

The constable turned his palms up. "That's between you and Baloo. You look after the boy any way you want. Share out the riches with him if you care. I'm just here to tell you what Baloo's offerin'."

Nacky looked down at the gems and the deed. The constable changed his tone and addressed him warmly, almost as if he were a friend. "That boat's a fool's errand, Patcher," he said. "It ain't going to get built. Keep it up and the people of this town won't have no place to live come fall. Do it Baloo's way and the builders get to keep their homes, you go live by the sea and your purse fills up fatter than you ever dreamed."

Nacky swallowed. It was a hateful bargain, a shameful bargain, below even the lowest thief—and he was a thief no more. He'd tell the constable that too, as soon as he could find his voice. Before he could, the lawman took the stones and the deed back out of Nacky's hand and tucked them back into his jacket.

"Puzzle on it," the constable said, patting his pocket where the riches once again rested. "You've got a short spell of time yet. You want to talk to me, you light off this."

The constable then reached back into his jacket once more and pulled out something he'd not revealed until now. It was a small fruit rocket. Nacky had never seen one this close, but he'd heard Teedie describe them enough times that he'd know one not only by its shape and size, but by its acrid smell. "Color of dusk apples," the constable said. "My favorite. Don't care for that blackfire type."

The constable stood, handed Nacky the rocket and left without another word. Nacky watched him retreat and then sat for long minutes after. Then he bent forward, slid the rocket under the front step and rose. He hopped quietly back inside and was pleased to see that Teedie still appeared to be deeply asleep. Teedie was content to let him think that.

BOOK FOUR

CHAPTER TWENTY-FIVE

It would not be easy for the likes of
Nacky Patcher to persuade the likes of Emma Hay to conduct business
with him, and yet he would have to persuade her all the same. Ever
since the boatbuilding got under way, Emma had been a tick less cool
to Nacky, flashing him fewer crooked-toothed snarls when she passed
him on the street or in the Rain. Now and again, she even shared a few
words with him—but only a few, and never without the narrowed-down
look in her eyes that told him that while he might have put his thieving
past away for now, a purse-pincher he'd once been and a purse-pincher
he'd always be, never mind that the rest of the town seemed to have been
convinced otherwise.

If Nacky was going to persuade Emma to help him with his boat,
he thus knew he'd best not come calling on her alone. Teedie, of course,
would insist on joining him, and that was fine with Nacky, who knew
he never counted higher in Emma's estimation than when he was looking after the boy.

Bara too would be important to have along. The business Nacky had
in mind would cost dear, and when it came to questions of finance and
supply, it was Bara who had the ledgers in her hands and the numbers

in her head. But when Nacky raised the idea with Bara at the lake bank, she broke a bowstring.

"You give Emma Hay leave to see to any of this," she fumed, "and I promise you your boat'll never see the sea."

"Ain't the matter of the work that's troubling you," Nacky said, "it's the matter of Emma herself."

"And with reason. I seen what Emma Hay can do—seen it seven years ago when she set the law on Mary, and I don't care to see it again."

"This ain't about your sister," Nacky said.

"It ain't about nothing else," Bara snapped, "and it won't never be!" She turned on her heels and stalked off, barking out an order to a nearby gang of workers, who seemed surprised by the bite in her tone.

Jimmer had no such cross feeling toward Emma, but he was nonetheless chary about leaving the work he already had to do to visit the indigents' home—particularly given the new problem of the steambox. Building a steambox, Jimmer had known from the start, would be a difficult matter, requiring him to hunt up a supply of heavy iron and a pair of unusually accomplished smiths who could hammer the entire assembly together, not to mention locating a load of hot-burning hardwood that he could later use to fire the thing. He solved both problems using the wood from his part-finished home. Gathering up his stacks of beams, he carted half of them down to the lake to use for kindling and the rest up the road into Knockle, where he sold them off for money to buy the iron and hire the smiths. Working from plans in two of Dree's books, Jimmer explained to the smiths what he wanted and stayed around for half a day to make sure they got the whip hand on the work. Then he hurried back to Yole, trusting their promise that in a week he could return and pick up his finished steambox.

During those seven days, the work on the boat proceeded quickly. For all the laughter that spilled over the lake when the plank smacked the Dreeboys off their ladders, the tumble the brothers took left them and the other builders sobered. Dree, it was said, had tongue-lashed the boys fiercely when she found out about the accident, and when they returned to the lake the next day, it was with a new air of respect for the job they were doing. To Nacky's, Jimmer's and Teedie's surprise, the crowd followed their lead.

All at once, there was no more reckless racing to get the frames put up, no more angry grumbling about getting parts hauled. Instead, there was a quiet doggedness to the work as the builders carried in part after part, carefully raising each one into position and hammering it in place. Now and again, Nacky's mind would wander back to the visit the constable had paid him and the marvelous things he had offered him, and when it did, he'd feel the thief heat rise inside him sure as the sun. But then he would look back at his boat—with the skeleton of teak taking clearer and clearer shape, climbing and arcing and caging the void in the air like rows of prison bars defining a cell—and the larcenous urge would cool, at least for the moment. Even the hunt for the eighteen missing plugs and trunnels picked up its pace, as a new crop of volunteer searchers began combing the undergrowth on the sides of the lake trail and found seven of the small parts. With the job moving so fast and sure, Nacky was reluctant to be away from the lake, lest the mood be broken and the discipline fall away. But his business with Emma could keep no longer, and thus it was that he and Teedie and Orro the pig set off for the indigents' home the very morning after Jimmer returned from his visit with the smiths in Knockle, leaving Jimmer and Bara alone to mind the building.

Nacky took more time getting ready to leave his house that day than he usually did, combing his hair first to the right and then to the left and scowling into his little mirror as his red-orange wisps flopped lightly all over his head. He put on the rough cotton shirt he always wore when he worked at the lake, then took it off and replaced it with the good blue one shot through with white thread that he'd bought from the Pounds.

"Wearin' that fine shirt just for a little boat business?" Teedie asked with a smile.

"There's business and there's business," Nacky said.

"And then there's business with Emma Hay."

Nacky snorted, shooed Teedie and Orro out of the house, and the three of them headed down the padroad. They had risen so early that by the time they reached the top of the hill descending into the business center of Yole, they saw little sign of morning life. The sky was still mostly a deep, iridescent blue, and the long dawn shadows had only begun to appear. Far at the end of the street, they could see a thin curl of white wood smoke rising from the chimney of the Albert T. Rain, likely from a small breakfast fire Dree had just lit for herself. To the left, they could see a feeble orange light leaking through the window slats of Gilly Boate's Shop at the Top. Everywhere else on the street, the blinds were closed tight and the lamps were unlit—everywhere save the indigents' home.

The home, as it so often was, was ablaze with light. The shutters that lined the front and sides of the building were shut up tight, but a bright gold glow poured from around the edges and through the slats. Another bright stream leaked out from under the front door; a fine needle of gold even flowed through the keyhole. The combination of the yellow house light and blue dawn light stopped Nacky and Teedie where they were.

"Can't reckon how they do that," Nacky said.

"Don't know," Teedie answered. "Only ever been on the porch."

The man, the boy and the pig approached the building and climbed the steps, Nacky wincing at each step-*clump* and *clack-clack* sound he and Orro made. When they reached the door, Nacky prepared to knock, then looked at Teedie uncertainly. He had done a lot of honey-talking and favor-trading in the short time he'd been working on the boat, but this was the first time he'd felt wholly unsure of himself.

"She awake by now?" Nacky asked.

"Always," Teedie answered.

"She cross at this hour?"

"She will be if she hears us hurklin' about out here."

Nacky turned back to the door, gave three tentative raps and waited for a response. He got none. He tried again and there was still no reply. Then the door opened.

Nacky and Teedie had not known whether they would see Emma Hay or one of her girls when they got their first glimpse inside the home. What they saw was light—more gold light, rushing out of the crack in the partly opened door and casting a bright gold slash on the porch. Nacky and Teedie blinked several times, and a piping voice emerged from the gold.

"H'lo," it said.

A small girl was standing in the doorway, her hand reaching up to hold on to the knob. Her hair was dark and cropped short just below her ears, a light dusting of freckles was scattered about her nose, and her eyes were a deep berry blue that played prettily against the gold light. She wore the familiar yellow canvas dress with the words "Property of the Yole Indigents' Home" stenciled at the hem. Nacky had never been good at guessing children's ages, but he put this one at a few months shy of four years old. She took Nacky, Teedie and Orro in at a glance, and then smiled.

"H'lo," she said to Nacky again. "I like your pig."

"Thank you," Nacky said. "His name's Orro."

"My name is Lassa. Is the pig yours?"

"He is."

"Do you like him?"

"I do."

"Is your name Nacky Patcher?"

"Yes, it is," Nacky said, surprised. "How did you know that?"

"Emma!" the little girl called out over her shoulder, "it's just as you said."

The girl ran back into the house without another word, and an instant later, Emma Hay took her place at the door. In the combination of morning light and house light, Emma's features had less of an edge than they usually did, and the amused glance she gave the girl as she ran away

203

softened them further. Her hair was tangled, and a lock of it was falling toward her eyes. Her right cheek bore a slight sleep crease, as if she had come from bed not long ago. Nacky felt his cheeks and temples blaze.

"Nacky Patcher," she said. "You look well-preened."

"So do you," he answered uncertainly.

"And you brought Teedie."

Teedie smiled.

"And Arrow," Emma added.

"Orro," Nacky corrected.

"The girls will like him."

"I can see."

"I reckoned you'd be coming soon," Emma said.

"You did?"

"Of course. You're in need of sails, aren't you?"

"Yes," Nacky answered, faltering a bit.

"You're in need of rope, aren't you?"

"Yes."

"So I reckoned you'd be coming soon."

Nacky fumbled for something to say. "That's not the only reason I come," he said. "I imagine I'd've come anyway. I mean even without the sails. I mean even without the rope."

Emma's smile broke fuller and a little snaggly. "Maybe," she said. "But it's business what brought you here." She turned to Teedie. "And it's breakfast what brought you."

Teedie nodded and smiled.

"I expect I can satisfy the breakfast easy," Emma said. Then she turned to Nacky. "As for the rest of what you're here about, I'll talk to you. But I don't want to do it down by the boat nor down at the Rain nor anywhere else we might be seen. That means we got no choice but to do it inside."

Nacky nodded, and Emma then fixed him with a sharp look. Near as he could identify it, it was a look of clean, pure will, one he'd never seen out of her before—and may never have seen from anyone else, either.

"But this here is my home, Nacky Patcher. And it's home to these girls as well. We like it fine, and we don't want anyone carryin' tales or tellin' stories that will change that. Do you understand?"

Nacky nodded yes.

"You?" she said to Teedie.

Teedie nodded as well.

Emma fixed them both hard for another moment, then, at last, took another step back and opened the door to the indigents' home full.

The first thing that struck Nacky and Teedie as they stepped into the big room behind Emma was the lanterns lining the walls—dozens of them, one every foot or so in two rows circling the room. The higher of the two rows was about five feet off the floor; the second was about three feet. All the lanterns were lit, and all were producing faint wisps of oily smoke, which were being funneled into a length of metal tubing and vented through a fitted hole in the wall. The lamps were thus able to keep the room fully illuminated without the smell or stain of the black exhaust.

The walls and floor of the room were made of polished planks, which by their color and grain looked to be hard pine. Half a dozen worktables that appeared to be made of sugar maple planks filled the room; four maple chairs were positioned at each table. The room was open all the way through to the back of the house, and along the rear wall was a large bank of windows. A pair of girls who looked to be about eight or nine were opening the windows' shutters, letting in a flood of morning sunshine from the eastern hills behind the house. As the light came in, a bigger girl and a smaller girl circled the room, snuffing the lanterns in the row of lights each could most handily reach.

"We like to light them before dawn for the girls who help lay the breakfast table," Emma said, "but we put them out when the sun comes up."

Nacky and Teedie nodded mutely and looked off toward the right side of the room. There they saw that a fine breakfast was indeed being laid. Another polished, planked table, this one long enough for at least two dozen girls, was crowded with trays of freshly baked yalla buck, hot tureens of mixabout, platters of sizzling breakfast meats and bowls of fruits. Mag and Gurtee were carrying out the utensils and plates, while two more girls, twelve or so, were seeing to the food. A dozen or so other girls—the youngest no older than four, the oldest no older than sixteen—were standing by their chairs, looking at Nacky, Teedie and the pig and whispering to one another behind their hands.

"I told them you'd be coming, so they've been setting two places near me," Emma said, pointing to a spot at the head of the table and a pair of empty ones to its left. "If you'd come later in the week, we might've had sweet brick, but yalla buck will have to do."

Emma gestured toward the table, and Nacky and Teedie started to follow her. Then Nacky remembered himself, turned around and addressed Orro, who was *clack-clacking* on the pine planks behind him. "The porch with you," he said.

Emma waved her hand. "I don't mind the pig," she said, "and I reckon the girls won't either, long as he doesn't want a place at the table."

The girls giggled and shrank back, both delighted and nervous. A few of them cast an uneasy look at Nacky's clumping wooden foot and whispered to one another anew. Teedie's hand they didn't seem to notice at all anymore.

Emma, Nacky and Teedie took their spots behind their chairs at the end of the table as Orro curled up in the corner of the room. Emma then clapped her hands, summoning the lantern girls, the window girls and a few other stragglers to the table. When all of them were positioned at their chairs, Emma looked out over them, shushing them with her eyes, and then, with a wave and a smile, bade them to sit. With a great scrape of chair legs and a great outbreak of chatter, the girls dove for their places and began passing around the food. Emma, Nacky and Teedie followed.

"What are you operatin' here?" Nacky asked Emma, as a six-year-old girl with a mop of red-blond hair reached for a plate of bacon rashers, grabbing it happily before Teedie could get hold of it.

"Don't slide it, Lomi, lift it," Emma said gently to the girl, "and pass some to Teedie Flinn." The girl glanced at Teedie and blushed. Teedie didn't notice, looking at the bacon hungrily as he took the plate. Emma then turned back to Nacky. "It's an indigents' home, just like the sign on the door says."

Nacky looked at the sizzling meat on the serving dish and the bowl of melons in front of him and the tureen of mixabout laced with runnels of honey that the red-blond girl named Lomi was now pulling toward her. Then he looked at the girls themselves, with their flushed cheeks and their clear faces and their matching yellow canvas dresses creased from a recent washing and folding.

"Don't look especially indigent to me," Nacky said.

"All the same," Emma answered, spreading fruit jam on a clump of warm yalla buck, "that's what they call us, so that's what we must be."

Nacky speared himself two wedges of melon and passed the plate to Teedie, who waved it off. "Fruit for you," Emma said to Teedie sternly, "or no yalla buck." Teedie did as he was told.

"So how do you keep yourselves the way you do?" Nacky asked her.

"We work."

"What could you work at that could outfit you like this?"

Emma put her yalla buck down on her plate and chewed for a moment. Then she wordlessly turned in her chair and inclined her head toward the north end of the workroom. Nacky and Teedie turned, followed her gaze and looked to the far wall. Their jaws fell open. There, mounted just above eye level, was a small, framed oil painting of a girl who looked for all the world to be Bara Berry.

"That's—" Teedie began.

"No it isn't," Emma said. "Look again."

Nacky and Teedie looked, and the picture came into focus. The girl was indeed not Bara Berry. She was broader of face than Bara was, with darker hair and more-deliberate eyes. She was, of course, Mary Berry—and not the Mary Berry anyone in Yole had ever seen, the girl who had come to such a sad end seven years ago. She was Mary Berry as she would look today, older and grown and fully come into herself.

"How much do you know about Mary?" Emma asked.

Nacky and Teedie shrugged. They knew a little, about as much as anyone else in Yole. Mary and Bara came to live in the home shortly after their parents took sick and died, an unfortunate turn for the girls, since the life the home offered—at least back then—was a bleak one. Bara was too young to do much about it, but Mary routinely tried to run away, promising Bara that she would set up house somewhere else and send for her when she was settled.

The fathers of the surrounding towns who had established the home did not care for girls running off, fearing that they would wander back to their own towns and become a burden on the local purse or a nuisance on the local streets. Since the law did not give the towns any leave to keep girls in the home against their will, the fathers devised a rule of their own. The yellow workhouse dresses and the heavy workhouse shoes that were the only clothes the girls were allowed when they came to live in the home did not, technically, belong to them, but to the towns. While a girl who escaped could never be charged with the mere act of leaving, she could thus be charged with stealing civic property. A girl who grew too clever and decided to shuck the dress and shoes and escape in her shimmy or in clothes of her own devising could be similarly arrested on charges of indecency or creating a public scandal.

On no fewer than three occasions, Mary Berry tried to escape the home with the dress on her back and the shoes on her feet. All three times—so the tales went—it was Emma who carried the news to the constables, and all three times, Mary was apprehended and sent to the tower. Her stays there were short and her treatment was gentle, but the idea of a child—never mind a girl child—spending so much as an hour in the tower alarmed even the unshockable people of Yole. As the new manager of the home, it was Emma Hay, more than the equally deserving town fathers, who was roundly cursed for it. On Mary's fourth escape attempt, she at last succeeded, fleeing the country entirely and settling in places that were variously rumored to be Bretony, Andala or perhaps even Ferize, depending on who was passing the tale. There were other, darker stories—that Mary had not made it at all, that she had taken sick like her parents and expired shortly after she escaped. Since nobody ever heard from Mary again, over time more and more folks assumed the sorrier stories were true. And for those accounts too Emma took the blame, most people guessing that if she'd just kept still, Mary could have settled in a nearby town like the M'crooms on her first escape and satisfied any debt for her clothes and shoes when she grew older.

Nacky now turned to Emma. "You know what happened to her?"

"I know a little."

"Is she alive?" Teedie asked.

"She is."

"Is she close by?"

"No."

Teedie and Nacky looked questioningly at Emma. She sized them up for a long moment, then plunged ahead.

"Mary Berry is in Bretony," she said, "just as some people reckoned. Landed there straight from here seven years ago after silk-talking her way onto a merchant boat. There wasn't much work in a country like that for a girl so low, but after a time, she found herself keep in a dress shop. The family that took her in was a good one and saw to it that the work stayed light and Mary's belly stayed full. They even tried to feather her up a little with new shoes and new clothes. Mary was mulish, though, and insisted that she came from a workhouse and would dress like that until her purse allowed her otherwise. Every night after work, she would clean and hang her yellow canvas dress, and every morning she'd wear it into the shop."

Emma stopped and took a bite of bread, and Nacky and Teedie, having entirely forgotten the food in front of them, waited for her to go on.

"The dresses Mary sold were fine ones, and the women who came in to buy them were right well-tinned. They'd ask Mary about her own yellow dress and she'd tell them, and they'd ask her again the next time and she'd tell them again. Pretty soon, the well-tinned women were bringing in other women with equally fat purses to coo at Mary and hear her story. Sometimes on Sundays, they'd even bring her over to their homes to give her tea and treats and coo at her some more. And pretty soon they started deciding that it might be nice if their own little girls could have the same yellow dress Mary wore made the same rough way hers was, figurin' they could wear it now and then and maybe grow up with some of the same iron Mary had in her.

"Seein' no harm in givin' them what they wanted, Mary stitched up a few of the dresses out of yellow canvas, and even took care to ink the indigents' home name along the hem. The dresses sold fast and dear, and the shopwoman made it a point to give Mary some of the money. Soon more women were comin' in for more dresses."

Emma now stopped again as an argument broke out at the far end of the table. Two girls were quarreling over a final wedge of melon in one of the serving bowls. Emma flashed them a scolding glance and they immediately quieted, apparently knowing that they had both now lost the fruit. A third girl speared it happily up.

"About five years back," Emma went on, "I got a letter from Mary tellin' me that if the girls here could make up a shipment of canvas dresses and send them out, the Bretony ladies would buy them quick and the fat-man's share of the money would come back here. We hunted up the canvas and stitched up the dresses, and true as she said, not long after I sent them over, a payment came back. Pretty soon, Mary asked for more dresses, some the same as before, but some cut different, just so long as they were all made from the same yellow canvas. For five years now, we been shippin' her crates of dresses and she's been shippin' us back pay, and no one outside this house has caught wise yet."

Emma sat back, turned her palms up and smiled. Nacky pushed his untouched plate away and stared at her. Around the table, the girls continued to giggle and talk and gobble up food.

"And them people in Bretony don't just take it into their heads to stitch up their own dresses?" he asked.

"Not just Bretony anymore. We're sellin' to Andala and Ferize too.

And no, they wouldn't think of makin' their own. People livin' soft lives like the feel of things that come from hard ones."

"How do you move your shipments out?"

"At first I hired a wagon from Knockle and paid in consignments or money. Lately, them friends of yours, Brigg and Constance Keeper, been helping us out, carrying cargo to the docks in the M'crooms, bringin' money envelopes back, and tellin' everyone they're just off to the coast to get more of their old newspapers. Folks here don't see much more than they want to see."

Nacky looked around himself and nodded slowly. "You must be fat as pirates."

"There's money," Emma said, "but most of it ain't bein' touched yet. Each of these girls got some put aside." She indicated the red-blond Lomi sitting next to Teedie, lacing her mixabout with spoonfuls of honey. "Expect she's got more to her name than you do right now," she said to Nacky.

"They don't get schoolin'?"

"More than they want, as the boy can tell you," Emma said, and Teedie nodded in agreement. "They practice reading, writing and numbers in the morning, and they sew up the dresses in the afternoon. When they're ready to leave here, they won't have to do workhouse work for anyone."

Nacky smiled. "Seems your cheepin' to the sheriffs and gettin' Mary run out of the country turned out fine for everyone."

"That's no credit to me. I broke up Mary and Bara—the last scraps of a family. Even knowing how things've turned out, I'd've kept mum if I could've."

"Why didn't you?"

"Constables wouldn't have it. They used to come in here and count my girls every week. If one went missing and I hadn't told 'em, it would've gone hard for the ones that were left. I couldn't make twenty-three suffer to spare the one." Emma now paused and glanced toward the picture of Mary hung on the wall. "All the same, I had this painted by someone who recalled Mary's face. I keep it there to remind me that there's a wrong that was done and that it's still my job to figure out a way to undo it."

"Doesn't Bara know any of this?" Nacky asked.

"Not a bit."

"She's not sharin' in the money?"

"She is, she just doesn't know it yet. Bara moved to the Baloos' right before we heard from Mary. I was goin' to tell her straightaway, but Mary asked me not to. Bara runs hot and doesn't always think out what she says. If she knew about the dresses and the money, she'd sure let it spill, then Mally Baloo would demand his share, the revenue collectors would buzzard the rest, and my girls would be back to real workhouse livin'. That's why we work with the shutters shut and the lanterns on. A few more years and a bit more coin and we're goin' to close down and move all the girls away—Bara too. Meantime, Mary sees that I keep an owl eye on the Baloo house to make sure Bara never gets worked too hard."

Nacky sat back in his chair and smiled admiringly at Emma. "Spend my life learnin' how to thieve, and look at the light-fingerin' you've been able to work."

Emma stared at Nacky with her mouth suddenly tight and her eyes gone cold. Teedie noticed and looked at Nacky in surprise. Nacky wasn't sure what he had said, but he wished he could pull it back.

"Hear me, Nacky Patcher," Emma said, leaning forward on her elbows and speaking in a voice that sounded like dry twigs snapping. "What we're doin' here ain't thievin'. What you did with your dreamed-up cows and your all-talk silver, that was thievin'. That's the reason I'd never have any business with you before, and that's the reason I didn't want to let you in here today."

Nacky drew back, surprised by her tone, and spoke apologetically. "Why did you, then?"

Emma paused. "Because you been good to the boy. Because you and him are after something different now, and it's something worth havin'."

Her tone softened a tick. "Maybe something worth even more than that foot you lost at sea."

Nacky nodded. "It is."

"But if word gets around about what I told you today, and if anything happens to these girls . . ." Emma trailed off and let the flint in her eyes take over where her words gave way.

"It won't," Nacky said. "It won't."

Emma gave him a crisp nod. "Now you're needin' sails, and you're needin' rope," she said. "You figured with all this yellow canvas the girls wear, I must be able to lay my hands on fabric cheap. And you figured where fabric is, rope might follow."

Nacky nodded.

"You was part right," Emma said. "The sails I can get you, but you're going to have to pay. The rope I can't get, but it can be had, long as you're willin' to travel for it. You good at holdin' figures in your head?"

Nacky nodded again.

"Good," she said, "because there's some arithmetic you have to do."

Emma started scattering numbers at Nacky that seemed to concern themselves with square measures and straight lengths and costs per foot or yard, but for the moment, Nacky was not taking hold of any of them. He was thinking instead about Bara Berry, of how she hated Emma, and of how far off the mark it was possible for one person to be about another. It was left to Teedie, sitting at Nacky's side, to do the listening and add the figures.

CHAPTER TWENTY-SIX

It took Nacky several hours to emerge from the dreaminess he felt after he left Emma Hay's house. The remarkable story he'd been told, the promised solution to the problem of his sails, the intoxicating presence of Emma herself, all lingered stubbornly with him. It was full noon before the half-smile he was wearing at last melted off his face and was replaced by the expression of furrowed worry he usually wore when he was down at the lake and tending to his boat.

Teedie Flinn didn't take nearly so long to get fretful. Even before he left the indigents' home, something had begun to nag at him. The feeling stayed with him throughout his day at the lake and lingered into evening time. He didn't fully work out what was troubling him until that night when Nacky was off having his supper at the Albert T. Rain and Teedie was alone in Nacky's parlor, working on one of the school lessons Emma had given him to do.

Even after the boatbuilding had gotten fully under way, Emma had made it clear that Teedie would still be expected to hold to his studies, particularly his reading and writing. She had always told her indigents that girls who couldn't make their way through a printed page could never know much of anything else—words being the things that made up thoughts, and thoughts being the things that made up ideas. She saw no reason the rule shouldn't apply to a boy too. Every night with the exception of Sundays, she thus sent Teedie home to Nacky's house with storybooks to read from and instructions to come back the next day with one full page of what he'd read copied down neatly and accurately.

The work was terribly slow going for Teedie. Letters were a puzzle he could never crack easily. He was always turning his *b*'s backward and his *t*'s top-bottom and getting his *s*'s and *c*'s tangled up entirely. With help and time, he could wade through a page of anything he had to—as he did when he and Nacky and Jimmer were reading Dree's ship books—but when he was done, his head ached and his eyes felt like stones.

Numbers, however, proved to be a different matter. If Teedie's brain moved like cold mixabout when he was trying to make sense of a printed page, it moved like sparkfire when he was adding up a column of figures. Emma would read him out a string of ten or fifteen numbers she'd expect him to copy down and add up, but no sooner would she finish reciting the list than he'd give her back the sum. Suspicious, she would make the numbers bigger and the list longer, but Teedie, if anything, just got faster, seeming to build up speed the harder the ciphering got. He moved the same way through his subtraction work, and did even better with his times tables and division, the last of which he taught himself one night when he was lying in bed and the cricking of the tree-bugs outside his window was keeping him awake.

"They didn't give you a bit o' this in that half-home you were living in?" Emma asked when he came for his breakfast the next day and showed off what he'd learned.

"They didn't give me much more than lantern-makin', rocket-stuffin' and a bit of readin'," he answered.

It was Teedie's way with numbers—or, more specifically, what those numbers were telling him—that was causing him such worry tonight as he sat in Nacky's parlor fighting with his reading. With summer unspooling fast, the boat was nowhere near done, and the job was actually getting bigger, not smaller. There was the Dreeboys' bad planking to undo, the warped boards to be steamed straight and now the sails and ropes to get stitched up and spun out. Of the twenty-four girls in the indigents' home, perhaps eighteen had the strong hands needed for the heavy sail work, but that was sure to be fewer than were required. The steaming, replanking and rope braiding would call for more workers still.

Those hard facts kept whirlpooling in Teedie's head until finally, on his fourth go at a story that, near as he could tell, had something to do with a bird, a button and what was either a magic cow or a magic sow, he pushed the book aside, snatched up a sheet of writing paper and began scribbling out figures. He tallied up the number of builders who reported to the lake each morning, ciphered in the hours of sunlight in a summer day and the number of days remaining before fall. He took away the amount of time that would unavoidably be lost on account of injury, shirking workers and plain bad weather. He added the time it occasionally took Jimmer to puzzle out a passage in one of Dree's books, then subtracted the minutes that were saved if Nacky read the book page aloud so Jimmer wouldn't have to climb down off his ladder and come read it himself. Finally, Teedie weighed all of that against the small share of the boat that had so far been built and the larger share that was still to go.

He looked at what he had on his page and frowned. According to his ciphering, his and Nacky's ship could be not possibly be ready to sail until the twenty-fourth of October—or more than a full month after the day on which Mally Baloo and his beat-men would come to cart off the parts.

Teedie chewed his lip, returned to the page and tried stretching out the hours the builders worked each day from fourteen to seventeen, but that cut less than a week from the job. He calculated what would happen if no days were ever lost to rain and no workers were ever lost to a turned ankle or a crown-smacked head. He saved a week more. Finally, he eliminated the plank steaming, sped up the rope-weaving and pretended that all twenty-four of Emma Hay's girls—even the ones who could not yet comfortably manage a knife and fork, much less a needle and thread—could somehow lend a hand to the sail-making. Still the work spilled into early October.

Throwing down his pencil in disgust, Teedie turned away from his calculations. No matter what the townspeople did, the boat was going to fail, beaten not by bad planks or poor weather or even Baloo himself, but simply by the hard wall of the unmoving calendar. The only answer, Teedie knew, was to find more workers, and not just any workers. The new ones would have to be nimble enough to scamper up into the masts to run ropes and hang sails when the time arrived. They would have to be accustomed to hard work, needing no time to adjust themselves to the long hours and the short sleep they would surely suffer. And Teedie would have to have at least two dozen of them—more still if he wanted to be absolutely sure the work could be done by the time Baloo came calling.

Teedie stared at his numbers in despair. Then, a broad smile crossed his face. Springing to his feet, he pulled open his bedroll, where he'd tucked the small kerchief filled with the bits and bobs he'd taken from the curio shop. He'd never bothered peering inside the cloth before, and with good reason. The fear of tower time had loomed large in his mind since the night he untied the black rag, and his worry had only grown worse after he listened in on what the constable whispered to Nacky the morning he came to call before dawn. *Mally Baloo's got other plans for the boy,* the lawman had said. Teedie had no doubt those plans were not good, and even looking at the things he'd taken from the curio store would only have set him brooding on the matter. Besides, he knew the kinds of sorry merchandise the Pounds had always offered for sale and reckoned he couldn't have taken anything of value. But now, he realized, he might need to lay his hands on anything he could possibly sell, and the contents of the kerchief were all he had.

Picking up the rumpled cloth, he noticed it had more heft to it than he'd remembered. He opened it, peeked at what was there and saw just the dreary kinds of things he'd expected—a watch chain, a porcelain brooch, a worry stone, a belt buckle. At the bottom of the pile, however, something glinted up at him. He dumped it all onto his bedroll, and to his surprise, out tumbled a large, shiny coin.

Teedie lifted up the mirror-bright thing and turned it over and over in his hand. He had never seen silver before, but he knew, as surely as he'd known teak and blackfire when he'd first seen them, that this was it. He examined the design on the front of the coin—the usual class of unrecognizable duke or prince who always found his way onto metal money. He turned it over, and his eyes went wide. Struck into the hind side of the coin was the image of a ship, a sailing ship with its canvases blown full and its pennants streaming back. The ship, to Teedie's astonishment, wasn't sailing on the sea, and it wasn't sailing in a lake. It was on dry land inclined at a mountainous pitch, a pitch that looked lick-alike the incline of the Yole mountains themselves. It was a scene of the Songs, made real in silver.

Teedie stared at the coin for several mystified moments. Then he wrapped it carefully in his kerchief and stuffed it in his trouser pocket. He'd be making a trip before long, he knew, and he now had all he'd need both to pay his way and to complete the work he'd have to do when he got there. The coin, he was sure, would be ample for all that. As someone had once told Nacky and as Nacky had often told Teedie, no matter how fancies may change, people will always have an eye for a bright bit of silver.

CHAPTER TWENTY-SEVEN

Meddo Brinn never much cared for visitors in his home, and he reckoned he had good reason. The tiny two-room house was barely large enough for his wife, his three sons and himself, never mind guests crowding inside and needing a place to sit or a hook for their coats. What's more, visitors tended to expect something for the trouble they'd taken to call at all—a glass of this or a plate of that or something else to fortify them after the trip they'd made. Since there was barely enough to fortify Meddo's own family when mealtimes came about, he didn't care to share out what he did have with strangers.

Worst of all, it was the nature of guests to want to pass the time with pointless talk about a man's work, but it had been a long while since Meddo had worked at all, as his untouched mailbag hanging by the front door attested. That was a fact he rarely discussed even with his family, never mind with a lot of unwanted people who had little business in his house in the first place.

Meddo was thus especially put out one evening when he was preparing to snuff his lamps for the night and heard a *tap-tap-tap* on the front door. His wife and sons had already retreated to the bedroom and fallen into the quiet of full sleep. He couldn't puzzle out who would be bothering him at this hour, but he'd surely make it clear he didn't care for the intrusion. His pique froze hard inside him, however, when he swung the door open and saw on his step the tall figure of Mally Baloo.

Meddo gaped, but before he could say anything, Baloo put his fingers to his lips, as if he'd guessed that Meddo's family was asleep and didn't care to disturb them—never mind that it was he himself who'd chosen this hour to call. Meddo nodded mutely but stood frozen in the doorway, blocking the entrance. Baloo looked at him balefully, and Meddo remembered himself and stepped aside to let the great man in. Baloo entered the parlor and looked around at the small room a bit sorrowfully, taking in what little there was to take in. His eye fell on Meddo's unused mailbag and lingered there for a moment. He clucked at the sight of it.

Meddo pulled a straight-backed chair away from the dining table, taking care not to scrape it on the floor and wake his family, and bade Baloo to sit. Baloo, however, declined the courtesy. He could stay only a moment, he explained in a quiet tone. He had some work for Meddo to do, and it would have to be done soon. Meddo nodded yes and inquired what the work was. It was only then that he noticed Baloo was carrying a small satchel. Baloo opened the bag, reached inside and produced a shiny metal hammer. He passed it to Meddo, who turned it over and over in his hand and was surprised to feel that the thing was far heavier than it appeared to be. It had an unusually narrow, oval-shaped head as well. It was a hammer designed for hard tasks but precise ones.

"Never seen one like it," Meddo whispered, looking at Baloo questioningly.

"It's suited," Baloo said, "for the job it has to do."

Baloo reached back into his satchel and produced something else— something Meddo couldn't identify. It was about the size and color of a hard pecan, but it gave off a faint, sulfurous wisp. Meddo looked at it dubiously, reluctant to touch it, but Baloo extended the thing to him.

"It don't look safe," Meddo said uneasily.

"It's suited," Baloo repeated, "for the job it has to do."

Baloo closed up his empty satchel and fixed Meddo with a hard look. Then slowly and carefully, he described what those jobs were. There would be three of them—one requiring Meddo to make proper use of the hammer, one requiring him to make proper use of the pecan-like thing, one requiring him to make proper use only of his words and his wits. Baloo left no doubt that he expected Meddo to do the work precisely how it needed to be done, nor any doubt that there would be consequences if he failed. Meddo assured him he would not fail, and Baloo nodded crisply as if he expected no less. Then he turned on his heel and left the house as quietly and quickly as he had arrived.

Meddo regarded at the shiny hammer and the pecanlike thing and looked around the room for a safe place to put them. He settled on his mailbag and tucked them carefully inside. No one, he knew, would have cause to touch that anytime soon.

CHAPTER TWENTY-EIGHT

Jimmer Pike's steambox arrived at the lake, and straightaway nobody liked it much. The main thing that made it such a disagreeable object was the fact that it was just plug ugly.

The steambox was actually made of three different parts. The heaviest piece was the stove itself, a tall, fat furnace about as large as an oversized chest of drawers. Its iron-gray mass was held together with berry-sized studs; its front and sides were scored with ventlike slats cut high and low. When the door was swung open, it revealed a giant maw that looked able to consume several cords of wood in a single swallow.

On the right side of the oven, sprouting horizontally from its flank, was the second piece of the assembly, a fat pipe with a round reservoir bulging in its center. At the top of the bulge was a small door that could be lifted open and flipped shut. Connected to the other end of the pipe was the third and final component: a coffinlike iron box with a door in its front end.

According to the design, when a fire was lit in the oven, the heat would travel up and across the pipe, putting the boil to water stored in the reservoir. The steam bubbling up from the water would then be forced farther along, streaming into the coffin box, where timbers from the boat wrapped in wet rags would be waiting for it. The mist and heat would then penetrate the wood, softening it up like young bamboo.

That was the idea, anyway, but whether it would work was another matter. For the week the smiths in Knockle were building the steambox, Jimmer had worried that they might not be clear on all the details in Dree's books, but when he returned to their shop and looked at what they'd made, he saw that they indeed appeared to have put together precisely what was called for. If Jimmer was thrilled to see the thing, however, the smiths themselves seemed uneasy.

"Know how to operate a steamer like this?" one of them asked as Jimmer was walking around the oven, admiring its ugly bulk.

"Just what I read in the books," he answered.

"Same as not knowin'," the smith said. "Know what to do if it looks set to blow?"

Jimmer paused. "Snuff the flame?" he answered uncertainly.

"If that's the best you can guess, then I did right givin' you the extra door," the smith said.

"What extra door?" Jimmer asked, alarmed. "The books didn't call for that."

The smith regarded Jimmer impatiently. "Steamers ain't bread hearths," he said. "That oven's meant to burn hot, and hot ovens are inclined to burst. You ever operated one before, I'd believe you could manage it. But a man like you what reads things in books—you get an extra door."

The smith stepped to the oven and laid his hand on its top where Jimmer indeed saw a small, vented door that was not in Dree's diagrams. "Things start to overheat, this ought to let the pressure off," the smith said, "provided you use it right. Open it before you're supposed to and your flame'll go cold. Open it after you're supposed to and it may be too late to keep it from blowin'."

"How do I know when to do it?" Jimmer asked.

"Listen to it. If it's whistlin' like a songbird, you're fine. If it ever starts screaming like a raven or a shrike, it's gettin' ready to burst."

Jimmer nodded, picturing the dreary black and gray birds that filled the Yole trees everywhere but the places August Ren's songbirds sat. The smiths, satisfied that Jimmer understood what he was doing, loaded the steambox into the back of their wagon and prepared to drive him back to Yole. Just before they rode off, however, the second smith hopped down, ran back inside the shop and returned with a four-foot pole with a large hook attached to its end.

"You ever need to open that emergency door," he said, handing the pole to Jimmer, "stand back and use this."

Jimmer nodded, assuring him he would—and he knew he meant what he was promising. If the iron oven ever started screaming like a shrike, four feet away was already much closer than he'd want to be.

Jimmer hauled the oven and steambox down to the lake bank and mentioned nothing about the shrikes or the vent door to the workers, allowing the forbidding look of the thing to serve as sufficient notice that it should be approached with respect. The boatbuilders seemed to understand, circling the giant piece of ironwork cautiously, occasionally reaching out to touch it, but rarely moving much closer. In short order, however, they forgot all about the steambox and turned back to the ship. It would take several days before they could finish their deck-beaming and lower floor-laying and turn their attention to heating and bending the hull planks. Wasting time now giving egg-eyes to the steambox was not something they could afford to do.

Jimmer spent that week studying up on the steaming and marking the planks that would need the treatment, while Teedie tended mostly to his own small team of builders at the lake. He said nothing to anyone about the coin he'd found or his plans for it, knowing full well that Nacky or Emma would stop him before he set so much as a toe out of town. He'd have to pick the right moment to go, and this was not it. Nacky himself divided his own time that week between overseeing the boat construction and working with Emma Hay on the calculations for the sails and ropes.

As Emma had explained to him, she could not provide the cord the ship needed, but she knew of a net and line workshop in Little M'croom that could. Unlike most local businesses, which operated on a strict cash basis, the workshop conducted nearly all of its transactions on credit. The practice was a risky one since there was always a danger that a boat with loaned rope would come back with an empty hold, or worse, not come back at all. If the ship returned full, however—which most did after dropping their fishing nets in the rich seas off Twelve Points and the M'crooms—there was plenty of revenue to pay for every inch of cord that had been advanced. When Emma sent word to the owners of the workshop that a vessel as large as the one in Yole would be needing rigging, they agreed straightaway to talk with Nacky and provide what was required, but only if he came to Little M'croom himself and impressed them that the boat was a worthy vessel and he was a worthy owner.

Finding the cloth for the sails was easier than finding cord for the rigging, since Emma herself could lay hands on all the fabric the builders might need. Sails were generally made of one of two kinds of cloth—flax and canvas—both of which Emma could get. Flax was the lighter of the pair and thus the better, since hanging sails on masts put a lot of weight up in the air, and it didn't do for a vessel to become too top-heavy. For a boat that was as jitter-built as the Yole clipper was likely to be, such a featherweight cloth was the best choice. The problem was that flax also cost dear—much dearer than canvas and other humbler materials.

"It's gonna have to be canvas, no matter what the weight," Nacky told Jimmer, "and we're gonna have to do this business on credit too, same as with the ropes. If the cloth supplier don't advance us all we need, I'll have to pay for the rest."

"With what coin?" Jimmer asked. "You've got nothin' but your wages from your *Walnut Egg*."

"That ain't nothin'."

"That's your pay-up for your foot. You lose that, Mally Baloo's gonna be sendin' the wagon to your house too when the fall comes."

"Then I reckon we better have the boat built before then." Even as

Nacky said that, he went a little cold and felt a little sickened at the prospect of an empty purse come autumn. The constable's gems and deed of land swam up unsummoned in his mind, and he pushed them back down.

Emma urged Nacky to be off to Little M'croom to meet with the cord men as soon as possible, and he agreed to go—but not until the steaming got under way. He was still worried about trusting even Jimmer with so perilous a business and wanted to make sure the work was well in hand before he left. The day the steaming finally did start, Nacky, Teedie and Orro appeared at the lake early and were surprised to find that Jimmer, Bara, Chuff and several of the other builders were already there—the prospect of firing the oven apparently having stirred all of them up so much that sleep had come hard. The rest of the workers arrived shortly after, as did an unusually large crowd of people gathering on the rim of the bowl.

Jimmer had already positioned the oven and steamer as close to the edge of the lake as possible, figuring this would provide a handy source of water to fill the reservoir in the pipe. He and Nacky also made it a point to move their table and books only a dozen or so feet from the oven, the better to oversee its operation, as well as to make it clear to the builders that they were completely sure they could manage the infernal thing—even if they weren't. Teedie, Bara and Orro joined Jimmer and Nacky at the table, as did Chuff, who seemed especially curious about the steaming. The other workers hung cautiously back near the wood piles.

When all was in place, Nacky turned to Jimmer and asked for workers from the sort-and-carry teams to bring the first stack of teak planks over for bending. Several volunteers, including Meddo Brinn, stepped forward, hauling a large pile of parts and depositing them on the ground in front of the mouth of the steamer. At a nod from Jimmer, Teedie then stepped to the edge of the lake and scooped several gallons of cold water into a spouted bucket. Opening the vented door in the pipe that connected the oven and the steamer, he poured the water into the reservoir.

Then, he gathered up a few of Jimmer's dry roof timbers, loaded them into the oven and looked back at Jimmer.

"Reckon I'll see to the rest," Jimmer said.

As Teedie retreated to the table, Jimmer stepped toward a small smoldering fire he had left burning on the bank. He picked up a fat piece of lit kindling, advanced toward the oven and put the flame to the dry cedar. The wood caught and began to flare a bright orange, producing a soft, gunpowder popping. Jimmer tossed the kindling inside and closed the iron door with a clang, watching as the vent windows in the front and sides of the oven started to dance with bright, striated light. He took a reassuring look at the closed vent door in the top of the oven, then stepped back to the table.

For several long moments, the people on the bank and ridge remained still, watching as the fire grew brighter and brighter. As it did, the oven began drawing in air from the outside, causing one of the lower vents in the big door to produce a fine, high whistle like the trill of a songbird. The single whistle was joined by two more, as the other lower vents began drawing breath and producing their own clear tones. A moment later, the air being inhaled through the bottom vents was exhaled through three upper ones, causing these to whistle an entirely different three-note tone. All together, the six vents produced a perfect, piping chord, the sweet sound of it rising up to fill the lake bowl and echoing off its walls. On the bank, the workers emitted a small gasp of surprise. In their big wagon cage, August Ren's birds began to flap and twitter, answering the trilling from the lake with a song of their own.

"Them smiths," Jimmer said, nodding in admiration. "Them Knockle smiths."

Jimmer turned to smile at Teedie, Nacky and Bara, who nodded back. Chuff saw none of them, standing utterly still with his eyes closed, the familiar blank look on his face now replaced by one of quiet peace.

The oven chord continued to play, and when it had grown a bit louder, Jimmer turned to the Dreeboys and called out.

"Now," he said.

The brothers stepped forward, snatched a teak plank from the pile, and swaddled it in wet rags. Then they slid the wrapped board into the maw of the steamer and slammed the door. If the oven worked true, the wood should not take long to drink up the heat and vapor and loosen up its grain. Jimmer waited several minutes, then turned to the Dreeboys and nodded again. The brothers wrapped their hands in more wet rags, opened the steamer door, pulled out the hot plank and stripped the swaddling from it. Then they placed one of its ends against the bank, lifted the other end up and began pressing down in the middle. Slowly, the wood began to bend.

"Give it less," Jimmer called. "Not any more than we said." The Dreeboys eased back, allowing the wood to straighten some.

"Less still," Jimmer said. "It can't take no more than six degrees." The brothers loosed their hold even further, and Jimmer leaned forward, squinting at the plank and angling his head this way and that. Finally, he saw the angle he liked. "Hold!" he shouted.

The Dreeboys did as they were told, bracing the wood with precisely the arc Jimmer wanted and waiting as its grain gave up its heat and its steaming slowly stopped. Then they relaxed their grip, shook the rags off their hands and righted the wood. The plank held its curve like a well-strung bow. The bigger Dreeboy held the plank above his head triumphantly, and a cheer erupted around the lake. Nacky threw his arm around Jimmer's shoulder. A grinning Bara embraced them both.

"Just as you said!" she called to Jimmer over the cheering. "Bends just as you said!"

Over the next hour, the workers transformed themselves into an efficient steaming and bending team. Some of them took on the job of keeping the wrap rags wet, others saw to the business of swaddling the wood, still others oversaw the matter of loading the cedar kindling into the oven. It was the Dreeboys alone, however, who did the actual bending, eventually producing a small pile of half a dozen perfectly shaped planks. As the seventh was being readied for the steamer, Jimmer grew concerned and turned to Nacky.

"I'm not sure I like the state of that oven," he said. "We been pushin' it hard for a while now. I say we steam one more bit and then vent it for a while." Nacky agreed and Jimmer turned to the Dreeboys and held up an index finger. "One more," he mouthed.

The brothers nodded, slid the plank they had just swaddled into the steamer and closed the door. As the board warmed, the people on the bank at last began to lose interest and slowly dispersed into the day's other work teams. The people on the ridge retreated too, their heads disappearing from over the rim of the bowl. Even Bara turned away, looking out over the work site to see what construction would need doing first this morning. Only Nacky, Teedie and Jimmer kept their eyes on the oven, unwilling to turn away until the plank was withdrawn and the fire could be cooled. Suddenly, from behind the table, Chuff spoke up quietly.

"Whistle's changin'," he said to no one in particular.

With his soft voice and indifferent tone, no one heard what he said. At the top of the lake bowl, however, there was an odd disturbance, as the birds in August Ren's wagon broke off their trilling and began chirping fretfully, flapping toward the rear perches of their cage. Nacky, Bara, Teedie, Jimmer and even Orro the pig turned toward the bird clatter.

"Whistle's changin'," Chuff repeated, louder this time. Jimmer swiveled his head to face him.

"What do you mean changin'?" he asked.

"Don't know," Chuff answered. "I don't like it, though."

As he said this, the sound coming from the oven changed indeed. Its register began to slide and shift. Its piping notes began to jump off their tracks, skidding into minor keys and grating and scraping against each other. Nacky and Bara winced and felt their teeth go on edge. Jimmer's eyes widened. The new whistle, he recognized, sounded precisely like the call of a shrike.

"The hook!" he shouted to Teedie. "Give me the hook!"

Teedie reached under the table, pulled out the four-foot pole with the metal attachment that the smiths in Knockle had made and handed it to Jimmer. Jimmer grabbed the pole and held it in front of himself like a spear. He began advancing cautiously toward the oven.

"That ain't safe!" Nacky shouted as Jimmer inched forward.

"It ain't safe to leave it be!" Jimmer shouted back.

The just-forming work teams dropped their hammers and turned back to watch, and the just-dispersed townspeople on the ridge once again poked their heads over the bowl. From the corner of his eye, Nacky thought he saw one person in the crowd not moving toward the oven, but backing away from it. It looked like Meddo Brinn, and he looked to be carrying an odd sort of shiny mallet, one entirely different from those the other workers used. No sooner had Nacky noticed Meddo, however, than he forgot all about him, Jimmer's approach to the oven holding his attention so.

Jimmer crept closer to the hot box of fire, feeling the heat rise in front of him and the air start to melt and swim. Through the vents in the top of the oven, needles of smoke began to stream. Through the lower vents in the door, bright, yellow-white flame began to emerge. If Jimmer hadn't known better, he'd have even thought the oven as a whole was turning a dull, shimmering red. When he was just a step or two away, he poked the pole forward and caught its hooked end on the latch of the safety door. Pulling with his shoulders and upper body, he gave it a hard tug. Nothing happened. He changed his grip, planted his feet and tried again. Still nothing. Closing his eyes against the searing heat, Jimmer smelled something foul and realized with alarm that it was the forward wisps of his hair and eyebrows curling and melting away. The shrike-scream of the oven filled his ears. He gave the pole a final pull—one as useless as the two before it—shook it free and staggered backward, stumbling toward the table.

"It's froze!" he shouted over the noise of the oven as Nacky and Teedie caught him. "It's froze tight!"

"Can we douse the fire?" Nacky called back.

"Can't get the water in them slats fast enough!"

"Can we push the whole thing into the lake?"

"It's too hot and too heavy!"

The oven noise now grew even louder, and the iron body of the thing began to shake and jump, causing the people on the bank to back away. Nacky turned and pushed Bara, Chuff, Teedie and Orro back. The girl, the dwarf and the pig obeyed, but Teedie resisted, standing beside Nacky and Jimmer. Nacky, casting an anxious eye at the oven, now gave Teedie another push, inadvertently causing the boy to lose his footing and stumble over Chuff. Teedie hit the ground and landed next to a heavy mallet one of the retreating workers had dropped. He snatched it up, leapt back to his feet and began to force the handle down into the clawed grip of his ruined right hand. He winced as the fat wood dowel worked its way into the clenched fingers, and, with a throaty groan of pain, he tensed the hand's hard and scarred muscles even tighter around it. Then he spun back around and charged the oven.

"No!" Nacky called.

"Stop!" Jimmer cried.

Teedie ignored them both and in several quick bounds was directly in front of the fire. The big door of the oven was no longer a dull red but was brightening into an angry orange. Smoke and flame were streaming through the riveted seams in its sides and bottom. Teedie felt the heat hit him like a wall, and from the front of his shirt, curls of smoke began to rise; his eyebrows vanished in an acrid puff, and his eyelashes followed. Heedlessly, he reared back and took a great swing at the vent door, hitting the latch square with the mallet head. The clumsy hammer gave off a loud clang but moved the latch only a splinter of an inch. Teedie swung again and felt the latch give again, feeling at the same time the hair on his arms and across his temples flame and vanish. He thought he felt his cheeks begin to burn and blister too. Crying out furiously, he pounded the latch again and again, no longer sure if he was opening it up or merely mashing it to uselessness. Finally, with a last great swing, he struck a dead-on hit. With a loud screech, the latch popped back and the safety door the Knockle smiths had taken such care to cut blew open with a clang. A huge, rectangular column of bright white fire roared up from it.

Teedie was blown backward by the force of the burst and landed on his back on the ground, his eyes wide open, his hair singed black, his shirt and trousers streaming smoke. The crowd on the bank surged toward him, but Nacky, Jimmer and Bara reached him first and fell around him, shouting out his name and patting out his smoldering clothes. The heat Teedie gave off was horrible to feel, and the charnel-house stink of burned skin was awful to smell. But Nacky could also see that the boy was awake and aware and breathing evenly. Very faintly, he also seemed to be smiling. In the background, the shrieking of the oven returned to a trilling, and the trilling silenced itself altogether. Nacky looked down at the ground and let his eyes fall on Teedie's ruined right hand. Even now, he could see, it was tightly gripping the heavy mallet.

CHAPTER TWENTY-NINE

In the moments after the oven erupted—
as Teedie lay smoldering and smiling on the bank—the ship workers re-
acted fast. Grimm and Anna Bland dove for the pile of wood-wrapping
rags and with the help of Bara and Nacky, sat Teedie up, stripped away
his shirt and wound the wet, cooling cloth around him. While they
worked, the Dreeboys snatched up two teak beams and still more cloth
and fashioned a crude stretcher that would have likely torn under the
weight of almost anybody else but would be more than strong enough
to carry a leaf of a boy like Teedie. When the Blands had Teedie fully
wrapped, Nacky, Jimmer and the Dreeboys laid him on the stretcher and
carried him across the bank toward the lake path, with Orro scrabbling
fretfully behind.

As the group moved through the crowd, the workers pushed close
to get a clear look at the scorched boy, and the Dreeboys protectively
stiff-armed them away. Most of the people needed only one rough shove
from the brothers to keep their distance, but Meddo Brinn was oddly
persistent. He fought his way through the crowd and appeared at the side
of the stretcher, his features creased in an expression that went beyond
worry and appeared more like a look of guilt.

"Ordinary oven don't go like that," Meddo mumbled, hurrying beside the group and nearly getting his feet tangled up with the older Dreeboy's.

"Stand clear!" the brother snapped, giving Meddo a hard push.

"But an ordinary oven don't go like that," Meddo repeated.

The Dreeboys and the others rushed on with the stretcher, leaving Meddo behind on the bank. Nacky, his attention fully focused on Teedie, did not notice Meddo at all.

For the rest of the trudging trip to Dr. Mull's house, Teedie remained neither fully awake nor fully unconscious, looking blankly ahead with a serene expression on his face, the hammer held tight in his twisted fist. Nacky had a hard go of it as the group struggled along, fighting both to support his share of the stretcher and to keep his footing on the rutted padroad, as the heat of the early August day caused his ankle to sweat and the socket of his loblolly foot to grow damp and uncomfortable. When they at last arrived at the doctor's house, the group struggled up the porch and clambered inside without knocking on the unlocked front door, calling out to Dr. Mull as they entered. The doctor appeared a moment later, hurrying down the stairs from the second floor. He was a small man with dark hair and a plump, pink face—plumper and pinker than Nacky had remembered.

"What happened?" he asked.

"Bad burn," Jimmer answered.

"More of this boat business, I s'pose," the doctor said, pushing Nacky, Jimmer and the Dreeboys aside and crouching over Teedie. "Might've known a bird-boy like Teedie wouldn't be safe around that thing."

"The boat ain't responsible," Nacky said. "It was the oven."

"Same work," Dr. Mull said, with an unpleasant look at Nacky, "same result."

The doctor looked at Teedie appraisingly, unwrapped his wet swaddlings and spent a moment taking the measure of his burns. Then he lifted up the boy's claw hand and, with a surer touch than Nacky would have expected, coaxed the fingers open and removed the mallet. He turned the hand over and over in his own, examining it for a moment.

It was the first time he'd had cause to tend to Teedie since he'd tried to mend the broken hand and done such a donkey's job of it. Nacky couldn't tell now if he was looking at the thing with pride of workmanship or shame at the mess he'd made of it. Finally, the doctor rocked back on his heels and looked at Nacky and the others.

"I expect I can make him right again," he said. "I expect it'll take a week or so."

Dr. Mull pointed to a cool back room off the parlor and instructed Nacky, Jimmer and the Dreeboys to carry Teedie there and lay him on a small cot. The doctor then disappeared and returned with water, clean bandages, shears, a razor and several bottles of liniments. As Nacky and the others watched, he cut Teedie's shirt and trousers away, then washed him down, gently swabbing off scorched cloth and stray ash and revealing red but surprisingly unmolested skin underneath. He then soaked the bandages in a combination of the liniments and wrapped Teedie tight in them. Finally, he took the shears and razor to the boy's remaining hair, cut it clean away and wrapped his scalp in the same treated cloths. Then he turned to Nacky.

"Take those," he said, gesturing toward the teak beams and the dirty rags that had been the sling. "Hammer that wood back into your boat where it belongs. Come for the boy in seven days."

CHAPTER THIRTY

In the week Teedie Flinn was recov-
ering from his burns, Nacky never got a clear night's sleep. A boy like
Teedie who'd already taken so many hard blows surely didn't deserve one
more, and it was Nacky's boat that had dealt him this one. It had been
a fool's choice to allow the steaming to take place at all, never mind to
allow Teedie anywhere near the angry oven. It even seemed like folly for
Nacky not to have simply accepted the constable's offer and walked away
from the boat—keeping the boy safe and giving them both newfound
riches to share.

But it was in the service of the vessel that Teedie had been so seared,
and now it would seem all the worse to make him bear that pain for
nothing. In short order, Nacky and Jimmer thus saw to it that the steam
box that had nearly taken Teedie's life went straight back into operation.
There were fewer than seven weeks left before autumn arrived, and
there was no more time to waste if the builders were going to get about
the planking.

Before Jimmer dared light another steam fire, he examined the oven
closely and determined that despite the accident, the vent door fit its
opening perfectly, swinging on its hinges with no resistance. The only

thing that could have caused the door to jam then would have been a bent latch; and the only thing that could have bent the iron hook and eye in the first place would have been a hammer heavily applied to them—one with an odd head, meant for hard but precise work.

"Can't reckon it," Jimmer said.

"Easy enough to understand if you quit thinkin' it was careless damage and take hold that it was purpose damage," Bara said.

"You're comin' unpinned," Nacky responded.

"Believe what you will," Bara answered. "But I notice you ain't seen Meddo Brinn around since the oven went wrong."

Nacky peered around the bank and realized she was right. It was only then he recalled the maybe-memory of Meddo backing away when the oven slats first started making their shrike calls.

The cause of the accident aside, the steambox soon went back to work, with Jimmer mastering how to measure out his kindling pile precisely, producing a fire that was neither too mean nor too weak for the hot-tempered oven. Once Nacky was assured the steaming was again under way, he was free to turn his attention back to Emma Hay and the work on the ropes and sails.

In recent days, Nacky had been spending all of his free time either visiting Teedie at Dr. Mull's or dropping in on Emma at the indigents' home. More and more, it seemed, he scheduled those visits to the home around mealtimes. The girls' lunches and dinners, he discovered, were as fine as their breakfasts, consisting of thick stews or soups, roasted fish or game, boiled vegetables and fried potatoes, crusty breads with yam or berry pastes, pickled ginger and little sweetcakes at the end. The fact that Nacky and his pig always seemed to arrive just as the table was being laid did not escape Emma's notice, and after a few days, she took to waiting until he was inside and then calling out to the girls, "Seems as if Orro and Orro have come to visit again." When the girls would laugh in delight at the hungry Nacky being confused with his pig, Emma would look about in mock surprise and ask, "You mean these two aren't brothers? The girl who picks which one is the man gets an extra sweetcake." So dearly did the girls love this game that the ten-year-old Mag and the eight-year-old Gurtee never again did call Nacky by his proper name, always addressing him as Orro and laughing until their eyes watered as they did.

But Nacky dropped by the home for more than the food, and in the week Teedie was recovering, Emma and her girls made remarkable progress on his sails. Emma had only to send one of the oldest girls into Bowfin with a bank draft and a letter of request for a quantity of cloth, and within three days, a pair of wagons loaded with canvas arrived at the home. The wagons appeared after dark to prevent any wide-eyes in town from prying into the home's dealings. In the event that someone did notice the hitches clattering up, the drivers were instructed to keep their cargo covered and to explain that they were delivering bran meal for mixabout and stump stones for repairing the foundations of the house.

No one in Yole did bother to challenge the wagons, and when the drivers arrived and threw back the tarps concealing their cargo, Nacky beamed at what he saw. Filling the wagon beds were dozens of long cloth rolls, stacked in piles like giant loaves. Even in the pale light of the gibbous moon, their rough texture and telltale yellow were visible. Each roll of material looked fearfully heavy, and all of them together caused the wagons to ride low on their axles. It took the two drivers and one cargo man to unload all the cloth, wrestling the rolls up the steps of the home and depositing them in the main room—Emma shushing them all the while so that they wouldn't awaken the girls sleeping upstairs. Nacky watched the rolls being carried from the wagon and briefly—and somewhat surprisingly—felt the thief heat well up inside him. Unbidden, his mind had begun calculating and recalculating the worth of the cloth and reflecting on how easy it would be to filch it all and sell it off. He blinked several times until his head cleared.

When the wagons were empty and the men were gone—their palms well covered by some folding money Emma insisted Nacky pay them for their trouble—Nacky at last went inside and took a good, close look at the cloth in the light of the brilliant workhouse lanterns. When he did, he frowned. Stenciled along the edges of every roll, like the border work on a bolt of damask, were the words "Property of the Yole Indigents' Home."

"What is that?" Nacky asked in a voice louder than he intended.

"Sshh!" Emma answered and lowered her own voice to a whisper. "It's the cloth for your sails."

"My sails with your name," he hissed.

"Your sails with the home's name. That's the way they store it for us. You want it unmarked, you wait a month, maybe more."

"Those sails go up the way they are, Mally Baloo will know for sure what goes on in this home."

"Not if we seam the stencil inside the hem so no one knows it's there."

"And if he looks inside or puts the yellow color together with your girls' yellow frocks?"

"I'll see those sails burned before I'll let him raise a hand to touch them," Emma answered flatly.

Nacky looked at the rolls again, running his eyes over them slowly. "There ain't one that ain't branded," he said mournfully.

Emma smiled and nodded agreeably. "And a good thing, as I see it. The moment we cut cloth on them things, my girls own a piece of that boat. If you were ever inclined to forget that fact, I reckon you won't now."

It was the very next morning that the cutting and stitching began. With the help of the two oldest girls, Nacky and Emma moved all the worktables to the edges of the main room to open up space for the rivers of cloth on the polished floor. Working from diagrams in Dree's books and notes written in Jimmer's hand, they unrolled and sheared off several lengths of canvas and opened them up wide. With little more than a glance at the books and a word or two of explanation from Emma, the girls then converged on the cloth, hemming and stitching along seams and edges, their hands moving deftly and their needles flashing meanly. Even with the diagrams to consult, Nacky could make no sense of exactly how the sails were taking shape, but Emma and the girls obviously could, standing back and smiling as the work progressed, seeing not just the piece of canvas in front of them, but the entire sail laid out in their minds. The girls worked through the week, developing a surer and surer hand with the canvas, while Nacky watched and fretted.

"You reckon you know what you're doing?" he'd ask Emma, glancing back and forth between a sail diagram in his hands and a stretch of canvas on the floor.

"I reckon I do exactly," Emma would answer. "You want to speed things along?"

"I do."

"Then go off to Little M'croom like we discussed. There's rope that needs gettin' still."

"Not with them sails unfinished."

"The girls and I will see to the sails."

"Not with Teedie in bed and bandage."

"The doctor will see to Teedie. It seems there's only one person here not tending to his business."

Nacky nodded. "I expect that's true," he conceded with a sigh. "I expect I'll go."

Emma took the sail diagrams from his hands and shooed him toward the door. "Girls!" she called out. "There'll be plenty of food at table tonight. The Orros will be off to the coast." From around the room the girls laughed delightedly.

That same morning, Nacky and his pig stopped at the doctor's house, said good-bye to Teedie and set off for the half-day trip to the town of Little M'croom.

CHAPTER THIRTY-ONE

Teedie was impatient for a lot of things during the long week he spent at Dr. Mull's house, but most of all, he was impatient for Nacky Patcher to get out of town. It was only when Nacky was gone that Teedie could at last get about business of his own.

As such things went, Teedie's recovery was a pleasant one. Whatever was in the liniment Dr. Mull spread on his burns, it proved to be remarkable stuff, cooling him when his damaged skin felt too hot, warming him when his raw flesh grew too chilled. The heavy paste even smelled agreeable, sometimes carrying the whiff of cut cucumber, other times giving off the scent of grape or mint. Several times Teedie asked what the liniment was made of, but Dr. Mull's answer was always the same.

"What you need," he'd say. Since Teedie's burns were healing fast, he couldn't argue the point.

The better Teedie began to feel, the more he squirmed to get back to the lake. To keep the boy in harness, Nacky would spend his daily visits describing that day's boat work and the plans for the next day, even inventing a problem now and then so that Teedie could turn his mind to coming up with a solution—one that Nacky would pretend to carry down to the lake that very afternoon and that would, to hear him report it later, have worked perfectly.

When Nacky wasn't dropping by, Mag and Gurtee from the indigents' home were. Their visits, Teedie supposed, were more agreeable than Nacky's. They didn't scold him about staying in bed and getting his rest the way Nacky did, though they did whisper and giggle to each other a great deal more than he cared for, especially when Dr. Mull would show them in and announce them as Teedie's "lady friends."

Mag and Gurtee would typically come to call late in the afternoon, having fibbed to Emma that they were going down to the lake to watch the boat get built. An unaccompanied visit to such a dangerous place as the lake did not seem to be the kind of outing Emma would permit—at least not if she really believed that was where the girls were going. Yet Mag and Gurtee kept showing up, often bringing along a small basket of sweetcakes Emma had packed for them with instructions to hand the treats out at the lake if anyone there looked peckish. Teedie couldn't help noticing that the cakes Emma chose were his favorite kind, and while there were never nearly enough for a lake bank full of hungry workers, there were just the right amount for a boy and two girls passing an afternoon visit.

But Teedie was grateful to Mag and Gurtee for more than the cakes. More and more, he was thinking about the journey he needed to make out of town, and more and more he was convinced they could help him make it.

During one of the girls' visits, Teedie sat up in bed, swung his legs over the side and drew close to them—something that started them giggling more heatedly than ever. Then he reached under his mattress and pulled out the bright silver coin wrapped in his small, tattered kerchief. The coin had been in his pocket during the explosion at the lake, and indeed every moment since the evening he'd found it. When he woke from his injuries, he found that Dr. Mull had returned it to him just as it was, still inside the kerchief that was still inside the shredded pants he had cut off him when he arrived. The doctor may or may not have been a very gifted physician, but he was surely an honest one. Teedie unwrapped the coin and displayed it to the girls.

"Silver," he said, watching their eyes go wide, "and a fine grade of it too." He was not at all certain that last part was true, but since the girls would be even less knowledgeable about the matter than he was, he could say what he pleased. Handing the coin to Gurtee, he explained what he had in mind.

That very day, Mag and Gurtee traveled to the edge of Yole and flagged down one of the noddy drivers who made the regular run from the mountains to the coast. The man was ruddy-faced and sour looking, but his horse was magnificent—an orange and white beast with a high head and ink-black hooves. Mag told the man what Teedie needed and produced the coin from her apron. The expression on his face told her that he appreciated the value of the thing, and though she briefly feared he might simply snatch it for himself, stealing from girls was beneath all but the hardest highwaymen, and the driver did not so much as move. He assured Mag that he cruised these roads every day, and if Teedie required his services, all he'd have to do was appear here and wait a bit.

The day Nacky left for Little M'croom, Teedie asked Dr. Mull if his burns had healed enough for him to leave his care. The doctor examined the boy and pronounced him well, and Teedie lit straight out for the padroad. Within an hour, the wagon man indeed drove by.

"You the boy with the coin?" the driver asked.

"I am."

"I'll need my payment before I set to work," the man said.

"I'll need your work before you'll have your payment," Teedie answered.

The two resolved to cut the melon in the middle, with the driver agreeing to wait for his pay until he took Teedie to Knockle, and Teedie agreeing to trust that the man would also deliver four other wagons when needed and share the wealth out among all the drivers. They shook hands on the arrangement—the driver pulling back at the feel of Teedie's claw-fingers. Before hopping aboard the hitch, however, Teedie paused and took the horse's tail in his hand. Then he raised it to his mouth, bit off several long strands and stuffed them in his pocket.

"Here now!" the man cried. "What are you after?"

"Only one horse like yours about," Teedie answered, "and near as I know, only one coin like mine. You take my money and light-foot on our deal, I want to be able to put the man what fleeced me together with the silver he took."

The man gave Teedie a long hard look through his heavy-lidded eyes and gestured him sharply up into the wagon. Within a moment they were jouncing down the road and off to the town of Knockle—a place Teedie hadn't been since the time of the blackfire.

CHAPTER THIRTY-TWO

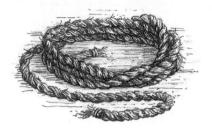

Nacky Patcher's trip to Little M'croom
was slower than he'd reckoned it would be. With no wagon to call his
own, he had arranged to borrow Grimm and Anna Bland's—a rattly hitch
pulled by an equally rattly horse, neither of which could move very fast
without threatening to break down. Anna regarded Nacky with a cool
eye as he climbed up into the seat and prepared to leave, the sure look of
a townsperson who—even now—worried whether property lent to Nacky
Patcher would ever be seen again. Nacky sighed and plodded off. Even
he could not summon up much thief heat over a horse and wagon the
likes of these.

It wasn't just the state of the conveyance that made the going slow,
it was the state of the highway too. Unlike the road that led in and out
of Yole, which was principally traveled by the people who lived in the
town, the long, main road that ran out of the mountains and down to
the coast was a well-trod one. Commercial wagons from all around the
region traveled along it daily, carrying goods into and out of the busy
fishing villages. Townsfolk from Yole, unaccustomed to driving such a
popular thoroughfare, were regularly warned to maintain a sharp eye for
these busy hitches, whose drivers often raced along at dangerous speeds,

heedless of the slower, less certain rigs picking their way along the route for the first time.

Nacky and his pig had been on the road in their jouncing wagon for what seemed like little more than minutes when they heard a clattering from behind and looked back to see a red cloud of road dust advancing toward them, the snout and forelegs of a galloping horse rhythmically poking through it and disappearing. The horse-and-wagon cloud drew closer and louder, spooking Nacky's own horse, who whinnied fearfully and picked up the pace of his trot. Within seconds the approaching horse was nose-to-tailboard behind Nacky's rig. Then it heeled left, clattered past and sped noisily ahead, causing Nacky's horse to veer and shy. In the bed of the receding wagon, Nacky could see a great ball of tan cord more than five feet across, rolling and thudding from side to side, with only the high rails of the speeding hitch to keep it from bouncing into the road. Nacky had heard about these cord wagons, which ran daily to the coast, supplying the fishing fleets with raw rope and other gear. He counted the sight of the hitch a good omen, since it was likely heading for the same net and line workshop Nacky himself was planning to visit today.

It was not until late in the day that Nacky at last arrived in Little M'croom. As always when he visited, he was struck by both the size and the sense of industry of the place. The business center of the bright coastal community was far larger than Yole's modest stretch of shops, and even had something of the feel of a proper city about it. The streets were paved with new brick and stone, and Nacky's horse found the footing unsettlingly slick. On several occasions, Nacky had to pull back suddenly on the animal's reins as another wagon came racing out of a side street, cutting Nacky off and causing the horse to whinny and wobble.

"Hold hard!" Nacky would shout at them.

"Rig or walk, rig or walk!" the other drivers would answer, which Nacky took to be a recommendation that he either learn to drive his hitch properly or abandon it altogether.

Nacky imagined that the hurried people on the crowded sidewalks would have noticed these scrapes, but if they did, they didn't show it, so preoccupied were they with whatever late-day mission they were on at the moment. Judging by their clothes, Nacky took most of them to be fishermen, racing to or from the quay with only the sea on their minds. Occasionally he saw better-dressed men whom he took to be involved in the mercantile trades. The women of the town appeared to be of two groups as well, married either to the boatmen or the money men. The fishwives were recognizable by the tackle or other gear they carried and the fish blood that flecked their aprons. The rich wives wore what looked like Sunday clothes and carried nothing but baskets for their shopping.

The places that shopping could be done seemed as numerous as the people themselves. As Nacky poked along, he saw shops that sold clothing, dry goods, food, fabric, shoes and high-cost horse rigging. There was a shop that sold musical instruments, a shop that sold parlor furniture, a shop that sold glassware and a shop that sold—near as Nacky could tell—nothing but buttons. There were also at least three pubs or restaurants, all far bigger than the Albert T. Rain and all finer too.

When Nacky finally reached the quay, he stiffened, this being the first time he had returned to the docks since the darkly recalled days after he bumped ashore on his *Walnut Egg* door. He saw the harbormaster's office where he had confronted Alfred Puddemsey, the infirmary where he had spent so many thrashing nights, the black wall of slick retaining stones that his door had fetched up against when he at last struck land. He closed his eyes against the memory, and next to him, Orro the pig seemed to shrink back too.

"Them's stones," Nacky said, patting Orro's bristly flank, "only stones."

Well beyond the infirmary, past a bend in the quay Nacky had never explored before, was a small knot of people and a cluster of wagons, several of which carried tan cord balls just like the one he'd seen on the road. The people and rigs were gathered in front of a large, low building with a sign painted above the door that read "Little M'croom Net and Line Works." Nacky pulled his wagon as close to the building as he could get and carefully jumped down to the street, hearing his loblolly foot clunk against the paving stones and wincing as the concussion traveled up into his ankle. He helped Orro down and the two of them made their way toward the shop.

Nacky had grown accustomed to clump-walking the streets of Yole with his pig trailing behind him, but he had neglected to consider that the two of them might not pass so unremarked upon in unfamiliar Little M'croom. Heads turned as he and Orro limped and scrabbled along, Nacky's dead foot tattooing on the paving and Orro's hooves clattering in counterpoint. Nacky didn't much mind the stares, but he didn't much care for them either, especially when they were joined by laughter, barely masked by hands covering mouths.

"Don't mind them, Orro," he said to the pig. "Ain't worth whatever thought you're givin' them."

Nacky and Orro wove through the crowd, reached the front of the net and line shop, and stepped inside the big, barnlike building. The interior space was cool and shadowed—much cooler and more shadowed than the open quay in the predusk August sun—and it took Nacky's eyes a moment to adjust to the gloom. The air in the room was filled with the scent of rope, and all around him, Nacky could hear the sounds of hurried work, as uncounted voices called out to one another. Blinking about, he began to make out the shapes of at least thirty people bent over worktables, snipping off lengths of cord and braiding up stretches of nets or coils of line. The workers were a varied group—some old, some young, some with the leathery look of onetime fishermen, some with the milky look of full-time shop help. Nacky saw nothing at all to distinguish any of them until a single worker, an ox of a man, rose to his feet at a corner table and turned in his direction. Nacky faced him and instantly felt his knees turn to water. His pig emitted a squeal of pure animal fear. A silence fell over the workshop.

Standing by the table gazing straight at Nacky was Orro, the lost Orro, Orro the man. He was a near-giant like Orro had been, the full of a door, with hammy upper arms that looked as if they had been built

248

for work. The man's hands, even from a distance, looked to be unfortunate things, big and damaged, with a pewter ring flashing dully on one finger. His face was framed by a heavy beard and a generous head of hair, though both were silver-gray, unlike Orro's, which had been a sooty black.

Nonetheless, Nacky had no doubt it was his friend he was seeing. In the hold of the *Walnut Egg*, Orro had told him they just might meet again, and now, it seemed, they had. He turned to the other Orro—the small and scrabbling animal at his side—to see if he saw the same. Orro the pig, however, had crumpled on his haunches and closed his eyes, as if the sight of the big man across the room had simply overcome him. In an instant, Nacky too saw everything go dark and felt the world tumble away.

When Nacky regained his senses, he was sitting on the floor of the net and line shop with his pig lying beside him and a half-dozen faces staring down at him. The faces were swimming dizzyingly, and he recognized none of them except the one framed by a cloud of silver hair and beard. When he saw that one, he jolted upright and struggled to stand.

"Easy there, easy there," the bearded man said to him, and many pairs of hands reached down to hold him in place. "It don't do to move without your wood part."

Nacky looked down and saw that his pine foot had somehow slipped off his ankle and was lying on the floor next to him. He reached out protectively for it, scooped it up and began strapping it back in place, his face reddening. He looked up and the silver-haired man turned away to give him his privacy. The others continued to stare. When Nacky finished, the big man spoke again.

"Stand away," he said to the others. "Man's gonna need room to right himself, ain't he?"

The other people took a few steps back, and the big man reached out his huge, damaged hands and took hold of Nacky by the forearms. The hands, what was left of them, felt warm and powder-dry. With the man's help, Nacky rose up on his good left foot, hopped once to regain his balance, then tried his pine foot against the floor. It was strapped true and would take his weight, so he relaxed and let it carry it. His pig stood up beside him.

"You're Orro," Nacky said hoarsely, looking the man square in the eyes.

"Don't know no Orro," the man said.

"But you're him."

The man nodded. "No. The name's Weaver—or least that's what they call me here." He turned to the people around him and they nodded in agreement. He then flicked his head slightly—a perfect, practiced movement Nacky had seen at sea from seasoned officers who knew how to command men with only the subtlest signs. The other workers read the signal and dispersed, returning to their tables. Weaver turned back to Nacky. "I ain't who you believe I am," he said. "But that don't mean you don't have cause to think you seen me before. I suspect I seen you too."

Nacky looked unconvinced, and Weaver pointed him and his pig out into the August light. The three of them stepped onto the quay and Weaver indicated a piling near the water. Nacky limped to it and sat.

"You been to sea?" Weaver asked.

"I have."

"That's your answer, then. There's lots of big men who look like me on ships."

"You got the right arms."

"Lot of men have me arms."

"You've got the right hands."

"Lot of men ruin their hands."

Weaver held his hands out and turned them over and back. Nacky looked at them and saw the familiar sausage fingers and the familiar missing ones. Even the pewter ring was identical to the one he'd remembered. All at once, however, Nacky jolted. They were Orro's hands all right, but the wrong way around. It was Orro's right hand that was missing the index finger and wore the pewter ring, and it was his left hand that was missing the middle finger. Weaver's hands were reversed.

"They ain't the same hands!" Nacky said.

"No," Weaver answered levelly. "Like I said, they're mine."

Weaver now pulled up a pair of stacked fish crates and sat down on them with a grunt. The slats of the top box bent underneath him. "What's your name?" he asked.

"Nacky Patcher," Nacky responded.

"Nacky Patcher," he said quietly, "I ain't the man you think I am. But I'm told I have a son. He'd'a grown up in a coastal town, fair a bet as any. And he'd'a probably gone to sea—fair bet there too. What he'd look like, I don't know; what name he'd'a took, I don't know either. But if you seen anyone at all, that might be who it was."

Nacky looked in Weaver's face for a long moment and saw the face of the lost mate Orro staring back at him. He spoke softly. "He'd'a looked like you," he said. "And he'd'a called himself Orro."

Weaver smiled slightly. "So you said. A friend of yours?"

Nacky paused. "He was."

"He's dead?"

"Yes. I'm sorry."

"I suppose I'd reckoned that," Weaver said. He looked back at his huge hands and then spoke without looking up. "I said I seen you before too, and I have, in a dream. You was limping like you are; you had your pig like you do. There was a lot of stormy water the color of berries."

"I know that kind of water."

Nacky and Weaver fell silent and looked out across the quay. At length, Weaver spoke. "You come here lookin' for something?"

Nacky nodded. "Rope, rigging. Got me a boat."

"Fishing vessel?"

"No. Clipper."

Weaver whistled softly. "You the captain?"

"Don't have a captain."

"The owner?"

"Own a piece."

"You must be rich."

"Got almost nothing," Nacky said.

"How do you expect to pay for rigging, then?"

"I was told I didn't have to, leastways not right away."

"You was told more or less right. Think you can make money with that boat?"

"I don't know."

"If you can't make money when you got a clipper under you, you can't make money with anything."

"I imagine I can, then."

"But you don't have a captain," Weaver said, and then trailed off.

"No," Nacky answered, "we don't."

"Nacky Patcher," Weaver said, "suppose I fix you some supper?"

Nacky nodded and rose unsteadily to his feet. The two men then walked slowly and silently back to Weaver's home with Orro the pig trailing after. When they got there, the shadows were long, the sun was falling, and Nacky and Weaver grilled up cod steaks and boiled up potatoes and poured some mugs of bark draught. Then they stoked the fire and talked through the night while Nacky's pig ate their scraps and dozed by the hearth. Weaver told Nacky about his long voyages at sea and his recent arrival in Little M'croom, about the *Duchess Isabel* and its odd *plink-pops*. Nacky told Weaver about his short ocean voyage—about the *Walnut Egg* and the storm that unbuttoned it, about the time he spent in the hold of the boat and the time he spent adrift with the two Orros. Then he told him the story of the broken ship in the berry-blue lake, of the work he was doing to put it together. Finally he spoke of the dry-land boats and the curse over Yole and how all might be well if only he could finish his ship and see it hauled safely to the coast. Weaver listened quietly and smiled occasionally and, Nacky was certain, believed him completely.

When Nacky had told his entire tale and morning had almost arrived, Weaver rose and summoned him to the door. "I got something you need to see," he said. "Outside."

Weaver then walked Nacky across his stretch of land to the small shady patch with the perfectly round bubble basin filled with perfectly clear water. In the predawn light, the water shimmered a deep blueberry, and though Weaver might have expected Nacky to look surprised at the pocket pond that was so much like his giant lake, Nacky merely nodded, as if he had anticipated such a thing all along. As the men stared at the water, Nacky thought he saw something glint at him once, then twice, off at the opposite edge of the basin, at the spot that would be just after three on a clock.

"What direction is that?" he asked, pointing to the spot.

"Sharp east," Weaver answered.

"And how far off the mark is that?" he asked, pointing to where he'd seen the glint.

Weaver pondered. "Five degrees, maybe a tick more."

Nacky nodded and grinned broadly. All at once, he was anxious to eat some breakfast, wake his pig and be back on the road as soon as he could get there. He was coming home to Yole with a captain for his ship and the rigging for its masts. And he believed he now knew just where he'd have to look to find the last of his missing boat parts.

OOK FIVE

CHAPTER THIRTY-THREE

Teedie's trip to Knockle was a quick one, the surly driver turning out to be good at his trade and the orange and white horse moving nimbly on its ink-black hooves. As they drew closer to the coast, Teedie felt his heart pick up, trip-hammering both with the fear of returning to a town that had held so much sorrow and the thrill of once again seeing a place that—for everything else it was—had also been his home. When they finally arrived in Knockle, however, the first thing he noticed was that he didn't recognize a whit of it.

In the time Teedie had lived in the half-home, the boys had been kept so busy they never much left the grounds. The only part of the town he thus recalled with any clarity was the route out of it—the long walk he'd made on the morning after the fire, trudging from the burnt grounds to the outer edge of Knockle proper, with the angry expressions of the villagers trailing after him like hornets. When the carriage driver reached Knockle this morning, Teedie therefore had him slowly circle the town until they came upon the end of the street from which he'd emerged on that long-ago morning.

"That's it," he said.

"High time," the driver grumbled.

Teedie hopped down, paid the driver the silver coin and reminded him once more that he'd expect him to honor the remainder of their bargain. Then he patted his pocket where the orange strands of horse tail still lay, in case the driver needed to be reminded of that too. The man nodded his promise crossly and clopped off. Teedie headed straight into town at double-time speed, having no idea what he'd find when he got to the half-home. It was barely fifteen minutes later when he did arrive there, and what he saw shocked him.

The hated half-home had been rebuilt just as it had always looked, made of precisely the same wood and even occupying precisely the same spot, as if the fire had not occurred at all. The land around the house, however, was another matter entirely. The blaze that claimed the home may have taken place three years earlier, but from the look of the grounds, it could have been just hours ago. The soil and grass were a blackened mat, the bushes were shrunk to bones, the few small trees that stood near the house were burned to brittle kindling. Everywhere, the sharp scent of fresh fire hung in the air, and if Teedie looked close and listened hard, he was certain he could even see the occasional wisp of lingering smoke and hear the odd pop of cooling timbers.

This, he knew, was precisely what a blaze caused by blackfire was said to do. Unlike other flame, which burned off whatever it touched but left the ground free to push out green again, blackfire not only murdered anything in its path, but destroyed the ability of the soil to support so much as a shoot ever again. New trees or bushes planted in blackfire land wouldn't just die, they'd die back black, shriveling up as if they'd been freshly put to the torch. Casting his glance around the grounds, Teedie recognized the small new trees and shrubs that the town fathers had planted in the hope that they would take hold in the damaged earth. All of them had quickly died, consumed by the flameless flame the blackfire left behind.

"Frightful," Teedie muttered to himself, the ghost smoke from the dead ground stinging his eyes. "Frightful."

Teedie took a few steps onto the brittle cinders, uncertain what he ought to do next, when he noticed a flutter in the corner of his vision. Flicking his gaze in that direction, he saw a boy crouching on an outcropping of rock, carefully shaking a large cloth in his small hands and looking closely at the ground around him. Teedie recognized the boy's fair hair, pale skin and sticklike limbs.

"Dal!" he called out. "Dal Tally!"

The boy looked in Teedie's direction and creased up his face in a squint. Teedie lit off across the grounds, crunching through the blackened earth and kicking up small soot clouds as he went.

"Dal!" he called again as he drew closer.

"Teedie Flinn?" the boy asked in a loud whisper, looking around himself anxiously as if someone might be listening.

"It is," Teedie answered, matching the boy's hushed tone and bounding up onto the rocks where he stood.

"What in the seas?" Dal said, standing up and clutching his big cloth in his arms. The two boys beamed at each other, but for Dal, this apparently called for some effort.

In the three years since Teedie had last seen him, the always-sickly Dal had become frailer still. He hadn't done much growing that Teedie could discern; his complexion, if anything, had become even sallower; his arms and legs, if anything, had grown twiggier. His thatchy hair poked up this way and that, and his breathing, always weak, sounded more labored still.

"What are you doing here?" Dal asked.

"I come to see you," Teedie answered. "You and the others."

"You shouldn't have. It ain't safe."

Teedie looked around at the empty grounds and the silent house. "Don't look too dangerous to me," he said. "Don't even see no headmaster."

"It's bad, all the same. Things've took a hard turn, Teedie. There ain't just one headmaster no more, there're four. And it ain't just fruit rockets and candles we're makin' now. They've got us tendin' the fish ruts."

Teedie swallowed; that was a hard turn indeed, one that he had feared might be coming. The mercantile men of Knockle had been complaining for years about the hold the local fishing fleet had on the commerce of the community. If only they could grow their own fish, they reckoned—catching a few in the open ocean and then breeding them in giant brick ponds near the coast—they could take at least a piece of the industry for themselves. Getting such a concern going would not be easy. Somebody would have to dig and line the oversized ponds, then run long ruts, also lined with brick, into the sea, so that the fishes' water could be freshened each day by the tides. An iron door with a wide grate that could be opened and closed would permit the seawater to flow in and out of the pools while preventing the fish from escaping. The doors and grates would be built and tended by the same people who dug the ponds and ruts.

"They made them things?" Teedie asked incredulously.

"*We* made them," Dal said. "They started us diggin' and linin' a month after you left, and we ain't stopped since."

"Is that where everyone is now?"

Teedie nodded. "All except me. I ain't deemed fit for the work, so I'm kept tendin' house and layin' table for the headmasters. Often as not, there are scraps on the cloth when I clear; makes for half a real meal if I shake 'em out and collect 'em up."

With that, Dal resumed flapping the cloth he'd been holding in his arms and a few bits of what appeared to be bread, meat and boiled potato scattered on the rocks. Dal moved to pick them up, then looked at Teedie and stopped himself short. Teedie bent, gathered the food and handed it to the smaller boy.

"It ain't right," Teedie said as Dal turned away and ate. "It ain't gonna stand."

Teedie knew he would need at least a few days to study on the circumstances of Dal and the other boys if he was going to come up with a way to free them from the twin prisons of the fish ruts and the half-home. He spent that time staying largely out of sight—sleeping in a stand of trees beyond the blackfire ground at night, slipping out to the quay during the day and hiding on the flat roof of a nearby building to watch the boys at work. He quickly saw that things were even harder on them than he'd imagined.

There were three working fishponds on the quay, each about twenty-five feet across and each connected to the water's edge by a long rut, wide enough and deep enough for a boy to stand up in and spread his arms out. A fourth pond and rut were under construction close by.

The three smallest of the two dozen boys were given the comparatively light task of managing the three working pits—operating the gates, repairing cracks and loose bricks, diving down into the water to clear away dead fish and loose debris. The first of the ponds held three-foot-long princefish, gray and sickly looking things that appeared to be languishing in their brick pit. The middle pond held larger queenfish, which looked healthier than the princefish, but only a bit. The left-hand pond held the true prizes: stonefish—a big, splashing school of them, their broad sides shining like white mica, their big tails breaking and slapping the water. Stonefish were known for meat that tasted sweet, cooked up clean and cost dear. And these particular stonefish seemed even better than most, taking readily to their captivity and breeding so fast the mercantile men could barely take the full-size ones out in time to make room for the young they produced. Whatever line of stonefish this school sprang from was a priceless one indeed.

The twenty-one boys who weren't minding the working ponds were building the new one. The bricks that lined the pits and ruts were each about the size of a bread loaf and had to be carried down into the hole in bags strapped to the boys' backs. A loss of footing could lead to a nasty spill, and if a boy hit the ground face-first, he could easily lose backbones to the brick falling on top of him.

One of the four headmasters supervising the work was the willowy man with the sweet-potato-shaped head who had run the half-home during the fire. He was joined by a shorter, stouter man and two younger, bigger ones. All of them paced the quay with long whipping straps hung from their belts. The willowy man and the stout man usually took at

261

least an hour for lunch at a pub on the quay at about one o'clock. The sturdier men took their break later. The boys themselves worked straight through the nine- or ten-hour days, receiving water every few hours and a lunch of mixabout and bread at noon, which they were expected to finish in ten minutes or less. How they had already managed to build three pits under such conditions Teedie could not imagine.

"It's a wonder ain't no one got killed," he said to Dal after the first day he spent watching the work.

"It's sure to happen in time," Dal said. "Everyone knows it."

But Teedie believed he had come up with a way to prevent that. On the third night he slept in the woods, he waited until Dal came to bring him a few bits of food from the headmasters' table, then kept the smaller boy there while he described his plan. He laid out the idea carefully, quizzed Dal on it once, then twice, then told him to return to the house and creep from cot to cot, explaining it to the other boys—especially the three small ones who tended the working ponds, since they'd have the most to do. Then he quizzed Dal once more.

"I've got hold of it, Teedie!" Dal whispered hoarsely.

"See that you do," Teedie answered. "Because it's the tower for me and likely for you if it don't work."

Dal then went back into the house, and Teedie slipped out of the woods to go find the wagon man and make sure all was in order.

CHAPTER THIRTY-FOUR

The next morning broke clear and
warm, and even before the sun was fully up, it was evident it was going
to be an oven of a day. The boys awoke at dawn and trooped out to the
quay, already panting from the thick morning air. Teedie trailed behind
them and hid on the roof of the nearby house as he had the previous
three mornings. Dal, as always, stayed behind at the half-home.

By eleven o'clock, the day had already turned as fiery as it had
promised it would. Up on his roof, Teedie felt as if he were being grilled
whole by the hovering sun. Down on the quay, the boys worked wordlessly as they were required to, but the sweat that soaked through their
shirts and the desperate way they gulped their water when it was brought
to them said what they could not.

The headmasters were under no contraints to suffer silently, and
even before noon, the willowy man and the stout man were grousing
loudly about the heat, stopping frequently to mop their faces and drink
draughts of water. As soon as their lunch hour arrived, they fell away
from their posts and staggered off to their nearby pub. An hour later
they returned, and the two bigger men retreated. Those two did not go
to the pub as they usually did, however, instead taking shelter under

an overhang of rocks and unpacking a meal and an ale bottle they'd brought with them. If needed, they could bound back to the ponds within seconds. Teedie frowned when he saw this, and the small boy at the queenfish pit looked over his shoulder up to the roof and cast him a nervous glance. Teedie looked back and offered a reassuring nod he did not entirely feel.

Over the course of the hour, Teedie watched as the boys worked, the smaller headmasters paced the quay and the sun angled sharper and burned still brighter. Under their rock ledge, the bigger headmasters worked through their lunch and their ale and then produced a wineskin and drank still more. Then they lay on their backs and rubbed their bellies sleepily.

The small boy at the queenfish pond looked at Teedie again, this time with a smile. Teedie held out the open palm of his good hand in a quieting gesture. At that moment, he heard a clattering of horse hooves from the quay. He looked back and broke into a wide grin. Approaching along the cobblestones was the carriage man and his orange and white horse. Behind him were four more horsemen and four more carriages. In the last carriage was Dal Tally. Teedie wheeled back toward the ponds, smiled at the boy looking up at him and then sprang to his full height.

"Flood the rut!" he shouted as loudly as he could.

The two headmasters guarding the boys wheeled in the direction of his voice. The willowy man with the potato-shaped head saw Teedie's face and went crimson.

"Teedie Flinn!" he shouted angrily.

"Flood the rut!" Teedie repeated.

With that, the boy tending the princefish leapt into the pond, disappeared under the surface and pulled a lever. The grated gate opened full and a great flood of water poured into the brick channel. The huge school of fish followed, flapping and thrashing toward the sea.

"Here now!" the stout headmaster shouted, fumbling for his whipping strap and lunging toward the boy as he broke the water. The willowy headmaster pulled his own strap off his belt more smoothly and began snapping it menacingly. Some of the boys at the other ponds backed away; others held their ground. The boy at the second pond—the queenfish pond—looked at Teedie intently. Teedie shouted again.

"Flood the next!" he said, and on that cue, the boy leapt into the water and opened that gate. The bigger, healthier queenfish spilled into the channel and began flowing away as well.

"Shut that thing!" the willowy headmaster yelled and lunged toward the pond.

Now the two sturdier headmasters awoke, saw the disturbance and ran toward the boys. They were not nearly so awkward as the other two men, sprinting lightly over the stones and swinging their whips with deadly ease. The crack of the straps sounded like tree limbs breaking, and even the boys who had stood their positions before backed away. The headmasters drew closer and closer, the whistling whips grew louder and louder, and Teedie now shouted out once more.

"The last rut!" he called. "Flood it."

"No!" the willowy headmaster shouted.

At that, the small boy tending the stonefish pond dove into the water, just dodging the lick of the biggest headmaster's whip. He vanished beneath the surface for an instant and then the biggest flood of all—filled with the most precious fish of all—poured into the brick channel. The headmasters cried out in a rage and then turned back to the boys, standing frozen between them and the fish. Saving the stonefish, they knew, meant losing the boys; holding the boys meant losing the fish. They could not have both, and for a splinter of an instant they remained rooted where they were. But in truth, it was no choice at all. It was the leaping stonefish, bred for their strength and the price they could bring, that were the true commodities here. Hollow-cheeked orphan boys who languished in captivity could always be replaced. As one, the headmasters flung down their straps and leapt into the rut, fighting to shut the wide-open gate and block the exit of the streaming fish.

Teedie immediately gave out with a loud whistle, and all of the boys scrambled up the quaystones and ran for the wagons. Leaping from his roof, he ran after them, hurrying them along. It was not until the very last boy had reached the hitches and climbed safely aboard that Teedie did too, jumping up next to the lead driver and giving the word to go.

Half a day later, Teedie Flinn, Dal Tally and the rest of the Knockle boys arrived safely in the town of Yole.

CHAPTER THIRTY-FIVE

Emma Hay's weekly visit to the Albert T. Rain to fetch back her girls' end-of-the-week sweet brick was always a chore to her, but to the girl who accompanied her on the mission it was a thrill. Emma made her trip to the Rain late on Friday afternoons, and the indigent girls—or at least the younger ones—took pride in the sober sense of duty that came from helping her bring the beloved bread home. To keep them from quarreling over who would be chosen for the adventure on any particular week, Emma had recently posted an alphabetical list of names so that all the girls would know whose turn was coming due. For those girls who didn't yet know their letters, this was one more reason to learn. On the second Friday in August, the dark-haired, freckled girl named Lassa was due, and this, Emma decided, was a good thing.

Lassa was typically a penny-bright girl, given to constant chatter and occasional mischief. In the days since the sail canvas arrived, however, she'd turned uncharacteristically glum, saying little, picking at her food and wearing a deep fret-line on her forehead. The first several times Emma asked her what was troubling her, Lassa said nothing. It was only two days ago that she at last gathered herself up and mentioned what was on her mind.

"I don't like the boat," she told Emma one evening as she climbed up into her lap after dinner.

"Why not?" Emma asked.

"It don't seem like it'll hold together. Suppose them parts come unbuttoned?"

Emma smiled and worked up a such-nonsense laugh. "Boats don't just unbutton themselves," she said.

"Some do."

Emma was troubled by the exchange. Nacky Patcher had confided in Emma about the final minutes of the *Walnut Egg*—the flying trunnels, the tumbling planks and all the rest. She hadn't yet settled out whether she believed him or not, but she had forbidden him to mention any part of the dark tale to her girls, and she trusted he had obeyed her. Lassa's fears, however, sounded awfully like the death of the *Egg*.

In the nights that followed, the girl grew more frightened still, waking well before dawn and crying aloud about collapsing ships and dying sailors. Emma kept a close watch on her after that and was pleased that the weekly trip to the Albert T. Rain would give them a bit of time together.

Emma and Lassa set out for the Rain earlier in the afternoon than they normally would have, Emma guessing that the girl might prefer it if the restaurant were quiet. As their walk down the business street began, Lassa seemed to come back to herself, chirping to Emma with much of her accustomed brightness. The closer they drew to the Rain, however—with its shiplike bowsprit poking out over the street—the quieter Lassa grew, clinging close to Emma's side and responding to questions with only a nod of the head. When they entered the restaurant, Emma was pleased to see that it was indeed empty, save for Dree herself, bent over the smaller of her two hearths.

"That Emma Hay?" Dree called into the hearth without turning around to look.

"It is," Emma answered.

"I imagine you come for your sweet brick," Dree said, her back still turned. "Hope you can carry both them trays with just that wee freckled girl."

Emma looked down at Lassa and smiled in exaggerated wonder at the seeming clairvoyance of Dree, who over time, had come to know which girls would be coming in when. Lassa smiled back less certainly. The two of them stepped toward the bar, Emma running her eyes over the tidy shelves of plates and mugs on the wall behind it. Her gaze came to rest on the slate board used to count the trunnels. A white number five was scrawled on it. Dree turned around, smiled at Lassa, then followed Emma's eyes.

"Forty thousand parts to start," she said, wiping her hands on her apron, "and just the five now shy."

Emma nodded. "I expect they'll get the thing built before long."

Dree grunted and turned back to her hearth. Wrapping her hands in cloths, she lifted out two trays and set them on a stone slab on the bar to cool. "Be a moment before you can handle them," she said.

Emma nodded and sat on a nearby bar stool. Lassa wandered a step away to the white-wood *Lamplighter* table and began tracing her finger in a wet spot on its surface. Dree pulled up a stool behind the bar and sat.

"Been followin' those numbers, have you?" Dree asked, inclining her head to the slate board.

"I know a bit," Emma answered, feigning unfamiliarity. She had always admired Dree as a woman as sturdy of character as she was of build, but that didn't mean she'd confide even in her about her girls' work on the sails or anything else.

"I read a lot of books about buildin' boats meself," Dree said. "A lot about how long it takes to put 'em together."

"I hear Nacky Patcher says they're halfway done," Emma answered.

"They ain't. Looks like halfway because the boat's took on the shape a boat's supposed to have. But them's just the big parts. Every frame you hammer in place, you still got ten boards or fittings to follow. And they ain't got but six weeks till fall." Dree looked square at Emma and fixed her with a glance that might have passed for friendship if it had been a little softer and might have passed for menace if it had been a little harder. "Even if they do manage to get it built, there'd still be the matter of the sails. Don't expect you know much about them, either."

Emma felt her breath stop and her skin turn marble. She looked back at Dree, who said nothing.

"Warm as a quilt in here with them ovens goin'," Emma said. She turned to Lassa with a smile. "Suppose you sit at a table near the door and busy yourself with a piece of sweet brick."

Lassa looked up from her tracings and beamed, and Emma broke off a piece of the flaky bread from one of the trays. Dree slipped a plate underneath it before any crumbs could fall on the bar. Lassa took the plate and retreated to the table Emma had pointed to.

"What do you know about sails?" Emma asked Dree in a firm, low tone.

Dree regarded her seriously. "Glad you come when things are quiet," she said. "I don't know for sure what you been busyin' yourself with lately and don't nobody else know either. But I been payin' attention. Boat needs sails, you got lots of spare hands, and Nacky Patcher don't come here for his dinners no more. Maybe it means somethin'. Maybe it don't."

Emma flashed a fire look and her snaggle teeth showed. "What it means is what it means. If it concerns my girls, it ain't anybody's affair."

"Ain't sayin' I disagree. But other folks may start askin' all the same."

"What other folks?" Emma asked.

Dree paused. "I had a visit last week," she said. "From Mally Baloo."

Emma blanched. "It ain't so unusual for him to come by," she said.

"No, it ain't. Comes maybe once a year, usually at dinnertime, just to show his face. Last week, though, he come at about this hour, when it was just me. Talked around things at first. But after a time he got 'round to the boat. Wanted to know what people say at my tables when they've got a few malts in 'em—if they really think the thing can be built."

"What did you tell him?"

"Same as I tell anyone what asks me that kind of question. Malt talk is useless talk, and even if I listened to it, I wouldn't believe it."

"I imagine that closed the matter."

"It didn't," Dree said. "Baloo believes what I believe, that six weeks ain't enough time to complete a boat that big. I been hearin' stories from the meat man and meal man who cart in me supplies. Baloo's jump-boys been all over Knockle, Bowfin, Twelve Points and the M'crooms, talkin' to constables. They say he's gonna need as many lawmen as he can find sometime in September for a big seizin' job—one that's more than just a few houses. He's talkin' about roundin' up some of the builders for tower time too, even the boy Teedie Flinn. Baloo seems to have a special quarrel with that child."

"Mally Baloo isn't coming near that boat nor any of those build-ers—least of all Teedie Flinn," Emma hissed quietly so as not to be over-heard by Lassa. "Pick a fight with a pack of people carryin' mallets and hammers and you'll get what you deserve to get."

"Push it off if you care," Dree said. "But with enough help, Baloo will take what he wants, and that means rope and sails too. And don't think he won't guess where them soft parts come from, neither, nor which girls was responsible for makin' 'em."

Emma fell silent and looked away.

"I ain't tellin' you this just to spook you, Emma Hay," Dree said. "I'm tellin' you this because you're a good customer, and you're good to them girls. It's only right that you know what I know." Dree patted Emma's forearm roughly. "Now collect your sweet brick before it turns cold."

Emma paid Dree for the bread, wrapped her hands in her apron and lifted the hot trays off the bar. She turned to take a step toward Lassa, and as she did, heard a sound behind her. It was a low creak, almost like a fat timber reseating itself as a boat rocked in the sea. She flashed her eyes in the direction of the sound and saw that it came from one of the weathered beams hammered into the ceiling from the original *Albert T. Rain.* Dree, who had already turned back to her hearths, did not seem to notice a thing. When Emma turned back to Lassa, however, she saw the girl staring at the ceiling, her eyes narrowed, her brow furrowed, her jaws absently working the bite of sweet brick in her mouth. For the first time, Emma had a taste of the girl's nighttime fears.

Emma did not have a hard time getting Lassa to laugh off the creaking beam in Dree's ceiling. It didn't take much more than a comical face and a whispered warning that a pot-walloper like Dree would whittle the timber down to picks if it ever tried to crown-smack one of her customers. Emma and Lassa left the restaurant and headed back up the road—the girl in the lead and Emma walking behind, trying to balance the two big trays. When they were just a few steps from the home, they heard a clattering up ahead and looked to see a wagon jouncing toward them. Emma recognized the hitch as Grimm and Anna Bland's and the driver as Nacky Patcher. In the seat next to him was a person she had never seen before. He was an ox of a man with a great silver head that bobbed heavily with the motion of the wagon. Emma squinted curiously; Lassa stared in wonder and her cloud-pale skin went a lighter shade still. The wagon rattled up to them and slowed to a stop.

"Nacky Patcher," Emma said approvingly, regarding the hitch and horse, "you brought back the wagon."

"Of course I brought it back," Nacky said a little crossly.

"And you brought back a friend too. Care to share his name?"

"This is Weaver," Nacky said. "Sea captain from Little M'croom. Come here to help us with our rope." Weaver looked at Emma and said nothing.

"Emma Hay," Emma said to him with a nod. Weaver inclined his head to her in a gracious tilt that called to mind the polite tipping of a hat, even though he wasn't wearing one. Then he turned his eyes to Lassa.

272

"This here person have a name like Lissa?" he asked.

Lassa gaped and worked for a moment to call up a word that wouldn't come. "Lassa," she said at last.

"Lassa," Weaver repeated to himself. He spoke in a low grumble that carried a promise of something pleasanter just underneath. "Knew a girl with a name like yours once. Same blackbird hair, same berry eyes." He looked closely at Lassa and affected a scrutinizing expression. "Even think she had the same field of freckles, though I wouldn't know for sure unless I counted 'em up. Never expected I'd get to know one such girl, and here I find a second."

Weaver hauled himself out of his seat and jumped down from the wagon with a surprising nimbleness. He hit the ground with a thud that caused Lassa to back away, thrilled and frightened. Emma smiled, and Nacky, watching from the hitch, did too. Weaver knew no other black-haired, berry-eyed girl, but he had listened to the names and descriptions of the girls Nacky had talked about on the ride to Yole and had remembered enough to make up a fib that clearly delighted Lassa.

"Nacky Patcher," Emma said, "you didn't tell me you were bringing company. You'd best jump down here and help me with these sweet brick trays, then you and your friend best come inside for lunch."

Nacky did as he was told and took the trays from Emma, and the entire group clumped up the porch steps, Orro the pig scuttling behind. When they got inside, the girls stared at Weaver with the same open awe Lassa had, and Emma gave them a moment to look their fill before introducing him. Then she summoned two of the older girls and asked them to lay two clean places at the table and serve the men up what remained of that day's lunch—some still-warm stew, some chewy yellow bread and a plate of fat, yellow apples, wet and cold from a well-water bath. Weaver and Nacky took their places at the table, Nacky feeling uncomfortable as he tried to eat his lunch with two dozen pairs of girl eyes locked on them. Weaver did not seem to notice and turned to his meal contentedly. After he took his first bite, he made something of a show of putting down his fork and sitting back to chew, as if the only way to pay proper mind to all the fine flavors was to give them his entire attention. The girls took his meaning and giggled appreciatively.

When the lunch was done and the girls had tired of looking at the giant in their home, Emma clapped her hands and shooed them back to their sail work. Then she turned to Weaver, and her countenance changed from the relaxed one the lunchtime Emma wore to the stern one Nacky had seen her put on whenever she was doing business.

"I reckon Nacky Patcher told you how soon we have to finish his boat," she said.

"He did," Weaver replied.

"You expect we can get the rope and rigging in time?"

"Ain't gonna be no rope or rigging."

"That's what he went to Little M'croom for, isn't it?"

"And that's what you'll have, provided you weave it up yourself. Rope and rigging costs dear. You'd never earn it back fast enough for the creditors, no matter how big this boat o' yours is. You're gettin' hemp cord—balls of the stuff; you make what you need from that."

"Can you teach us how to do it?"

"I can teach you what I know."

"Is that enough?"

"No."

"Your books got the rest?" Emma asked, turning to Nacky.

"Expect they do."

"Expect won't carry. Best make sure."

Nacky nodded.

"And how long till the hemp balls come?" Emma asked, turning back to Weaver.

"Tomorrow a week."

"The boat has to be done by start of fall. That's only six weeks now, five weeks when the cord comes."

"Tomorrow a week's the best I can do," Weaver said. He reached in front of him, selected an apple from the plate and took in nearly half of it in a single bite.

274

"You have somewhere to stay while you're here?" Emma asked.

"Don't know. Nacky Patcher and I were just trying to settle that out."

Emma shrugged. "I expect you can settle it quick enough if you just stay at Nacky Patcher's. Nacky, his pig and Teedie Flinn can spread some blankets on our porch. There's still enough summer left that the sleeping should be good."

Nacky looked surprised but did not object. Weaver smiled and gave Emma another tip of the cap he wasn't wearing. "Thank you," he said.

"It's no trouble," Emma answered, and smiled for more reasons than she was letting on. Emma didn't know why Mally Baloo had such cross feelings for Teedie, but if Dree was right about the fact that he did—and Dree was rarely wrong about such things—she'd be just as happy to keep the boy close.

Weaver started to take another bite of his apple when all at once, there was a cry from the workroom. Nacky, Weaver and Emma turned and saw a slight, blond girl, no older than ten, standing in the middle of the great spread of sailcloth, holding her finger and howling. A large, glinting needle poked from the tip of the finger and a spot of cherry bright blood dripped down onto the yellow canvas. The girl's face was crumpled miserably, and her cheeks were already streaked with tears. The other girls started to crowd toward her, but Emma, moving with cat-footed speed, leapt from the table and in two or three bounds, got to her first. As Nacky and Weaver rose and watched, she gathered up the girl, cradled the injured hand, removed the needle, examined the finger and wrapped it in a clean cloth she produced from somewhere in the folds of her apron—seeming to perform all the tasks in the same moment. When the finger was swaddled and the girl was soothed, Emma kissed her on the top of her head and pushed her toward the kitchen with two of the other girls, where there would be clean water and a true bandage to treat the wound properly.

"Nasty poke," Nacky said to Weaver, wincing as he watched the girl retreat and looked at the small bloom of blood she had spilled on the canvas.

"Mmm," Weaver said, not seeming to have heard.

Nacky turned to him and saw that he was not in fact looking at the blood or the girl at all. He was looking instead at the sailcloth covering the floor in what appeared to be a great canvas acre. The expression on Weaver's face was the same one Nacky had seen the girls and Emma wear, using their true eyes to take in the sight of the cloth and their inner eyes to unfold it into the sail it would one day be.

"That a mainsail?" Weaver asked.

"Mainsail?" Nacky repeated, searching his mind for the pictures in Dree's books.

"No," Emma said from the canvas, rising to her feet and moving back toward them. "It's a shroud, topmast shroud."

Weaver looked at her in surprise. "This here ain't but a topmast shroud?"

"Piece of one, actually," Emma said, and then smiled at the cloud of wonder that crossed Weaver's face. "Nacky Patcher told you it was a right big boat, didn't he?"

Weaver nodded disbelievingly. "Expect we better hurry with the building like you say," he conceded. He took another bite of his fruit and looked at the bit of it that remained in his hand. "If you're gettin' your fall apples in already, we may not have much time, at that."

It was shortly after Nacky and Weaver finished their lunch at Emma's that Nacky realized Teedie was missing from Yole. He tied himself into worry knots for the next two days until Teedie finally returned, the twenty-four half-home boys in tow. At the sight of the procession Teedie was leading, the scolding Nacky was going to give the boy froze in his throat—even more so after Teedie described how the orphans had been living. Nacky's mood brightened still further when Teedie explained the ciphering he'd done before he left and how the extra pairs of hands would be needed if the town were to have any hope of finishing the boat on time. Nacky, who'd come to trust Teedie's way with numbers, didn't doubt them now.

Emma and her girls spent part of the next couple of days cutting and restitching twenty-four indigent home dresses into twenty-four sets of trousers and shirts. Nacky, Bara and Jimmer, meantime, circulated among the workers at the lake, looking for households willing to take any of the orphans in. The boys' dubious pasts and no-doubt enormous appetites would normally have made them about as welcome in the homes of Yole as a crowd of road cats, but Nacky promised that any family that opened its doors would get an extra half-share in the boat, which would come out of Nacky's own shares. All the families would also get help feeding any boys they took in, including a weekly tray of yalla buck, which would come straight from Dree's kitchen and be paid for from Nacky's pocket. Dree even offered one free stand of malt per week for the man of any home that opened its doors to the boys, an inducement that was less generous than it seemed since a customer given one free malt generally bought two or three more. Still, the bounty of boat, bread and drink was more than enough to get all the boys placed, some families even taking in two orphans in exchange for a full boat share, two trays of yalla buck and two malts.

The only Knockle boy who remained unclaimed was Teedie himself, whose fire past still sat wrong with the townspeople. Teedie preferred to live on the porch of the indigents' home with Nacky anyway—and Nacky preferred that too, reckoning he'd be able to keep a better watch on the boy. When the last few of the freshly combed and clothed orphans were sent off to their new homes, Nacky pulled Teedie aside and spoke to him sternly.

"Now," he said, "you done what you needed to do. After this, I expect you're shut of Knockle forever."

Teedie looked up and solemnly promised that he was. Nacky believed him entirely.

CHAPTER THIRTY-SIX

No one in Yole had ever tried the sweet brick served in the Edgar Forest in Little M'croom. That was just as well, because it would almost surely have been a disappointment.

There was a lot wrong with the Edgar Forest's sweet brick, starting with the sweetness itself. The ghost of honey that was supposed to float through the cakey bread instead lay flat in it, turning it cloying where it should have been pleasing, lead-heavy where it should have been light. The texture was all wrong too, chewy sometimes, crumbly others, but never the this-and-that balance that made it both a meal and a treat. To people brought up on the just-so sweet brick Dree baked up in the Albert T. Rain, the Edgar Forest fare would be an altogether unpleasing thing.

But the Edgar Forest had other things to recommend it above the Albert T. Rain, particularly the building itself. Like the Rain, the Forest was named for a legendary ship that had famously foundered in sight of the local shore, littering the coast with debris. Unlike the wreckage of the Rain, however, much of which was left to molder on the beach, the wreckage of the *Forest* was gathered up by dozens of Little M'croom residents, who used it to make tables, chairs, cupboards, stair rails, moldings, bed frames, nightstands, flower boxes, ceiling beams and even privy doors. The owner of the largest restaurant in the town gathered up most of the wood and put it to good use, filling his dining room with fine carved fittings salvaged from the vessel and building his entire front porch from its polished planks. When the work was done, he changed the name of the restaurant to the Edgar Forest in honor of the lost boat. Dree's Albert T. Rain, decorated with its scavenged bits of a few stray ships, was a dreary sight compared with the sparkling Forest.

Whether the letter carrier from the nearby town of Yole noticed the fine wood fittings when he dropped in at the Forest one day around suppertime was impossible to say. He blinked a bit at the noise and the crowd, but did not linger over anything he saw when he entered. Instead, he walked straight to the bar, bought a mug of bark draught and a square of sweet brick, neither of which seemed to interest him, and introduced himself to the man drawing the drinks. His name, he said, was Meddo Brinn.

The barman nodded hello and Meddo started in talking. He was visiting Little M'croom on business, he said, business on behalf of a Mally Baloo. Had the barman ever heard of Baloo?

The barman said he had. Baloo was the well-tinned fellow who owned all that land in Yole—not that land in Yole was much worth the owning, he added with a laugh.

The letter carrier named Meddo laughed agreeably, said that the barman had the right Mally Baloo and that Baloo was indeed as tinned as the stories had it. In fact, Baloo had so much money that he'd recently discovered he'd hired too many people to work on his estate—not even noticing the cost until the workers themselves began complaining that there weren't enough jobs for all of them to do. Baloo was thus interested in selling off the debts of some of the workers, starting with a particular young girl he'd be happy to send to another town where folks might be in need of shop help or a housemaid. Did the barman know anyone in Little M'croom who was looking for that kind of girl?

The barman thought and answered yes, then called out to two men eating at a nearby table. One of the men, the barman explained, owned a clothing shop on the main business street of the town. The other was a fisherman who owned one of the larger local boats.

The men came over to the bar and Meddo explained his business and then described the girl. She was a leather worker, he said, who went by the name of Bara Berry. Bara was strong, if a little mulish, but that could probably be trained out of her. She'd lately got herself mixed up in some mischief involving a boat, mischief Mally Baloo really had no use for. Since she seemed to fancy the idea of sailing, however, she might be just right for the fisherman. What's more, the debt she owed Baloo was a big one—cottage, food and clothes for several years now. With the wages she was earning, she had not paid much of it off. Anybody who bought her debt could thus keep her working for a good, long time.

The fisherman listened as the letter carrier spoke but eventually shook his head no. His boat was full up, he said, and even if it weren't, he had no use for a leather worker. The shop man was a different matter. He sold only suits and topcoats in his store and thus could not use Bara Berry's particular skills either. But he did know a shoe man in Twelve Points who was looking for help. If the debt the girl owed was indeed so high, he'd be pleased to buy it from Baloo now, then turn around and sell it higher still to the shoe man, making a fair profit in the bargain.

Meddo said that would be a fine arrangement—and a clever one too—and that he could have the girl sent over whenever the price of her debt contract was met. The shop man said he would draw up a bank draft and meet it straightaway—by morning if Meddo could find lodging in town overnight. Meddo said he could, and the shop man said that in that case he'd expect Bara Berry before the end of the week.

The two men shook hands on the deal, and for the first time since he arrived at the Edgar Forest, Meddo allowed himself a smile. Sitting back, he finally began to drink off his bark draught and taste his sweet brick. The draught, at least, he appeared to enjoy.

CHAPTER THIRTY-SEVEN

Weaver got his first look at the Yole boat not long after he arrived in town. Ever since he and Nacky left Little M'croom, Nacky had been imagining the wide look of wonder that would cross the former sea captain's face when he at last saw the half-done vessel for himself. But when they stepped onto the ridge overlooking the lake and peered down together, Weaver responded with only a thoughtful seaman's squint.

"Big, like you said," he muttered.

"Mmm-hmm," Nacky answered.

"Bigger, actually," Weaver allowed.

Weaver took a minute or so to gaze appreciatively down at the boat, then pulled his eyes away and turned himself to business. Taking a step back from the ridge, he began scanning the bank. He stopped his gaze at the sharp east point, counted off five degrees beyond it, and took Nacky by the arm.

"That," he said, pointing, "is the spot you seen in me basin. That's where you'll find what you're lookin' for."

Nacky brightened, looked down among the workers and spotted Grimm Bland. He halloed to him, and Grimm trotted up the trail.

Nacky pointed out the spot Weaver had indicated and asked him to go see if he could find the missing clutch of parts there. Grimm hurried back down, searched about in the scrub and mud, and within a few moments, popped back up with a holler and a wave, holding a handful of glinting wood. Nacky and Weaver hurried down the trail themselves, and Grimm handed over what he had found: three round plugs and two short trunnels.

Nacky whooped. "Forty thousand!" he said. "Forty thousand pieces and not one shy." He clapped Grimm on the shoulder and turned to beam at Weaver. Weaver smiled back, but skeptically.

"Forty thousand seems right for a ship like this," he allowed. "But somehow it don't seem right either."

"You reckon we're still short?" Nacky asked.

"Can't say why, but I do," Weaver said. "Just a tick, but short all the same."

Nacky looked at Weaver crossly, not just because of the way the big man had taken the puff out of him, but because he suspected he was right. He had found his forty thousandth part, and yet something still felt oddly incomplete.

Nacky looked down at the scrub, poking it with his toe as if to turn up a piece of teak Grimm may somehow have missed. As he did, Weaver looked across the bank and noticed the oven and steambox flaming and puffing near the water. He walked over to take a closer look. The oven had been lit since early morning, and Jimmer and the Dreeboys were still hard at work, feeding dry cedar in one end, pulling steamed teak out the other and carefully giving the wood planks the bend. Weaver looked on silently as one board was finished up and another was swaddled and laid in the steam. Then, without waiting for Nacky, he stepped over to Jimmer.

"You're lettin' good steam go to waste treatin' them boards one at a time," Weaver said.

Jimmer was jolted by the rumbling voice and turned to face the giant man with the lion head who had spoken to him. "Who are you?" he asked.

"Don't really matter. You're lettin' good steam go to waste treatin' them boards one at a time."

"Man's name is Weaver," Nacky jumped in, hop-running over to the steambox as fast as he could. "From Little M'croom. He's here to help us with our rope."

Jimmer surveyed Weaver and jutted his chin out. "Good," he said. "We need help with the rope. Don't need help with the oven."

"You do if you wanna quit wastin' your steam and your time," Weaver said.

"Ain't a waste. You can't heat more than one at a go, since they don't all take the steam the same. Surest way to ruin 'em is to let 'em soften up too much."

"That don't happen if you know how to stack 'em," Weaver said. He inclined his head inquiringly toward the steambox, waiting for leave to approach it. Jimmer did nothing; Nacky nodded and waved him over.

As Jimmer and Nacky watched, Weaver walked to the woodpile and shooed the Dreeboys off. He selected three planks, covered one completely in swaddling, the other halfway, and left the third bare. Then he stacked them in the steambox in a precise fan pattern with the unswaddled one at the top and shut the door. After several minutes, he opened the box, extracted the perfectly steamed planks, handed one each to the Dreeboys, and kept one himself. Together, they gave all three boards their needed six-degree bend.

"You stack and wrap that wood just so," said Weaver, "you can steam seven pieces in there at once. Then all you need to do is make sure you got seven people trained up in how to bend 'em." That very afternoon, Weaver was teaching Jimmer and the Dreeboys how to prepare the planks, and the Dreeboys were teaching the other workers how to apply the right bend to the properly softened wood.

Weaver saw other things he didn't care for on the bank and went about fixing them too. He showed the workers how to use the planks and trunnels to peg together a pallet on which beams and other, smaller parts could be stacked and then jigged anywhere on the bank with Jimmer's hoist. When the work was done, the pallet could be disassembled and the planks returned to their piles. Weaver also showed a keener eye than Jimmer had for recognizing which planks belonged to which part of the ship and found that many boards that had been marked for steaming were already bent right for the job they had to do.

With Weaver helping out, the pace of the work picked up so much that within two days, Jimmer at last agreed that enough of the boat's skeleton had been assembled and that it was time for planking the hull and laying the top deck to begin. That very afternoon, mallet-wielding workers clambered up the scaffolds and ladders and set about the long-delayed work. By the middle of the next day, growing patches of shiny teak hide began to materialize over the bones of the boat, and the first stretch of the glinting upper deck began to appear at the ship's aft end, creeping steadily toward the bow.

The burst of building went on for a week, growing even faster when Teedie's Knockle boys arrived and began doing their share, running planks and other parts to workers and clambering up into tight places in the boat frame where the full-grown builders found it hard to squeeze. The boys—clad in their matching canvas clothes—took happily to the work, particularly when Nacky promised that, like all of the other builders, they would receive a share of the boat in exchange for their labor. Even Chuff the dwarf helped out as he could, accompanying Bara to the lake each morning and lending a hand carrying bags of plugs and trunnels to the workers on the ladders. At first, Nacky allowed him to do the work only because Bara demanded it, though he feared Chuff would bollix the job, losing some of the small bits the builders had worked so hard to recover. But Chuff grew good at the chore, showing a sharp eye for tracking each worker's progress and bringing over the correct parts even before they were called for.

284

"He does a right fair job when folks don't keep reminding him he can't," Bara said.

Finally, early on the seventh morning after Weaver's arrival, the promised balls of cord needed for the ropes arrived. The workers were busy down on the bank as the hemp wagons made their clattering approach, but even from the depth of the bowl they could hear them coming. No fewer than seven wagons pulled by two horses apiece were needed to make the trip up into the sawtooth mountains with the fourteen giant balls of cord that would be required to start rigging so big a ship. The sound the wagons gave off silenced both the morning twittering of August Ren's birds above and the din of the mallets pounding away below.

When the workers heard the noise, they scurried down from their ladders and raced up the trail to the rim of the lake bowl, reaching it just as the wagons clattered into position and stopped side by side. The fourteen horses pulling the seven hitches stood in a cloud of road dust, pawing the ground and snorting—the fourteen balls of hemp lined up in the wagon beds behind them like a row of rust-colored worlds. The workers crowded toward the wagons, reaching up to touch the cord balls and heedlessly spooking the horses as they did. The drivers tried to swat the people away, but they kept moving closer. Nacky, Jimmer, Weaver, Teedie and Bara, who had been gathered around the book table on the bank when the wagons arrived, were the last to climb the hill and were startled at the scene that greeted them.

"Here, now!" Nacky called. "Leave off them horses!"

"That hemp ain't lashed secure!" Jimmer shouted. "Somebody's gonna get rolled flat!"

The crowd didn't respond, continuing to gather around the wagons. Finally, Weaver let out with a high whistle—a single, bladelike note that cut through the voices of the builders, the shouts of the drivers, even the snorting of the animals.

"Hold hard!" he barked, and the people stopped and turned.

"Them's thousand-pound balls. Those what cares to wrestle 'em alone, keep right on with what you're doin'. Those what has a bit more sense, stand aside."

The crowd looked uncertain and parted. The big, silver-headed man then approached the lead wagon, nodded to the driver and patted one of the horses roughly on the neck. The driver reached into his coat and produced a folded sheet of paper. Weaver unfolded it, scanned it once and walked back to Nacky.

"This is yours," he said, handing over the paper. "You're agreein' to use the earnin's of your boat to pay for this rope and however much more you need. You don't earn, it becomes their boat."

Nacky took a long look at the fourteen giant balls, then tucked the paper into his trouser pocket with barely a glance. Weaver turned back to the wagon drivers and nodded again. The seven men hopped to the ground and quickly set about unloading their rigs.

Nobody could ever say for certain in the years that followed just where Chuff the dwarf came from in the moments the balls were being lowered from the wagons. He had been working among the parts piles when the wagons arrived, and no one had seen him climb the hill with the rest of the builders. Wherever he came from, he was on the ridge nonetheless, standing with Orro the pig in front of August Ren's horse-less bird wagon. August Ren himself had gone off to fetch food for his birds.

Chuff watched closely like everyone else as the first driver let down the rear of his wagon and unfolded it into a hinged ramp. Three of the other drivers approached the wagon and produced long, harpoon-tipped poles that they jabbed into the front end of one of the two balls in the wagon bed. The first driver then climbed up into the bed, cut the cords holding the ball in place, and began pushing it from behind, slowly rolling it down the ramp as the men with the harpoons backed away, jabbing and rejabbing it in front. When the ball was on the ground, they rolled it a safe distance from the wagon and secured it with lines tied to a quiver of stakes they hammered into the soil around it. The men then turned to the second ball to repeat the unloading. This one, however, did not go as smoothly.

No sooner had the man in the wagon cut most of the restraint cords securing the ball than something in one of the morning cook fires gave off with a loud pop. The sound echoed like gunfire around the ridge. A faint whiff of sulfur followed the noise and a shard of some kind flew from the fire, striking one of the horses hitched to the wagon. The scared and stung animal spooked and reared up, lifting the front end of the wagon off the ground. The remaining ball rolled toward the hitch's open back—its final cord breaking with a loud snap—and pitched itself out onto the ground. In a blink, the three men with the harpoons scrambled out of the way and the ball began rolling clear, directly toward Chuff and Orro. Whether a man with a sharper eye or a brighter nature would have seen the half-ton sphere coming was impossible to say. Certainly Orro the pig—jumpy by temperament—did, and scrabbled away. Certainly Chuff the dwarf—sleepy by temperament—didn't. In a dark instant, the ball rolled toward Chuff and struck him a ferocious standing blow. Chuff vanished, and the ball collided with the horseless bird wagon behind him. The wagon jumped up and skidded sideways toward the edge of the ridge. Just a foot or so from the lip, its wheels struck a rocky rut, where they grabbed and held. The wagon and the ball came to a shuddering stop. The terrified birds in the cage fluttered upward and then dropped to their perches, stunned.

In the moment that followed, only one person on the ridge had it in him to move: Weaver, who bounded from the spot where he was standing and flung himself toward the ball. Striking the giant thing with the full of his enormous shoulder, he jarred it loose from the wagon and set it drifting toward the lip of the bowl. The ball rolled over the edge and then bounced down the hill, moving with a heavy rumble that caused the very ground to shake. When it hit the bank, it bounced once more, splashed explosively into the water, and came to rest there, floating twenty feet from shore.

The eyes of all the people on the bank then turned back to the bird wagon, and as they did, there was a small stirring beneath it. Blinking through the red dust and coughing in the dry soil was Chuff the dwarf, on his belly and badly shoggled, but apparently alive. A full-grown man—even a large child—would never have survived the force of the ball. But when the mass of hemp struck Chuff, it merely knocked him under the bed of the wagon, instead of crushing him against its hard wooden side. Weaver reached down and with a single sweep of his huge left arm scooped Chuff safely out and set him back on his feet, where he stood looking dazedly about. The people on the bank broke into a cheer. Bara Berry dashed forward, took Chuff into her arms and wept.

After that, Nacky, Weaver and Jimmer assigned six of the strongest builders to assist the wagon men in unloading the rest of the hemp balls and ordered all the other townspeople to stand clear of the ridge. Poking about in the fire, Nacky found the split halves of something that appeared to be about the size and color of a hard pecan, but one that emitted a faint, sulfurous wisp. An object like this tossed into the flames would surely have given off a gunshot pop like the one that spooked the horse—assuming there was someone here who'd wanted to do just that. Nacky looked about the ridge suspiciously, but if anyone was indeed responsible, he had slipped in and out unnoticed.

Chuff himself saw none of this, as Bara banished him from the lake, forbidding him to come anywhere near the boat again while it was being built. Chuff obeyed, and in the days after that stayed mostly on the grounds of the Baloo estate and out of sight. He would not show himself again until the remarkable day it was at last time to **haul the** vessel away.

CHAPTER THIRTY-EIGHT

Bara Berry was not nearly ready to put out her lamp for the night when she heard a sound at the door of her cottage. Bara's door was given to making a lot of rattly noises, and almost anything from a breath of wind to the slam of a drawer could set it to shaking. Tonight, however, the *tuk-tuk-tuk* she heard at the door was undeniably a knock—one that came too late and was made too soft to be anything but trouble.

Had it been almost any other night, Bara might have missed the quiet knock altogether, since she almost certainly would have been in bed, sleeping with the stillness of the fully dead. For most of the month of August, Bara found that she had been sleeping more and more deeply at night, mostly because she had been working longer and longer during the day.

Ever since the man named Weaver arrived in Yole, he had been driving the boat workers hard, and by the last week of August they had managed to get nearly three-quarters of the great teak boat covered in hull. The top deck was more than half laid as well, with only its forward portion, as well as the detail work around the wheelhouse, capstans and hatches, left to be done. With the weight of all the planks added to the ribs, Jimmer had grown concerned that such a top-heavy structure might simply topple over, despite its broad base of a keel. He had thus recently added a bristle of bracing beams anchored in the bank and propped up against both sides of the ship. From a distance, the beams looked sturdy enough, but viewed up close they still didn't look any more able to support so massive a boat than an equal number of kindling sticks.

At the same time the work was proceeding on the bank, the cord work got under way on the ridge above. Weaver had explained to the builders what he knew about winding rope, and from everything he told them, the task would not be easy. In order to make a proper cord without knots and tangles spoiling the weave, they would have to lay individual strands of hemp out to their full length and then braid them carefully together. The ropes that would be needed to rig a clipper ship were so long and numerous, however, that there was no stretch of clear lake bank that could accommodate them. Instead, the bowl of the lake itself would have to be used.

Weaver instructed the half-home boys—under the supervision of Teedie Flinn and Dal Tally—to hammer a bristle of thirty stakes along one stretch of the rim of the bowl, setting each of them about three feet apart. He then told them to unspool long pieces of cord from the hemp balls, carefully measuring all of them so that they could run from the top of the bowl down to the bank. Anywhere from twenty to one hundred of the strands would be tied to each stake—depending on the thickness of the rope that was needed—and laid out on the hill. The boys would then take up the strands and braid their way down to the bank, weaving the already-heavy hemp tied to any one stake into a stout, seaworthy cord. When a rope was done, its bottom would be tied to another stake hammered into the base of the hill, allowing it to be pulled taut to strengthen the weave.

The boys went about the rope work quickly, requiring Weaver to send to Little M'croom for another shipment of cord and then another. Some days the braiding proceeded so well that all of the stakes along the bowl were full by midday, with thirty completed ropes running down the hill like piano wires. Indeed, like piano wires too, the ropes could be plucked and made to give off surprisingly rich tones, the fatter ones sounding in the lower registers, the finer ones in the higher. The boys delighted in running back and forth along the bank, strumming a stick against the ropes and producing rising or falling chords that sounded throughout the entire bowl. If one of the ropes gave off a note that seemed bent or flat, Dal or Teedie tightened or loosened its stake as needed, tuning up the hill like a violinist tunes up an instrument. Sometimes, a wind would sweep through the bowl, giving the ropes an even louder strum than the boys ever could. When the oven was running and producing its own birdlike notes, the combination of steam music and wind music could stop the workers cold.

Helping to oversee all this building and weaving kept Bara awake far later than she was accustomed to, and most nights she would thus drop flat into bed the moment she arrived back at her cottage. Tonight, however, she was still awake, hard at work hammering together several pairs of boots so as not to fall behind in her shoemaking labors. It was for this reason she was able to hear the *tuk-tuk-tuk* sounding softly at her door not long before dawn broke.

Bara froze at the noise of the knock and stared at the door as if she could peer through it. The heavy oak panel gave up no clue as to who was outside, but Bara could see the floorboards under the door gapping and bending slightly as the person on the step shifted his weight.

With her hands suddenly cold, Bara softly put the shoe she was stitching down on her small worktable, held her breath and sat as still as she could. The *tuk-tuk-tuk* sounded again. Bara sighed and slumped. Pushing back from the table, she stood, puffed herself up, stepped to the door and flung it open. On the other side stood Nacky and Weaver.

"What in the seas–" Bara said.

"I'm glad you're about," Nacky whispered, glancing over his shoulder.

"Where else would I be?"

"I'm sorry for the hour," Weaver said softly.

"I don't even know the hour," Bara hissed.

Weaver squinted up at the sky. "It's gone five," he said.

"And you guessed that was a good time to come?"

"Didn't have no other time," Nacky said. "We need to talk to you. Need to do it now."

Bara looked askance at Nacky and then turned to Weaver, who nodded once. She stepped aside, and Weaver and Nacky entered the little one-room house. Nacky took another nervous glance outside and closed the door.

"I'd give you a place to sit yourselves . . . ," Bara said, then shrugged and gestured to the room, which, apart from her small chair and narrow cot, in fact had no such place. "Besides, got me boots to finish before sunup, so whatever your business is—"

"I don't guess you'll have time to finish them boots," Weaver said.

"Not them nor any others," Nacky added.

Bara looked at them suspiciously. "Estate manager ain't gonna see it that way," she said.

"Estate manager can keep," Weaver answered.

"He ain't gonna see it that way, either."

"We need you to come with us," Nacky said. "Straightaway."

"On what business?"

"Boat business," Weaver said. "We have to start gettin' ready to haul it, and Jimmer says we can't wait even another day."

Bara took the two men in through slitted eyes. "I don't expect there's anything we can do until we've actually got somethin' to haul," she said, "and last I saw, that ship ain't near done."

"Don't hurt to start," Nacky said.

Bara folded her arms. "I'll start when there's cause to start, Nacky Patcher. And if I know Jimmer Pike, he'd say the same." She fixed them both with a hard look. "Now it ain't haulin' what brought you two here more than an hour ahead of sunup when I got boots to make. So you best tell me what your business is or you can turn around and go the way you came."

Nacky turned to Weaver and shrugged. Weaver hitched himself up

292

and thought. Then he stepped over to Bara's cot, swept aside a few shoe scraps and leatherworking tools and sat. The thin mattress of the little bed drooped almost to the floor.

"Mally Baloo sold your debt," he said. "I reckon he knows what you're doin' at the lake, and I reckon he wants to put a stop to it."

Bara remained expressionless. "When'd he sell it?" she asked.

"Don't know exactly. Only know that he offered it up in Little M'croom and a shop man bought it. Shop man means to sell it to a shoe man in Twelve Points. Shoe man means to carry you there as soon as he can—maybe tomorrow, maybe today."

Bara spoke tonelessly. "How'd you come by this?"

"Cord man told me when he last drove in."

"How'd he come by it?"

"He knows a fisherman who was there when Meddo Brinn came callin' on behalf of Baloo."

Bara's lips went tight and she turned to Nacky. "Brinn," she spat. "Well, I don't care what he done. I ain't bein' sold off like a load of yams."

"It ain't you what's bein' sold," Weaver answered quietly. "It's your debt. And the law allows it."

"Don't matter what the law allows. I ain't leavin'."

Weaver turned his big, soft palms upward. "I don't see how you can fight it. I expect you're gonna have to leave, but it don't have to be to no shop man or shoe man in some other town."

"Ain't no one else payin' for me."

Weaver rubbed his heavy eyes and then looked at her. "Ain't so," he said. "I'm payin' for you. I'm doin' it today, soon as we carry you out of here."

Bara looked as if she'd been struck. Then she set her jaw and straightened herself up to the full of her height, a pose that only showed off the bird-size tininess of her frame. "Ain't no favor when someone pays money for me," she said. "And ain't no friend what claims to try."

"Bara Berry," Weaver said, with a faint smile, "you lower that chin now. I don't mean to hold your debt, I mean to tear it up. But I can't do that if I don't buy it first."

Bara softened and took a step back; she bumped the edge of her little worktable. "You'd settle my debt?"

"I would. I will."

"That's a round piece of money."

Weaver waved his hand. "I got money. And Nacky Patcher here's got a little left over too. I expect he'll pay a share."

Bara looked at Nacky. He felt a small wash of the sick feeling that always came over him when he imagined an empty purse. He pushed it aside, looked back at Bara and nodded a firm yes. Bara blinked a suddenly wet blink and turned away. Then, just as quickly, she wheeled back around. "And Chuff the dwarf?" she asked.

"We can't pay for you and Chuff both," Nacky said. "Even if we could, Baloo ain't shown no sign that that's a debt he wants to sell."

"I ain't goin' without Chuff."

"I expect you're goin', either way," Weaver said. "You come with us, you can still be close by. You don't, you go to Twelve Points. You run, it could be the tower. Then what happens to Chuff?"

Bara's face fell and her eyes filled again. She sat down at her little table, picked up her unfinished boot and turned it over and over in her hands. Then, without a word, she stood and slowly began moving about her cottage, collecting her few belongings and packing them in a small fabric bag. When she was done, she reached over to her worktable and put out her lamp. Nacky opened the door, allowing the faint light of the predawn sky to flow into the room. The three of them stepped outside and Bara closed the door behind them. They began trudging slowly through the wet grass, making their silent way off the estate. Well before they left the grounds, Bara turned around and looked behind her. Far off in the darkness, she saw the yellow light from a morning lantern leaking through Chuff's shutters. It was far earlier, she reflected, than she'd ever known him to awaken before.

CHAPTER THIRTY-NINE

The shop man eating lunch in the Edgar Forest in Little M'croom didn't know what to think when the homely giant with the silver beard and the ruined hands sat down next to him and placed a heavy purse of money on the table. The shop man suspected he had seen the giant before—down on the quay or in the streets—but he had never spoken to him. He had certainly never conducted any business with him that would involve such a purse full of coin.

The giant started in speaking straightaway and said he understood the shop man had just bought the debt of a work girl in Yole. The shop man was surprised at how soft the giant's voice was—softer than his great size threatened—and he smiled slyly. Might be true that he had bought such a debt, might not, he said. Where had the giant heard such a thing? The giant waved that off with one of his terrible hands and asked again if the shop man held the debt. This time the softness was gone from his voice. The shop man stopped smiling and said that yes, he had recently bought title to such a girl.

The giant sat back and nodded in a way that said he'd known that all along. Then he asked the shop man if he might buy the debt himself.

The shop man straightened his back and told him it wasn't for sale. The giant said he wished the shop man would think the matter through again. The shop man said he didn't need more thinking, and besides, he'd already promised to sell the debt to somebody else. The giant nodded in a way that said he might have known this too; then he gestured to the purse anyway. The shop man kept his gaze on the giant, hefted the bag and opened it up. He peered inside and spilled the coins out on the table. He smiled.

Was all this for one work girl? he wanted to know.

It was, the giant told him.

Must be an important girl, the shop man said.

The giant didn't answer.

The shop man lifted his fork and took a bite of his sausage and smiled his sly smile again. If the girl was so valuable, he said, maybe the money in the purse wasn't quite enough. The giant said he didn't have any more money to spend. The shop man shrugged and said that it wasn't only money that would round out the price to his satisfaction; there were other things that would serve too. Then he let his eyes fall on the pewter ring on the finger stump on the big man's left hand.

The giant looked at the shop man with no expression on his face and the shop man faltered. He reached for his mug and took several hard swallows of malt, making his eyes run rheumy. Then he put down the mug and laughed uncertainly. The ring and the money were his price for the girl, he said. What did a ring matter to a man like the giant, anyway? It wasn't as if it could do much to pretty up his awful hand.

The giant considered that for a long moment, and then nodded. Yes, he said, he reckoned that was true.

Without another word, the giant removed the ring and placed it on top of the pile of coins. The shop man swept them all up and stuffed them in his pocket. Then he paid his bill and led the giant back to his store, where he handed him the debt paper he held on the girl. The giant thanked the man, left his shop and returned to the Edgar Forest. He walked to one of the flaming hearths in a rear corner of the room, tore

296

the paper neatly in half, then in half once more and then once more. Then he placed the pieces in the fire and watched as they burned to ash. Finally, he sat down at a nearby table and drew a deep breath. He had driven a long way to come here today, and he had earned a few minutes of rest before heading back.

CHAPTER FORTY

There were a lot of changes in Yole
after Bara Berry left the Baloo estate, not all of them involving Bara herself. Nacky had hoped that once Bara was freed from the dreary prison
of the Baloo cottage, she'd be content to make a bed at Emma Hay's
indigents' home, and Emma herself had hoped so too. Bara, however,
would have none of it.

Grateful as she was for the good turn Nacky and Weaver had done
her, she made it clear that she could never accept any such kindness
from Emma. Nacky knew she'd be unmoveable on this point and that
pressing her on it would only distract her from the far more important
boat work she had to do. Bara thus moved straight from the Baloo estate
into Nacky's house, and Weaver in turn moved out, renting attic quarters
in Brigg and Constance Keeper's home, the money he had available to
spend easily overcoming the reservations the Keepers had about allowing the strange giant from Little M'croom to bed down under their roof.
Bara promised to use her expected earnings from the boat to pay Weaver
back what he spent for rent.

Nacky and Teedie meantime, who had been spending their nights
on the porch of the indigents' home, were now joined there by Dal

Tally, who had been staying with one of the families in town, but was as attached to Teedie as Teedie was to Nacky. Nacky had worried that Dal's weak wind would suffer badly on the sometimes chilly porch, but the clear night air—along with the fine meals Dal had been getting from Emma's kitchen—worked like a tonic on him, and he actually seemed to grow stronger for the time he spent outdoors.

On the whole, Nacky, the two boys and Orro the pig got on well on Emma's porch, though Orro at first had an unhandy habit of rising before the sun and pacing up and down along the planks, *clack-clacking* his feet and snorting fretfully until someone would wake up and fetch him breakfast.

"Nacky Patcher!" Emma Hay shouted down from an upstairs window on the third morning of the predawn noise, "you hush that animal up or sure as I'm standing here, my girls will be eating pork stew for the next week!" The laughter of the girls themselves floated down from the windows, but Orro apparently understood the iron in Emma's voice and never again made a sound before the first flash of sunup.

Orro, as it turned out, was not the only one who stirred up the indigents' home. Dal Tally did too. Mag, Gurtee and the other girls had always seemed to have a fancy for Teedie, but when Dal arrived, their attentions changed entirely. The slight, pale boy may have looked far younger than he was, but something about the way he carried himself made him appear older and more careworn. That, coupled with the fact that he at first seemed so sickly, somehow turned the girls dizzy. They fussed openly over him whenever he was about, appearing to forget anyone else was in the room. Teedie could never be sure if they wanted to kiss poor Dal or care for him as if they were Dr. Mull himself, and he wasn't sure the girls knew either. When the first autumn rains started to trickle in and Emma decided to break one of her usually unbreakable rules—allowing Nacky, Teedie, Dal and even Orro to sleep on the floor of the workroom so that none of them would take ill in the wet air—the girls looked fit to swoon.

If the turn of weather unsettled things in the indigents' home, it caused even bigger problems down at the lake. With September unspooling fast, the day was quickly approaching when Jimmer and the builders would have to begin preparing to haul the boat. Ships built inland—as Weaver knew from experience, and Nacky, Teedie and Jimmer knew from Dree's books—were pulled to the coast by teams of horses and humans. A vessel that was ready to be taken to the sea would be slid from its cradle and heeled over on its side so that one flank was resting on the ground. Animals and men harnessed to its hull would then slowly slip-drag it to the shore. To make the work easier, the hauling was best done in the winter months when the roads were iced over slick. Nonetheless, a trip to the coast of this kind was slow and terrible, with frequent stops along the way to make sure the hull was not getting gouged. It was not unknown for the odd man or horse to die of an exhausted heart long before the ship actually touched water.

The Yole boat, of course, would have to be dragged in September, when there would be no ice on the ground to ease the trip. The autumn rains could be counted on to slick up the soil enough to make the journey possible—and indeed, the more rain the better, Nacky believed, since Baloo and the dry-land curse could be beaten only if the boat made it the entire way to the coast and into the sea. But the trick was that the rain could not come too early. The horses and men would first need mostly dry footing to pull the boat up the bowl. Once they were at the top, the skies could open up as much as they cared.

"Too much rain comes along too soon," Jimmer told Nacky more than once, "and your ship stays just where it is."

As it turned out, the autumn drizzles turned to true autumn rains well before they ordinarily did, arriving on the sixth day of September. The noise of the downpour woke Nacky and Teedie earlier than normal, and they peered out the windows of the indigents' home workroom and frowned. They rousted Dal and Orro and joined Emma and a few of the lighter-sleeping girls for a quick breakfast of hot mixabout with honey and sweet mugs of tea. Then Nacky and the boys hurried out the front door with Orro clattering behind them. No sooner had they got down the stairs and into the falling rain than Emma hurried out after them.

"Nacky Patcher!" she called. Nacky and the boys turned; she ran out into the road and up to Nacky. "Behave yourselves today," she said crossly to him.

"We didn't reckon not to," Nacky said, confused.

"Never mind what you reckoned," she snapped, now flicking her eyes toward Teedie too. "I won't stand for any mischief this morning—nor any other time, come to that!"

"All right," Nacky said appeasingly, "all right." Emma huffed and turned on her heel.

Nacky and Dal turned to go, but Teedie remained rooted where he was. Emma, he'd discovered, sometimes seemed to know when he was bound for mischief even before he knew it himself. It was only when he was actually faced with possible trouble and saw her stern face floating in front of him that he knew what it was she'd foreseen. Today that face seemed sterner than it had ever been before. He watched Emma's retreating back, then slowly turned and followed Nacky, Dal and Orro.

When the little group arrived at the ridge overlooking the bank, they found Weaver there already, peering downward. The rain had eased back to a cold, steady drizzle, and the sight that greeted them all was a sorry one. Only a dozen or so soggy workers were on the bank, standing about with mallets dangling loosely in their hands, too wet or dispirited to get about any work at all. Most of them were streaked with red mud along the seats of their trousers and the backs of their shirts, and it took only one look at the slick, rutted lake path running with rivulets of water to guess the stumbling, slipping route they had taken to the bank. Near the edge of the water, the Dreeboys stood tending the oven and steambox, intent on treating a few remaining jambs and stanchions that still needed to be bent. Weak puffs of wet smoke came from the damp kindling inside the oven, but proper steam was nowhere to be seen.

"They been fightin' with that oven for the better part of an hour now," said Weaver. Nacky grunted in response.

Teedie edged toward the ridge and tried the footing. The mud beneath him immediately started to melt away and he stumbled backward and was caught by Weaver.

All at once, Orro, who had plopped contentedly into a red mud puddle behind the group, rose, wriggled through their legs and skittered sure-footedly toward the ridge. Dropping to his rump, he began to slide down the path, bumping and jolting as he went, but remaining upright the entire way. In seconds, he reached the bottom and skidded out onto the bank. Nacky and the others crumpled into laughter.

"Always knew he was a clever pig," Nacky said.

"Cleverer than that lot, anyway," Weaver said, indicating the workers on the bank.

With a smile, Nacky stepped to the edge, dropped to his seat, and made his way down the same way Orro had. The other three followed, all of them reaching the bottom with their rumps and heels muddy, but the rest staying mostly clean. Picking themselves up, they splashed toward the oven, where the bigger Dreeboy was bent over the sputtering fire.

"Don't seem to be catchin'," Nacky said, peering at the hissing cedar sticks in the cool oven.

"Don't nothing seem to be catchin'," the Dreeboy said, turning away from the oven with a disgusted look. "Flames ain't goin', workers ain't workin', boat ain't gettin' built."

"How long you brothers been here today?" Nacky asked.

"We didn't never leave yesterday. Last time we was home was two suppertimes ago."

Nacky gave them a reproachful look. "Well you're leavin' now," he said. "Long as you can get up that hill, I want you to go home to Dree's. I don't expect to see you again till tomorrow."

"Jimmer ain't gonna be happy about that," Teedie warned Nacky.

"I'll answer for it," Nacky said. "I don't see Jimmer anyway."

"He's in the kutch tent," the smaller Dreeboy said. "Been there near two hours, and he don't seem pleased."

Nacky nodded, shooed the Dreeboys off and told Teedie and Dal to see if they couldn't get some life into the oven. With Weaver and Orro following, he then made for the kutch tent at the edge of the bank. The tent, which was staked in the ground near the stern of the boat, wasn't really a tent at all—just a heavy canopy set up on four poles, protecting a small patch of ground. Underneath was a large metal barrel standing above a fire. The barrel was filled with a percolating stew of sticky kutch—a combination of pine tar, tapped rubber and linseed oil. Workers soaked long stretches of rope in the messy mix, then used wooden wedges and mallets to hammer the blackened cables into the seams in the hull and deck planks, making the boat watertight. A lot of progress had been made on the kutching in the last few days, but today was different. Nacky could see Jimmer slumped disconsolately in his chair near the barrel, his fire managing to stay lit but no workers coming to get the slowly bubbling kutch. Bara was pacing back and forth in front of her own chair, scowling into her ledger. Weaver, Nacky and Orro reached the tent and ducked inside. Above them, they could hear the soft tattoo of the rain pattering against the canopy.

"Devil's weather," Nacky said, trying a sporting smile.

Jimmer looked up and glowered. Bara stopped her pacing. "One spit of rain and most of 'em stay home," she said.

"More'n a spit," Nacky responded appeasingly.

"All the same, we got fifteen days left till the first of fall, and they ain't workin' a lick."

"You got nobody inside the boat?" Weaver asked.

"Them's the only ones doin' anything," Bara said, "and that's only 'cause they can stay dry. You'd think the lot of 'em would melt away like sugar-sticks if they felt a little drizzle."

"Think you can talk some life into the ones who're out there?" Weaver asked.

"I've tried," Bara said.

"Think you can try again?"

Bara sighed, dropped her ledger on the table and stomped splashily out of the tent. Nacky saw two workers spot her coming and immediately turn to the boat and affect a busy look.

Weaver faced Jimmer. "What's this rain do to the haulin'?"

"Ain't no haulin' if it keeps up," Jimmer answered.

"And if it stops?"

"One full day of sun after any rain's the best time to move. Ground with grass should be dry enough to give footing. The lake path should still be muddy enough to let the boat slide easy. And then we gotta haul fast if we're gonna get it to the coast before Mally Baloo can lay claim to it."

"How long you think that'll take?"

Jimmer thought. "With the horse muscle and human muscle we got, we'd need at least three days, and that's only if we work 'em all in shifts so we can haul 'round the clock."

"That means we got to start movin' the boat on the eighteenth," Weaver said. "Which means the rain's gotta break for at least a spell by the seventeenth."

Nacky looked alarmed. "You sayin' we only got eleven days left?"

Jimmer smiled apologetically. "That's what the ciphering says."

Nacky's shoulders slumped. He stepped soddenly over to Bara's abandoned chair and sat. The rain and mud, which had begun leaking into the socket of his loblolly foot, felt damp and gritty against the stump of his ankle. "Eleven days," he said sourly, "and this one's a tossaway."

Jimmer nodded in agreement. "I wouldn't say this to none but you," he said, "but we're hard against it. I don't reckon us finishing in time if we don't get some sun soon."

"How soon?" Weaver asked.

Jimmer peered out at the sky and smiled wanly. "I wouldn't say no to now." Nacky frowned at Jimmer, who shrugged helplessly. "I'm tellin' you fact. It's the weather what's in control now."

At that instant, as if to give the truth to what Jimmer had said, a bright gash of lightning cut through the sky. It was followed immediately by an ear-cracking explosion—one that caused the ground to heave and the air itself to shake. Nacky, Weaver and Jimmer jumped up. The sound followed the flash far too fast—and was far too loud—to be mere thunder. There was only one thing it could be.

"Lightning strike!" Teedie's voice cried out from the bank. "Strike on the ridge!"

Nacky, Weaver and Jimmer wheeled toward the sound of the boy's voice and saw him pointing up toward the lip of the bowl. The patch of ridge he was indicating had indeed simply ceased to exist—a ten-foot stretch of ruby-red soil now replaced by a ten-foot crater, steaming off its rain and bleeding off its mud. The smoky smell of cordite hung in the air.

"Lightning strike!" Nacky echoed. "Clear the bank! Clear it now!"

The workers did not need any persuading. The few who were working on the hull of the boat dropped their hammers and tore off for the ridge; the ones who'd been working in the cabins and passageways emerged from the hatches up on the deck and began climbing over the side on ladders and scaffolds. Nacky and Jimmer moved to run off too, but Weaver held out his arms to keep them back.

"No!" he barked in his seaman's tone. "You ain't gonna outrun lightning, least of all on an open road. Stay here! Stay low!"

He pushed Nacky and Jimmer behind him, then faced the bank and whistled loudly for Teedie and Dal. The boys turned at the sound and sprinted toward the kutch tent, where Nacky and Jimmer grabbed them and pulled them inside. At that moment, another bolt of lightning flashed, striking the ground on another part of the ridge and shaking the air with an even louder roar. And as that happened, the rain-softened trail up the side of the bowl that the ship would have to climb in just eleven days' time seemed to melt whole, running red like a downward-streaming river. The trail, for now at least, had vanished. Nacky looked at Jimmer beseechingly. Jimmer looked back and shook his head in a slow, disconsolate no.

CHAPTER FORTY-ONE

It took Nacky more than two hours to
fight his way off the bank, up the lake bowl and back down the padroad
to his house. It was, he realized, the first time in a long time he'd been
there alone. The lightning that struck the bank stopped as quickly as
it had started, and though the rain kept drizzling down, the danger
seemed past. Bara thus decided to stay at the lake for a while to oversee
any builders who might return for an afternoon work shift. Weaver sent
Teedie and Dal off to Emma's for a change of clothes and a plate of
hot food, then decided to follow them there to make sure they didn't
go hurkling in the mud ruts on the way. Before he left, he turned back,
took Nacky by the arm and gave him a narrow look. He did not appear
to like what he saw in Nacky's eyes.

"What are you about?" Weaver asked.

"Goin' home," Nacky said.

"On what business?"

Nacky pulled away, annoyed. "To get a set of clothes what ain't covered in rain and mud."

Weaver did not seem satisfied. "See that changin' your clothes is all
you do," he said. Nacky looked hard at Weaver—harder than he'd ever

looked at him before—and stalked off. The big man had taken the same warning tone with him that Emma Hay had taken earlier this morning, and Nacky wasn't sure he cared for it from either one of them.

Chilled and shivering, Nacky finally arrived back at his house, clumped up the front steps, shooed Orro over to the hearth and wearily followed him there. There was, of course, no fire burning, and there were only a few sticks of kindling lying nearby. The true firewood was outside, likely now too wet to burn. Nacky muttered to himself, then unbuttoned his muddy shirt and tried to strip it off. The twisted fabric clung to him like pine tar. Nacky fought to free himself, feeling the cloth pull against his skin and the anger grow inside him. As he struggled, his wooden foot, which provided poor purchase even when it was dry, skidded suddenly on the floorboards, causing him to fall on his hip and back with a great crash. Nacky wailed in surprise and pain—and then in rage. He pulled at the shirt until the right sleeve simply ripped away, then turned on the hated loblolly foot. He yanked it from his stump of an ankle, heedless of the way the wet leather straps raked at his flesh, then flung it as hard as he could against the warped door of the *Walnut Egg,* still leaning next to the hearth. The door tipped forward and fell to the floor with a crash even louder than the one Nacky had made. Orro scrabbled backward in terror, and Nacky dropped his head into his hands, weeping.

His teak boat would never be. He knew that now. There was too much wood still to hammer, too much rain still to fall. And there wasn't nearly enough time to manage any of it. What's more, Nacky wasn't nearly enough man. He'd been a poor thief, a poor sailor and now he was a poor builder too. This time, though, when he failed, he was going to cause the entire town to fail along with him. Yole had been a sad and broken place before, but it was a sad and broken place where most people at least had their homes. Come the twenty-first of the month, that would all change. The boat would still be on the bank, Baloo and his beat-men would come to fetch it, and any builders whose rent was in arrears—which was most of them—would promptly be pitched. The townspeople's lots had never been good, but Nacky Patcher and a vengeful Baloo would soon make them far worse.

But there was an answer to all that. The beat-men didn't have to come; the builders didn't have to lose their homes. Baloo could be appeased and the town could be saved—made no better perhaps, but surely made no worse. What's more, Nacky himself could have true wealth—gems in his pocket and a deed to his name—for the first time in his life. That would surely sit poorly with the townspeople, but did the state of his purse truly matter if he saved the builders their homes? Why, in time they might even think him a hero for devising such a clever way out of their problems. And if all that meant that the town would never emerge from the curse of the dry-land boats, perhaps that was not such a worrisome matter after all. Even Jimmer said the stories were just cradle tales, and Jimmer's opinion on most things counted high in Nacky's esteem.

It all seemed so surprisingly simple, and the more Nacky thought of it, the more sense it made. As those thoughts came over him, so too did the warm, thrilling feeling of the thief heat—filling his mind with images of riches and his ears with the sound of his own pulsing blood. Somewhere under the stone steps outside his front door was the dusk apple fruit rocket that could make those riches his. Nacky scooted on his rump over to where his wooden foot lay and expertly strapped it back into place. He rose quickly and turned to go, but before he could move farther, the front door swung open and Teedie Flinn stepped inside. The man's eyes met the boy's—and then Nacky broke the gaze.

"What are you about?" Teedie asked suspiciously.

"I thought you was at Emma's," Nacky said, looking down.

"Been there, then came lookin' for you. What are you about?" Teedie repeated. Nacky still didn't answer, and Teedie gave him a long look, taking in his torn shirt, the toppled door from the *Walnut Egg,* Nacky's flushed face. At last the boy spoke. "Boat ain't never gonna get full-built, is it?" he asked quietly.

Nacky slumped, and the thief heat he'd been feeling cooled. "No," he said simply.

"There ain't no hope for it?"

"I don't see how."

Nacky did not know how Teedie would react to such news, but so young a boy, he reckoned, would likely cry. Teedie, however, remained silent, chewing what Nacky had said. Then, less like the child he was than the man he was still years from being, Teedie answered. "I don't see no hope for it, neither," he said. "What do you reckon to do now?"

Nacky was surprised. "I don't guess I know," he said, averting his eyes again.

Teedie looked at him skeptically. "I expect you do. I expect you know precisely."

"What are you saying, boy?"

"You still got yourself a fruit rocket under them steps?"

Nacky looked shocked. "What do you know about such things?"

"I know enough. You learn to sleep light in a place like a half-home, and it ain't a habit you lose," Teedie said. "Constable comes calling here early one morning with a rocket and a deed and bagful of gems, I'm not likely to miss it."

"That ain't your affair," Nacky snapped.

"It's half my boat," Teedie said, "it's half my affair."

"All the same, this ain't fit business for a child."

"Bein' a child don't have nothin' to do with it," Teedie said. "It don't take a full-up man to know that what the constable said was truth. If we can save them builders' homes and fill our pockets too, I can't see how anybody gets hurt—especially if the boat is lost no matter what."

Nacky looked at Teedie forlornly. The boy was right, of course, and he reckoned he admired the way a child so young came to a conclusion so straight and cold. But then he looked at Teedie again and saw that there was more than just a man's good sense behind the boy's thoughts—there was a man's greed too. Teedie's face was smooth and untroubled. There was a cool glint in his eye, and he wore an odd, uneven smile, as if he'd taken strong drink. Nacky went cold. This was the way he imagined he himself looked when the thief heat flowed through him. It was the way he imagined he'd looked only a moment ago. His Pippa had always been able to spot the expression coming over him and had always scolded him to stop—a thief showing such a face being a thief showing his plans. Nacky had never learned to mask his feelings, and Teedie, a mere child, could not, either. The boat had left the boy's thoughts altogether, and the gems and land had taken its place.

Nacky stared at Teedie in something close to sorrow. The boy had always talked about learning thieving, and now Nacky reckoned he was. He gave him a gentle shove on the shoulder. "Outside," he said simply.

Teedie beamed, then hopped out the door and down the front stairs. Nacky took a match from the cup on the mantel, and followed him out. The boy was already lying on the ground, peering under the steps. Nacky nudged him aside, crouched down and reached into the cool, shadowy space as far as he could. He felt the rocket, pulled it out and looked at it. This was the first time he'd seen the thing in full daylight. It was about a half-foot long with a half-foot launch stick protruding from its bottom. It had a small, inch-long fuse. Teedie regarded the rocket approvingly.

"It's fine made," he said. "It'll fly true."

Nacky poked the stick into the ground, struck the match on the dry understone of the stair, and touched the flame to the fuse. There was a loud hiss, and the tube of bright powders leapt from the ground and shot into the sky. It arced high over the padroad and burst in a dark, brilliant shower of dusk apple red. In morning light, the color was not as rich as it would have been at dusk, but it was still bright enough to catch the constable's eye—and to hold Nacky's fast.

"Beautiful," Nacky whispered.

Teedie winced at the sight—and at the terrible memories it still conjured.

Nacky did not know where the constable was staying in the long days since he'd come to call on him, but he had no doubt Baloo had kept him close, likely on the estate itself. He had no doubt either that Baloo had instructed the lawman to set out for Nacky's the moment he saw the fruit rocket fly. It was a twenty-minute walk from Mally Baloo's estate to Nacky Patcher's house, provided you went briskly—something else Nacky was sure Baloo had ordered the constable to do. Nacky summoned Teedie inside, made a pot of tea and changed his clothes while Teedie sipped at his mug.

On the twenty-first minute there was a knock at his door. Nacky opened it to find the constable on his step.

"Reckoned I'd hear from you on a day like today," the lawman said, peering around Nacky and spying Teedie inside. "Didn't reckon I'd see the boy here too."

"It's the boy's affair same as it is mine," Nacky said. Teedie nodded.

"As you say," the constable answered indifferently and made a move to come in. Nacky blocked his way.

"Outside," he said. "This ain't fittin' business to conduct in a home."

The constable looked at him and laughed. "Thief's honor, I expect," he said, standing back to allow Nacky and Teedie to join him outside. "It don't matter to me where we do business, long as you understand the terms. You keep them builders off that bank tomorrow. Tell 'em the mud needs clearin' or the ship needs dryin' or some such. Give us two full days and we'll have that teak chopped to beams and every stick hauled clean. For that, you get the gems and the land, and the builders get to keep their homes."

The constable reached into his pocket, took out the jewel bag and gave it a shake. He produced the deed and held it out invitingly. Nacky felt the thief heat run through him, hard enough to make him sway slightly. The constable looked at him and grinned a cheerless grin.

"Take them," he said. Then he looked at Teedie and laughed. "You don't grab 'em fast," he said to Nacky, "I expect the boy will."

Nacky turned to regard Teedie. The lopsided smile was back on the boy's face, bigger and more crooked than before. His eyes were fixed on the bag and the deed, filled with the look of dreamy greed. Teedie's face was usually a sunny thing—smart and sharp and lit from within. Now it had been replaced by something slow and dim and hungry. Nacky felt sickened. And with that, his own thief heat, which had been surging so powerfully inside him, instantly turned to cold stone. Without thinking, he snatched the gems and deed from the constable's hands.

"What are you about, Patcher?" the constable demanded, alarmed.

Nacky ignored him and in a blink, ripped the deed in two pieces and tossed it in the soil, then tore open the bag and poured the gems into his hand. He cocked his arm back to hurl the sparkly stones toward the thick stand of trees next to the padroad. The constable's arm shot up and he grabbed Nacky's wrist and held it fast.

"Are you away to the hills, Patcher?" he screamed, going red-faced. "Are you away to the hills?" The constable pushed Nacky up against the side of the house and with his free hand grabbed him half by the collar and half by the throat. "That deed can't be replaced!"

The enraged lawman looked ready to choke Nacky where he stood, and a terrified Teedie leapt toward them. He threw himself against the muscled constable, who barely moved at the impact of the small boy.

"Stop!" Nacky croaked to Teedie. "Back to the road!" Teedie stayed where he was. "To the road, I say!" Nacky barked with the last of his breath as the constable tightened his grip on his throat. Teedie obeyed, taking several steps toward the padroad. Then Nacky twisted back toward the constable, whose furious face was only inches from Nacky's own, running with sweat and the still-drizzling rain.

"Any harm comes to me, the boy will light out," Nacky said hoarsely. "And it won't be no good settin' off after him. There's cats what can't run with that child. Now, you ain't committed no crime yet, constable, but throttling me would surely be one. What's more, the boy would cheep about the kind of business you was here on today and you'd be run out of this town and any other. So think on what you want to do next."

The constable stared at Nacky hard, and Nacky stared back harder. Then the lawman slowly loosened his grip and pushed Nacky away with a rough shove.

Nacky straightened himself up and handed the gem chips and the bag back to the constable. "Now you're going to have some sortin' out to do with Mally Baloo," he said, squaring off his shoulders. "And what you tell him ain't my worry. I still got a boat to build, and now I got a boy to set straight as well. You'd best leave my land."

The constable glared at Nacky, bent and scooped up the ruined deed, then stomped off to the padroad, almost losing his balance in the slick mud as he went. Nacky followed him with his eyes, then looked sternly back at Teedie. "We got matters to discuss, boy," he said. With an angry tick of his head, Nacky gestured Teedie back into the house—an honest man's house, he thought, as he followed him inside.

CHAPTER FORTY-TWO

Almost the moment Baloo's gems vanished back into the constable's pocket, the wet weather that had been melting the lake bowl began to subside. The clouds crumbled away, retreating to the edges of the sky where, over the course of the next several days, they'd occasionally close in with a misting of rain but never a true downpour. This was precisely the kind of half-dry, half-wet weather that was right for this time of year. It would be possible to build a boat in such conditions, and while the work that lay ahead would be terribly messy and sometimes slow, it could at least resume. Whether the soil had already soaked up too much water to allow the great ship to be hauled from the bowl was impossible to say.

Jimmer, nonetheless, moved fast to take advantage of the improvement in the weather. He assigned a small team of workers to repair the damage to the lake trail—smoothing out the rain-rutted soil, scattering gravel to improve the footing, digging a wide trench straight up the center to give the boat a smooth path up. While this work was going on, he also relit his kutch fires and saw to it that the hot caulk got used in a hurry. Most of the workers not busy with the trail work were told to put aside anything else they were doing and help with sealing the hull and deck. In order to get the most out of every day, he erected a series of torches down the lake bowl and along part of the bank so that even the fall of night would not prevent the work from proceeding. The two dozen half-home boys joined in the kutching, their nimbleness serving them well on the ladders and scaffolds.

Barely four days after the messy work began, it was almost complete. The builders were then free to turn their attention to the business of hanging the now-completed ropes and sails from the spars and masts. It was a matter Nacky had done his best not to think much about.

The merchant fleets were filled with stories of boatbuilders who got fumble-fingered on masts a hundred or more feet in the air and came tumbling down to land bug-flat on hardwood decks. Nacky could not abide the idea that his workers, who had neither builders' skills nor builders' wages, should take on such risks. What's more, the sails they would be wrestling up the masts would be much more cumbersome than anyone had imagined. The yellow canvas seemed coarse and heavy when it was used to make a child's dress, but spread out to sail size and opened up to the fist of the wind, it was as delicate as a lady's kerchief. For that reason, the indigent girls had to make some of the sails out of two or even three layers of cloth, depending on just where each would be hung on the boat. Every one of those sails would thus be two or even three times harder to lift than it looked.

To minimize the danger of hanging such unwieldy things, Nacky took a couple of precautions. First of all, he ordered that a cargo net be woven and hung over the side of the ship, so that the sail riggers could use it as a ladder, making it easier to climb aboard while muscling the heavy canvas with them. He and Bara then spent a long night by lantern light, going over Bara's ledgers and reviewing which folks were best suited to the dangerous work and which weren't. The next morning, they came to the lake with a list of the twenty-five people they had chosen and announced to Jimmer that those would be the only ones allowed to take part in the rigging and sail hanging—and that only the strongest among them would be allowed to climb anywhere near the top

315

of the masts. Just two of the half-home boys were deemed big enough and serious enough to manage such work, and they were assigned to rig only the mizzenmast, and the bottom half of it at that. Teedie was left off the list entirely.

"It ain't right," he groused. "I'm at least as fit for climbin' as them others."

"You already ruined your hand and burned off your hair, and you ain't yet twelve," Nacky said. "I ain't gonna let you break yourself up any more."

Teedie fussed but knew it was useless, and that very dusk the sails arrived at the lake—fat, yellow wedges finished and folded by the fine hands of the indigent girls. Over the next several days, the twenty-five riggers busied themselves climbing up and down the masts, adding cloth muscles and rope tendons to the high bones of the huge ship. Nacky went flutterguts watching the dangerous work, and finally, on the morning of the fifteenth, an exasperated Bara ordered him into the passageways inside the ship to help out with the final parts-fitting and door-hanging, guessing that what he couldn't see in the masts above wouldn't frighten him. Teedie remained outside on the bank, still grumbling about being banned from the masts, but keeping himself busy overseeing the remaining sort-and-carry teams, so that those builders who were doing the sail-hanging had all the canvas and rigging they needed.

"That boy works better in a foul mood than most people do in a good one," Bara said to Weaver.

Finally, on the morning of the sixteenth—just two days before the boat would have to be pulled—the rope-hoisting slowed, the hammers fell silent, the fires under the kutch barrels were allowed to cool. As the sun rose over the rim of the bowl and the torches that had lit the bank grew smoky and cold, the workers, most of whom had labored through the night, backed away from the vessel and regarded it quietly. Nacky, who had been working in the 'tween deck, appeared at the rail, climbed over the side and made his way carefully down the cargo net. Teedie and Jimmer were waiting for him at the bottom. They helped him hop the last two feet down to the pebbly soil, then the three of them also stepped back and gazed up at their ship—a rampart of blond teak made almost gold by the early sun.

"She ready to launch?" Nacky asked Jimmer quietly.

"A few lines to test," he answered. "A little more work with the tar pots, maybe. But if we had to sail today, we'd be rigged and ready."

"Rigged and ready," Nacky repeated softly to himself.

"Forty thousand pieces," Teedie half-whispered, staring up at the wall of teak, "come to this here one piece."

"One piece that ain't yet touched the sea," Jimmer reminded. "We got a day and a half till we haul it out of here, and I aim to spend most of it sleeping. I expect you two ought to do the same."

Nacky nodded, turned Teedie by the shoulders and gave the boy a shove toward the lake trail. "You heard what he said," Nacky instructed. "Back to Emma's for a scrub-up and bed-down."

"You ain't comin'?" Teedie asked.

"I'll be along. I need to have a word with Bara Berry first."

Teedie nodded and ran off. He expected he knew what Nacky and Bara needed to discuss.

For several days now, Emma Hay had been talking about holding a grand meal at the great table in the indigents' home. She knew from the start that she wanted to hold the dinner on the evening of September the seventeenth, the day before the boat would have to begin being hauled from the lake. This, she figured, would be a proper night for the people who had worked hardest on building the thing to take a supper together, and while she was still chary about letting outsiders into her home, these few were also the ones she could most trust to keep the secret of her girls and how they lived. If she didn't hold such a meal now, she worried that she never would. With so big a ship to drag up so slick a bank, there was no telling who might still be about when the hauling was done and who might have been sent off to the tower or chased off by the chain-and-ladder wagon or finished off altogether if the vessel toppled midway through the pull.

Teedie was thrilled when Nacky told him of the plan. Having enjoyed so many fine meals from Emma's simple baskets, he went half dizzy thinking about what she might produce when she decided to lay out a true feast. Nacky himself did not much care for the idea, reckoning that he would prefer to eat little and sleep long on the evening before such punishing work was to begin. But when Emma had her mind set on an idea, she was not likely to be dissuaded. The dinner would thus be held just as she planned it, one hour before sundown on the night of the seventeenth. Nacky would be expected to invite Weaver and Jimmer, as well as Teedie and Dal. Emma even suggested that Bara Berry attend, if Bara would see fit. Nacky promised to extend the invitation to Bara, but he did not look forward to what her answer would be. Now he saw her approaching on the bank and hallooed her over.

"You ain't going off to sleep?" she asked him.

"In a tick," he answered. "I need you to do me a turn first."

She looked at him dubiously. "What sort of turn?"

"I need you to take dinner at the indigents' home tomorrow night."

Bara stopped. "Emma Hay's indigents' home?"

"Yes."

"And Emma Hay'll be there?"

"Of course."

"Then I reckon I won't be."

Nacky sighed. "Ain't it time to put all that aside?"

"It won't ever be that time."

"One evening's all I want."

"One evening's too much."

"She asked for you special."

"I said no," Bara answered flatly.

"Now see here, Bara Berry!" Nacky snapped. He startled himself with his tone, and from the look on Bara's face, he surprised her too. "A long time ago, Emma Hay done you and your sister wrong—or that's what you believe. But nobody made Mary run off. She done that herself. And Emma didn't set out after her or send her to the tower. Others done

318

that. Emma ain't done nothin' but look after her girls since. And she ain't done nothin' but help us with our boat all summer. So you point fingers where you will, but I won't have you pointin' them at her any longer. You hear?"

Bara looked at Nacky and said nothing. Nacky had always known her to be a girl who could tell precisely when it was time to stand up for herself and, just as important, when it was time to stand down. As far as he could remember, he'd never seen her make the wrong choice.

"As you're askin'," she said quietly, "I'll be there."

Nacky had expected no less from her.

CHAPTER FORTY-THREE

In the day and a half leading up to the grand dinner at the indigents' home, Emma and her girls would have much to do. Dal Tally agreed to help out—a fact that surprised nobody at all, since Mag was at the indigents' home, and wherever Mag was, Dal increasingly contrived to be. Mag, for her part, was entirely thrilled with the attention. Teedie too offered to help out, reckoning that he'd enjoyed so many fine meals from Emma's baskets, it was only fitting that he help her get ready for the finest she'd ever lay on her table. The night before the dinner, Emma sent Teedie and Dal to the Albert T. Rain to borrow a large tureen Dree had promised to lend her. Mag volunteered to accompany Dal. Gurtee, who liked to do whatever Mag did, insisted on accompanying them all. So it was that the four children set out in the full-night hours when most folks in Yole were preparing for bed.

The evening was warm and clear, and while Teedie was enjoying the night air, Dal was enjoying the quiet walk with Mag—or as quiet as the chittering Gurtee would let the moment be. When they got to the Rain, Teedie prepared to run in alone, knowing that Dree never took kindly to one child in her restaurant, never mind four. He hadn't taken more than a single step onto the porch, however, when the four of them heard a wet coughing from the shadows. They froze, then turned as one, and the dark shape of a man emerged. Standing—slouching, really—in front of them, the man was swaying slightly and muttering something he appeared to intend them to hear but also seemed unable to say properly. Even from several steps away, Teedie, Dal, Mag and Gurtee could smell the cloud of malt coming off of him. It didn't take much to guess that the man had had many mugs more than his share this evening. It also didn't take much to guess who he was. Even in the dark, the stout shape and hard, nasal voice were unmistakable.

"Meddo Brinn!" Teedie said.

The other three edged away, placing themselves behind Teedie's shoulder. Teedie stood his ground.

"Brinn I am," Meddo said, peering at Teedie. He closed one eye against the drink that was causing him to see eight children in front of him instead of the four who were properly there. He turned his open eye toward Dal. "You're one o' them boys what come from Knockle to build the boat," he said.

"Don't matter who I am," Dal answered. "What's your business spookin' the girls?" Mag drew closer to him.

Meddo laughed at Dal's brass, then coughed wetly again in a way that made the girls wrinkle up their noses. "I don't guess it does matter," he said. "Don't guess it matters who none of you is—nor what none of you does, neither."

"See here," Mag said, finding her voice, "you shoo or I'll fetch Dree. She'd be pleased to pot-wallop the likes of you."

Teedie held his hand up to hush Mag and looked at Meddo, narrowing his eyes. Something about what the sodden man said had troubled him. "What do you mean it don't matter what none of us does?"

Meddo nodded. "Boy's smart. Even a man in his malt deserves a hearing."

Teedie waved that off. "What did you mean it don't matter?"

"Your boat," Meddo answered. "It don't matter what none of you figures to do with it, because there ain't no boat—not a whole one, anyway."

"That boat's whole—whole as any what ever sailed."

"No it ain't," Meddo said. "It looks whole. But a part's missin'. May not be an important part. May be so important the whole thing'll shake itself to timbers soon's you try to move it. Can't say. I can say it's as pretty a piece of wood as I've ever seen."

Teedie narrowed his eyes. "How's the likes of you come to know such a thing?" he asked.

"I seen the part. Seen it in the hands of the man what took it. I can tell you this: He reckons it's important."

"Baloo," Teedie spat.

"Just so," Meddo answered.

"What's he want with one piece o' boat? Can't reckon it'll do him no good," Dal said.

"That's what he reckons too—or part reckons. But there's people in this town what believes in curses, and I suspect he's one o' them—leastways that's what I see in his face. I expect he thinks if he can keep hold of one piece, he can keep the rest from leavin'. He watches over it fierce when he's at home. When he's not, he gives it to the stable boys to look after. You find them boys, you'll find your piece."

"Why are you tellin' us all this?" Mag asked. "Emma Hay says you don't mean nothin' but misery for this boat."

Meddo laughed again, this time so hard his face reddened. But it was a dark laugh, one without mirth. It reminded Dal of the laughter of the Knockle headmasters when they'd crack their whips at the boys working the fish ruts. It was the laugh of a coward.

"I'm tellin' you so that maybe you'll tell the others I did," Meddo said when he'd finally caught his breath. "Baloo said he'd look after me—my family too—if I helped him out. But I don't think he's the kind what'll keep his word. If he turns us out, and if none others will have us, then where'll we go? I tell you where you can find that piece, maybe you'll talk kindly of me." Teedie gave Meddo a hard look, and Meddo fairly crumpled, seeming to fold in on himself even more than he already had. "I got boys too, lad," he said pitiably.

Teedie glanced at Dal and the girls, then looked at Meddo and ticked his head yes. Meddo smiled a weak smile. "You'll have to go to Baloo's," Meddo began, "and you'll have to be right careful about how you do it."

Meddo went on, slowly describing the lay of the estate and the look of the missing boat part and what would have to be done to retrieve it. It was a job Teedie resolved to do himself—he and Dal, if the other boy was of a mind. Nacky Patcher would never let him undertake something so risky. But Nacky himself liked to say that charms are broken when the chances present themselves. This chance had just presented itself, and they alone, Teedie guessed, were meant to pursue it.

CHAPTER FORTY-FOUR

At precisely one hour before sundown the next night, Nacky, Bara, Weaver, Jimmer, Teedie and Dal gathered on the porch of the indigents' home, all of them looking more combed and tucked than anyone could remember. Weaver was wearing a pair of buffed black boots and a stiff white shirt and had combed back his silver hair, giving him even more of a lionheaded look than he usually had. Teedie had applied a bit of hair oil to the bristly brush that was growing back on his shorn scalp, and though neither he nor Dal owned a proper dinner shirt, both had worn the cleanest shirts they did have and rolled the sleeves down full rather than keeping them pushed above the elbows as they usually did. Nacky too had combed and slicked his feathery hair and had made it a point to wear his fine blue shirt shot through with its fine white thread. For this evening, he had also left Orro back at his house. Only Bara had not dressed special for the dinner.

The evening air was pleasant enough, and the six guests didn't mind idling on the porch—a good thing, since, as Nacky knew, Emma would assume they'd appear on time but would further assume they knew not to disturb her until she was ready for them. As they waited, Nacky looked down the road in the direction of the Albert T. Rain and was surprised to see Dree struggling up the hill toward them. She was dressed not in her accustomed poppy red, but in her less-common plum purple, a color she wore only when she wanted to put on the feather. She was carrying three heavy trays of what appeared to be her breads and looked like she was having a difficult time managing them. Nacky had suspected for a while that the walk up from the Rain would eventually be hard on the stout Dree, but this was the first time he'd ever seen her struggle. Weaver noticed Dree at the same moment Nacky did and spoke up immediately.

"Hey, hey," he said to Teedie and Dal, pointing toward Dree. "Lend a hand there, lend a hand."

The boys quick-stepped off the porch and hurried down to Dree. From a distance, Nacky could see them reach out for the trays and Dree fuss at them and resist. They pressed and she still resisted, but eventually she handed the heavy breads over with a glower. The three of them then began walking up the hill, Dree staying between the two boys and saying nothing to either one of them. At one point she appeared to lose her balance and leaned into Teedie, who held her straight with a discreet brace of elbow, doing her the kindness of pretending not to realize it was happening at all.

"I didn't truly need no assistance," Dree puffed as she reached the porch steps and struggled up them.

"Didn't anyone say you did," Nacky answered. "I just couldn't bear seein' that fine bread get dropped. You was walkin' without 'em, we'd'a let you alone."

Dree grunted. "Shouldn't've brought 'em at all. Emma Hay come down about midday to ask me up to supper. Her girls like their sweet brick, so I guessed I'd bake some up. I didn't recall 'em being so heavy." She looked around at the group. "You six all that's comin'?"

"On top of Emma and her girls," Nacky said.

"I'm pleased to see you combed up, Teedie Flinn," Dree said with an approving expression. Teedie looked down and smiled. "You too, Nacky Patcher," she added. Bara stood silently, talking to no one.

From behind them, there was a sound of a latch being pulled back and they turned around to face the door. It opened to reveal the four-year-old Lassa looking back at them straight and square. Her black hair was pulled back with a bright bit of ribbon, and her face was flushed as if she had just washed it. Her dress—one Nacky had never seen her wear before—was made of the familiar yellow canvas, but with a scalloped collar and a similarly fancy finish around the short sleeves. She seemed puffed up with the idea of wearing it.

"Emma says there should be seven people here," she said in her piping voice.

"There are," Nacky said.

"If there aren't seven people, you can't come in."

"There are," Nacky repeated.

Lassa nodded, satisfied. "Then you can come in."

Lassa stepped aside and opened the door full, and the boys and the men stood back to let Dree and Bara enter first. Dree went ahead without hesitation, but Bara stopped and turned to Nacky.

"Ain't been here since just after Mary," she said.

"I know," Nacky answered.

"Didn't never want to come back."

"I know that too."

Nacky smiled at her and nudged her through the door, and the rest of them followed. For this evening, Emma had lit all the lamps in the main workroom, but had turned them down to half their brightness, filling the space with a soft shimmer. Off to the right, the dining table was fully set and decorated with yellow candles in pewter candlesticks. The small flames gave off a lemony light of their own. Most of the girls were already lined up at their places, all of them wearing the same fancy dress Lassa was. Those whose hair was long enough to take decoration also wore bright bits of ribbon. For this evening, the picture of Mary Berry had been removed from the wall opposite the table on the other side of the workroom, a faint, rectangular patch marking the place it ought to have been. Emma, of course, would not have cared for Bara to see such a thing, and Nacky was pleased she'd remembered to attend to the small matter before they arrived.

"House didn't used to look like this," Bara said to Nacky in a wondering whisper.

"A lot ain't the way it used to be," Nacky answered.

Emma emerged from the kitchen with Mag and Gurtee and walked toward the workroom. She smiled easily, her eyes playing over her guests. The two girls looked mostly down, though Mag did sneak a glance up at the group, then sneaked a second one, this time directed at Dal. Even in the owl light of the workroom, she appeared to blush.

"I'm pleased everyone's here," Emma said, speaking more formally than she ordinarily did. "I'm not terribly good at hellos. Everyone knows me. Over there are my girls. I'll leave you all to share out your names. Bara Berry, I expect a lot of them know of you already."

"Expect they do," Bara grumbled.

"I'm happy you're here especially."

"Expect you are."

Nacky winced, but Emma paid Bara no mind. "I've got places set for everyone at the table," she said, then turned to Mag and Gurtee. "You two take the sweet brick trays. The rest, take a seat."

Dal and Teedie handed the girls the trays, and Emma showed them all to the table. Emma's own seat at the head of the table was empty, and to Nacky's surprise, she pointed Dree there. The spot to her left was also free and she gave that to Weaver. Teedie and Dal were given two empty seats in the middle of the table between Mag and Gurtee. At the far end were four more empty seats, and Emma, Nacky, Bara and Jimmer took their places there.

The atmosphere in the room was quieter than usual as the big group settled themselves in their chairs, but as soon as Emma's food was brought to the table, the stuffy mood broke. The girls attacked the platters and bowls of fowl and potatoes and yams and greens and breads and barley and relish as soon as they were laid down, and the guests did much the same. Teedie and Dal ate hungrily and began to talk excitedly to the clutch of girls seated around them. They chattered on about the boat, describing the number of parts and the weight of the keel and the remarkable places the huge vessel would sail, their eyes sparkling as the girls' eyes widened. Though Dal and Teedie did not let their speaking interrupt their eating, their plates never seemed to grow empty. Mag and Gurtee continually filled them and refilled them, sometimes jostling each other as they fought to be first with the serving spoon.

At the head of the table, Dree and Weaver dished out food as well, filling up the youngest girls' plates first and then their own. Lassa, who was seated next to Weaver, paid her food little mind. She was far more interested in climbing onto the giant man's lap and shoulders than working at her supper. At the far end of the table, Jimmer tried to keep up a lively stream of conversation first with Nacky, then with Bara and finally with Emma, but the three ate in comparative quiet. Emma was busy watching over things with her usual tend-to-business eye. Bara was busy avoiding Emma's roving gaze. Nacky was silent for other reasons entirely.

As the sun vanished and the meal commenced, he began to realize fully the awful business that was to begin in less than twelve hours' time. Nacky and Teedie had not set out this summer to build a giant ocean boat, but build a giant ocean boat they had. Tomorrow that boat would begin to move. The likelihood was high that it would founder well before it ever saw the sea. Nacky had understood that all along, but now, so short a time before the fate of the vessel would actually be known, he understood it in a much more terrible way. Whenever Nacky's mind turned toward this thought, his stomach turned against the food in front of him. He ate what he could so as not to give offense to Emma, but he wondered how it was that nobody else in the room was as troubled as he was.

All at once, however, he recognized that someone else was just as disturbed. Looking toward the other end of the table, he saw that Lassa had suddenly given off climbing over Weaver and settled back into her seat. She was staring over her food, across the workroom, and toward

328

the far wall. Her eyes were fixed on the pale spot where the picture had been hanging and she was wearing an expression of frightened wonder, the same one Emma had seen when the girl heard the ceiling beam creaking in the Albert T. Rain. Nacky looked at her face, followed her gaze and saw the part of the wall that held her fast. As he did, he was filled with understanding. He suddenly realized why Emma had insisted on this supper in the first place. As he was realizing that, there was a sound at the front door, and all eyes at the table turned toward it. The door opened full and Mary Berry stepped inside.

Mary Berry in the flesh looked precisely like Mary Berry in the portrait. She was seven years older, seven years straighter, seven years surer-looking than she was when anyone in Yole had seen her last. To- night, her hair appeared tangled and windblown, and her dress—a pale yellow canvas with the faded words "Property of the Yole Indigents' Home" stenciled around its hem—looked rumpled with travel. Even from a distance, her cheeks seemed flushed, her breathing seemed fast and her eyes—the same dark color as Bara's—appeared to be brimming. She looked out at the room, standing just inside the door in the lemony light of the workroom, scanning the supper table and the people seated there. Then she clapped her gaze on Bara Berry.

At Nacky's side, Bara made neither a move nor a sound. Then a single howl escaped her—a sound like none Nacky had ever heard before, but one he understood completely. It was the sound of whole joy.

Bara leapt from the table, tears streaming from her eyes, and bounded across the room toward Mary; Mary ran toward her as well and they col- lided in the workroom in a clawing embrace. They spoke unintelligibly, they wept uncontrollably. Bara buried her face in Mary's shoulder and Mary—taller, stronger—held her close. Some of the girls at the table leapt up to join them, but Emma, her own eyes full, held up a restraining hand and they obeyed her. Nacky swallowed and blinked and felt tears well up in his eyes too.

After a long moment, Bara turned back to the table, ran to Emma and flung her arms about her, covering her head with laughing kisses.

Then Bara returned to Mary and the two of them made their way out the front door, around the porch and into the complete stillness of the dark yard. There, for the better part of the night, Mary told Bara a long, long story. When the evening ended and the supper table was cleared, the sisters were still lost in a talk that would go on until sunup.

CHAPTER FORTY-FIVE

Most of the people who attended the
grand dinner at the indigents' home slept like the fully dead that night.
The late meal, the rich food and the prospect of the terrible work they
would undertake in the morning sent them straight to their beds and
into heavy slumber. Even Nacky was able to enjoy a long night's rest in
his own bed in his own home, Bara having no intention of returning
there this evening. Emma, perhaps, slept best of all. It was she, of course,
who had summoned Mary from Bretony tonight, bringing the Berry girls
at last back together. She had undone the thing she'd done seven years
earlier and was drawing her first clear breaths in all that time. On this
night in all the town, it would thus be only Teedie Flinn and Dal Tally
who had no plans to sleep. Meddo Brinn and the things he had told
them were still sitting heavy on their minds.

When the dinner was done, Nacky instructed both boys to come
home with him straightaway; however, they insisted they'd prefer to stay
and help Emma and her girls clear the mountain of plates and scraps
the hungry guests had left behind. Nacky, guessing it was the girls themselves who truly had the boys' attention, agreed but told them to follow
him home as soon as they were done. Teedie and Dal promised they

would. But when the dishes were done and they at last left the home, they turned not in the direction of Nacky Patcher's little house but toward Mally Baloo's far finer one.

Meddo may have been clouded with malt when he spoke to the boys, but his directions to the Baloo lands were clear and good. Even in the half moonlight, Teedie and Dal were able to make their way along the padroads and out to the edge of town where the estate lay. Meddo had told the boys that the first thing they'd see when they approached Baloo's home was an enormous front gate, one with heavy iron bars, each as big around as a man's leg and rising a full twenty feet up. Such a thing would look unpleasant enough in full daylight but would look flat-out fearsome at night. If anything, the boys discovered, it was worse than what Meddo had described.

The gate door was crowned by what appeared to be spearheads, deadly to anyone who attempted to climb over. The door was locked by a huge latch, which was itself as fat as one of the bars. While this was an obstacle that could neither be opened nor scaled, the rest of the fence that surrounded the estate was a different matter—not so high as the front gate, and absent entirely in places where clear ground met thick woods. The night Nacky and Weaver came to take Bara away, they had entered through such an unfenced but densely wooded patch. Teedie and Dal found a similar spot and crept in the same way.

Trespassing on Baloo's land was actually something of a pleasure, partly because of the very danger of the thing, partly because the lushness of the grass and soil felt so different from the dead, patchy ground everywhere else in the fallow Yole. Before long, the boys came upon the spot on a hummocky hill where Meddo had told them the stables should be. The shadow of a boxy building just visible through the gloaming and the smell of horse on the night air told them Meddo was right.

Teedie and Dal picked up their pace and pad-padded through the grass, and the building grew bigger. When they reached it, they half-felt their way around the walls until they got to a small side door behind which they guessed people, not horses, would live. Teedie opened the door, wincing at the loud creak it gave off, and he and Dal stepped inside. Far off, somewhere in the building, they could hear the deep, heavy-chested sound of horses breathing. Up close, they could hear the higher, slighter sound of boys breathing.

The absence of light inside the stable seemed total, but then, about ten steps away, Teedie thought he saw something glint at him. He locked his eyes on that spot, waited while his vision sharpened in the darkness, then saw the thing again. It was something shiny, something polished, something about half the size of the darker, lumpier shape lying beside it. He had some idea what the shiny thing was; the lumpy thing was certainly a boy.

Teedie tiptoed forward with Dal trailing, knelt down and shook the lumpy shape. A boy jolted up, too surprised to speak. Teedie put his hand over the boy's mouth anyway.

"You one of them stable lads what Chuff calls Birl?" he asked. The boy nodded yes. "Good," Teedie said. "Then I reckon you got the thing I come for."

Teedie kept his voice low and his eyes fixed and quietly described the business he was here on. He could see that he had not only startled the boy but was frightening him too. That was just as well, since he'd need him to do precisely what he told him to do when he told him to do it. The stable boy listened and nodded silently to show he understood. Teedie looked at Dal, who nodded too. Wordlessly, Teedie stood, turned and sprinted back off the estate so that he could be back at Nacky's house before he was missed. What happened here he'd have to leave in Dal Tally's uncertain hands.

 OOK SIX

CHAPTER FORTY-SIX

Nacky was the first to stir in his little
house on the day of the hauling. Rising quietly so as not to wake Orro or
Teedie, he lit a small fire in the hearth, heated himself a pot of tea and
slowly drank it off, contemplating the work that lay ahead. When he was
done, he rousted Teedie and Orro from sleep and gave them biscuits to
eat and milk to drink. He asked Teedie if Dal had decided to spend the
night at the indigents' home. Teedie said yes, that was precisely what Dal
had done, and he would in fact be spending the entire day there since
he was feeling poorly. Nacky clucked his tongue at the poor boy's frail
health. Then he waited until Teedie was finished eating and snuffed the
fire with a shovel of ash. Then he, the boy and the pig left the house to
go tend to the matter of the boat.

The walk to the lake that morning was a pleasant one, with the
air cool and the eastern sky taking on the first dim shimmer of dawn.
When they arrived at the ridge overlooking the bank this morning, a
shadowy light filled the bowl. Even with the sun still as weak as it was,
the boat was impossible not to see, a great, peaked shadow blotting out
much of what was around it. From somewhere in the morning gloaming,
the singing of August Ren's birds was clearly audible—the nightingales,

it sounded like, taking one final flap at the ends of their tethers before August tugged them in and sent the morning birds out in their place. Now and then the wind stirred, strumming a soft chord on the thirty ropes running down the bowl. Nacky and Teedie smiled at the sound.

Much sooner than either of them had imagined, they heard the crunch of approaching footsteps. The other workers were not expected here until after dawn, and even Jimmer had said he was going to try to claim as much sleep as he could before beginning the back-snapping labor the day held for them all. Nacky and Teedie turned and saw the shadow of a solitary person coming toward them—a person carrying a bundle. The shadow drew closer and resolved itself into Emma Hay. Nacky smiled into the darkness. Emma approached, wearing a soft expression. The bundle she carried was wrapped in yellow canvas.

"Nacky Patcher," she said, keeping her voice low to match the light. "I expected you'd be here first." She looked at Teedie. "And I reckoned you'd be alongside him."

"Didn't seem like much point stayin' in bed," Nacky said, speaking as softly as Emma.

"You fixed for what's ahead?" Emma asked Teedie.

"Fixed fine," Teedie answered. "No strain to it."

"There'll be plenty of strain," Emma said. "So you stay careful, you understand?" Teedie nodded and then Emma pointed him to a spot several steps away where a cook-fire left by last night's workers still glowed dully. "P'haps you can wait over there for a moment. I've got business with Nacky Patcher."

Teedie did as he was told, and Emma took a step closer to Nacky, peering down into the bowl. He could feel the lick of air she stirred as she moved and could smell the rough soap she used to wash her clothes. It was, he guessed, the finest soap a man could imagine.

"Can you make it out down there?" Emma asked, gazing at the great ship.

"Mostly."

"It's a beast of a boat," Emma said, "a marvelous boat."

"Only hope it floats," Nacky answered.

Emma fell quiet and looked down at the bundle in her hands. Then she extended it to Nacky. He took it and hefted it, and Emma indicated a twine tie holding it shut. Nacky pulled the tie and the canvas spilled open, and even in the dim light the first thing he could see inside were colors—bright berry blue, bright cherry red, green, yellow, orange, peach, pink, purple and more. What Nacky was seeing, he knew at once, were pennants—dozens of fancily stitched ones strung together by cord, enough to form a taut line of snapping colors all the way from his boat's bowsprit to its highest mast.

Nacky's throat closed up and his eyes went full and he held the bright bundle in his arms, unconscious now of the weight of it. To his surprise, Emma then leaned forward, took his face in her hands and kissed him once square on the mouth. Nacky shut his eyes, and Emma held the moment. Then she pulled back, breaking the kiss first and at last releasing his face. She looked bright and flushed.

"Boat deserves such a thing as those pennants," she said. "You deserve such a thing as that boat."

Nacky nodded and tried to speak, but nothing would come. A moment later, he could hear more footsteps approaching the ridge as the other workers at last began to arrive.

Jimmer and Weaver were the first to appear, followed by Bara and Mary Berry. They in turn were followed by Dree and the Dreeboys, the Grimms and the Blands and the twenty-four half-home boys. After them came all the other people who had raised so much as a single board or hammered so much as a single trunnel all summer long. For a moment, the swarm of people on the bank let Emma and Nacky be. Finally, Emma put on her tend-to-business face.

"You've got affairs to mind," she said.

"I do," Nacky answered.

"Then mind them." She turned and walked off toward Mary, Bara and Dree. As she did, she caught Jimmer's eye and signaled to him. Jimmer in turn signaled to Teedie, and the two of them hurried over to Nacky; Weaver followed at a slower pace.

"I never thought you'd free yourself up there," Jimmer said with a smile.

"I ain't sure he wanted to," Teedie added.

"Never mind all that," Nacky said, handing Teedie the bundle of pennants. "You take these and see that they get strung fast and proper." Teedie peeked inside the bundle, smiled and ran off. "And I want them pennants strung by someone other than you!" Nacky called after him. He watched the boy go and then turned to Jimmer and Weaver. "Believe we're ready to haul?" he asked.

"Ain't important if we're ready," Weaver said. "We got to haul, no matter what."

"Is the ground suited to it?" Nacky asked Jimmer.

"The trail and bank ain't as slick as I'd like. The brush beside the trail ain't as dry as I'd like."

"And the weather?"

"I don't care for them clouds," Jimmer said, frowning up at the sky. "This ridge takes up any more water, it could slide out from under us altogether. But like Weaver says, we got to haul."

Whether the builders would actually be able to do that hauling was still to be learned. As Jimmer had planned it, the huge vessel would be dragged up the bowl the same way the huge keel had been dragged out of the water, with a capstan—actually, four capstans. Up on the ridge, Jimmer had chosen four stout trees and shaved away a patch of their bark, the same way he'd stripped down the tree on the bank. He then had a heavy, four-spoked wheel built around each of them and equipped the spokes with harnesses for four horses each. Tied to the capstans were dozens of long ropes that ran down the lake trail and up to the flanks of the boat, where they'd been strung through portholes and tied in place around the vessel's sturdiest ribs. Also secured to the boat's bones were seventy additional towropes with loops at the ends that would be harnessed not to horses but to townspeople on the bank. When the people and the beasts pulled together, so the thinking went, the boat would follow.

In order to keep the ship from tipping as it was hauled, the workers had dug a deep trench in the ground across the bank, connecting to the one that already ran up the trail to the rim of the bowl. As long as the vessel was pulled properly, the trench and the broad keel should keep it upright. In the event the ship didn't move as easily as Jimmer hoped, he had also decided that the main sails on the three tallest masts would be opened up full, allowing them to catch any wind that might come along and provide an extra push along the slick ground. When the ship was at the top of the hill, the workers could gather in the sails, ease the entire vessel onto its side and prepare for the long pull to the coast.

That, at least, was how Dree's books and Jimmer's calculations said it could be done. Jimmer left Nacky's side and hurried to the capstans, where he set about getting the horses secured properly to the spokes. Then, along with Bara and Emma, he began herding the people down to the bank to get them secured to the towropes. Weaver and Nacky stayed on the ridge to collect the last stragglers. To their surprise, among the final people to arrive was Chuff the dwarf.

Nacky had not set eyes on Chuff since the day the little man was struck by the great ball of hemp. Chuff approached him today with the same flat expression and aimless gait he always exhibited. This day of all days, that sleepiness could put him in real danger. Nacky and Weaver hurried over to him.

"Chuff the dwarf," Nacky said. "I thought Bara told you it weren't safe for you to come here."

"She did," Chuff answered and offered nothing more.

"Why'd you come then?"

"I heard the wind blowin' in last night," he said. "Wanted to hear the music up close." He looked toward the harp scale of ropes on the bank and smiled.

"All the same," Nacky said, "this close to the edge is too close. Once them capstans start movin' you'll only get yourself hurt."

Nacky walked Chuff over to the spot where Mary and Dree were planning to wait out the hauling, and clucked his tongue for Orro to follow. "Watch these two?" he asked Dree.

"I'll watch 'em," Dree answered, looking at the pig with lingering distaste. "I won't chase 'em."

Before Dree could change her mind, Nacky returned to the rim of the bowl and spent a final moment with Weaver, who, it was agreed, would stay on the ridge during the pull to supervise the capstans. The former sea captain may have been a bull of a man, but there was no denying he was an old bull, one not necessarily suited to work that required both a stout back and a stout heart. Nacky had worried Weaver would not hear of being left out of the pull, but the former sea captain had a keen sense both of those things he could do and those things he couldn't, and he agreed to remain above. Now he and Nacky watched quietly as the workers slipped into their tow loops down on the bank and the pennant riggers finished their work up in the spars, moving about as dark and quick as tree bugs on branches. When the flags had been strung and the mainsails had been dropped, they knew it was time to go to work.

"You'll see to the capstans?" Nacky asked Weaver.

"I will," Weaver answered.

"Look after Dree and Chuff and the rest?"

"I reckon Dree will manage that herself."

Nacky gazed at the lake once more and took in the full sweep of what he and his builders had accomplished this summer, and for the second time this morning, his eyes went full. His Pippa had told him he'd need to like the people he intended to lead, but what he was feeling for them now was far beyond liking. Weaver cast a glance at him and seemed to read that on his face. The big man smiled slightly, then covered it with the gruffness that had helped make him the fine ship's captain he'd been.

"You've got a boat to see to," he said simply.

"Yes," Nacky answered. "I expect I do."

Nacky stepped onto the lake path and hurried down as fast as his wood foot would allow him. Bara and Emma had already made their way down the trail and were standing with Jimmer and Teedie, their hands on their hips, scowling up at the masts. Nacky ran-hopped up to them.

"I don't know if it was smart to drop them sails," Bara said when she noticed Nacky. "Ain't no wind gonna move a ship this size on land. And if a true gust catches and the boat don't go, you might blow out the cloth altogether."

"That true?" Nacky asked Emma.

"Any cloth can tear if you push it too hard," she answered.

All of them looked back up at the sky, and the wind—as if responding to their worry—spun itself up to deliver its biggest gust of the morning. A deep *whoosh* sounded from the top of the ridge and flowed down the hill, producing the loudest chord yet from the harp scale of ropes; the gust raised a watery mist from the lake and a cloud of grit from the bank. The workers blinked and grabbed their hats, and the sails filled and pulled hard against their spars. As they did, the boat suddenly, groaningly, lurched forward.

Nacky, Teedie, Jimmer and the others stared dumbfounded at the vessel. The ship hadn't moved much—only a few inches—but move it had. The sight of the thing shifting itself was a spectacle far more frightening than it was thrilling, and a few screams went up from the crowd. Nacky looked at Teedie with an astounded expression. Then he looked back at the crowd with his blood pumping fast.

"Anyone what ain't in harness, get in now!" he shouted. "Them what are, brace up to pull!"

The workers responded fast, scrambling into the ropes and digging their feet into the soil. Teedie halloed to the half-home boys to make sure they were safely harnessed, and then, along with Jimmer, Bara and Emma, found four free ropes directly in a row and climbed into them. Nacky seized a fifth rope behind them, then looked up into the masts to the last of the sail riggers.

"You comin' down from there?" he shouted. The men waved and

scrambled down the masts, onto the deck and over the cargo net that still hung from the side of the boat.

"You set with them horses?" Nacky called as loudly as he could to the ridge, waving his arms in a big, swooping gesture to Weaver.

Weaver, his silver beard and hair visible even at this distance, waved back with the same wide whip of arms. He then turned and shouted something to the men at the capstans, and all at once the long ropes running from the wheels to the ship went fish-line taut, rising up off the bank with a loud snap. Nacky called out to the workers all around him.

"Pull!" he shouted as loudly as he could. "Pull!"

The workers responded as one, yanking on their ropes in a single tug. The wind that had just struck had not fully died, and with the sails still fat and the people pulling hard, the groaning boat leapt forward once again—this time a full foot or two—freeing itself from its rearmost braces, which collapsed into one another and clattered onto the bank.

"Pull!" Nacky shouted once more.

Again the workers dug in and again the boat lurched, plowing the fore end of the keel into the soil in front of it. Weaver raised his hand above his head, spinning it around, and shouting to the men at the capstans to keep the horses moving. Nacky, Teedie and the others strained as hard in their rope harnesses as the horses did above, digging one foot into the soil, driving themselves forward, and planting the other foot hard. Nacky felt the stump of his bad ankle press hard against his loblolly foot, causing him to wince.

"Pull!" he shouted again, feeling the boat move and hearing another set of braces fall. The hull and frames groaned loudly, and the mainmast emitted a terrifying crack as it swayed like a willow and shifted in its socket.

"Smooth pullin'!" Jimmer shouted through gritted teeth. "Don't jerk! Haul it even!"

The workers changed their step in response to Jimmer's call, trying not to tug at their ropes but to stride in them in a way Jimmer had said would tow the ship without shaking it. The wind seemed to answer

Jimmer's call too, giving off with another big gust, but a longer, slower one that didn't come up quite so suddenly or drop off quite so fast. The boat moved ahead with a heavy slide.

The workers now needed no more calls from Jimmer or Nacky to do their pulling. They trudged forward inch by inch, the wind blew again and again, and the boat ground slowly ahead, dropping another pair of braces behind it, then another and then others, until it was free of the last of them and moving on clear bank. As the horses went 'round and 'round above, the people struggled two more feet, five more, twelve more, until the very tip of the boat's bowsprit reached the edge of the bank and pointed its way up the trail. Nacky saw the little path come within reach and felt he could go no farther. All around him, the rest of the workers began to stagger too. "Hold!" Nacky shouted out suddenly. "Hold! Hold!"

At once, the workers quit their pulling and fell wheezing to the bank. The boat ground to a stop and shuddered above them. The workers lay where they were, unable to move, fighting merely to regain their breath. After a time, they wrestled themselves to a sitting position, their faces red and their chests heaving.

"It's horrible heavy," Teedie gasped. "Horrible."

"It can't be done," Emma said. "Can't be moved up that hill."

Nacky tried to speak, choking for air. "Has to be," he said. "We moved it this far, we'll move it the rest."

For a blessed minute, the wind stayed low and the workers remained crumpled, recapturing whatever strength they could. Then there was another loud chord from the strings on the bowl and another sudden swelling of sail, and Jimmer leapt to his feet. "Back in harness!" he shouted. "Pull, pull, pull!"

Once again, the capstans turned first and the workers pulled next. This time, however, the boat seemed to be sliding more easily. As the bow nosed onto the lake trail and the tip of the keel sliced into the soil of the hill, the entire mass of wood seemed almost to want to move. One by one, the workers advanced, stepping onto the rough scrub on either side of the trail, while the boat, still murderously heavy, slowly rode the slick mud path between them.

"Ain't possible!" Nacky shouted to Jimmer's back. "It should be harder."

"It's the wind!" Jimmer called back without turning around. "Hits the bank and rides up the bowl faster than it come down!"

If it was indeed the wind that was driving the ship, it was doing a passremarkable job, pushing harder and harder as the workers climbed higher and higher and the harp scale on the bank sang louder and louder. The wind snatched off caps, pushed on backs and caused Emma's rainbow of pennants to snap like gunshots. But slowly it caused the lip of the bowl to draw closer and closer and Weaver—standing on the hill—to grow larger and larger. Finally, the fore portion of the keel crested the hill and the first of the straining workers reached the flat ground of the high ridge. One by one, the rest of them followed, climbing farther onto the ridge until the entire mass of the boat was brought to safety far above the lake and bank where it had been found and built.

The workers came to a stop without Nacky's call and threw off their harnesses almost as one. Then, in a gale of their own, they whooped and wept and embraced, dancing about their ship and howling up into the sky as the kind wind continued to blow and blow around them.

It was only then that the people noticed Mally Baloo. He was striding toward the ridge from the padroad, followed by a dozen armed constables, a dozen ruddy beat-men and a dozen chain-and-ladder wagons. The crowd went instantly silent as Baloo and the lawmen closed to within a few feet of them and stopped, the clattering wagons and the snorting horses forming a menacing rank behind them.

Baloo was dressed as Baloo always was—in his soft clothes with his cloth buttons. He appeared comfortable, his hands clasped behind his back and a pleased expression on his face. The constables and beat-men appeared far less friendly, all of them big and cross-looking and wearing thick work gloves as if they had a job of lifting to do. They eyed the ship with fish-gape expressions. The horses toed the soil nervously. Baloo cast his eyes across the crowd, and the workers shrank back.

"I expected I might find a group here this morning," he said, not unpleasantly. "No one seems about in the town—not in the streets, not in the shops, not in the Rain." He looked across the crowd, and his eyes caught Dree, who didn't react. He flicked his gaze toward the Blands, who offered nervous smiles, and then toward Bara, who remained expressionless but backed partway behind Mary. "I see a lot of familiar people here, a lot of people I'm surprised to see here." Then his gaze came to rest on Nacky. "And I see Nacky Patcher too."

Nacky felt his heart pick up but managed to look at Baloo square. Even without straightening his sapling of a spine, he stood taller than Baloo. He straightened his spine anyway and found his voice. "Not hard to find me," he said. "Ain't hardly been nowhere else."

Baloo nodded. "I can see that. I don't have to ask how you've filled your time since you were last released from the tower. You were released, weren't you? Didn't wriggle free on your own?"

"I was released," Nacky said.

"You built this after?" He waved his hand generally in the direction of the ship.

"I did."

Baloo seemed to consider this. "A big job for one man." He tipped his head in polite admiration. Next to Nacky, Jimmer stepped forward.

"You want the one what learned to build it, you want me," he said.

Teedie looked at Jimmer and then stepped ahead as well. "And me," he echoed.

Baloo cast a cold eye at Teedie, then surveyed the group again. "And the rest?" he asked. "The rest are the haulers and fitters and sailmakers and the like?" He affected a look of genial confusion. "A remarkable job, though I don't imagine work like this earns any income, and income is what so many people here need—if only to get their rent paid up."

The crowd shifted at that.

347

"Rent ain't due for three days," Nacky said.

"Rent is due every month," Baloo answered, in a harder tone.

"All the same," Nacky said, "you can't do nothing about it till autumn comes on full, and that's three days from now."

Baloo shrugged. "I can wait," he said. "In the meantime, I'm free to make some arrests." He cast his gaze over the crowd again as if selecting a veal calf for supper. "There's been some lawbreaking in this town of late, particularly concerning the rule against tampering with black rags. Those knotted cloths are the only way I can keep track of my new properties. It doesn't do to fool with them, as most of you know." His eyes came to rest on Teedie once more. "It may be time to learn the wages of breaking the rules."

Baloo nodded at the constable behind his right shoulder. The beefy man nodded back and took a few menacing steps toward Teedie. Instantly, Nacky shoved the boy behind him and leapt forward.

"You don't lay hands on that child!" he barked.

"I'll lay hands on who the law entitles me to lay hands on, Nacky Patcher," the constable said.

"Not so long as I'm standing!" said Nacky.

"Nor I," echoed Jimmer, stepping forward.

"Nor I," said Emma, showing all her snaggle teeth.

"Nor I," rumbled Weaver.

Weaver spoke more quietly than the others, and unlike them, he took not a step forward. But he didn't have to. At the sound of his voice alone, the constable seemed to falter and the crowd seemed to stand straighter. The constable cast a glance to Baloo, who sighed and with another tick of his head, motioned him back behind him.

"As you all wish," Baloo said wearily. "I'll wait the three days till autumn and content myself then with taking what I need to settle your debts. That will include a sailing ship, of course."

"Three days from now this ship will be gone," Jimmer said.

"Three days from now, this ship will be somewhere along the padroad, half broken from the dragging and most of the people worn out and gone home," Baloo said. "You don't have the backs, you don't have the horses, you don't even have the wind to give you a push."

Baloo looked up. The air had indeed gone still, and heavy clouds had begun to gather. The builders began shifting again, looking from the sky to the boat to Baloo, calculating the weight of the vessel against the weight of his words.

"Now," Baloo went on reasonably, "these wagons can serve as carting wagons, carrying chopped teakwood to market, which would both fill my pockets and help settle your debts. Or they can serve as chain-and-ladder wagons, doing an entirely different kind of work. It doesn't matter to the men and horses. They'd as soon pull down the wall of a house as cart off a load of wood. It seems it's up to you what they do."

The people eyed Baloo, and then slowly began to shift their gaze, turning as a body back toward Nacky Patcher. Nacky looked back at them full. He collected himself and drew his breath.

"Then your boys'd best go tend to the houses and start with mine," he said to Baloo. "Folks here got a boat to sail."

There was an instant's pause, as the townspeople, Baloo and even Nacky himself absorbed what he'd just said. Then, a cheer burst from the crowd, even louder than the one they'd given off a moment ago. Nacky kept his gaze fixed on Baloo—a position the two of them might have held indefinitely, had Chuff the dwarf not suddenly spoken up.

"Ridge is givin' way," he said in a small voice nobody but Dree and Mary heard.

"What?" Dree said, alarmed.

"Ridge is givin' way," Chuff repeated, unaccustomedly loudly.

Nacky and Teedie snapped their heads toward him. "What do you mean givin' way?" Nacky asked.

"It's givin' way," Chuff said. "I can hear it meltin'."

As he spoke, the rain-softened soil that all morning had looked wet and slick but fully solid indeed began to change, going quick and runny under the twin weights of the people and the boat. A thick ooze of dark red mud began to flow around the keel and stream down the path. A narrow fissure opened up in the ground and started to widen. It was followed by another and then another. The people felt their purchase slipping as the earth itself seemed to shift and roll. The ship gave out with a low groan and swooned heavily backward.

"Take the ropes!" Nacky shouted. "Hold the boat!"

Heedless of the dissolving ridge, the workers did as Nacky said, springing to their abandoned posts and climbing back into their harnesses. Hurrying to the capstans, Weaver shouted at the men and the horses, slapping the nearest animals on the rumps to get them moving. The ropes stretching from the four wheels tightened, as did the ones the workers themselves were pulling, but the boat resisted the tug, listing farther and farther backward. The people pulled harder, Weaver shouted louder, the horses dug deeper, and slowly, the vessel began to level itself, its nose settling back down toward the ground and its stern rising from the abyss.

"Keep pullin'!" Nacky shouted. "Keep pullin'!"

The people and beasts did as he said, and the boat edged a yard from the ridge and then two yards. Nacky grinned through gritted teeth as he felt the vessel slide. "It's workin'!" he shouted. "It's holdin'!"

But at that same instant, there was a great, wet, slipping sound and a chunk of ridge beneath the stern calved away and melted down into the bowl. The boat listed sickeningly backward.

"Hold on, hold on!" Teedie screamed in his high voice.

As the ship swooned, another loud chord sounded from the thirty strings on the hill. This chord, however, played not up the scale as it should have, but down it, meaning that the wind was blowing the wrong way, from the bow of the ship to the stern, filling the fronts of the sails and pushing the vessel backward.

When this inverted gust struck, it slapped the boat hard, causing it to rear higher and drop back down like a spooked horse, carrying the people holding the fore ropes with it. The crowd shrieked in terror, and even Baloo's constables and beat-men backed away, stumbling into their horses and falling against their wagons. Only Baloo himself held his ground.

A second wrong-way wind followed the first, filling the sails again and pushing the boat harder. A third wind then struck, and when this one hit, there was a loud ripping sound as the biggest sails were torn from their riggings. The mainsail on the foremast pulled entirely free of the boat, soared into the sky and flew off. It was followed by Emma's marvelous pennants, which swirled away from the masts and flapped down into the bowl like a flock of bright birds. No sooner had they gone than a flock of real birds followed, as the ridge fell away under August Ren's wagon, causing it to topple on its side and tumble down the hill, releasing songbirds and night birds alike, their perches and bars snapping and their tethers tearing free.

When that last gust struck, it brought with it the largest, darkest rain cloud of all—a black and oily-looking thing that blotted out the sun almost entirely. Teedie was the first to notice the shadow swallowing the bank and looked up in the sky. He gasped at what he saw. It was a thunderhead of blackfire. All the workers turned their faces to the sky and cried out at the sight, the half-home boys—who knew blackfire too well—the loudest of all.

No sooner did the cloud appear than it split wide and began dumping its rain. This was nothing like the warm sky-bath the blackfire clouds had released on the lake the morning after Teedie and Nacky discovered the wood. This was an icy curtain of water pouring everywhere and on everything at once. It penetrated the people's clothes and the animals' hides. It pounded down on the deck of the ship. It turned the dirt that had not yet flowed away into a torrent of ruby mud.

The horses hitched to the capstans reared up in protest; the ones pulling the chain-and-ladder wagons did the same. Several of the stronger beasts snapped their harnesses and galloped off into the padroad. Most of Baloo's constables and beat-men scattered as well. Baloo himself did not follow them, but stood and watched silently.

Nacky, clinging to his rope as his boat fought to escape him, cried out to the workers: "Hold the lines! Hold the lines!"

But holding the lines was useless. Teedie, gripping his own rope, looked up and down the starboard side of the ship as dozens of workers struggled for both the boat's life and their own. Then he looked up into the sky and felt one more terrible fist of wind and one more cold explosion of rain, an explosion as deep and as awful as the sound that had roared up from the cellar of the half-home so long ago. And at that, he knew the boat was finished. He looked back at Nacky, who was straining in his harness with his eyes tightly closed—an expression that said he'd hold his rope until the giant vessel wrung the life from him, which it surely would. Nacky would never admit that the ship was beyond saving. Teedie already had.

"Release!" Teedie shouted from deep in his belly. "Release! Release! Release! Release!"

Nacky stared at the boy in horror, but it was too late. All around them, the people heard the call, jumped from their harnesses and scrambled frantically away. The boat, with neither horses nor people holding it in place, swayed violently on the knife-edge of the ridge, teetering back and forth. Nacky reached out and took hold of Emma and Teedie, Emma in turn grabbed Bara, and together with Jimmer they all raced off the ridge and back toward the road. The remainder of the people did the same, abandoning the dying ship and stumbling away. Mally Baloo retreated too, but not nearly fast enough and not nearly far enough.

It was on the port side of the boat that Baloo was standing when an explosive crack sounded from the deck and the huge mainmast, with its riggings and sails clinging to it, snapped at the base and fell toward the ground. Baloo vanished beneath the avalanche of canvas and rope and wood. As he disappeared, the last of the ridge on which the boat rested did too, collapsing spectacularly into itself. And as that went, the gigantic teak ship, with its ruined sails and its fractured spars and its lines of kutch filling the seams in its carefully planked flanks, went with it, rolling port over starboard, fore over aft, down the hill and toward the lake, smashing itself to splinters on the wide, abandoned bank.

CHAPTER FORTY-SEVEN

It was only half an hour before the boatbuilders who had fled the ridge in terror could safely return to it, but that short time did not pass easily. From the moment the skies split open, the rain came down in an unbroken gush, with explosions of wind driving the downpour harder still. One or two folks tried to run down the padroad in the teeth of the tempest, but the sheer power of the thing slapped them off their feet and back to the ground. The rest simply flung themselves down on the sides of the road, where they covered their heads and waited out the worst of the storm's bursts.

Nacky and Teedie were only faintly aware of the people around them in the half-hour they lay in the storm. They did not attempt to speak or stand, remaining still in the road just a few feet apart, with their fingers laced behind their necks and their faces in the torrents of water and mud.

Their boat, of course, was finished. It would never leave the town in which it had been built, much less make the trip all the way to the coast. That fact, oddly, did not seem to move Nacky or Teedie at the moment—the drumming of the cold rain, which could so easily numb the body, apparently did the same to the brain. Whatever the reason, so lost were they to sensation and thought that at first they didn't notice when the black storm clouds began to crumble and the wind and rain began to retreat. It was only when Nacky felt a heavy hand on his shoulder that his attention returned to the things around him. He rolled over, looked up into the subsiding rain and saw the red-streaked beard and mud-caked face of Weaver looking down at him.

"You need to breathe some," Weaver said.

"I know," Nacky answered.

"You need to take your face out of the water to do it."

Weaver reached down and seized Nacky under the arms. With a mighty heave, he pulled him to his feet. Then he turned to Teedie and lifted him as well, using only one hand to hoist the small boy. Teedie came up coughing. Beside them, Orro wriggled up from the mud.

"You fit?" Weaver asked Teedie, setting him down on his feet as easily as if he were putting down a cat.

Teedie nodded, choking but breathing.

"You?" Weaver asked Nacky.

Nacky waved off the question. "How are the others?" he asked.

"I don't know," Weaver answered. "Ain't taken an accounting."

Nacky peered up and down the road and, as far as he looked in either direction, could see dozens of other forms struggling out of the mud and rising up unsteadily. With a flicker of fear, he searched for Emma, then breathed with relief as he spotted her. Then he scanned about for Mary, Bara, Chuff, Jimmer and Dree and found them all. Teedie looked about himself and saw the yellow-clad half-home boys climbing out of the mud as well.

"Most seem to be about," Teedie said.

"Most," Nacky said, "but that don't mean all. Mally Baloo is layin' somewhere on the bank. No tellin' who else was claimed with him." He turned to the builders as a whole and called out. "Pick yourselves up and shake yourselves out," he ordered. "Then we got to take a count. Them what came here with somebody today, make sure they're still about. Them what came alone, look for the last person you saw. Weaver and I will go back to the ridge to see if we can find anyone what didn't make it through. Jimmer and Teedie will stay here and tally up heads."

Nacky looked toward Jimmer, who nodded. Teedie frowned.

"I'm comin' with you," he said to Nacky.

"No, you ain't," Nacky answered. "People may be broke to bits over there. That ain't a fit thing for a boy to see."

"It's fit if it's my boat what broke 'em in the first place," Teedie said. "What ain't fit is if I hang back safe."

Nacky looked at Weaver.

"Boy's right," the big man said. "It ain't but boatman's decency that he comes along."

"If Teedie comes, the others'll want to follow sure," Nacky said.

Weaver shrugged. "You're the one what gave 'em shares in the boat. Don't you reckon they got a right to see what become of their property?"

"And if that ridge gives way under a crowd this big?"

"It'll give way all the more if they stampede it behind us. Best to walk 'em over slow and together."

Nacky looked at Weaver doubtfully but turned and called back to the crowd, "Them what's fit and wants to come along, you're free to come. Them with more sense can stay." The crowd made a general noise of assent and began to surge forward. "But go slow, go slow!" Nacky called. "Don't push past Weaver nor Teedie nor me."

With the two men and the boy in the lead, every one of the wet, shoggled people trudged off the padroad and back toward the lake. Walking even a few steps on the ridge was torturous, with the thick mud grabbing hold of the townspeople's feet and emitting a loud, whooshing suck as they pulled free. Nacky worried that he'd lose his pine foot altogether, but he'd strapped it on especially tightly this morning in anticipation of the boat haul, and so far the belts appeared to be holding true.

The group closed in on the ridge, aware of what they'd find but not wanting to see it. Somewhere, they knew, would be the remains of Mally Baloo; everywhere, they knew, would be the remains of their boat. As Nacky, Teedie and Weaver drew closer, they craned their necks forward to peer down into the bowl, while Weaver waved his hand behind him to hold back the crowd. They caught sight first of the far side of the lake, shining a clear berry blue with no sign of ruin. Their line of vision widened as they moved farther, with more clear water and bank revealing themselves. The three exchanged puzzled looks, took another tentative step forward, and all at once saw a slash of color. They stepped again and looked full down. What lay beneath caused Nacky's legs to buckle under him and Weaver's and Teedie's jaws to fall open wide. The crowd pressed forward, and Weaver tried to signal them back, but not before they too saw what was below.

Floating on the water, twenty yards from the lake's near shore, was the great teak sailing ship, whole and unhurt and flying her countless colors. The vessel was the same one the people of Yole had built, but it was a different one too. Its wood was buffed to a higher shine, and its grain had turned a richer color. The kutch streaks that in some spots had leaked from the seams and stained the hull were gone and the planks themselves ran straighter and truer. The mainmast, which Teedie had always worried looked a bit shy of center, rose clean and fixed, and the yellow sails and cargo net were far more tidy and squared than before. The only thing amiss was Emma's string of pennants, which was absent entirely.

"It can't be," Nacky whispered.

"We saw it break apart," Teedie said.

Nacky rose unsteadily to his feet and took a step toward the edge. Immediately, the patch of ground on which he was standing began to melt away. He stumbled back and Weaver caught him.

"I can't reckon it," he said, staring at the boat and heedless of his near fall.

Weaver nodded mutely.

"Here now," Grimm Bland called out loudly behind them, "what's the meanin' of this, Nacky Patcher?"

Nacky turned around to face the crowd and saw them all staring at him with the same questioning expression Grimm wore.

"What *is* the meanin'?" Bara asked softly.

"I don't know," Nacky answered. He looked toward Weaver inquiringly.

"Never seen its like," the big man said.

"This here ain't possible," Anna Bland called out.

Weaver looked at her and frowned. "It is possible, seein' as it's there," he said. "That don't mean we understand it."

Weaver turned back toward the lip of the bowl and took a tentative step forward. The ground groaned even louder under him than it had under Nacky. He backed away. "Won't hold a lick," he said with a nod of his head.

Teedie craned his neck forward. "Reckon it'll hold me," he said.

"Reckon it won't, and you ain't gonna try it noways," Nacky said.

"We can't stand up here hidin' from our own boat," Teedie said. "Someone's got to take the measure of that thing up close."

"This mud already buried Mally Baloo today," Nacky said, staring down the dizzying bowl where Baloo was all but surely interred. "You fancy joining him?"

Teedie shrugged. "We slid down there on trouser seats once before and we can do it again."

Teedie took two quick steps forward—easily dodging Nacky's reach—and plopped on his seat in the mud at the edge of the bowl; the wet ridge held his feather of a frame without moving.

"You come back here, boy," Nacky said sternly.

Teedie ignored him and planted his hands in the mud, preparing to push over the edge, when suddenly there was a halloing from the padroad. The crowd turned to see Dal Tally running toward them and waving. Behind him trailed a panting stable boy carrying a large, heavy object in his arms. The object was wrapped in a gray woolen horse blanket.

"Dal!" Teedie exclaimed.

"What in the seas?" Nacky said.

Teedie leapt back up and started running toward the padroad. Nacky, Weaver and Jimmer followed, and the rest of the crowd surged after them.

"We got something, we got something!" Dal shouted. "Something pass-remarkable!" He came skidding to a stop in front of the townspeople.

"Where have you been?" Emma asked sternly. "I thought you were at Nacky Patcher's house."

Nacky looked at her in surprise. "I thought he was with the indigents."

"We got something!" Dal repeated, ignoring them. The stable boy caught up with him and stopped, panting. "I been to Baloo's estate," Dal said.

"You been where?" Nacky asked, alarmed.

Dal waved him off. "I didn't never see Baloo up close, but we spied him as he was leavin' this morning. All the same, I couldn't leave meself till I was sure he was gone. It wouldn't do for him to see us makin' off with this."

Dal nodded to the stable boy, who threw back the blanket that covered his bundle. Lying in his arms—though appearing ready to spring from it—was a graceful carving of a winged pig, braced in a frozen moment of flight. It was a lean pig like Orro, but larger, with the muscles and sinews most pigs keep hidden seeming to burst from the grain. The wood itself was a rich, butter-colored teak, the richest and butteriest of all of the boat pieces so far. The pig's wings were inlaid with mother of pearl, as were its hooves. Its eyes were dark like Orro's, but made of hard onyx. It was a carefully wrought thing, and it was lovely.

"The figurehead piece," Teedie whispered.

"Forty thousand and one," Nacky answered softly.

The townspeople gathered around to look at the pig, cradled like a child in the stable boy's arms, but none reached forward to touch it. Chuff, who had woven his way near the front of the crowd, now looked at the boy with a flicker of recognition. He spoke a single syllable, and this time he spoke it without reproach.

"Birl," he said.

The boy smiled. "Birl, if you wish," he answered.

Teedie, standing beside Nacky, looked up at him with a questioning expression and then looked down the lake bowl. Nacky followed his eyes to the bow of the boat, where the bowsprit extended like a great teak spear.

"No," Nacky said. "It still ain't safe."

"Boat's waitin' for its final part, Nacky," Teedie said. "There's gotta be a reason it weren't swallowed by the storm."

Nacky looked long at the boat, then at the boy, and finally ticked his head yes. Teedie brightened, grabbed Dal and the stable boy and the three of them, grinning, broke for the ridge in a run. The wet soil beneath the three boys groaned, but it took their weight easily. They dropped to their seats at the rim of the bowl, slid down the hill to the bank and ran into the water. Pushing the figurehead in front of them, they kicked and paddled out to the giant boat. When they got there, they seized hold of the cargo net and climbed up it, wrestling the heavy teak onto the deck with them. From there they sprinted to the bow.

The bowsprit of the teak ship was one of its most decoratively carved parts, with flourishes and curves running along most of the twelve-foot length where a figurehead should be. The last three feet were empty, but a number of the carved curls reached ahead like bent arms, almost as if they were cradling the air. The boys crowded to the prow of the boat, then Teedie took the figurehead in the crook of his right arm and crept along the base of the bowsprit on his good hand and his knees. On the bank, Nacky and the others gasped as Teedie crawled forward. When the boy reached the empty spot on the figurehead, he reached down and fit the rump of the carved pig into the bent arms. It snapped into place and it held true. The carving's widespread wings with their mother-of-pearl feathers caught the sun and flashed it all over the lake bowl, spangling the people on the ridge with reflected light.

Teedie and Dal beamed at the sight, sought out Nacky and waved to him. No sooner did they do that, however, than the boat began a fearsome trembling. The movement started at the tops of the masts and traveled downward, rattling the sails, then the rails, then the deck, then the hull, sending fine, round ripples out across the water. It was almost as if something had taken hold of the vessel and was shaking it—something that would not let go until it had sunk whole. Teedie clung hard to the bowsprit. Birl and Dal held fast to the rail. The three boys looked up to the top of the lake bowl, suddenly terrified.

"Get off, get off!" Nacky and the townspeople shouted to them, waving their arms. "Jump, jump!"

For an instant, the boys stayed frozen. Then the boat gave a mighty lurch, one that seemed to be trying to pitch them off entirely. Just as they had hurled themselves through the window of the half-home three years before, Dal now leapt unthinkingly into space and Teedie dropped straight down from the bowsprit. The stable boy followed them. They all plunged to the lake below, hit the water and splashed frantically away. When they were fifty yards off, they turned back to look.

Looming before them, the shaking ship slowly began to sink, its hull descending below the water one plank line at a time. It dropped farther and farther and the water rose higher and higher, climbing up the hull until it reached the glassless portholes and flowed inside. The water began rising faster, spilling over the deck and rails, swamping the wheelhouse and hatchways, climbing up the spars, the sails, and finally, the very point of the mainmast. Then, with a great burp of air from the surface of the water—very much like the great rising bubble that had created the lake itself so long ago—the vessel was gone, taking the magnificent, flying figurehead and its mother-of-pearl wings with it.

Absolute silence fell over the people on the ridge. Stunned and chilled, Teedie, Dal and the stable boy slowly paddled back to shore. As they reached it and staggered onto the bank, a solitary voice from up on the ridge broke the stillness. It was Chuff the dwarf, speaking out in the same uncommonly clear, unaccustomedly strong tone he had used on that day months earlier when he recited his poem in the Albert T. Rain. As on that day as well, there was an unfamiliar light in his watery green eyes.

The mouth of the fool
and the mouth of the wise,
have little to set them apart.

There is tongue and there's voice
to tell truth and tell lies.
The difference depends on the heart.

A tale is now done
and a page is now turned
in a nautical history grand,

in a story of vessels
all harbors once spurned,
and which sailed all their days on the land.

The darkness descended
some twenty lives back
when the mountains were bled of their sea.

But the full sun can finally
break from the black,
and the folk under yoke are now free.

A boy who saw light,
in the ink of a cloud,
and a thief who believed in his Songs,

were all that was needed,
to lift a dark shroud,
and to right the most grievous of wrongs.

The vessel they built
surely longed for the sea,
surely yearned for the taste of a wave.

But it came to its end
in a manner less fine,
in the maw of a mountainous grave.

Still it's but a small thing
that their boat never sailed,
that it smashed on a hard earthly shoal.

What matters far more,
what will always be hailed,
is that somehow that boat was made whole.

Chuff finished speaking and slowly lowered his head. For an instant there was silence, and then a great fluttering sound began, one that seemed to come from everywhere at once. The fluttering turned to a flapping and then, all around the townspeople—from the lake bowl, from the trees, from the mountains themselves—rose a vast, black cloud of ravens and starlings and sharp, noisy shrikes. They burst and burst from thousands of invisible nests and branches, swirling up in a mammoth, churning mass that briefly blotted the sun. They climbed higher and higher, shrank to a smudge and then a shadow, and at last they vanished entirely.

"It's over," Nacky said quietly. "The charm has quit."

"It has," Weaver answered.

Nacky nodded his head wonderingly. "The ship didn't never have to get to the ocean after all," he whispered.

"No it didn't," Weaver said.

A dazed murmur rose from the blinking townspeople. They looked up at the sky where the flock of blackbirds had been and down to the lake where the teak boat had floated. Both were now utterly empty and utterly blue. Teedie, Dal and the stable boy scrabbled up the lake bowl, which was already growing dry again. They reached the top, and Teedie came to Nacky.

"Our boat," he said sorrowfully.

"It weren't never ours," Nacky said, "not to keep noways."

Teedie looked down at the empty lake. "It ain't right," he said.

"Right's just what it is, son," Weaver answered quietly. "It's proper that the sea takes a boat. It ain't proper if the people take a sea. A long time ago, folks here had it backward. I reckon it was up to you and your boat to make an apology for that." He looked down at the water, where the vanished vessel no longer floated. "I reckon it was accepted."

"So what are we about now?" Teedie asked.

Nacky shrugged. "Whatever we want, I imagine," he said. He looked at Weaver, who nodded in agreement.

At that, there was a sudden gust of wind, one accompanied by a low, loud, musical chord. The townspeople looked toward the lake where a dozen of the rope lines strung down the bowl had survived the storm and were once again being played by the wind. A second chord sounded, and then a third. And then, from somewhere nearby, another cloud of birds—this one a riot of colors—seemed to take wing. The townspeople squinted at the flock and watched it go and realized that they weren't swirling birds at all. They were Emma's pageant of pennants, torn free and given wing. Nacky, Teedie, Dal, Emma and the others followed them with their eyes until that last bright bit of their wondrous ship had vanished into the sky. Then they turned away from the ridge where their work was finished and back toward the town, where it all at once seemed they had much to do.

EPILOGUE

A few years on

The first thing Nacky Patcher did when his daughter was born was look at her feet. He knew, of course, that they would be normal feet. A one-footed man did not have to produce a one-footed child, after all. But Nacky had had the single foot for so long now it was hard to imagine anything that came from him taking shape any other way. So when his daughter was born, he looked straightaway at her feet and was pleased to see that they were both as they should be. He named the girl Shira, partly because it sounded pretty, partly because it was the same name his grandmother—his Pippa's wife—had carried, and partly because someone had once told him that it meant "song," which may or may not have been true but which pleased him nonetheless.

If Shira didn't have her father's feet, she certainly had her mother's hair. She was born with a dusting of cherrywood-colored fuzz over most of her head, a dusting that grew surprisingly thick before she had even a full year on her. Nacky guessed the girl might grow up with Emma's snaggly teeth and strong-willed ways too, and that pleased him as well, since Emma herself had always made those things work in her favor. Shira was not born until three years after the storm at the lake and the death of the teak ship, and that made sense. There were a lot of other things that had to be attended to first—things that claimed the attention of the entire town.

The people of Yole spent a good spell of time hunting for the remains of Mally Baloo without ever finding them, and eventually concluded that he was interred forever in the deep mud of the lake bowl. The laws under which the Baloos had ruled the town provided that if no senior member of the family stepped forward to claim title to the estate within thirty days of such a death, the wealth of Yole would be passed back to the people who lived there. Baloo, who had long lived alone, had not foreseen his end coming and thus could not have notified any of his widely scattered relations. The townspeople saw no reason to do so either, and at the end of the month, the entire community, which had just been freed of the dark charm of the dry-land boats, was formally freed of the dark curse of the Baloo family too.

The Baloo estate workers took over the running of the land, with the kitchen girls overseeing the manor, and the stable boys—who now felt great shame over how shabbily they had behaved toward Chuff over the years—managing the fields and the animals and vowing to treat even the slowest and dimmest worker or beast with a fair hand and a gentle voice. All the workers labored hard in that first season, and by the very next harvest, the land exploded with fruits and vegetables in ways they never had before, and the soil was heavily trod by robust herds of animals, healthier than any a Baloo-managed staff had ever raised.

Such abundance produced more than enough food for the workers to feed themselves as well as to sell at markets both in Yole and outside it. Some of the money this raised was used to pay off the boatbuilders' debts to the net and line shop and the canvas supplier. The rest was spent in the few businesses that remained in town, with Gilly Boate finding new buyers for his dry goods, Jenner Rind finding new demand for his roofing work, Dree finding new customers for her food and drink—causing her to open up earlier in the day, take on other workers besides the Dreeboys, and pay them all handsomer salaries than she would have been able to before.

Other people too benefited from the changes in Yole. A bit of the light that filled Chuff's watery green eyes when he recited his second poem lingered there, and while the little man would never have his full complement of wits, there was a clarity and thoughtfulness to him he'd never shown before. More and more, he'd leave off the menial work he once did in the fields and retreat to his cabin, where he'd labor with pen and creamy white paper to produce more poems like the ones that had sprung from him—all of them full of song and color and all written in a small, neat hand.

Chuff showed his poems to Brigg and Constance Keeper, who carried them to Greater M'croom, where a bookseller took a liking to them and agreed to print and bind several dozen copies and credit them to Chuff. The books sold well, and the bookseller printed more, passing the largest portion of the earnings back to Chuff. Soon more and more copies were printed and sold throughout the local towns and beyond, generating more and more income.

Chuff shared his earnings with the Keepers, since he had little use for money, or interest in it either. Brigg Keeper was powerfully interested, however, and decided that he'd had his fill of reading old newspapers and instead would now start one of his own for the people of Yole and anyone in the surrounding towns who wanted to read fine accounts of current circumstances. Brigg hired on writers to produce the paper's stories and even made space available in the pages for readers who wanted to take out a public notice or two—for which they would pay an agreed-upon sum. Constance, who still preferred past circumstances to current ones, spent her time converting a portion of their home into a lending library, making more trips than ever to communities like the M'crooms, where she bought up the finest books she could find and made them available to anyone in Yole who wanted to indulge—or develop—a taste for reading. Chuff would spend the rest of his life among the shelves, keeping the books organized and the lending records tidy and, in quiet moments, reading other writers' poetry and composing more of his own.

Jimmer Pike, whose love of building only grew after the construction of the boat, traveled to the M'crooms and Twelve Points with Teedie Flinn, where he and the boy spent several weeks in the towns' larger libraries, learning all they could about the business of building fishing vessels. The story of the great teak ship had spread beyond Yole, and though few people in the coastal towns believed it, one wealthy fisherman was intrigued enough by both the tale and the builders who claimed to be behind it that he commissioned Jimmer and Teedie to build him a new fishing boat—with payment to be made only upon satisfactory completion. Jimmer and Teedie accepted the work, provided they would be permitted to build the boat on the ridge overlooking the Yole lake where the locals could share in the job and the pay, without having to waste what they earned finding lodgings on the quay. When the work was done, they would haul the boat to the coast, this time on a wheeled cradle to make the trip easier. The fisherman agreed, so Jimmer and Teedie recruited the best of the workers who had assembled Nacky's ship, and in short order had designed and constructed a fine fishing vessel, for which they were well paid.

Shortly thereafter, the newly named Pike Boatworks received another contract, then another, and a thriving business rose up on the ridge. Jimmer promised Teedie that when he came of age, he would own half the business and the Pike name on the boatworks' sign would change to Pike-Flinn. It was a promise he faithfully kept. Nacky visited the boatworks often, spending many long afternoons watching the ships slowly take form. When Jimmer and Teedie took on their largest job—building a small clipper ship—Nacky gave them his door from the *Walnut Egg*, which they sanded and smoothed and oiled till it shone, then installed in the new ship's captain's quarters. The little clipper sailed for many years, perhaps protected by the luck of the door, perhaps not, but always riding safely, all the same.

The indigents' home prospered as well. With no Mally Baloo to fear any longer, it threw open its shutters and doors and renamed itself the Yole Garment Concern and Girls' Home. So impressed was Mary with Bara's leather work that she asked her to make a collection of shoes and boots for the thriving business, which brought in even more revenue and allowed the home to expand and take in more orphan girls, and eventually boys as well. Emma and Nacky oversaw the local operation of the company, Mary and Bara Berry traveled back and forth between Bretony and Yole to tend to foreign markets, and all of them grew comfortably tinned on the money the work brought in.

The girls from the indigents' home and the boys from the half-home all continued taking lessons from Emma, spending their other hours working on boatbuilding at the lake or dressmaking at the home and earning a fat share of what both businesses collected. Dal Tally, who somehow seemed to grow taller and look sturdier after the day he brought the figurehead to the lake, might have had a position at the boat-works, since it was a job he was now fit to do. But he decided instead to work at the garment concern, since that would keep him close to Mag. It was an arrangement that suited them both fine, and would for the rest of their lives—which, as it turned out, they spent together.

Weaver, who felt no real connection to his big home with its bubble basin in Little M'croom, sold it and bought another house in Yole. He spent part of his time at Jimmer and Teedie's boatworks, training and overseeing the rope weavers, and part of it down at the Albert T. Rain, helping Dree manage her new crush of customers and filling her ear with tales of the sea whenever she asked, which she did often. The Dreeboys—who Dree ultimately acknowledged were indeed her own—also took a liking to Weaver's stories and decided they might enjoy living the same kind of life he had.

With Dree's approval, Weaver made several trips to the coast, investigated many available ships and secured both of the boys good commissions on sturdy vessels that would take them to many interesting places and bring them home for frequent visits. When he felt the time was right, he also sat Dree down and persuaded her that it wasn't proper to make the kind of use she did of the bits of lost ships she'd collected. One by one, Weaver helped her replace each scavenged piece with fresh parts cut from new trees, and together they carried the older ones to the coast. There, they dropped them in the water, where they bobbed and crashed up against the rocks and at last had the chance to melt into the sea as they were meant to. The restaurant kept the name of the *Albert T. Rain* as a tip of the cap to the lost ship but surrendered any other claim to it.

Elsewhere in Yole, other townspeople made other uses of the suddenly available bounty, opening shops and farms and dairies and even a small accounting firm to help manage the new wealth. Teedie sent word to Knockle for Audra and Stolley Pound and their two boys, who promptly returned to Yole, tore away the black rags that bound their curio store, and reopened for business. August Ren never did find a horse to replace the one he had lost, nor birds to replace the ones that had gone free. Many of those birds, however, settled in a stand of trees not far from the lake and seemed to like it there fine. August spent so much time nearby listening to their singing and watching them hatch their colorful young that Teedie and Jimmer built him a small house on that spot, where he lived the remainder of his life in the knowledge that the birds could now carry their own songs about town and he could give up the job.

Dal, Mag, Teedie and Gurtee kept their promise to the broken Meddo Brinn, informing the townspeople that it was he who had told them where to find the figurehead. The Brinn family remained in their home in Yole, and while Meddo's wife and boys fared well enough, Meddo himself never regained the spine or the will he'd given so freely to Mally Baloo. He grew increasingly beaten with the passing years, rarely speaking unless he was away to the hills on malt and then having nothing much worth hearing to say.

It was only when such matters in Yole had begun to sort themselves out that Nacky had at last set his cap on wooing Emma Hay properly.

And it was only after a year of his trying that she agreed to marry him. Another year after that, the cherry-haired Shira was born.

Nacky Patcher lived to be a very old man, surviving well into his nineties and possibly beyond, though no one was ever absolutely certain of his age. He never traveled much beyond Yole, except on the occasional trip to the coastal towns, when business matters required it, or the occasional holiday to Bretony or Andala, when a restless Emma demanded it. Nacky ultimately outlived Emma—though not before they had shared many years and produced several more children in what became known as Greater Yole.

In Nacky's final years, when he could rarely bear hobbling on his old wooden foot and his weak, weary ankle, he would ask his eldest grand-daughter, who precisely resembled Emma, to walk him to the Albert T. Rain, which had long since passed from Dree's hands. He would sit at a table near where an old ship beam used to hang, drink a malt, and listen for the creaking of the lost vessel's timbers. His granddaughter never heard it, but now and again, when the room was quiet, Nacky himself was certain he did.

ACKNOWLEDGMENTS

The town and people of Yole do not exist—and yet in a number of meaningful ways they do. Most of the events in this book are entirely imagined; many are based on or inspired by real events. For helping me find what there was to find and acquire the tools to invent the rest, I owe thanks to a number of people.

Much appreciation goes to the talented boatbuilders of the New England coast, particularly Maine's Maynard Bray, Eric Dow, Steve White and Bob Stephens. Thanks too to Matt Murphy, publisher of *Wooden Boat* magazine, and to Mystic Seaport's Quentin Snediker, the designer of the reborn sailing ship *Amistad*.

I owe even greater gratitude to the wonderful people of southern Ireland. Patty Joe Morrisey, John Baldwin, John Tatten and Sheila Egan taught me much about the world of the fisherman. I learned much as well from Michael Cuddigan, the butcher in the town of Cloyne; Tom Neville, a tavern owner in Fethard on Sea; John Young and Nicholas Graves, lay historians in the town of Dungarven; and Brendan Gallagher, proprietor of the restaurant Alfred D. Snow, in Dungarven East. Much appreciation also goes to the people of the Ballymaloe House in East Cork: Myrtle Allen, Darina Allen and Yasmin and John Hyde. It is on the grounds of the house that the real Chuff the Dwarf lived and where the poem that inspired the ones in the book can be found. Great thanks to Tom Hickey of Fethard on Sea and his good friend Tedie Finn. Though Tedie Finn and Teedie Flinn differ in age, gender and story, they are equals in both grit and richness of character. I am indebted to Tedie for inspiring Teedie.

Numerous books also aided in my research, including *New England Sea Tragedies*, by Edward Rowe Snow; *The Famine Ships*, by Edward Laxton; *The Book of Cloyne,* edited by Pádraig Ó Loingsigh; *Diaries of Ireland,* edited by Melosina Lenox-Conyngham; *Slanguage: A Dictionary of Irish Slang,* by Bernard Share; *The American-Built Clipper Ship,* by William L. Crothers; and *Desperate Haven,* by William Fraher, Bernadette Sheridan, Seosaimh Ó Loingsigh and Willie Whelan.

More personal thanks go to the people closer to home who made this book possible. There would be no *Nacky Patcher* at all if not for Michael Green of Philomel Books, who embraced the story I wanted to tell, edited it with gentleness and extraordinary care, and even took the time when he had read just fifty pages of the manuscript to call and reassure me that he liked what he'd seen so far—a gesture of sublime empathy. Michael would have had no manuscript to read at all, of course, if not for Joy Harris of the Joy Harris Literary Agency. If there is another agent anywhere like Joy, I've surely not heard of any sightings. For reading this book in all its incarnations, for staying with it in the years it took to complete and for never losing patience with either it or me, I owe her more than I'll ever be able to calculate. Thanks too to Joy's talented associates, Leslie Daniels and Robin London, who also read and nursed the book along. Much love also to Byron and Maria Cooper Janis, for the music and magic they bring to our lives; and to Hilde Gerst, who never saw the finished book and yet, I suspect is seeing it all the same. Deep gratitude to the small group of people who offered generous time and wise counsel throughout the writing process: Steve Kluger, Richard and Phyllis Kluger, Lori Oliwenstein, Donn Weinberg, Alison Friesinger and Bob Strozier. They have my thanks and love.

Finally, my greatest thanks to those who have my heart: Alejandra (my Emma Hay) and Elisa and Paloma (my Mary and Bara). It is Alejandra who helped me open up to the world of enchantment; it is Elisa and Paloma I found when I did.